ADVANCE PRAISE

"Grabs readers and leaves them hanging on for dear life... excellent dialogue and non-stop action."

— *Suspense Magazine*

"A classic legal thriller in the mold of Scott Turow, with a fiery heroine, a monster of a mobster, corporate villains, and a young lawyer fighting to win his first big case. The action is compelling in and out of the courtroom. Taut, lean storytelling with a great finish."

— Michael Sears, award-winning author of
Black Fridays and *Mortal Bonds*

"With the backdrop of *Mad Men*–era New York, *Pardon the Ravens* never fears to get dirty with style. Alan Hruska brings it all— sounds, smells, tastes, and attitude—to life with passion. Bravo!"

— Cara Black, author of the *New York Times*
bestselling Aimée Leduc series

PRAISE FOR *WRONG MAN RUNNING*

"As good as the best offerings of Turow, Grisham, and other legal-thriller hitmakers."

— *Booklist*

"Beautifully written and beautifully imagined, this dark, spiraling, Kafkaesque nightmare might be the best psychological suspense you'll read this year—or this decade."

— Lee Child, author of the *New York Times*
bestselling Jack Reacher novels

PARDON THE RAVENS

BY ALAN HRUSKA

PROSPECT
·PARK·
BOOKS

Published by Prospect Park Books
2359 Lincoln Avenue
Altadena, California 91001
www.prospectparkbooks.com

PROSPECT
·PARK·
BOOKS

Distributed by Consortium Book Sales & Distribution
www.cbsd.com

Library of Congress Cataloging-in-Publication Data

Hruska, Alan, author.
 Pardon the Ravens : a novel / by Alan Hruska.
     pages cm
 Summary: "Gifted young New York lawyer Alec Brno gets the career boost of a lifetime: the opportunity to try a huge fraud case making international headlines. But he risks it all when he falls for an alluring young woman whose estranged husband is a sadistic Mafia don—and the criminal mastermind behind Alec's case."— Provided by publisher.
 ISBN 978-1-938849-40-4 (hardback)
 1. Legal stories. 2. Suspense fiction. I. Title.
 PS3558.R87P37 2015
 813'.54--dc23
                                    2014013284

Cover design by Howard Grossman.
Book layout and design by Amy Inouye.
Printed in the United States of America.

For Julie

ONE

September 1961. New York. Wall Street. *Center of the universe.* Bounding up from the subway, Alec Brno sails forth.

He's noticed and noticing, this gangly young man, his longish face questioning, his brown hair awry. Heading toward Water Street into the sun, he pauses at Broad. Rivers of boaters—white straw hats with bright silk bands—stream on currents of lawyers and brokers. And there are guys rushing, like Alec: hatless, eager. Guys thinking, *I'm ready!* Depression babies in their ill-fitting suits.

To the magazine columnists, they are "The Silent Generation," which misses the point while unintentionally abetting it. Graduates of the Fifties aren't shouting slogans down the corridors of power. They're too busy quietly taking over what the Establishment has.

And Alec Brno is especially motivated. He's a poor kid from Queens with an unpronounceable last name—the Czechs, for obscure reasons, having disdained the need to make explicit indispensable vowel sounds. To those in power, a person with such a name coming from such a place has sizable obstacles to overcome—a fact of life of which Alec is well aware.

In point of fact, Alec's family is more Organized Labor than ethnic. Union Socialists, almost Communists, for whom Wall Street has particular abhorrence. These are people, Alec has always known, with big hearts, intolerance for injustice, and little understanding of economics. They would regard the firm employing him as the Mecca of depravity, and its presiding partner, former judge of the federal court of appeals Ben Braddock, as the socialist equivalent of the Antichrist. By their standards, those assessments would be dead accurate. Kendall, Blake, Steele & Braddock is not simply the most-feared legal weapon wielded by American big business; in important respects, it runs the institutions it services.

Two years earlier, Alec had signed on with Kendall, Blake right out of law school. Then, the firm had been housed at 25 Broad Street—a squat pile of some twenty floors, deco in style, serviced by elevators that made a great deal of clanking noise and took forever to go in either direction. But new buildings continually arise in the city, and its successful inhabitants grow into them. Now, every morning, Alec speeds soundlessly to the heights of a sixty-story glass tower on Water Street. He has his own small office on the fifty-eighth floor with a spectacular view of almost the entirety of Manhattan.

Alec is drawn to that view as soon as he enters his office and stands admiring it for some minutes before settling down at his desk. The partner he works for, Frank Macalister, is in Miami, finishing a trial. It's the only Macalister case Alec isn't assigned to, which means he's expected to deal with the rest of Mac's caseload. It can be time-consuming, keeping everything from blowing up in his face, but it's a lot easier dealing with Mac's opponents and co-counsel than with Mac himself.

For the last several days, Alec has been covering for Mac, representing Biogram Pharmaceuticals in a five-defendant price-fixing trial, one of the few government actions brought under the state antitrust laws. Normally, Alec would be in court an hour beforehand to get everything ready for the first chair. As it is, he has to swing by the office first for Mac's letters and messages. He leafs through them, then moves the stack to a corner of his desk. None requires immediate attention. He's got the luxury of a few minutes to think about what the morning might bring about.

He leans back and visualizes the courtroom. He sees, facing the bench, a semicircle made up of six small tables. Behind each will sit the senior trial counsel for each party accompanied by one or more junior partners, or in the case of the state attorney general's office, several less senior trial attorneys. Behind them will be their associates, and behind them, patent counsel, for there are charges in the case of monopolization by the fraudulent procurement of patents. And behind each of those tiers there will come and go the various experts, paralegals, and other support personnel for each team. At the table for Biogram, in splendid isolation, Alec Brno will reign: a second-year associate, first chair temporarily, at the first trial he's ever seen firsthand, much less participated in.

The witness for the day, and probably several more, will be J.J. Tierney, the chief executive of Pharmex Pharmaceuticals, holder of the principal patent. According to the government, it was Tierney who masterminded the price fix. The possibilities that Alec might cross-examine the case's pivotal witness in Mac's absence are slim to none. What Tierney will say on direct examination has been heavily negotiated and agreed upon. If Alec were to speak at all, it would most likely be to read the statement that Mac wrote out for him with a smirk: "No questions for this witness, your Honor." Alec hopes he can manage to get that out without embarrassing himself.

One of these days, he thinks, he'll head up a litigation team and be comfortable enough in court to command attention, not let it command him. At his present level of inexperience, however, his view of trial practice is still influenced by the movies.

He packs his black leather litigation ("lit") bag and makes for the elevators. The image in his head is of Raymond Burr's district attorney in *A Place in the Sun*, slamming his cane on the counsel table. Were such histrionics even conceivable in *State of New York vs. Pharmex Pharmaceuticals, et al.*? Emerging from the elevator, Alec laughs out loud, almost in the face of Judge Braddock, a long, gaunt, white-haired man in a black homburg, waiting to get on. Disapproval flickers in the judge's sharp gaze, with no sign he knows or cares who Alex is.

TWO

At a tower window of an oil storage facility in Bayonne, New Jersey, manager Whitman Poole stands riveted, watching. It is one thirty-seven in the morning.

Miles of marshland breathe in the night. Moonlight flares the tops of marsh reeds. In the yard, thirty-foot-high storage tanks row up like a mustering of UFOs.

Eventually, an oil truck appears, bumping along the potholed road to the facility. Front gates swing wide. The truck splashes through puddles and sidles up to a tank. Two men jump out. They attach a truck nozzle to the tank and open a tank valve. With each exertion, their breath fogs the air. They work fast, with an occasional glance over their shoulders.

Poole, a tanned, hair-combed-back dandy, observes intently. He looks jumpy, displeased that the men below aren't moving faster.

Poole's attention is diverted by a silver Cadillac Eldorado pulling into the compound. He remains fixed on the car as it stops near the tower. The driver springs forth to open the passenger door. Uncoiling from the seat is a tall, black-haired figure in a leather jacket, who, with indifference to his surroundings, carries a lighted cigar. As he looks up to Poole's window, the power and pathology of the man are evident on his broad, flat face.

Poole, anxious to please, jerks his thumb upward in a gesture of success. The tall man grimaces, flips the cigar away in a splash of embers, and gets back in his car. His driver scurries to stamp out the sparks.

"Where to, Phil?" the driver asks through the open back

window of the vehicle.

"I'm staying in town. Call a meeting for the morning—nine thirty."

"Sure." Still thinking, settling into the driver's seat. "What's up, boss?"

"Just call the meeting, Vito, all right?"

Vito blinks several times and cranes around. He's a pear-shaped man with a large head, but with the sort of bulging muscularity that suggests serious devotion to a workout routine. He knows he's slower than his boss in comprehending most anything, but he does like to have things explained.

"His face, Vito. I don't like his face."

"That's it?" says Vito.

Phil's frown shows the edge of his patience. "We've let it go too long. Everyone's too fucking greedy. And smug. Okay?"

"Whatever you say, boss."

"And another loose end."

"How's that?"

"Aaron Weinfeld," says Phil.

"The lawyer?"

"He's in Narragansett, Rhode Island. I'll want you to go up there this weekend. The boat's up there. The fifteen-footer. Or it'll be out of Newport by the time you arrive. You can use the boat."

"The boat," repeats Vito.

"You know what I'm talking about, *use the boat?*"

"Like last time."

"Exactly… like last time."

"Why's he in Rhode Island?"

Phil summons his patience. "He's scared, Vito."

"What's he done?"

"I've seen the transcripts. He's lost my trust. I think he knows."

Vito heaves a sigh. "Okay."

"Start the fucking car, will you?"

THREE

For a brief time, Carrie Madigan, wife of Phil Anwar, mob boss of Manhattan, Brooklyn, and Long Island, has some respite from the beatings her husband inflicts. She's at the rehab facility of the Payne Whitney Hospital in Manhattan. They, too, administer pain. They call it detoxification, and they do it cold turkey. Rages like a toothache in the gut and every appendage. Lasts two weeks. Then she goes home for more drugs and sporadic beatings. She's under no delusion about the nightmare quality of her life.

In the hospital she sometimes thinks of how it was when Phil had her heart, when she was barely nineteen, and he—smart, good-looking, powerful—flashed all the trappings of a romantic rogue. They met at a large gathering Phil hosted at a restaurant in the Fulton Fish Market called Sloppy Louie's. The affair was meant as an offering to the mob boss of Staten Island. One of his lieutenants invited Carrie's father, Conner Madigan, a small-time Staten Island lawyer who was known for a willingness to carry bags of cash to the local judges and politicians. Conner brought his daughter to the party and dangled her like bait.

Didn't take much for Phil to lead her off to one side. "You give a party like this," he said, "you don't really expect much. Then what do you know! Out of the blue, an angel appears."

"You're referring to me, are you?" said Carrie.

"I see none other in this room."

"Well, this room," she said. "In *this room*, anyone normal would look angelic."

Phil laughed. He liked clever women, especially those who bit. "So, is your being here a matter of coercion?"

"Coercion stopped working with me a long time ago."

"You wanted to come."

"I was curious."

"About *mobsters*," he said, brightening his eyes in self-dramatization.

"About you," she said.

Later that night, Phil took her for a spin in his long, finned, sky-blue Caddy and showed her a Manhattan club life she'd only read about: the Stork Club, Birdland, the Copacabana, and a Bowery dive featuring lip-synching transvestites, with Judy Garland in the audience. Wherever they went, a table materialized next to the stage, with a bottle and two glasses, but never a check.

Phil was not quite forty and already the boss, the *capofamiglia*. She was a Loyola sophomore majoring in marketing, so he talked to her, in the weeks that followed, about his own principles of management—how he kept his teams small and delegated authority—and about his long-range plans for legitimatizing his businesses. He shared his early history: St. David's, Lawrenceville, Brown, NYU Business School; as well as a revisionist history of his rise to power: his father's death, his uncle's abdication, Phil's bloody coronation and the much bloodier warfare to solidify his reign. He took her to his apartment on Central Park West, his estate on the North Shore of Long Island, and his weekend retreat in Lyford Cay. It was like Gatsby flinging down his wardrobe of shirts. And he solicited her love with kindnesses and charm.

They were married in her family church near her home on Staten Island. On Phil's tab, her dad was allowed to play the munificent host at the banquet following. Phil had been generous from the moment she'd met him. And he completely co-opted her parents.

Conner was easy. A weak man with a love of Irish whiskey, he was on the block for anyone feeding his appetite or his pride. Her mom, Katherine, however, was a sharp-tongued stalk of a woman, who initially regarded Phil with scorn. He wasn't Irish—he was, in her words, a "fancy-man crook"—and he couldn't possibly attain the gentility which she claimed as her own birthright and therefore her daughter's. Phil understood her perfectly. He agreed that she had every reason to be resentful of her circumstances in this country and a perfectly appropriate need to return to Killarney as a woman of property. So he booked her first class on Aer Lingus for an all-expenses-paid three weeks at the Dunloe Castle Hotel.

Carrie and Phil could laugh together at this smoothing of Katherine and Conner, at her parents' readiness to take over the wedding preparations, at the FBI's shooting pictures of the wedding guests, at the comical appearance of wiseguys in cutaways, at the over-exuberance of the catering, and the enormity of the cake. Phil was clever about people; he could size up immediately what anyone wanted. He could also laugh at himself, even his power, and he plainly loved his young Carrie.

They had a child in nine months, a girl they named Sarah after Phil's mother who had died giving birth to him. Several months after the christening of their daughter, Phil began exhibiting passions that wouldn't have shocked those subject to his actual managerial principles but were stunning to his twenty-year-old bride. He liked tying his young wife to the bed naked and stropping her with a leather belt. The belt, he told her, was how his father once taught him life lessons. So he himself took pains explaining to Carrie why punishment was being administered. The beating was always for her own benefit, according to Phil, and rarely done with the buckle end.

Often the beating was said to be for something she did, or more commonly failed to do, while under the influence of the drugs to which Phil himself had introduced her. He wasn't unaware of the irony, Carrie thought, or the hypocrisy. He was simply indifferent to both.

Providing drugs, mainly heroin, is the way Phil controls her. She's often left him, but invariably comes back. Drugs are the core of Phil's business. His supply is inexhaustible. And Phil always apologizes a day or two after each beating, promising never to hit her again.

Carrie's skin is translucent. Blue veins run visibly beneath it like a roadmap to her heart. Phil never breaks her skin. He seems to know the precise shade of discoloration that precedes bloody sheets and a permanent scar. But there can be little question that he takes great pleasure in thrashing her. She'll catch him reacting intently to the way she twists and turns her wisp of a body on the mattress to avoid the blows, the way she screams when they land. Eventually, as his blows become rhythmic, he'll close his eyes as if transported to a place of indescribable serenity.

A nurse at Payne Whitney arrives with a needle. Her name is Terry, and she's from the Deep South. "You got a choice," Terry says. "Your father's here—a man who claims he's your father, Conner Madigan by name, and I believe him, 'cause he's good-looking like you. So you can have this needle or the man, but if you choose the man, he can't stay long 'cause you need this needle. You following this?" Hovering over the bed, Terry—black, squat, upbeat, and professional—waits for an answer.

"Show him in."

"Will do, honey chile," Terry says, deliberately mimicking the stereotype.

Carrie looks around her. A double room, but she is its only occupant. The room has faded lime-colored walls, vinyl floor coverings fatigued to a mud-like hue, and a window. She's been out of bed only once to check the view. It's of an alley of dirty brick, black fire escapes, and unwashed panes. Moving is still very difficult for her. Of course she's on the verge of feeling wonderful. Addicts call it the "pink cloud."

"Hi, baby," says her father, with Nurse Terry hanging for just a moment to make sure he's who he says he is. A stooped, well-dressed man of middle height and curly, somewhat oily, gray hair, Conner appears to be cheerful, which means he's had a few "liveners," as he calls them, at a local pub.

Sitting on the chair next to the bed, he takes a closer look at her disfigured face and frowns, his own once-fine features now bumpy with large pores and flushed with broken blood vessels.

"Phil," she says, by way of explanation. "He beats the shit out of me whenever he likes, which is often."

"Jeeze, baby." Her father is terrified of Phil, though he was happy enough with the connection when she married him. "I thought he'd stopped that."

Carrie laughs to cover her bitterness and yanks the hospital bathrobe around herself more tightly.

"I could talk to him again."

"Oh, great," she says. "That'll fix it."

They both stare into the futility of such a suggestion.

"How's Mom?"

Conner winces. "The same." He fumbles in his pocket for a Chesterfield, lights it shakily, finds an ashtray on the window sill, comes back to the chair.

Carrie thinks about sending regards, then decides not to waste her breath.

"I'm leaving him," she says.

"Jesus, Carrie."

"Yeah."

"Maybe—" Conner starts.

"What? He's not going to do it again? It's my fault? It never happened?"

"I didn't—"

"I'm not stupid," she says. "He's not gonna change. I've had enough."

"Where will you go?" He already looks frightened.

"I have a place. That's what the last beating was about. Supposedly."

"Oh, jeeze, baby. What about Sarah?"

"I'll take her with me."

"You will?"

"Phil has no rights."

"Oh… rights," he says, with a deep drag on the Chesterfield.

"You remember what Sarah was like as an infant?"

"Of course."

"The happiest kid, almost never cried, loved to be held."

"She cries a lot now?"

"No," Carrie says. "But she doesn't laugh much either."

"You're saying Phil—"

"He adores her."

"So?"

"He's making *me* miserable, what do you think! And beat up! You think a child can watch that?"

"He hits you in front of the child?" Conner says, squirming.

"Jesus, no. He doesn't have to. You're not getting any of this. Or don't want to. I can't have Sarah living in a house where her mom's getting beaten up every other day."

"I dunno, Carrie, I dunno."

"What are you worried about, Da, Phil cutting you off?"

He shows a pout. "Needn't be unkind."

"No worries about yourself, is it?"

"That's the least of it. I'm thinking of you."

"That right? Be a first."

"I can protect you."

"Oh, yes?"

"Yeah, you and Sarah. Come live with us. Maybe…" he begins.

"Maybe what?"

Conner sits up in the straight-backed chair. "I could get an order of protection?"

Her laugh belittles him.

"You think I can't?"

"He'd probably kill you," she says.

"Let him try!"

"Oh come on, Dad."

"What about you?" says Conner, his hand trembling ashes over her bed. "He'd probably beat you to death."

"No way," she says. "Guy like Phil doesn't actually kill his wife. Much less the mother of his kid. It's a sign of weakness. He goes up to that line. That's a sign of expertise."

A low groan comes from deep in the man's throat.

"Stuff it, Dad, will you! You're a fucking broken record."

"Isn't there anything that can be done?"

"Oh sure, you got a cannon?"

"Maybe...."

"Will you stop with the maybes!"

"Maybe he's not totally hopeless."

"Didn't you hear what I just said?"

"Yeah, but maybe"—Conner looks away—"if you were... nicer to him?"

Her eyes get squinty and dark. "Boy."

"I'm only saying...."

"You're out of your depth."

"What then?"

"What do you think?" she says. "What do you think stops a guy like Phil? An abuser like Phil? You think he likes just sex? He likes the beatings. That's his sex. That, he gets off on. And he's what? One of the twenty most powerful guys in the whole fucking world. So how do *you* stop him from doing what he most likes to do?"

Conner's brow bunches. "Maybe...."

"Oh shit."

"Maybe when he's in one of those moods—you know, when he's apologizing—you could suggest... I don't know... therapy?"

Carrie, dazed for a moment, lets out a guffaw. "One thing about you, Dad! Always good for a laugh."

FOUR

Alec and Darcy met senior year on spring break in Bermuda. Outside the army barracks, where the rugby teams stayed, Alec was perched on a low stone wall, face up to a light tropical rain, trying to distill the rum punches out of his brain cells. Darcy came screeching up the driveway on a motorbike, yellow slicker billowing, pale hair wet and wild. "Where's the goddamn party?" she demanded to know in a voice made at prep schools and New York cotillions.

They still get on reasonably well. The world, according to Darcy, is peopled largely by dimwits with whom she communicates on terms of sweet insincerity. With persons she likes, she banters. Fun, but never relaxing. And Alec never knows what the girl wants.

The Stork Club is their hangout. For them, the velvet rope always comes down. And in that blue-and-gold room glistening with silver and crystal, they congregate with their fellows and an occasional celebrity to the beat of Lester Lanin refrains. If Sherman Billingsley, the owner, is there, their dinner is comped. Darcy, a recent Smith graduate, was a classmate of Sherman Billingsley's daughter at Miss Porter's.

Darcy's willowy Botticellian form packages the appetites of a mink. "If I like the boy," Darcy would say, as when she showed Alec her favorite masturbatory technique in a bathtub in the old Taft Hotel in New Haven. "Running water?" asked Alec. "Oh, yes!" she said languidly, the V of her legs poised under the spout. "But the temperature has to be perfect."

In the cab taking her home from the Stork Club, Alec says, "I'm afraid I'm about to become even busier."

"Great," she says. "Even busier than totally inaccessible."

"Looks that way."

"Then you'd better come up," she says. "Mummy and Daddy are away."

Alec had never been on good terms with either of Darcy's parents. As the son of impoverished socialists, he embodies their worst nightmare. And to Alec, the von Hammerts seem like birds of prey, maneuvering beyond their means on the fringes of New York society.

They keep a tiny apartment in a Park Avenue co-op for which a listing in the Social Register is a minimum requirement. Their bedroom, despite their absence, Darcy declares off-bounds. This leaves a slender cot in Darcy's room, the sort of six-by-four cell in which Park Avenue families used to torture their servants. Alec and Darcy, having shed all clothes, squeeze together on it as tightly as they can. Until Alec, attempting something overly ambitious, falls out of the cot.

"Oh, shit!" Darcy declares. "If we could only live our lives at the Stork Club, everything would be fine."

Alec starts getting dressed. "I'd better go. I actually have to work tomorrow."

"Oh, well, in *that* case!" she says.

When he kisses her goodnight, she says nothing, and doesn't move from the cot when he leaves.

Outside, in the elevator vestibule, Alec pushes the button and waits. Eventually, the elevator doors open. A uniformed gray-haired retainer appears, his expression implacable. They both hear the scream inside the apartment—a sound of raw anguish. The doorman's face remains impassive. "I'll be another few minutes," Alec says, and goes back inside.

He finds Darcy sitting on the edge of her cot, with a nightgown bunched at her shoulders. "What happened?" he asks.

"Whatta you mean?" she says, getting her arms through the sleeves and the nightgown into its normal and more useful position.

"I heard a scream."

She gives him bright eyes and a hard shell, as if to say she couldn't imagine to what he might be referring.

"Not you, huh?"

She bats her eyes and shakes her head twice.

"Must have been some other apartment," he says.

"Must have been."

"You okay?" he asks.

"Well," she says in an upbeat voice. "I'm not having what you'd call a really great day."

He doesn't know what to say.

"Go," she says.

"Darcy, I'm sorry. I'll call you."

"Go already! Get out of here!"

"We'll talk about this."

"Like hell we will!"

"See you Sunday?"

She shrugs.

FIVE

In a Narragansett diner, a man eating dinner in a suit and vest is conspicuous, no matter how ordinary he might otherwise appear. Aaron Weinfeld has no leisure clothes, however. He's a widower, has no hobbies or even much leisure, and devotes himself to the practice of law, which he rarely enjoys. For Aaron, it's an activity engaged in solely to make money. He is not physically attractive, being a portly man with a protruding brow and an inadept comb-over. He likes sex with women and pays for it. He also feels invigorated on occasion by elements of danger, which his work offers him as well as making him rich. He isn't consigliere to any one crime family, but rather, in his fields of expertise—market manipulations and commodities law—he acts as outside counsel to several families in New England, New Jersey, and New York. Of course representing potentially conflicting interests places him in a precarious position.

The day before, his young office manager, Carrie Madigan, had come to him with news that made his situation untenable. She'd been away for two weeks, he thought on holiday, so he was surprised to see her normally pleasant face lined with distress. Carrie's husband, Phil Anwar, was Aaron's principal client. Aaron assumed Phil's aim, in placing his wife in Aaron's office, was to allow her to spy on other families. For that reason, Aaron didn't want to hire her, and all his other clients were furious he had, but Phil left him no choice. Now Aaron was glad he had taken her on.

"You've got to run, Aaron."

"Run?" he said. "I haven't done a thing."

"Doesn't matter," Carrie told him.

"What's happened?"

"It's subtle."

"Maybe I can fix it."

She shook her head. "As I understand it, Little John has turned sour on the Bayonne thing. It's too close to him."

"I know this."

"Because of Bayonne and other reasons, Little John's also turning on Phil. At the same time Phil thinks you've gotten way too close to Little John. Which is dangerous to Phil because of what you know."

"I haven't done anything! I've been very careful."

"Not the way Phil sees it. And he's had your phone tapped."

"*My phone!*"

" 'Fraid he has."

"I haven't said anything."

She gave him a look.

"One can always be misinterpreted," he uttered in an agitated voice.

"I said it was subtle."

"Subtle? That's it? That's enough for Phil to have me killed? After all I've done for him?"

"Just go, Aaron. Today. And don't tell me where."

He left. Carrie knew what she was talking about and gained nothing by telling him except risk to herself. Aaron was touched. She was trying to save his life.

He thought she had done so. And he'd been congratulating himself on having chosen Narragansett as a place no one would dream to look for him. *I won't stay here for long*, he thinks. *I'll keep moving around.*

Aaron is no fool; years ago, when there could have been no suspicions or reasons for phone taps, he prepared himself with an escape hatch: alternate identities, different bank accounts, places to stay. *I'll be all right*, he thinks.

Then Vito walks into the diner.

This muscle-bound menacing figure slides into the booth across from Aaron. He simply stares into Aaron's startled eyes. The lawyer is too shocked to say anything.

Finally, Vito speaks. "Narragansett?"

"I'm here vacationing."

"That right?" Vito says.

"Love it off-season. The sea air."

"Know what you mean," Vito says, nodding sagaciously.

"How'd you happen to know where I was?"

"Oh," says Vito, "usual ways."

"You've put the tap on me, Vito? When?"

"Not me, no."

"Those are confidential communications you're intercepting. Lawyer, client."

"What can I tell ya?"

"So what's up, Vito?" Aaron asks, shifting his weight on the hard wooden seat of the booth. "What the fuck's happening?"

"Not here. I've got the boat at the boatyard."

"You want me to get on a boat with you?" Aaron manages to say, fear tightening his throat.

Vito shrugs.

"I'm not getting on a boat with you."

Vito's look is apologetic.

"That's crazy! A fucking boat! No fucking way!"

Vito spreads his hands and smiles, as if to say, *you don't have much of a choice about this.*

"You here alone?" Aaron asks.

"No, couple of the guys came along. They're outside."

"Front and back?"

"That's right."

"You're here to kill me, Vito?"

"Absolutely not. Just talk."

"Why do we have to get on the boat?"

"The sea air," says Vito. "I love it too."

Four miles out to sea, Aaron throws himself around Vito's ankles, crying in panic and grief. "I haven't done anything, Vito! Please let me see Phil."

There's a young hood on board named Joey Forcaccio. He's rocking with Vito on this fifteen-foot craft, helping to untangle Aaron from Vito's legs. Together—sea spray and wind whipping their faces, the older man struggling pitiably—they prop him at the aft railing. Aaron is sobbing, pleading for his life, offering them all his money, promising forever to be loyal and good. *This is so sad*, Vito thinks, then shoots the top of Aaron's head off with a Smith & Wesson 1911 semi-automatic .45-caliber pistol.

It's not a job Vito enjoys. He thinks of himself as a paramilitary organization man and would always prefer a pitched battle. Now—even though they'd taken the trouble of dragging Aaron to the rail—given the direction of the wind, the deck needs some swabbing. It's a job Vito dislikes even more.

SIX

Sunday morning. Darcy opens the door to Alec's apartment, which would depress anyone, especially when it rains. The apartment had been advertised as a "street-level with yard" in a "charming brownstone" between Madison and 5th. The address was accurate, and the building itself charming for those living above ground. For Alec, living in the basement, there was little charm, but the price was right, and he knew he'd be there only to sleep. The "yard," though, turned out to be a small slab of concrete. Darcy refers to it as a "guano factory," in view of its attraction to pigeons. What disturbs her most is the incessant cooing.

She storms into Alec's tiny bedroom, making as much noise as she can. "How can you sleep with that pigeon racket?" she says.

Startled awake, he blinks at her.

After breakfast, which they have at Soup Burg, the rain stops, and they go for a walk in Central Park, taking the path up to the track around the reservoir embankment. Few joggers. It's seven-thirty on a wet Sunday morning. Darcy plainly has something on her mind.

"What do you feel," she says, "when we make love?" She stops and reconsiders. "Or maybe that's loading the question. When we have sex?"

"Making love with you is wonderful," he says carefully.

She resumes walking. "That's it? Makes you feel wonderful?"

"It's not a weak feeling."

They walk in silence.

There's a lane leading down to the bridle path, and she takes it. In front of them stands an ancient tree, a London Plane, whose roots sprout out of the ground like ganglia. Darcy puts her ear to the trunk.

"What do you hear?" Alec asks, thinking she's clowning.

"Listen!" she says, beckoning.

He puts his ear to the bark too, humoring her, then comes away. "What?"

"The forest goddesses."

"You hear goddesses conversing in trees?"

"Of course," she says.

"What do they tell you?"

"To get the hell out of this relationship."

He puts his hands on her shoulders. "Those goddesses..."

"Yeah?"

"Never know what they'll say."

"They have a point, though, don't you think?"

"It's questionable."

"Should be clear."

Alec knows the banter has stopped.

"I'm sorry, Darcy."

"Me too."

"Hard to understand."

"Not to me," she says. "I'm not what you're looking for."

"You know what I'm looking for?"

"Wild guess."

"So let's hear."

She purses her lips. "Someone softer, I think. Not as all-together. Maybe someone you can mend."

"How could you know that?"

"Dunno, Alec. Just radiates out of you. Maybe 'cause you need mending yourself?"

SEVEN

In his office, Alec deals with letters requiring answers that day, messages requiring return calls that morning. Macalister was scheduled to fly in the night before, and they've arranged to meet in court at nine a.m. Good timing. The witness, J.J. Tierney, still hasn't given the testimony that his lawyer, Hal Richardson, promised.

Alec stuffs his lit bag with papers he thinks he'll need in court; then, halfway to the elevator, on an impulse, he goes back for some additional documents. Adding them to the bag, he's about to take off again when the telephone rings.

"Brno," he answers.

"Good thing I caught you."

"Mac?" says Alec. "You're in court already? I'm just on my way."

"I'm still in Miami, kiddo. Hearing here's been put over to this afternoon."

Well, well! What an interesting development!

"You know Tierney hasn't come through yet," Alec says.

"Don't worry," says Mac.

"I think there's a risk he might not."

"There's always a risk, kiddo."

"So what should we do?" Alec says. "Get an adjournment?"

"Why would you want to do that?"

"Me?" says Alec. "Adjournment? Hell no. I'll handle it."

Macalister's laugh rasps into the receiver. "Wouldn't sweat this, dear boy. We've got a deal with Richardson *and* Tierney. Double confirmed. Tierney's to tell the damn truth. Piece of cake for you."

"Walk in the park."

"So, you okay with this?"

"Absolutely."

"Good. Break a leg, kid."

Alec is left holding the receiver, wondering whether he'll be left holding the bag.

On the street, he passes up cabs, choosing to walk. Fast-paced, almost a jog. Gets the blood running. Works down the nerves. The nerves are the problem.

Jesus Christ! I may have to cross-examine a witness!

Walking north, there's the Federal Courthouse on Foley Square, the remnants of FDR's gold-leafed pentahedron roof flashing its phony image of prosperity. Behind it looms Alec's destination: the dark-domed State Supreme Courthouse, its outer walls the color of dried blood.

Carrie Madigan stands indecisively at the top of the stairs of the State Courthouse. To go down for some coffee before her ten-thirty hearing? To go inside and wait in the courtroom? To wander to Chinatown, knock on some doors? She looks in her handbag. A lipstick, makeup, some cash. Not what she now needs, but enough money to buy it. So she'll go down the stairs. At least think about Chinatown.

She begins her descent.

She would not strike everyone as being beautiful. Her face, a small oval, is too pale, her bones delicate and sharp. Her mussed dark auburn hair is in need of a brushing. She gives the impression of being taller than she is, since she's leggy, her shoulders narrow, sharply bladed. But to Alec, ascending the stairs, there is, as they pass, in one brief unguarded exchange, an insistent shock of recognition.

Alec turns as he reaches the top of the stairs and looks down for her. Carrie, having arrived at the pavement, is negotiating her way through the crowd. Just as he turns back to enter the building, she stops to look up. Sees him go through the doors. Doesn't consider re-climbing the stairs, but does rethink the Chinatown plan. She heads for the coffee cart on the corner where she knows, from experience, jelly doughnuts are sold.

EIGHT

B en Braddock rasps into his squawk box. "Mac?"
  "Yeah, Ben?"
Braddock leans back, his legs resting on the top of his desk, his hands clasped behind his neck. "What the fuck you doing, Mac?"

"How's that, Ben?"

"Your secretary. She's saying you're still in Miami."

"That's right."

"So J.J. Tierney? You gonna let him cross-examine himself?"

"Got it covered," Macalister says.

"Oh, yeah?"

"Alec's handling it."

"Alec?"

"Brno."

"Brno? Whatta you know! What's he, second-year?"

"I know what you're thinking."

"You mean that you're outta your fucking mind?"

"In the first place, Alec's ready to do this."

"That right?" Ben says. "A second-year associate?"

"Have you seen his record?"

"Why would I have seen his record?"

"You ought to take more interest in who we're hiring here, Ben."

"And I'm going to learn that by reading law school records?"

"Well, this one's unusual."

"What?" Braddock says. "He didn't go to Yale or Harvard?"

"He was at Yale."

"Then don't tell me—he wasn't first in his class."

"Actually he wasn't," says Macalister, "but he did pretty well. What's unusual is, after the first two weeks, he stopped going to class. Drove the faculty crazy. Some of them refused to read his exam papers, just graded them D, or he probably would have been first."

"What was his point?" Braddock asks, getting mildly interested.

"Time. He was editor-in-chief of the *Law Journal,* running two businesses to pay his way, and teaching a tax class."

"A law student? Teaching? At the law school?"

"Even more unusual, right. The tax professor—after working with Alec on an article for the *Law Journal*—was so impressed he partnered with him to teach the advanced course in corporate reorganizations. Then he just let Alec do it on his own. In fact, Alec holds a record at that school that will never be broken. He taught more classes than he attended."

"It ain't trial work," Braddock snaps.

"I know. But Alec is the smartest associate we've had in at least ten years, maybe longer. And the fact is I worked out a deal with Richardson. Tierney will confess to having authorized the tapping of the Biogram phones. So there shouldn't be any reason to cross-examine at all."

"That's all you need from Tierney, that admission?"

"The last piece, yeah. The state attorney general is claiming that Tierney's company could have used its patent to stop our client, Biogram, from entering the market but let us in because we agreed to fix prices. The reality is Tierney let us in because we caught him red-handed tapping our wires. Not only would that have put Tierney in prison, it gave us a patent misuse defense to his suit for patent infringement."

"You say Tierney will admit this?"

"Sure. It's their defense as well as ours. To the price-fixing claim. And Richardson has made him understand there's no risk he'll be prosecuted now for illegal wire tapping. It's too old, and we're not complaining."

"And you trust this kid? If things blow up?"

"If we're ever going to think about making him a partner, Ben, we'd better find out what we have."

NINE

Four men in dark suits and fedoras arrive in a limousine at the locked gate of the Bayonne oil storage facility. They're all smoking, so the car windows are open a bit. A slender, fiftyish man of medium height and sallow complexion gets out of the car to try to improve his view of the grounds. Dropping his cigarette and grinding it out on the pavement, he gets back in and instructs the driver to blow the horn. Finally a car from inside arrives, and Whitman Poole, hatless, steps out to open the gate.

After the limo rolls into the compound, Poole signals the driver to stop and open the window further. "You're a little early," he says to the four men, "but we're ready for you."

Poole, his men, and the four visitors assemble near the office tower. No one is smoking now. Poole introduces himself and points to the nearest tank. "We thought we'd start here."

The slender man speaks. "Hank Sturrage, Senior V.P., Chemical Bank. I'm in charge of the operation. We'll start at the edge of the field and work our way toward the center."

"We're already set up here," says Poole.

Sturrage gives him a look of impatience.

"Surely," says Poole, "you don't have to check every single tank. It would take all day. More. You'd be here through tomorrow."

"Look, mister. I have no idea yet whether the other tanks are empty or full. But the only tank we don't have to check is the one you've set up on. I've got a fair notion that one's bulging with diesel."

"Are you accusing me?" asks Poole with outraged incredulity.

"I just want to get started. So if you could tell your men to bring the rods, we'll all climb up that tank over there, near the gate."

TEN

In a shabby courtroom packed with reporters, Pharmex's chief executive, J.J. Tierney, is being examined by his lawyer, Hal Richardson. The examination has taken up most of the morning. It's now twenty-seven past twelve, and they've reached what appears to be the end of the subject on which they've spent the last half hour. Richardson hesitates and looks upward with a pensive expression. He then puts to the court the question foremost on everyone's mind.

"Would this be a good time to break for lunch, your Honor?"

Judge Robert Locklear, heavily jowled and large-bellied, stares down at Richardson and the army of lawyers arrayed behind counsel tables. The jurist quickly picks out the least experienced lawyer in the room, to his surprise occupying a first chair.

"Where's Macalister?" barks the judge.

Alec rises, for the first time ever, to speak in a courtroom. "Called away, your Honor. Unexpectedly. An emergency."

"And you—how do you pronounce your name?"

"Burr-know, your Honor."

"You plan to cross-examine Mr. Tierney when we get back from lunch, after Mr. Richardson finishes up?"

Alec's right leg begins to twitch. The counsel table starts shimmying before Alec realizes it's his knee that's partnering the dance. A young lawyer named Jed, an associate from another firm, makes a heroic catch of the water pitcher as it flies from the table.

"I'm considering it, your Honor."

"Ever cross-examine a witness before, Mr.… Bruno?"

"No, your Honor."

"Jed, give him back that water pitcher, will ya? He's gonna need it. Dry mouth!"

All laugh. The judge has cracked a joke.

"All rise!" chants the bailiff as his Honor descends, ponderously, from the bench.

The lawyers pack up their lit bags. Alec is halfway down the hall when Richardson, racing to catch up to him, calls out. Alec slows, and the two walk in tandem toward the elevators in the building's rotunda.

"I just told the clerk," says Richardson, slightly winded. "I've decided I have no further questions for Tierney, and the state's done with him. So what do you say? Can I let him go back to his office?"

"Whoa!" Alec says, pulling up short. "You told us he'd admit to the wire-tapping."

"He's changed his mind, Alec. Sorry." Practiced smile.

"Tierney doesn't give that testimony, then what the hell's our defense?"

"It's not that serious," Richardson purrs.

"Not serious?" says Alec, fighting panic, trying to be patient. "Whatta you mean, what am I missing?"

"The state's case is not that strong."

"You gotta be kidding. You guys let us into the market either because we caught you tapping our phones—which happens to be the goddamn truth—or because we agreed to fix prices— which is the state's theory. Which this jury is all too ready to buy. In which case people in both companies will be going to prison. Because this judge can't wait to be in the headlines. So—Hal—to me, it looks pretty damn serious."

"I don't know what to tell you, kid. Tierney's not going to cop to it."

"Why? You think they're going to prosecute Tierney for authorizing a wiretap? Seven years after it happened? When we're not complaining about it?"

"Not likely." Another smile. "I've told him."

"But he thinks they can't touch him personally on the price fix, just nail the company and his subordinates."

Richardson shrugs.

"So he's willing to sell them out," Alec says. "Who are you representing, Hal? Tierney or the company? Seems to be a conflict here."

"You know I can't talk about this."

"We had a deal, Hal."

The smile with another shrug, this one more apologetic.

"Okay," says Alec. "I get it. Macalister's gone. You don't think I have the balls to cross-examine Tierney myself. Well, let me tell you—I have no fucking choice!"

In another corridor of the courthouse, Alec is on a pay phone with Macalister's secretary.

"Jane, can you reach Mac? I need him immediately."

"He's in Miami, Alec."

"I know he's in Miami, but his hearing wasn't scheduled to start until later."

"He's not… reachable."

"Jane. Enough with the code. Where is he?"

"He said to say… he's in court."

"Ah."

"So you see."

"Not reachable."

"What I've been telling you, Alec."

"All right," says Alec. "Switch me to Braddock."

"He is in court. But Madge can reach him."

"Okay," Alec says. "Switch me to Madge. I'll hang on." He reaches into his pocket for another couple of dimes.

ELEVEN

B en Braddock strides into Foley Square Park, leaving his entourage in front of the Federal Courthouse packing lit bags
into the trunk of a limo. Spotting Alec walking across Centre
Street, Braddock beckons him toward a bench in the middle of
the park.

"Yes?" says Braddock. Neither man sits.

"Tierney's welshed on the deal," Alec says. "Won't admit the
wiretapping. And Richardson's just letting him walk—screw his
client, and screw us."

Braddock looks impatient. Like he never believed in Mac's
deal. Like this is exactly what he expected of Tierney. And so
far as Richardson is concerned, it's hardly news that a lawyer is
willing to sell out the company he represents for the CEO, the
person who actually retained him. "Who's in the courtroom?"
Ben asks.

For Alec, the question seems off the point. "Whatta you
mean? The eighteen lawyers for the other defendants?"

"No, no," says Braddock, his impatience mounting.

"The twenty, thirty reporters?"

Braddock settles down on the bench, his long legs stretched
out. In his dark suit and tie, he looks like a preoccupied pall-
bearer. "You know what you lack?"

Alec sits next to him. "Brains?"

"I'm talking about something important."

"Ability? Experience?"

"Christ!" Braddock says. "You people don't get it. Reputation! You need a rep! How can you be a great trial lawyer when

no one's ever heard of you?"

"I haven't been doing this very long," Alec says.

Braddock makes a deprecating sound. "When I was your age, I'd already tried high-profile cases. Got lots of press. See! That's what you need. People reading your name in the newspapers. You don't have to be any good. You just need the ink. It makes people think you're good. You following this?"

Alec nods.

"You nervous?" Braddock asks.

Alec's look denies it.

"Litigation, you know, is just sublimated violence."

Alec, laughing, says, "Violence runs in my family."

"Then you're suited to the work."

"You understand," says Alec, "with Mac in Miami, I'm the only lawyer from the firm who's in that courtroom."

"And what? You consider yourself understaffed?"

"No. I can handle it."

"Then why the fuck are you wasting my time?" Braddock says, rising to his feet.

"Right," Alec says, watching the old warrior head back toward his limo.

But then Braddock turns with a thought. "What's the name of that wiretapper?"

"Carl Raffon," Alec says.

"You want him in court?" Braddock asks.

"We have his affidavit."

Braddock consults his watch, then the heavens. "Okay," he says and heads off.

Alec, having taken the stairs two at a time to the second floor of the courthouse, realizes he's in a sweat. He heads toward the men's room, douses his face with water. Stares hard at his image in the mirror. Tense.

He makes for the counsel room. During lunchtime it's deserted. He pulls the stack of documents out of his briefcase. The top three, the ones he went back for, he deals to the table and stares at without comprehension. What he sees in his mind is Richardson's smug face. Then he focuses, and knows what to do.

Someone has left that morning's *New York Times* on a chair. Alec cuts out a story at random, brings the clipping to the Ozalid copying machine set up in the room and reproduces it on eight-and-a-half-by-eleven copying paper. Now he's ready for the two lying bastards inside.

Judge Locklear, reassuming the bench, looks downward. "Mr. Bruno?"

Alec stands. He feels a curious, euphoric sensation. No nerves—they've miraculously vanished. In their place, a little adrenaline, which is good, and confidence, which is splendid. "Burr-know, your Honor. And I do have some questions for Mr. Tierney."

The judge looks surprised, then indulgent. "Do try to leave the table intact, son."

A wave of courtroom laughter washes over Alec, reddening his face but doing no damage.

"Yes, your Honor."

Alec crosses over to the court reporter, handing him a document.

"I ask the reporter to mark as Biogram's Exhibit 1 for identification—and show to the witness—an affidavit sworn to by a Mr. Carl Raffon."

Alec waits as the document is stamped and given to Tierney who glances at it briefly with disdain. Tierney's a homely man with a pockmarked, bulldog face, but he seems to take such pleasure in his own appearance one is led to believe something pleasurable might actually be found there.

"Mr. Tierney, do you personally know Mr. Raffon?"

"Do you mean, have I met with him? I have no such recollection."

"Really!" says Alec, removing another document from the top of his stack. He holds it up, glances through it, finds the place that he wants. "You don't remember meeting him some years ago, and referring to him as a 'possibly useful fellow?' "

Tierney, now wary, studies Alec anew. *Does the document actually say that?* Uncertainty marks the witness's demeanor. "No," he says finally.

Alec again swoops down on the reporter. "I ask that this document be marked as Biogram's Exhibit 2 for identification, and be shown to the witness. The question, Mr. Tierney, is, does it refresh your recollection?"

The reporter dutifully stamps the one sheet of paper and places it before Tierney who regards it as something repellent.

Alec waits. The judge waits less patiently. Tierney finally picks up the memo. Perusing it, he finds something he likes.

"As it happens, it does refresh my recollection. It seems I did meet with Raffon. And I also recall—as it says here—that he worked on projects for a lot of major companies in addition to mine."

"Okay. You remember there was a meeting. I want you to read paragraphs eight and nine of the affidavit where Raffon describes what was said at that meeting. And then tell us, Mr. Tierney, whether those sworn statements are untrue."

Richardson rises to object, his manner condescending. "We've been over this, your Honor. Asked and answered. Mr. Tierney's already testified he recalls no such conversation."

"That's not quite what he said," says the judge. "In any event, I'm going to allow this. You may answer, Mr. Tierney."

"Well, all right," says Tierney, shifting into a friendlier pose.

"There was a conversation with Raffon about his doing an investigation of Biogram. We were in litigation with those people. So naturally.... But if he tapped anyone's wires.... I never authorized that. He did that on his own. He was way out ahead of himself." Big phony smile. "Okay? Got what you wanted? Can I go back to work now?"

Alec feels a jerking on his sleeve. It's Jed, who pulls him into a hurried whispered conference.

"Stop here! You've got enough, Alec. Go further, you could lose it."

Alec nods—it's the safe course—but when he straightens up, he sees Tierney's look of triumph. "Had you ever used Raffon before this job?" Alec asks.

Tierney displays his disgust: "I don't believe so."

"Had you used other investigators with whom you were satisfied?"

Tierney glances at the judge, as if to ask to be relieved of this annoyance, but gets only a stony stare in return. With a sigh of tedium being borne, he says, "My company is… large. Large companies use investigators. Some of them do satisfactory work."

"So before the Biogram job, you had had satisfactory experience with other investigators and no experience with Raffon, yet you hired Raffon."

To Tierney's discomfit, Alec picks another document from his stack and fixes his eyes on it for a moment. "Had you ever personally been informed by a memorandum that Raffon's specialty was wiretapping? In fact," says Alec, running his finger along the bottom of a line, "that the man was incapable of doing anything else?"

Tierney, twisting a bit in his chair, cannot resist a swift glance at his lawyer. And Richardson cannot resist giving a negative signal, a slight twitch of the head.

Now Tierney has two problems. The signal's ambiguous. Does it mean, *No, he's bluffing, he has no such document, so you're free to lie*? Or does it mean, *No, don't lie, he has such a document.* Far worse, the signal, whatever it meant, was seen by the judge.

"Mr. Richardson," intones Judge Locklear, causing the back of the lawyer's smooth neck to splotch purple and red. "I want to see you at the break. And let me remind you, sir," he rasps at Tierney, "that you are under oath." Locklear turns to the court reporter. "Read back the question."

"I'll repeat it, your Honor," says Alec, waving the document warningly before him. "Had you been told, Mr. Tierney, that Raffon's only specialty was wiretapping?"

Tierney stares at Richardson, who looks away.

"Yes," says Tierney, with barely suppressed fury.

"So for the Biogram job," says Alec, "you personally hired a known wiretapper?"

"Yes!" Tierney fairly spits the word in Alec's direction.

"I have no further questions of this witness, your Honor," Alec says, turning the document down on its face.

Judge Locklear looks curious. "You want to offer that exhibit in evidence, son?"

"Be no point, your Honor. It has nothing to do with this lawsuit."

TWELVE

In another, smaller courtroom on the second floor, Carrie Madigan stands waiting with dark, wondering eyes. Another judge—another tired, black-robed middle-aged man—studies her file with increasing consternation. His turning of pages is the only distinct sound. Carrie's hands drift now and then to objects on the counsel table or to the buttons of her blue dress. An assistant district attorney, approximately the judge's age, fidgets beside her. The room is otherwise empty except for the bailiff, standing to the judge's right, and one large dude, sleek as a Buddha, seated on the aisle in the last row of benches. The sun lowering through the window catches his cufflink diamond, the glint making the judge raise his head.

"The People's recommendation is a bit surprising, Miss Madigan, this being your second offense. However. If they see some hope for you…." The judge glances again at the papers with mixed weariness and disbelief. "Probation, then," he says, looking sharply at the ADA. "Three months. Straighten it out, Miss! Get yourself into rehab! This is a courtroom, not a revolving door."

"All rise!" says the bailiff, although only the large man in back had not already done so.

The ADA, traversing the aisle, bestows on the man a slight smile of acknowledgement and a small squeeze of the shoulder. Carrie, observing the exchange, is taken aback and not pleased by it.

Her displeasure flares when she finds the man following her ponderously into the corridor outside the courtroom. "Did you fix this?" she says, turning on him. "Is this Phil's doing?"

"No, to the second." His manner and voice imply the absurdity of the question.

"Who are you, and what do you want?" she says.

"A very small amount of your time," he says. "Given the circumstances." As she stares at him, he adds, "My name is Harvey Grand."

Alec, at that moment, rushes out of his courtroom, trailed by a pack of reporters. "Look," he says. "I told you guys. What was in that document is not for publication."

"I saw it," says a reporter with a lumpy nose. "Some article from the sports page. I'm gonna print that. I assume you're not going to deny."

What the hell is Harvey doing here with that young woman?

"Later, okay?" says Alec. "Someone there I've got to talk to."

Alec strides across the hall. "Harvey," he says, with his eyes now entirely on Carrie. "Careful of this guy."

"What about you?" she says.

His smile is quick. "I'm real easy."

Harvey says, "Carrie Madigan, Alec Brno." Then, to Alec, as the two continue to pay him no attention, "You get to use that Raffon affidavit?"

"That was you? Getting Raffon to sign?"

"Who the hell do you think?"

"You did good. I mean it." Alec looks at his watch. "Gotta get back to the office." Turning once more to Carrie, "Harvey'll have your number, right?

"I don't even know this guy," she says.

With a laugh, Alec gives Carrie his client routine. "This was a great first briefing, but I'll need to see you again." Heading off, he gives her his warmest smile.

"Okay," she says, bemused by it.

Alec moves toward the stairs, jabbing his finger in a gesture to Harvey and silently mouthing the words, "Get her number!"

THIRTEEN

Fifteen minutes of fame. Page eight of the *News*, which would boost any young lawyer's reputation. Page six of the *Post*, which was more a slam at Tierney for having been so easily taken in. Page three of the *Times* business section, which might mean more to the people who, to Alec, count. Like the firm's partners who now seem to know who he is. Or his fellow associates, some of whom, strangely, now seem not to want to. Or maybe Carrie Madigan, whose number, it turns out, is for a phone that's been disconnected.

Everything published on the case is read with interest by a fifty-six-year-old former union organizer on Long Island. He hasn't just clipped the stories; he's saving the whole papers, including the one he's carrying with him to an interview at the Syosset shopping center. But he's carrying that one because of the classifieds.

He parks an old Ford coupe a few yards from a storefront occupied by a firm called Syosset Security and rings the bell for admittance. He's a tall man with a bit of a stoop, yet wiry and with a full head of sandy hair, belying an overall appearance that is older than his years. At the welcoming buzzer, he enters.

Abigail Vaccaro, a trim woman of forty-nine, stands up from her desk. "Are you Sam?"

"I am."

"Sounds like the Dr. Seuss."

"The who?"

"That's another Dr. Seuss."

He looks puzzled.

"I'm talking children's books—*Green Eggs and Ham? Horton Hears a Who!?* Didn't you read Dr. Seuss to your kids?"

"Never heard of him."

Two people standing, which is awkward to begin with, so both try to think what to say.

She asks, "You have kids?"

"A son," he says.

"Well," she says, sitting, beckoning to the chair in front of her desk. "You're here for the job. Let's talk about that."

He plunks down on the indicated chair, trying not to be distracted by her fine features, hazel eyes, plentiful freckles, or literary references. "Good enough," he says, extracting a Camel, holding it up. "Mind?"

"No," she says, passing a metal ashtray.

He takes it, lights up.

"You killed a man," she says. "That I might mind. We should start there."

Big puff of smoke. "Right."

"You weren't prosecuted."

"No."

"Self-defense?"

"It was a fistfight. He had a hemorrhage. It was waiting to happen. I didn't know that. Neither, I'm sure, did he."

She sits back, runs one hand through a mane of undyed salt-and-pepper hair. He likes trim figures and admires hers.

She says, "You wrote about this on the form you dropped off. I thought, when I put on the form 'anything else I should know,' I'd get a lot of self-congratulatory bullshit. 'I killed a man'—that's different."

"I thought you should hear it from me."

"Good thinking. But you're still a risk."

"I can see why you'd think so."

"He was a security guard, the guy you killed?"

"Yes."

"Does that have anything to do with your application here?"

"No."

"Why are you applying?"

"Need the work." He drops an ash in the tray.

"Just read the ad, called, came in?"

"That's right."

Her mouth scrunches up in thought. "Ever work for a security company?"

"Haven't, no."

"Are you a college graduate?"

"No."

"High school?"

"No."

"You don't seem to be an uneducated man."

"I read a lot. Though not children's books."

"Self-educated," she says.

"You might say."

"Can you be trusted with weapons?"

"I know my way around weapons."

"That's not what I asked."

"Am I likely to use 'em?" he says, taking another deep puff of the Camel. "No."

"To defend your own life?"

"Well, there, hard to say."

"You wouldn't fire a gun to protect yourself?"

"Possibly not."

"Someone else?"

"Maybe. Depending."

She studies him. "Do you know what the word *laconic* means?"

Sam smiles. "Yes."

"You want a cup of coffee?"

"Sure," Sam says.

She gets up again. "Then let's go out and get one."

There's a coffee and bagel shop a storefront away that's been fashioned from an old-style diner. They sit at a booth in a window.

After a great deal of thought, she leans forward. "I should think that incident would render you almost unemployable."

"It has," he says.

"So why'd you tell me about it? I might never have found out."

"I said."

"I know. Still a risk. Why should I take it?"

He shrugs.

"Tell me," she says.

"Well, I didn't want the fight."

"He came at you?"

"With a bat."

"What were you doing, that he came at you?"

"Talking to the men."

"Where?"

"In the company cafeteria."

"You were warned off?"

"I was always warned off."

"So this was where, some industrial plant?"

"Steel plant in Akron."

"You always worked for the steel union?"

"Up to then."

"After?"

"Dockworkers. New Jersey."

She nods at that knowingly. "How long?"

"Couple of months?"

"What happened?" she asks.

"I didn't like who was running the union."

"The mob. You didn't know that going in?"

"It was the job available. I thought I'd try keeping my

distance."

"Didn't work?"

"No."

She reflects for a moment. "You have another one of those cigarettes?"

"Sure." He takes two out, hands her one, lights hers, then his, watches her inhale, figures she's a regular smoker.

"What did your father do?" she asks.

"Is that relevant?"

"I'm looking for… something."

"You probably won't find it there."

Her look presses the question.

"My father and his father were…." He makes a guttural sound. "They found labor wars and fought in them. My father was killed when I was nine."

"Not a risk-reducer."

"Actually it is. To essentially zero."

"It wasn't zero in Akron."

"It's because of Akron that it's now zero, full stop. It was low before Akron, but that wasn't low enough, was it?"

She sits back, has a puff, finishes her coffee. "We do two things. We supply security guards, and we install security systems. Your form also says you're experienced in those."

"That's right. One of the things I did. In addition to organizing."

"Including motion detectors?"

"Of course."

"I don't know why, but I believe everything you've told me."

"I don't know why either. But what I've told you is true."

"You know my husband started this business."

"Did he?"

"It's very successful, which is why I need someone to run crews."

"Glad to hear it."

"He died two years ago, my husband. A boating accident. Some stupid fishing trip up in Rhode Island."

"I'm sorry."

"He may have had too much to drink. He did that. They all did." Her eyes water up and she says with a flourish, "Just went over the rail."

"Wow."

"Yeah. And you're a widower?"

"Right."

"Mind saying how…."

"She was an alcoholic," he says. "She died of pneumonia, but it was the drinking that killed her."

"Boy."

"You could say that, yeah."

"There's something weird about all this."

He laughs for the first time in their meeting.

FOURTEEN

Alec's in the habit of getting to the office too early and leaving too late to conduct much of a personal life, let alone catch up on the news of the day. His reading consists of judicial decisions, interoffice memos, documents, and briefs. With Mac still in Miami, however, Alec finds time, on the way downtown, to flip through the morning papers.

The New York Times is filled with stories about Kendall, Blake clients. Telemarch News, Braddock's big media client, is involved in a humongous libel action brought by the police chief of a Milwaukee suburb who was accused by *World Week* magazine of stealing the department's Christmas fund for underprivileged children. Alec's already worked on two Telemarch libel actions with Mac. He knows that the burden is on the publisher of the accusation to prove that it's true, though most of the litigators at Kendall, Blake, Steele & Braddock work tirelessly to convince the courts that a public-figure plaintiff should be required to prove falsity. If they succeed in shifting this burden, it will cut libel litigation down to a trickle of easily winnable cases and destroy most of Harvey Grand's business. Telemarch is also said to be near a deal to serialize the autobiography of the Japanese mogul Spike Ikuda, written with the help of a hack writer named Leland Franks. Alec mulls over that story. A notorious recluse such as Ikuda publishing an autobiography? Doesn't ring true. Somehow, Alec thinks, there'll be litigation coming out of this one too.

The lead story of the day, however, dwarfs anything else in the newspapers or, potentially, in the American courts. It seems that an old-line financial institution, United States Safety Vault &

Maritime Company, headed by World War II hero Gen. Marcus Rand, had recently created a subsidiary for the warehousing of diesel fuels. By means as yet unclear, that company and a flock of banks had allowed themselves to be swindled out of $1.2 billion by notorious con man and ex-convict Salvatore Martini.

The U.S. Safety Vault story stays on Alec's mind as he comes out of the subway and marches down Wall Street. While the details might yet be surprising, one outcome is highly predictable. There will be tons of litigation. He wonders who represents U.S. Safety. Whatever the firm, they're about to get super busy. And rich.

Alec turns left on Water, crosses to the east side of the street and heads into the lobby and elevator of his own building. In that brief trip he passes several hundred hatted, vested, prosperous-looking men of all ages, many of whom may already be engaged in rescuing U.S. Safety from this debacle. No women, however. The working women in this building are secretaries or clerical help who arrive early; not lawyers or bankers. Only a tenth of Alec's law school class were women—at Harvard it was one percent—and the top-ranked girl, who happened to have had the highest grades in the class, is still looking for her first job.

As Alec streams toward his office, his young secretary, Joni, tries to warn him: "He's in there!"

"Who?" Alec asks, naturally enough, but not stopping.

Should have. Swiveling around to face him, in Alec's own cushiony desk chair, is Alec's boss, Frank Macalister.

"You lucky son-of-a-bitch," Macalister says, bright blues radiating. "That cross-examination stunt on Tierney—the oldest fucking trick in the book."

"Had I been able to get you on the phone," says Alec, recovering, "you might have put me in touch with something more current."

"You did just fine. Exercised the one authority you always have."

"Not to fuck up."

"That's the one. Just don't start believing your own press."

"You mean, despite my smashing victory for Biogram, I'm not being made partner after a year and a half at the firm?"

Mac laughs at the ridiculousness of that statement and derricks himself to his feet. He's a large man with coat-hanger shoulders, a prodigious head, leathery skin, and a smile known to warm opponents into submission. "What do you know about the storage of diesel oil?"

"About what?"

Mac, letting his laugh trail off, says, "We got a meeting to-morrow morning at nine in Gen. Rand's office. United States Safety Vault & Maritime Company."

"We?"

"Seems some oil there has gone missing. One-billion-two-hundred-million-dollars' worth."

"That's yours?" says Alec, not hiding his excitement. "The biggest goddamn case on the Street, and I'm on it?"

"Should I get someone else? You too busy?"

"No, Mac. I think I might be able to squeeze it in."

"Good," says Macalister, making for the door.

"We have a defense to this mess?"

Mac gives him a look.

"Right," Alec says. "If it were that easy, any firm could be doing it."

"Y'know," Macalister says, on his way out of the office, "there might be hope for you yet."

FIFTEEN

At a lunch in a private room in a steakhouse on 116th Street, Phil Anwar, at the head of the table, listens to ten angry men squabble. Better this, he thinks, than the alternative. Every one of these guys is a short-fuse executioner and commands at least thirty equally violent assassins. The way they know to express themselves verbally is to shout, but it's beginning to get on Phil's nerves.

"All right, enough. Enough!" Phil says. "I've talked to the man. He'll go quietly like he always does. He'll be out in eight years, and inside be treated like a fucking potentate."

Eddie Ragno has qualms. And he's the third most powerful man in the room. "You trust this, Phil?"

"I do, Eddie."

"Why's that?"

"He has a son, Martini does."

"And where's the boy?"

"Palermo."

"How old?"

"Fourteen."

"Ah. And he's being watched, this boy?"

"He is."

"Martini knows this?"

"He does."

"So you've been careful?"

"Always, Eddie."

Anwar looks around the table. The faces aren't pretty, nor do they look convinced. At the other end sits an enormously fat man with a bulbous nose and glossy black hair, "Little John" Cuitano, who controls all Jersey mobs but the dockworkers' union and was let in on the Martini deal. His own men sit silently behind him.

"See Phil," says Cuitano, "I don't worry about Sal Martini. He's a pro. This is what? Third time he's going up? He's tested out. It's early retirement for him, and he's funded. You know who worries me? With all due respect. Your wife. Sorry. But that's how it is. That's the reality of the situation."

Phil, keeping his temper, says softly, "What worries you there, John?"

Little John is a doodler. His subject is the submachine gun. He's proficient in most models, current and classic. His canvas, at restaurants, is a napkin, even a cloth napkin, on which he works with a ballpoint pen. "Word getting back to me," he says, looking up from his sketch, "is she's on the street."

"You've been misinformed, John."

"Aaron was worried about her."

"I wasn't aware of that."

"Haven't heard from Aaron in a while. Know where he is?"

"Aaron?" Phil makes a gesture of not knowing or caring.

"The man just disappeared. Not like him."

"No idea, John."

"She's not living with you, I hear. Your wife."

"For the moment," Phil says.

"Not even using her married name."

Phil looks at the man without speaking.

"You have her on a leash?" John asks.

"Very tight leash."

"Some place nearby?"

"That's correct."

"And where's that, Phil?"

"Sorry, John. Can't do that."

"She knows a lot, I understand. Maybe too much."

"It's not a problem. You have my word."

"She's doing heroin, they tell me."

"For the moment. A little. That's part of the leash."

"I don't like it, Phil."

"You're going to have to trust me."

Silence in the room. Tension with a lot of bowed heads. Little John observes them. Phil knows that everyone in the room knows that only Little John could have gotten away with the conversation they just had, but that any further intrusion would mean bloodshed.

"Okay, Phil," says John with a cold smile. "For now." He returns to his doodling.

No one but John's men care for his tone, but everyone but Phil wants the woman dropped in the bay.

SIXTEEN

Gleason's Gym. Center ring. Ray Sancerre, the United States Attorney for the Southern District of New York, pounds his sparring partner with a flurry of blows, taking violent pleasure in the pummeling.

The audience for this spectacle consists of a group of beat reporters and photographers who egg Sancerre on. Their cries ring out with each punch landed. A barrel-chested bald man in his fifties, Sid Kline, chief of the Criminal Division, watches with a dour expression.

Landing a particularly vicious shot to the head, Sancerre signals an end to the punishment. He whips off his face protector and, grabbing a towel, knifes out of the ring. Wending through the gentlemen of the press, he's a dark, saturnine, lipless man with the sort of thick neck, thick hip structure that steals from an appearance of height. In his big shoes, purple trunks, and sweaty tank top, he resembles an oversized, deviantly aggressive Hobbit. "So whatta you say, fellas? Still got a punch?"

"You could sure beat the shit outta the last U.S. Attorney!" wisecracks an unshaven reporter for the *Daily News*.

"Before or after he took off his dress?" responds Ray.

As the assemblage gives this a halfhearted cackle, Sancerre gestures to Kline to follow him into the locker room.

While Ray's in the shower, Sid waits on a side bench that catches a current from an air vent in the ceiling. After a few minutes, Ray calls out, "We alone, Sid?"

"Yeah, Ray."

Sancerre steps out in a towel. "What are you getting from the

Bureau on that U.S. Safety diesel oil scam?"

"The guy who did it—"

"Sal Martini?" Ray says, going to his locker.

"He's talking," Kline says. "Up to a point. What he's dishing us is how he did it."

Sancerre slips into his underwear. "That right? How did he do it?"

"Real simple. Martini goes out, buys, say, ten million dollars of diesel, takes it to one of the U.S. Safety Vault storage tank yards, says, 'Please, sirs, will you store my oil for me?' "

"Which they're happy to do."

"Of course. Guy running this operation, name of Whitman Poole, says, 'Sure thing, that's our business.' So Poole takes the oil and gives Martini a warehouse receipt for ten-million-dollars' worth. Martini then goes to the bank, borrows eight million dollars on the security of that warehouse receipt—and all's fine, except, in the dark of night, Martini goes back to the storage facility and siphons all the oil out of the tanks. Ain't that a fucker! So now Martini's got the original oil plus eight million dollars in cash which he uses to buy more oil. And guess what?"

"He does it all over again," says Ray, "this time with eighteen million dollars of oil, rather than ten. And keeps leveraging up. I'm surprised he didn't corner the market. How'd they catch him?"

"Market price fell," says Kline. "Banks got nervous about their security. Sent their own inspectors in to check out the oil tanks."

"Who backed him?"

"Funny," Sid says, allowing himself a trace of sarcasm. "That, Martini's not telling us."

"Had to be inside help. Who gave it?"

Kline shakes his head.

"We've questioned everyone? Thoroughly?"

"Short of physical torture," Sid says.

"You getting fastidious?" says Sancerre, deadpan. Then, buttoning his shirt, grins at Kline's reaction. "Just kidding. What about shaking the tree?"

"What tree?"

"This is a mob job, Sid. You might talk to Phil Anwar."

"You wanna signal a mob boss he's a suspect on this?"

"We got something to lose?" Fastening his tie in the mirror, the chief federal prosecutor admires his face, as if fleshiness were the new chic. "Seriously," he says. "The FBI's been on this a week. They've got nothing except how the thing was done—which we could have pieced together without Martini's so-called cooperation. The wiretaps are worthless. And nobody else is talking, nor are they likely to. What the fuck's the downside on this?"

Kline's face registers plenty of downside, including a risk to his own life, but he says nothing.

Ray, getting his shoes on, looks up. "There's a wild card in Phil's deck. A junkie wife who's now left him. I'm watching her; you talk to Phil; it'll give him a reason to shuffle some cards. Okay?"

"While we're shaking the tree," Sid says.

"What? You don't like mixed metaphors?"

Sid shrugs. "What's not to like?"

And Ray laughs. He likes Sid, likes his banter. But the best thing of all? Sid will never upstage him.

SEVENTEEN

Phil Anwar's principal residence is a three-story Tudor estate on the North Shore of Long Island. Its sixteen acres of lawn roll down to the Sound. The swimming pool and tennis court share a changing facility that would comfortably house a small family. Phil's study sports two Rothkos and a Twombly.

The entrance and main rooms are large, but graciously so: no drama to the fireplaces or moldings, or curvatures to the central stairs, though the gallery is two stories high and hung with other fashionable and expensive paintings. The furniture is contemporary, in keeping with Phil's collection of art; each sofa, chair, cabinet, and table is the signature piece of a well-known designer. The colors are muted, with just a splash here and there of something not primary but vibrant. The windows, though dressed, are carefully treated to afford individually framed views of different aspects of the property and, as now, the setting sun.

For Phil's associates, it's like entering Brigadoon. Some live in scaled-down replicas of mansions. Most have at least visited people in large and expensive homes. But few can explain the effect Phil's house has on them. Especially Vito, who lives in an apartment over the five-car garage. He thinks of Phil's house as "high class."

At the edge of the water, Vito, while patrolling the grounds, walks a big black mongrel of a dog, part Labrador, part English setter. It's a pound dog that Vito rescued and owns, and he's named it Friday after a character in a book he read in the fifth grade. At his first glimpse of the animal, Vito thought, *He wants to please me.* As Vito judges the matter, it would seem that, for

Friday, Phil's estate is dog heaven, and Vito himself, the perfect owner. He enjoys watching the dog romp around on the undulating lawns, scampering on the beach and hiding in bushes to look out for birds, other animals, and people. He even enjoys watching him play with the well-groomed pedigrees of neighboring estates. Someone trained Friday before he came to Vito, but the dog transferred allegiance to him almost with the first feeding and took to his further training. To run around with Vito, retrieve thrown balls or sticks, or simply stride alongside his human seems to fulfill this handsome creature's undoubted emotional life.

Vito hears a car pull into the driveway. No one, so far as he knows, is expected. He calls the dog while heading toward the house, and Friday turns from his inspection of a dark patch of lawn to race after him. There is an obvious analogue to the pet's devotion, and indeed his name, but that would no more have occurred to the master than it would have the dog.

Phil, at his desk, smokes an after-dinner cigar as he watches his four-year old daughter, Sarah, coloring pictures on the floor. His feeling is close to contentment. The spoiler, when he thinks about it, is his young wife, who slips the tail constantly. And he can't help but think about her whenever he sees Sarah.

Leaving the cigar in an ashtray, he kneels down to admire her work. An angelic auburn-haired beauty, very serious about her coloring book, she moves slightly to allow her daddy to admire.

"Exquisite," he says. "Better than a de Kooning."

"A de-what?" she squeals.

"Famous painter. But not nearly in your league."

They hear a doorbell ring. Vito appears in the doorway.

"Some guy named Sid Kline?" Vito announces in a tone he tries to make sound cultured. "Says you'll know who he is?"

"Sidney Kline," muses Phil. "U.S. Attorney's Office. Lifer. Ray

Sancerre's main man."

"What the fuck!" says Vito.

Phil shakes his head reprovingly, looking at his daughter who, however, seems lost in her work. "Vito! The mouth! I keep telling you."

"Sorry, Phil."

"Try to remember, will you?" says Phil, rising, putting out his cigar.

"Sure. The guy? I'll tell him to piss off?"

Phil rolls his eyes. "On the contrary. Show him in."

"You're gonna let him into your house? Talk to the son-of-a-bitch?"

"I'm going to listen, Vito. You listen, you learn. Sometimes you learn more than the other guy thinks he's revealing. You understand?"

"Of course, boss."

As Vito leaves, Phil kisses his daughter on the cheek, and a nanny materializes to gather up Sarah and her drawings. "Now go up to bed, sweetheart. I'll tuck you in in a sec."

"TV," Sarah says.

Phil looks at his watch.

"Mister Ed."

"All right," Phil relents. "One program."

"Yea!"

Nanny and child leave the study as Sid Kline enters, obviously distracted by the paintings floating on the walls. "Lovely place."

"What's up, Sid?"

"Give me a moment, will ya?" Kline says, eyes fixed on the larger Rothko.

"You know art?"

"I know of it. I know a Rothko when I see one. Who's the other?"

"Cy Twombly. Relatively new. You know the Leo Castelli

Gallery?"

"Heard of it."

"Well, Leo thinks Cy's the second coming."

"Of Rothko?"

"Of God, Sid." Phil resumes his seat behind the desk. "So what's up?"

Kline grips the back of the chair in front of him. "Thank you for seeing me, Phil."

"Cut the shit, will you? What the fuck you doing here?"

"First, I have to say, if you need a lawyer present for this, you can call one, or I can come back."

"I don't need a lawyer, fella. You got something to say, sit down and say it."

Sid pulls the chair under him. "You know Sal Martini?"

"Man of the hour," Phil says. "According to the media. Never met the gentleman."

"Thought you might have."

Phil gives this a puzzled expression, and Sid shifts his weight a bit. "Quite a scam he brought off."

"That right?" says Phil.

"Put the Atlantic Ocean in the tanks in Bayonne where there should have been diesel."

"My, my."

"Bayonne and elsewhere. Up and down the East Coast. More than a billion dollars' worth."

"And this," Phil asks, "relates to me how?"

"Martini—to get himself started?—needed a nut of ten million bucks. Not the sort of capital handed over, unsecured, to a twice-convicted felon... by a bank."

"So who gave it to him?"

Sid stares at Anwar until the younger man laughs. "If you had anything to back up that smirk, Sidney, I'd be looking at a subpoena right now, not your adorable face."

Phil gets up, forcing Kline to his feet, but the prosecutor isn't finished. "At this moment, Phil, a deal could be made. Later, when U.S. Safety goes belly-up, when fifty thousand people are out of work, and when thousands of shareholders lose their life savings—it's not going to be so easy copping a plea."

Phil, smiling, urges Sid by the shoulder toward the door. "Tell that guy you work for—Ray Sancerre, king of the G-men—I respect unusual approaches, I really do. Coming to a man's home. Implying he's a criminal. A guilty party would have thrown you out on your ass, Sid. Me? As I say. Always a pleasure." He shakes Kline's hand as Vito arrives to usher Sid out, then Phil turns his back on the both of them.

Vito watches Sid's government car pull out of the long driveway. Standing at the front door, he gives a single shout: "Come!" In two seconds, Friday skids to a stop at his feet, happy to be there, eager for the next command. So simple, thinks Vito. So right. So nice to be appreciated.

EIGHTEEN

Gen. Marcus Rand gathers himself up from behind his desk—itself the size of a small office—and points a gnarled finger at Macalister. "You're telling me I can be wiped out—my wife and family impoverished—because I didn't crawl on top of some fucking storage tank in Bayonne and stick my arm in up to the pit?"

Impressive, thinks Alec: the famous eye patch, the eagle beak, the perpetual scowl; and the framed photographs behind him, displaying these features on the covers of *Life* and *Time* magazines. The effect is not diminished by the enormity of the office, the thick Turkish rugs, the combat decorations and war memorabilia encased on pedestals or decorating the walls.

"That's the claim," Mac says off-handedly. And you're not being charged with simple negligence. The assertion against you, the other directors, and the company is fraud."

"Fraud! We haven't defrauded anyone! We didn't know a goddamn thing about it!"

"The offense of fraud," Mac says, "doesn't require knowledge of wrongdoing or an actual intent to deceive. If you publish rosy financial statements and recklessly disregard the material facts, you've committed fraud. And the fact you're charged here with having recklessly disregarded is that you were missing the oil the banks were loaning money on. One point two billion dollars' worth of oil."

"What the fuck you mean reckless?" spews Rand. "We had every conceivable security check in place. There were absolutely no signs of trouble. The manager of this business, Whitman

Poole, reported to the board every month."

"He's the guy the plaintiffs are saying was reckless. And if he was, you get stuck with it. As a matter of law."

"The lawyers who brought these lawsuits—they have no idea what we did or didn't do."

"Of course not. They read an article in a newspaper, they file a suit. Then they try to learn something about it."

"Ambulance chasers!" Rand says, finally sitting down. "No. What do you call them in your field? Strike-suiters!"

Now Mac gets up, walks pensively to the back of the office and turns. "Little lecture," he says. "There's a biological principle that, in whatever nook or crevice of the Earth life can be supported, some form of it will generate. A similar principle works for lawyers. You see a corporate misfortune, you'll find a species of lawyers in a frenzy to feed on it."

"And they feast," Rand says.

"While the victims get pennies apiece," says Mac, "and the corporation that suffered the misfortune in the first place suffers another one almost as bad by having to pay off the lawyers."

Rand eyes him with a small shake of his head.

"And as an additional result?" says Mac. "Of truly monstrous perversity? The stockholders who comprise most of the original victims still own the company that pays the damages and fees. So they get screwed again. By the lawyers who are supposedly representing them."

"Great system," the general mutters. He is used to a better one, in which he picks the judges, tells them how to rule, then decides all the appeals himself.

"You don't want to pay off the strike-suiters?" Mac says, returning to his chair. "Then you get the best lawyer you can find, hope for an honest judge with a functioning brain and take your chances with a jury."

Rand gives Mac a one-eyed glare. "And is that you? The best lawyer I can find?"

Mac stares back. "If you want it tried, General, we'll win the case for you."

Rand turns to Alec. "And what do you think, son? That your view too?"

"Yes, General. It is."

"Always agree with your superior officer, right? Ha!" He leans back, making a decision. "Listen to me, both of you. I want you to fight this case. No settlement. I'm not paying those bastards a penny. Not one red cent."

"You got it," Mac says. He's heard hard lines before, wonders how long Rand will stick with it.

"You understand," says Rand, "at the moment we're still not out of pocket. We've issued more than one billion dollars' worth of warehouse receipts for oil that Martini stole back, but the people he gave those receipts to—and borrowed money from—the warehouse receipt holders—they're the ones who haven't gotten paid."

"So you still owe them," Mac says. "Who are they, exactly? Banks, I assume."

"East Coast banks, mainly. And pretty much all of them. Large and small. Which reminds me," Rand says. "We've brought in special counsel to try to negotiate a settlement with them. Marius Shilling. You know him, I assume."

"I know him," Mac says with no enthusiasm.

"And while he's at it," Rand says, ignoring Mac's tone, "maybe he can give us some help on the litigation front, too."

Heading off Wall Street down William, toward the office, Alec asks, "Is Shilling going to get in our way?"

"Not unless we let him," Mac says.

"I can understand special counsel handling the settlement negotiations with the East Coast banks. But on the litigation—what do we need him for?"

"Don't worry. It'll sort itself out. Shilling's on somebody's list."

"List?" Alec says.

"For windbag lawyers who get to suck on the great corporate titty."

Alec muses on this for another half-block, then says to Mac, "That was a pretty bold prediction back there."

"You think?"

Alec mimics the Texan's drawl. *"We'll win this case for you, General."*

Mac, laughing, says, "A bit of showmanship. Tell the client you'll win, makes him easier to deal with. And if you lose, it doesn't matter what you've told him. You're never going to see him again anyway."

At the corner of William and Pine, Mac casts an eye to the Down Town Association, a half block away. "Want to stop for a drink?"

"Little early for me, thanks."

"Bad career move," Mac says.

At the look on Alec's face, Mac laughs out loud. "Kid, you got to lighten up."

NINETEEN

Alec had promised his father a visit, then delayed going until he could delay no more. He's on the verge of being too busy to see anyone for months. His dad won't understand that. The forecast all day had been warning of a freakish early snowstorm. Nevertheless, Alec makes his way to Penn Station.

The Long Island Rail Road terminal is a frantic hive of humans desperate to get someplace else. Since Alec's days of frequent commuting, the LIRR has changed the trains. They're double-deckers now, so that you either sit in a hole, as Alec does, or with your head bumping the car ceiling.

As the train emerges from its tunnel, snow begins to fall, the first large flakes impaling themselves on the grit of his window.

It was in high school and as an undergraduate that Alec rode this line often, back and forth to summer jobs, packed in among the sweaty businessmen, with their collars thrown open, breathing like frogs. They played gin rummy on knee boards for a tenth of a cent and chain-smoked cigars. One by one, through the years, they got off for the last time at Valley Stream or Babylon, while new commuters took their seats.

Alec gets off at the town he lived in until he was eleven. He'd moved all over the Island after that, but his father had recently moved back to the southeastern end of Queens. By the time Alec reaches his destination, the snow, exceeding all predictions, has blanketed the streets and buildings, braceleted the trees and wires. He looks around the square in front of the train station. He hasn't been there for years. The wooden railway platform has been rebuilt in concrete. New buildings have overgrown the old and caused them to shrink. The place, however, romanced in snow and emptied of people, has the quality of a dream.

Instead of waiting for a cab, he starts walking. He walks east on Center Street, the snow crunching beneath his shoes. Of course there are ghosts; he had chosen to walk in order to stir them. The one-story bank branch where he opened his first savings account at age ten. The candy and stationery store, the pharmacy, the cor- ner grocery. He had delivered packages from there on a swaying bike. Everything's closed, and every corner holds memories of good and bad times; but more disturbing, by far, are the changes.

On an impulse, instead of proceeding directly to his father's new home, he walks out on the beach road. A quarter of a mile toward the water he finds the driveway he's looking for: the en- trance to the grounds of a day camp. Past high hedges that offer privacy from the street, the land rises sharply to the old gray field- stone estate house the camp had converted, and then slopes down behind it, for thirty acres or so, bordered by marsh that leads to a bay and, beyond that, the ocean. A baseball diamond and bleach- ers sit on a corner of the grounds, buried in snow. He climbs to the top of the bleachers, clears some space on the plank and sits on it.

It's strange: this compulsion to be here without any clear idea why. He stretches his arms behind him and looks at the sky. The storm has ceased, and the clouds open to reveal a nearly full moon. It's extremely quiet and amazingly warm. The snow, wind-rippled, shimmers in the bluish-white light.

Alec glances across the fields to the house, once a grand man- sion, to the tennis and volleyball posts denuded of nets, to the wire backstop and the soccer goals. He tries to see himself as he had been when he was eight years old, sporting a new camp T-shirt, blue shorts, blue camp sweater tied around his waist. New boy, playing fiercely at games.

He remembers arriving home once with a bloody nose. His father, laughing at an old book he was reading, dropped it on the floor and took him into the bathroom. With his face being washed off, Alec asked what was so funny about that book. "This old Roman," said Sam. "Name of Juvenal. Poking fun at those who, as he put it, 'Pardon the ravens and censure the doves.' Know what that means, pardon the ravens?"

"Sure? Some guy keeps coming after you, it's okay to beat the shit outta him."

"Which is what you just did?"

"Otherwise he's not gonna stop," Alec insisted.

Sam studied his son as if seeing himself, not altogether pleased by the reflection. "I think even Juvenal," he said slowly, "would have pardoned that."

Alec gets up and tracks back through the snow to the main house. No one had bothered to lock it. It's dank inside, smells musty, and the downstairs rooms are stacked with benches. There's enough moonlight for Alec to navigate the staircase and the servants' stairs to the arts and crafts room in the attic. A long shop table still stands in the center with vises fixed to its corners. He sits in the dormer enclosure and peers out.

He used to come here at rest hours when the room was empty. From this window you can see almost the entirety of the grounds, the marsh, the bay, and clear to the sea. He remembers a view green to overflowing; and now, in the blanched shuddering of this landscape, he feels the disappearance of years. It's still inside him, that idea or notion he had come back to find, almost retrieved because he is there.

Tantalizing, it is so close, but not coming. He thinks, *People are all brazen on the outside, full of knowing better, protected by shells of smart-aleckness. Alone in a room, their insides come out soft, not knowing anything, whimpering a little, pitying themselves for having to live without knowing.* With one last lingering look he gets up from the embrasure of the window.

Alec retraces his steps across the room, down the stairways, through the halls, out onto the snow-laden lawn, then down the driveway to the street. He walks at a steady clip, not looking back. There is one more place he wants to see.

People are living there, of course. It's a big old comfortable three-story house with a wraparound porch, built after the First World War. By the time he'd moved in, it had been converted into a two-family dwelling, and it appears still to be that. Lights are on in both bedrooms on the first floor. Alec's old backboard and hoop have been removed from over the garage door; the bicycle rack his dad made is gone. His mother materializes on the front porch. He stands watching from across the street, listening to her call his name.

His mother was a mystic, although she would have been astounded by the charge. She was fond of saying that what we think of as "God" was in reality spirit—a sort of force that joins us; an essence of which we were all part. In the next moment she would tell Alec to do his homework and get good grades so he would grow up to be successful. More so than his father who had failed her in that way.

These, to Alec, were bewilderingly conflicting propositions. To what end were grades or success if we were all part of some mystical whole? And wasn't he special? He heard plants grow and the motion of stars. He saw thoughts before they were spoken. Wouldn't he stand out, change the world? He had thought about this to the limits of his mind's endurance, pressing against it like a headache. He had thought about it in that attic room, sitting in the dormer window.

Sam Brno opens the door to the upstairs of a split level.

"Alec."

"Dad."

The entrance is to a "front" room that's really in the back of the two-story dwelling. It has the look of a place furnished by the landlord: browns and oranges, thin cushions, spindly woods. Indistinguishable from a cheap motel room.

"What can I get you?"

Alec glances at his father's half-filled beer bottle on top of an ancient TV. "Got another?"

"Sure."

Sam heads to the small fridge in a kitchenette area at the end of the room, while Alec parks himself on the sofa. He moves to one side a TV tray on which sit the remnants of a frozen dinner. "So tell me about this new job," Alec says as his father hands him a cold Miller's.

"Well, it's in Syosset."

"That's a pretty good drive from here."

"I've had worse," says Sam, settling into a lounger.

"What about the work itself?"

"It's okay. Security systems, mainly. Burglar alarms, smoke detectors, you know the kind of things."

"You do the installations yourself?"

"We have crews."

"We?"

"There's a woman who owns it."

"The company?"

"Right."

"And what's she like?"

"Seems decent enough."

"Age?"

"Probably a little younger than me."

"Married?"

"A widow."

"Good-looking?"

"A handsome woman, yes."

Alec gives him a look.

Sam gives one laugh. "Right," he says.

They lapse into silence.

Sam says, "Your work?"

"I've got a new case."

"Oh yeah? Big one?"

"Pretty big, yeah."

"What's it about?"

"Huge swindle. Diesel oil. Guy stole more than a billion dollars' worth."

"Oh, yeah, heard about that. That yours?"

"Well, the firm's."

"Diesel. Whatta you know. And who you representing?"

"The company he stole it from. And its directors."

"The big shots."

"You could say."

"They want their money back?"

"It's more complicated."

"Yeah. Would be. So you'll be working those crazy hours again."

"Yeah," Alec says. "No doubt."

Silence.

Sam says, "There's a basketball game on tonight."

"That right?"

"Wanna take a look?"

"Sure."

Sam flips on the set, finds the right channel. They watch for a while until Alec looks at his watch.

"When's your train?" Sam asks.

"I've got a half hour."

"Half hour," says Sam. "Whatta you know." And they continue watching.

TWENTY

Mac and Alec enter one of the larger courtrooms in the State Courthouse on Foley Square. They're immediately mobbed by more than twenty lawyers serving them with affidavits.

Taking a seat on a back bench, Alec asks, "Want me to try to read these? Before the judge comes in?"

"That pile of recyclable horseshit?" says Mac. "Don't waste your time."

Alec looks about the spacious, once-elegant room. Paint peels from the ceiling; benches wobble out of their fastenings; once-carpeted floors gather grime on an institutional vinyl. There then appears through the doors a towering gray-haired figure to whom all eyes swing. He stands there a moment with a matinee-idol tilt to his aquiline nose and an attitude of proprietorship.

"Si Rosenkranz?" Alec asks Mac in a whisper.

"The one and only."

The other lawyers surge to greet him with the homage shown to a mafia boss. Si chats with each group briefly and moves on. He holds up fingers, shakes hands, sparks laughs with the kind of remarks deemed funny only when uttered by very important people.

Alec again leans over to Mac. "He's making deals?"

"Splitting the pie, baby. Doling out shares of the fee. I told you not to waste time with those affidavits."

A sharp knock quiets the room. The bailiff springs to his feet. "Hear ye, hear ye! All rise! The Supreme Court of the State of New York, New York County, is now in session, the Honorable Jacob Kaye presiding. Draw near, and ye shall be heard."

To the chant, the judge streams in, black robe swishing, equine face lined vertically with discontent. Assuming the bench, he peers into the assemblage until spotting someone familiar. "Mr. Rosenkranz?" he says in reedy Bronx tones.

Si stands decorously. "Yes, your Honor?"

The judge lifts a stack of affidavits, then allows them to fall with a thud. "I have here a considerable quantity of paper."

"You may put it aside, your Honor."

"Twenty-two, no, twenty-three affidavits. Each proclaiming the lawyer who wrote it to be the model of all men and uniquely qualified to be lead counsel in this action."

"All no doubt true," Si says.

"But you have arrived at an accommodation?"

"We have, your Honor."

"In which you will be lead counsel."

"I have that honor, your Honor. And we will be filing a new, consolidated complaint within three weeks."

"Sounds reasonable," the jurist says. "Defense counsel wish to be heard? Mr. Macalister?"

Mac stands. "Not at this time, your Honor."

A beefy man with a shaven head rises from the first row. One notices the suit. It could have been shaped to his form only by dint of many long fittings. "Nothing to add at this time, your Honor," he says with a soft Germanic burr. "We'll await the amended pleading."

"And what is your role, Mr. Shilling?" Judge Kaye asks.

"I've been retained by U.S. Safety as special counsel—to achieve a settlement with the banks, who, as your Honor knows, now hold the warehouse receipts originally given to Mr. Martini in exchange for oil. I've also been asked by the company to consult on this litigation."

Judge Kaye looks amused. "You are to advise U.S. Safety on Mr. Macalister's handling of the case?"

"A second opinion, your Honor. So to speak."

"How nice for Mr. Macalister. Another lawyer right at his back." Getting up, the judge looks sharply at the court reporter. "That was off the record."

"All rise!" sings the bailiff as the jurist escapes.

Coming up the aisle, Si Rosenkranz leans in toward Macalister. "Mac, let's talk."

The two older lawyers and Alec wind their way down a back hall and troop into an empty jury room, a low-ceilinged box with a long, battered table and twelve chairs. Mac goes into the lavatory but retreats quickly. "Christ! Nothing works in this place anymore. First the judges go, then the toilets."

"You think anything ever worked here?" Si says.

"Well, you know, you hear stories—" Mac gets a faraway look—"of real judges. Evenhanded. Smart. Dispensing justice like it was meant to be—in great rooms of which these are the mere ruins."

"A myth," scoffs Rosenkranz.

"I know," Mac says. "Pretty story, though."

Si turns to Alec. "You're the kid who got all that publicity in that Pharmex-Biogram price-fixing case?"

Mac does the belated introductions. "Alec Brno. Simon Rosenkranz."

They shake hands, then Si, taking one side of the table, gestures for the others to sit across from him. It's a time-worn ritual, Rosenkranz's play, but there are different ways for their respective roles to be enacted. "So tell me, Mac," says Si, "after you get Shilling out of your hair, what do you plan to do with this case?"

"Me? It's your fucking case. I didn't bring it."

"And I did. Which reminds me. Where's the thanks?"

Si turns to Alec. "With lawyers I don't like? I give warning, 'I'm never gonna sue your clients again.' Scares 'em shitless.

They'd fucking starve." Si appreciates his own humor with a rheumy guffaw. "Okay, Mac. Seriously. Whatta you gonna do with this case?"

"Try it, I expect."

"You're a lot smarter than that."

"I'm just a big dumb jock from Texas."

"I wish," Si says. "Look. Let me tell you what we have here, okay?"

"You gonna show your hand?" Macalister says. "Lay it on me, boy. You have my full attention."

Si gives a sympathetic glance to Alec. "What we have here is an unforgivable mess, okay? A major financial institution exposing itself to a one-point-two-billion-dollar risk—for the sake of what? A few million dollars in warehousing fees? I mean, Jesus!"

He looks at both men for effect; neither shows anything, though Alec's thinking, *The jury'll love this guy!*

"But not to worry, right?" Si continues. "Safe as houses. A ton of the company's paper—warehouse receipts, as good as money— is turned over to a real honorable guy. Sal Martini. Fresh from the slammer. What was the man in for? Fraud! Scheme just like this one."

Si gives Mac and Alec a moment to appreciate the humor. "So here's this white-shoe company," he continues, "with its white-shoe board in front of an immigrant jury. And who's the man on the spot, the guy the company gets to run the warehousing business? An Ivy League twit named Whitman Poole, who's recently been fired from two other jobs. It's Poole who gives this ex-con Martini more than one billion dollars in warehouse receipts for phantom barrels of oil. You think the jury's not gonna think that Poole was reckless? And that your board shouldn't be held responsible for letting him do it?" He smiles at Macalister, who gives nothing back. Alec, now standing, is peering out the one window in the room, over the rooftops of Chinatown.

"Oh, and Alec," Rosenkranz says. "You'll appreciate this. You won that price-fixing case by proving that a company CEO hired a shithead named Carl Raffon? I'm going to win this case the same way—on top of everything else I've got. Because guess who U.S. Safety hired to check out the security in Bayonne? You got it! Same shithead! Carl Raffon!" Si's phlegm-filled laugh is almost infectious. "I love irony! I really do!"

Coming from the courthouse, Alec says, "You know what I'm thinking?"

Mac, not breaking stride, shows Alec a pained smirk. "Probably."

"Guy running that warehouse business—Whitman Poole—wasn't just stupid."

"Nobody," says Mac, "is that stupid."

"Which is how we win," Alec says.

"Which is how we win. We may be legally responsible for the stupidity of our managers, but not for their dishonesty."

"So how do we prove it? That Poole was taking?"

"We call Harvey," Mac says. "Put him on two tracks right away: your buddy Raffon, the wiretapper; and anybody around Sal Martini—starting with his lawyer, the lawyer's secretary, etcetera. Maybe we'll get lucky."

TWENTY-ONE

Abigail says, "Turn right onto Goose Hollow Road," and the Ford pickup, slowing barely, swerves sharply, throwing her up against him.

"Little more notice would be good," Sam says, steadying the vehicle on the right-hand side of the road. He stubs out a cigarette in an ashtray already bulging with butts.

"Yeah, well, I just saw it," she says.

"So what's the name of the family we're seeing?" On the narrow winding road, he's doing about twenty-five miles an hour, but the old catalogues on the floor slide back and forth with each shift in direction.

"It's a big estate, half mile from here."

"You don't want to tell me the name?"

"Anwar," she says, bending to collect the catalogues. She stacks them in her lap, distractedly and unnecessarily. "The family name is Anwar."

"You're kidding," he says.

"You know them?" Her tone seems deliberately light.

"I know a Phil Anwar, at least of him."

"That's the guy."

Takes him a moment.

"Jesus, Abby."

"He's very polite."

"You work for the mob?"

"Turn right on Sycamore. Plenty of notice this time. Three blocks from here. And he's not even home."

"You think that matters?"

"Look. I'm not the D.A. The man needs a burglar alarm, I put it in."

"That's it?"

"What more?"

"How the hell did you get involved with this guy in the first place? Didn't you know who he was?"

She takes time before answering. "In the beginning, we almost went under. Bank had called the loan, we didn't have the money. There are a lot of home security businesses on the Island. At least there were then. Phil showed up. He's not going to go to one of the big companies. He trusted us more. Maybe it was the Italian name. Got along with my husband."

"One customer? That saved your business?"

"He's got a lot of friends."

Sam senses something's wrong here, or missing, and she sees that.

"All right," she says, "I might as well tell you. I get a lot of work from these families."

"Enough to pay off the bank loan?"

"I haven't paid off the bank loan."

"But the bank just dropped its demand."

"Yeah."

"When Anwar became your customer."

"That's right."

Sam doesn't even like the sound of her voice now. It's brittle. He says, "He runs the dockworkers' local I left."

"I know. He know you?"

"Never met the man."

"So it's okay."

"You think it's okay?"

"It'll do."

"I don't love it," he says, keeping his eyes on the road.

"I don't love a lot of things."

"That's great," he says sourly.

"You gotta love everything you do?"

"We're talking low-lifes here."

"Lotta people hate 'em," she says. "That's why they need security systems."

He's thinking hard. "What aren't you telling me, Abby?"

"Nothing," she says with resentment.

"It's dangerous, working for these people."

"You don't have to do these jobs, Sam."

"Oh right. Just leave you out there."

"We're civilians to these people. They don't mess with civilians."

"Unless you pick something up," he says. "Like information."

"Well, we'll try not to do that."

"While getting into their telephone lines to plug in our systems."

Sam pulls up at the front gate, and they sit there for a moment. He asks, "How tight was your husband with this group?"

"A little business socializing, that's all."

"Parties? He take you?"

"No. Fishing trips sometimes."

"What?"

"Stop, Sam!"

"Your husband died on a fishing trip!"

"Jesus! You're absolutely paranoid. You can't imagine how solicitous Phil was."

"Really. And was there some inquiry?"

"Of course. The cops were all over it. If there was any possibility of what you're thinking—"

"Would have come out? How? Anyone else on that trip other than mobsters?"

They sit in more silence.

"You wanna just drop me off?" she says.

"What I wanna do is keep going. Away from here. With you in the truck."

"I can't do that, Sam."

"Right," he says wearily.

She gets out to open the gate, like the opening of a box: one named for a more famous—and mythological—female.

TWENTY-TWO

Nighttime at the firm. Most of the associates have yet to leave. The desk and every surface of Alec's single-windowed office are littered with open case books and documents. When the phone rings, he has to find it from beneath some papers. "Brno."

Harvey Grand stands in an unlit phone booth in Queens. "All right, Alec, here's what's happening. Carl Raffon? There's probably something there. So far he's ducking me—which means he's scared and doesn't want to talk. I'll stay on that, of course. The other guy—Sal Martini's lawyer—is an individual practitioner on Duane Street, name of Aaron Weinfeld. This man's gone. Poof. Vanished. Doubtful Aaron's still among the living." He pauses to let a derelict weave by.

"Harvey?"

"His office manager, however? A twenty-four-year-old named Carrie Madigan? Who you've met. Still alive, if barely. She's a junkie."

"A drug addict? The girl you were with in court last week?"

"Two arrests for possession, which were dropped, and two federal charges for transportation with intent to sell, which are still pending. The U.S. Attorney seems to be taking a particular interest in her. I'm a couple of blocks from her building now, a three-family in Bayswater. She, however, ain't there. Guy who lives upstairs from her thinks she's staying with a friend of hers, who this guy once dated. A Thelma Rosbach, who lives at 1264 Grand Concourse in the Bronx. No apartment number. All I could get was fourth floor."

"Have you called Mac?"

Harvey's laugh is a rumble.

"It's only nine," Alec says.

"How long have you worked for him?"

"You're telling me what? He's asleep?" Alec pauses. "Blind drunk?"

"Let's just say, a conversation with Mac at this hour would not be productive. Or remembered."

"All right," Alec says. "I'll meet you up there."

Harvey hesitates. "We could let it go until the morning."

"You're kidding, right? We've got a potential key witness to a billion-dollar swindle who's floating around the drug pits of the city—could OD or get killed any second—and you think we can wait?"

"Killed?" muses Harvey. "If they—whoever they are—wanted her dead, she'd be gone by now."

"Like Weinfeld," Alec says.

"I'm still looking for him."

"I'm going up there," Alec says.

"I'll pick you up, then," says Harvey.

"No, look. On second thought, you're in the ass end of Queens—"

"Ass end? What do you know about where I am?"

"I grew up around there, Harvey."

"Oh… really."

"I'm on my way. You go home. I'll call, if I get something."

"The hell you will! Alec! I don't care where you grew up. You do not want to be roaming around some building in the Bronx in the middle of the night. Believe me, you do not want to be doing this."

"Bye, Harvey."

Alec, hanging up, takes one look out the window at the still-busy streets below, and grabs his topcoat from the rack. In a bound, he's out of the office, stopping only to pick up a stack of small bills from the messengers' emergency cash kitty.

Cabs are plentiful at this hour; traffic no problem. In about twenty-five minutes Alex is brought to the Grand Concourse address Harvey supplied. It's a six-story building with fire escapes down the front. The lobby is war-torn and silent with menace. The mailboxes lack nameplates. There are five fourth-floor apartments; Alec pushes all their bells. One rings back at him.

Cautiously, Alec makes his way up to the fourth floor on a staircase of broken tiles, which echoes intermittently sounds of grief or violence. A dark hallway looms, redolent of pot, one door slightly ajar. Alec hesitates, then knocks.

"Come in!" calls a female voice made sultry for effect. "Door's open."

It's a vestibule stinking of Chinese takeout and drugs. Alec parts the strands of a beaded curtain. On a sofa, among the remains of takeout containers, lies a rangy, young, thin-faced woman. She wears a rayon nightgown that leaves little to the imagination. And Alec is not what she expects. "You a cop?" she asks.

"That what I look like?"

"Maybe. Cops come in all shapes and guises. Like the devil."

"I'm neither. I'm looking for Carrie Madigan."

"Oh, yeah? You her date?"

"Nope. A lawyer. I want to talk to her. It would be to her benefit."

"And yours."

"Possibly."

"I'm an accountant, myself," she says, the effort of sitting up completing the exposure, for a moment, of her small breasts. "Also a professional person. I worked with a very distinguished firm downtown."

"Where was that?"

"Hundred Twenty-Fifth Street. I got sick, so they let me go. I'll go back to it soon, though. Plenty of good jobs for accountants."

"You know where Carrie is?"

"Oh, sure."

"Where's that, then?" Alec asks casually.

She throws her head back and laughs.

"How much?" Alec says.

"How much you got? I got bills to pay, honey pie." At Alec's look of annoyance, she says, "Gonna need twenty for my connect."

"The guy you thought I was when I walked in here."

"That's right. Flocko. Down there on the corner with my shit. You give me the money, then go down there. Tell him to come up. Then I'll tell you where Carrie is. Deal?"

Alec shakes his head, no. "You tell me where Carrie is. I'll give you the money. You stick your head out the window and get Flocko or whomever you want."

"*Whomever?*" she mimics in what she thinks of as an upper-class accent.

Alec laughs.

"You want a blow job?" she asks, scratching herself, wriggling a bit.

"No thanks."

"You look like you need a blow job."

He says, "That's probably right."

"I like you. I'll do it for fifty. Best you ever had." She smiles, and her voice lowers suggestively. "By an accountant."

"Rain check."

"You got twenty?"

"You got the information?"

She gives him a look, and he hands over the bill. She holds it up to the light, turning it in different directions.

"Stop screwing around, Thelma. Where is she?"

"Man!" she says, turning nasty. "What cause you have...? Who gave you that name?"

He holds up another bill—ten dollars—and she grabs it.

"Where?" he says.

"One Sixteenth and Lex." She's pulling some clothes together, preparing to go out.

"Street number?"

She's heading toward the door. "It's in the projects. Corner building. A shooting gallery. People will know."

TWENTY-THREE

Alec hails a gypsy cab, gives the driver the address. The man's bald head swivels sharply. "That's the projects," he says.

"I'm looking for someone. A woman."

The man laughs and propels the car into traffic. It's a plain car, black, with old, sagging leather seats, probably bought used five years ago, and steeped in the sharp smell of tobacco.

"Ain't it wonderful," he says. "There's always a woman."

"Yeah, well." Alec rolls the back window down so he can breathe.

"A woman—a white woman?"

"Uh-huh." They're headed for the Harlem River Drive.

"A white woman in the projects... you don't mind me saying... you looking for trouble, boy."

"I'm told she's in a shooting gallery. Which would be where?" Alec decides to play dumb. "Someplace on the ground floor?"

"Jesus!" says the driver. "Jesus!"

"I don't know anything, right?"

"Right," he agrees.

"A shooting gallery has something to do with drugs, and the last place it's likely to be is on the ground floor?"

"You got it."

"But you don't know where it is?"

"Hey! I look like a guy who takes people to shooting galleries?"

They drive in silence. Alec is deposited on the designated corner.

The cab pulls away. It's the middle of Spanish Harlem on a cold night. Alec looks about: rows of dark buildings, ten, maybe twelve stories high; many dark windows—though he's sure people are looking out from inside; bags and papers littering the paths; garbage uncollected in the entryways. On the street, lots of people go by in heavy outdoor clothing; vehicular headlights glare in his eyes. Alec, suited up for the office, feels conspicuously out of place. Eventually he moves closer to the corner building. Stands there for several minutes. Wonders how he can possibly find, let alone talk to, a woman who might or might not be in any one of the apartments in any of these buildings and would probably run in the opposite direction if she saw him.

An older man and woman come barreling out the front door. Alec approaches, and they sweep by. They have, unsurprisingly, no interest in talking to someone who is a lunatic or a cop, or both.

For almost an hour, Alec continues to entreat passers-by with an equal lack of success. He takes some bills out of his wallet and distributes them to various pockets. Why? Instinct. *Don't show a wad. This neighborhood, any neighborhood. At least in New York.*

It's getting colder by the minute, and his topcoat is thin. The alarming fact is that he has no plan. Calling her name out, up and down the corridors of any of these buildings, would probably get him shot.

He's finally rescued by a functioning market, the oldest in the world.

Appearing out of nowhere, a pretty young woman in a mini-skirt and boots, breasts flopping in a polka-dot halter, open fake-fur coat dangling on her shoulders, beelines toward Alec. He sees two other women swerve off, like cabbies after the first swoops in for a fare.

"Aye, guapo! Looking for somebody?" She juts a small round face with a button nose.

"I am, as it happens. Maybe you can help me."

"You bet, sweet pea. I'm the girl of your dreams."

"Tonight, alas, I really must find this other woman."

"Alas? Alas? What have we here? Shakespeare of the fucking projects?"

"Sorry."

"Don't be sorry, hon. What we need more of around here is people saying 'alas.' But you sure it's a woman you want?"

"Particular one, yeah. And she's here somewhere." He hesitates. "In a shooting gallery."

"Uh, oh!" she says, drawing back. "You either a cop or in deep shit."

"Well, I'm certainly not a cop."

"You have a wallet, honey?" Her tone now professional and dry.

"You'd like to see my wallet?"

"I'd like to have your wallet, baby, but a peek will do. For now."

As he takes it out of his pocket, she quickly restrains his arm. "Not here!"

She leads him to the entry of the corner building, where she inspects the contents of the proffered wallet, pocketing the remaining cash. "Okay. You're cool. I take you there."

"To the shooting gallery?"

"For another fifty, I take you to heaven."

"Heaven will have to wait."

"You need the woman in the shooting gallery?"

"I do."

"Okay," she says. "Let's go."

"There's only one here?" he says, pointing upwards.

"Hell no. But I know the one you want."

A guy Alec knew in college once told him about how he and a bunch of other guys had gotten picked up by a con man outside Jimmy Ryan's jazz club and taken to what they were told would be a bordello of beautiful young women. Outside an apartment, in the Harlem projects, the grifter took their money, ducked into the apartment and disappeared. It occurs to Alec, as he follows the girl's swaying butt up the stairs, that he's the mark of a similar scam. When, on the seventh floor, at the end of a long hallway, she holds out her hand, he's pretty sure of it.

She says, "This is the place. And I know you got some more money, or you wouldn't have let me clean out that wallet."

He unfolds a five-dollar bill on her palm. "I'm going in with you," he says.

She squints disbelief while knocking on the door. "What you come up here for, man, if not to go in?"

The door cracks open on a small vestibule. Swinging a bit wider, it reveals a mountainous bewigged woman almost too large to be female, draped in a muumuu and dripping with jewelry from Woolworth's or Grant's. She looks down at the streetwalker, then at Alec, then back to the girl. Alec inhales the apartment's sweet chemical fumes as they mix with the hallway smells of boiled vegetables and fried pork.

"He's cool," says the girl.

The guardian at the gate puts out her hand. Alec lays out another five-dollar bill. She doesn't move. Alec drops on her hand a ten-dollar bill and takes the five dollars back. With a smile, the woman lets him in.

It's a smoky living room with peeling walls. Two grizzled men nod on a sofa, and a woman of indeterminate age curls fetally in an upholstered chair. The proprietress lifts a lit Herbert Tareyton from the ashtray and inhales it as if taking a toke. "So, Daddy, what you want? This woman? This ain't no 'ho house.' "

"I'm looking…." Alec stops. "You know a young woman named Carrie Madigan?"

"Hmm. Could be. I know lots of young women. Lots of names. Hmm. This one… dunno. What you want her for?"

"Nothing bad. Good, possibly. To her advantage. Right now, I just want to talk to her."

"Dunno, dunno," the woman says. "Gonna cost."

Alec pulls out another five. With a negative wag, her earrings chime. "Not for this one," she says.

Alec puts a ten on the five, and she snatches both bills, jerking her head in a gesture to follow while pushing upwards her luxuriant breasts.

She leads them into the kitchen, where a waste of a man with bleary eyes and dreadlocks nods at a needle and bent spoon on the Formica table in front of him. By the sink, with her back toward Alec, a slim white woman in a sleeveless dress drinks water from a glass, holding onto it with both hands, while peering out the window. She turns, and a current circumnavigates Alec's spine. Eyes on him, she places the glass down carefully, as if trying to recall the precise location of the countertop, but still grips it with one hand until her knuckles whiten. She seems not simply troubled by her presence in this place, but uncertain of it.

"We've met," he says. "In court, two weeks ago. You're Carrie Madigan."

She looks at him blankly.

"My name's Alec Brno. You've probably forgotten."

Her hand, thin and white, floats free of the glass, fingers sensing the air like the tendrils of some exotic plant. "What are *you*," she says, "doing *here?*"

"It's a bit of a story."

"I'll bet!"

"Listen," he blurts out. "I'm a lawyer. But no matter what, I won't hurt you. I need to talk to you about Aaron Weinfeld and Sal Martini. You can tell me nothing or what you want. I won't use the information against you. I won't let anyone else use it against you. In fact, I'll do whatever I can to make sure you're protected at every turn. Christ! I'm throwing everything at you at once. I'm probably confusing the hell out of you."

Her sudden smile sends laugh lines to her cheekbones. "You're doing just fine."

"I am?"

"You are."

"Can we talk, then?"

"Here?"

"No. Definitely not here. Let's absolutely get out of here."

Alec takes Carrie's hand, and the two head out of the kitchen. Carrie stops, jerks her hand free, goes back to the kitchen, returns with her handbag and coat. The proprietress and the streetwalker stand watching in amazement. "No charge," says the fat woman finally.

Outside, it evidently had rained. The pavement glistens like bits of glass in black sand. Alec says, "Would you like me to take you home?"

"Whose?" she asks, unsteady on her feet.

"Yours?"

She shakes her head drowsily. "Too far."

"My place, then. 67th. Between Madison and 5th."

"Posh," she says. "Suits me."

They ride downtown in a rattling fleet cab, the driver's face, gaunt and criminal, staring at them from the photograph. Carrie turns away, toward the signs and storefronts flying past, her eyes gradually closing. At each halt, the stoplights reflect red, then green in the rivulets of rain still streaking the cab windows. She falls asleep in Alex's lap. Or passes out.

At 87th Street and Lexington Avenue, the cab, a big Checker, swerves to a stop. Men are working here, under flashing lights, on some great torn upheaval in the pavement. Carrie doesn't stir. The commotion, the lights, make no impression on her breathing. When they arrive at Alec's building, he has to shake her awake. She smiles and says, "Are we there yet?"

Inside, she makes directly for the bathroom, and, without bothering to close the door fully, has a long, audible pee. Emerging, she says, "I may be high, but I can tell you live in a basement."

"Right," he says, showing her the bedroom. "You'll take the bed."

"Good idea," she says, climbing right in. Within seconds, she's again fast asleep. Or passed out.

Alec takes her shoes off and, after a moment of study, covers her with the blanket rolled up at the end of the bed. He then uses the bathroom himself, gets his own clothes off and stretches out on the sofa in the living room. Where he lays awake for hours listening to her thrash.

TWENTY-FOUR

The phone ringing at nine surprises him with the realization he'd been sleeping. "I've talked to Harvey," Macalister's voice says. "You find her?"

Alec, dully sensing that Carrie's gone, peeks in his bedroom to confirm it. "And brought her here," he says, trying to rouse himself to full consciousness. "Only she crashed and has now flown."

"You took her to your apartment?" Mac says.

"I didn't really have a choice."

"Really!"

"That's how it was, Mac."

"And you learned nothing, except that she's a junkie, which we already knew."

"I've practically just met her."

"I think we ought to let Harvey take over from here."

"Why? I'll find her again and talk to her." Alec pauses. "We have a rapport."

"You have a what?" says Macalister.

Alec hears the man swallowing what is probably not coffee.

"Let me put this in context for you, kiddo. What we have here is one of the largest swindles in the history of the world. Fifty thousand people may lose their jobs. Thousands more are gonna get hurt. And there's a girl out there—a hophead, a junkie—who may damn well hold the answer to the problem." Mac sucks in his breath. "You fuck this girl, Alec, and you fuck up the case. You know what happens, you fuck up the case?"

"I got a pretty good idea."

"Dog meat, kiddo! You, dog meat! Get it?"

"Got it."

"Good!"

Her house is a three-family with a high stoop, on a tree-lined street of three-families with high stoops. The houses were constructed at different times but all with cheap sidings, a similar narrow upright style and no more than six feet between them. No person's doings on this block could be a mystery to his neighbor. The town itself, Bayswater, Queens, bounds Jamaica Bay, which is at low tide in the late afternoon, and Alec can smell it. He sits on the top step of her stoop for almost an hour and assesses the daytime activity of the street, which is to say, none. There can be few real families in these three-family houses. The neighborhood must rock at night.

It's mid-afternoon of an unseasonably warm day, and Alec dozes off. When he awakes, Carrie is standing at the bottom of the stairs. It's like having a hallucination. She is squinting up at him behind two bags of groceries. He lopes part way down with a smile he intends to be raffish and befriending. "So it's you," she says.

There is perspiration on her upper lip and forehead, and the late day sun haloes her hair. Her face is more angular than he recalls. Her body is made to seem more frail by the light cotton top and skirt she is wearing.

She, reasonably enough, breaks free from so much inspection. Passing him on the steps, she calls out from the landing, "Well, come on then, if you're coming." As he follows, she thrusts the packages into his arms.

Carrie's living room is littered with books, discarded clothes, old magazines, and newspapers. Alec grimaces; the place is a mess. "Yeah," she says. "Hard to find good help. Want some coffee?"

She grabs the grocery bags from him and takes them into the kitchen.

Alec looks for a place to sit down, finally settling on one of those canvas sling contraptions which hammocks him into its sagging depression. He hears activity in the kitchen, water being run, then water running in the bathroom. She emerges. Flash of blue, scrubbed clean, shiny face, forehead cowled with wetness at her hairline. "You look preposterous in that chair," she says.

He tries to look comfortable. She isn't fooled and strides off for the coffee. Then imprisons him further by handing him a cup. "Black?"

He takes it and tries to drink, but this is made difficult by the angle at which he is sitting. "Oh, come on," she says, looking at him impatiently. With one hand she removes the cup; with the other, she pulls him out of the chair. They sit on the carpet, knees to knees. She is taking his breath away.

"So," he says finally. "You know a guy named Whitman Poole?"

She gives him a look of surprise that turns questioning.

"I have a case," he says, "that hinges on whether this guy, Whitman Poole, was bribed. He was—I can win. For the company that got ripped off—U.S. Safety Vault and Maritime."

She considers this. "Maybe I need a lawyer."

"Maybe you do," he says.

"What about you?"

It takes him a moment. "Interesting idea."

Her head hangs low, exposing the nape of her neck.

Why is she doing that?

"If I were your lawyer," he says, fascinated by this view of her, "you could tell me what you know in confidence. I'll then be able to figure out whether there's a conflict. But whatever you tell me will be privileged. And you own the privilege, so I can't disclose what you tell me without your consent. You'll be protected."

Her head bobs up with a flurry of hair. "Wow! Lots to think about."

"Yeah, there is."

"Trouble is, hard to think right now."

"Why's that?"

"There's this guy coming around. He's already late."

"What kind of guy?"

"Kind of guy who brings things."

"I see. That kind of guy."

"You being judgmental?" she asks.

Before Alec can answer, there's a knock on the door.

She springs up like a gymnast. "Can I borrow twenty dollars?"

Alec, unhappily, fishes out a bill and hands it to her. Carrie, bounding to the door, quickly concludes her transaction in the hall. Alec hears a man's guttural voice but does not see him. The door shuts. Carrie returns, sits splay-kneed, displays a small bottle and downs the contents. "Methadone."

"Why not get it at a hospital?" he asks. "Get in a program? Or, better yet, kick it all? I could help you."

"Oh yeah? Why would you do that?"

"I dunno," he says.

"I'm broken, you're gonna fix me?"

"Don't," he says.

"What?"

"I like you." It just comes out of him.

"Not smart."

"Doesn't matter." He's in free-fall and, instinctively, leaning closer. He can feel her breath on his skin.

"So maybe you're not on a white horse," she says. "Maybe this is darker. Junkie girl—there for the taking?"

"Is that what you think?"

"You're not denying it."

"What I know is… I really… like you, okay? I'm just saying it. There's no plan here. In fact—" He laughs. "There is a plan, and this is against it."

"So maybe I like you too," she says. "But, of course, being a broken person—*unlike* you—I can't trust my feelings."

"You think I'm broken?"

"Falling for a junkie? What do you think?"

She smiles and closes her eyes for a moment. "Takes a while to hit. The methadone. When it does… umm… like a blanket of love." She laughs softly. Throwing back her head and laughing. Leaning back on outstretched arms and curling up around her chin her slender shoulders.

He's right in her face. Her breath this close smells of peppermint and coffee. In one deft cross-armed motion, she yanks her tank top over her head. Her small bare breasts and mussed hair completely undo him. She pulls him up and toward the bedroom. He watches her slide into bed.

"Hurry!" she says, shivering in a draft, gathering the covers over her—then, just like that, passing out.

Her sleep is not peaceful. Almost at once she falls into dreams that distort her face and make her legs thrash.

Alec lies on top of the covers beside her. He both realizes what is happening and questions his sanity for allowing it to occur. How could it be that a woman as delightful as Darcy could not touch his heart, despite years of lovemaking and laughter, while an unfortunate creature like Carrie, after a very few hours and those spent mainly with her being unconscious, could now be burrowing into him as if she were the missing part of his cells? He knows—no one has to tell him—how stupid it is to open one's life to an addict; how alluring a young woman this good-looking can be exposing such neediness and vulnerability. He knows it and yet thinks he sees more. In her face, though not calm, which he studies until he sleeps, he sees the beauty behind the disease.

TWENTY-FIVE

I t's raining in Carrie's bedroom. Alec wakes up and, for almost a
minute of sluggish consciousness, watches the drops drip down
from the ceiling. It finally dawns on him that he's lying under a
leak in the roof. Hauling himself out of bed, he realizes he's not
only wet, but alone.

He flips the light on in her bathroom to a surreal horror.
Floating in the pond the rain has made of the floor are bent hypodermic needles, glassine envelopes, and other drug paraphernalia.

He checks the living room and kitchen, though he already
knows she's gone. It's eight thirty-seven at night. The phone
now—amazingly—works. He calls for a Scull's Angels cab, waits
for it forever, and finally has himself transported to downtown
Manhattan, operating under the delusion he might still get some
work done.

Inside his office, he closes the door. Then he turns off the
lights and sits at his desk. Thoughts race about and collide in his
head like passengers in a terminal dashing for their trains. From
the darkness of a huge window, fifty-eight stories into the sky,
the city rises, bedecked in glints of far-off lights as dazzling as the
galaxy.

TWENTY-SIX

Friday morning. Phil is standing behind his bar, blending fruit drinks for his visitor. Since the house is built on the side of a hill, one end of the basement is not subterranean, but offers a view, through French windows, of an inlet to Long Island Sound. It's not the best time to be there, however. The sun bouncing off the inlet floods the entirety of the wide, knotty-pined room.

Little John Cuitano, on a bar stool, has his back to the sun, but the rays off the mirror flash in his eyes. He lifts his pen from the ink drawing he's committing to one of Phil's napkins, squints and shifts position. "You've lost her, I hear."

"Bullshit," Phil says.

"It's what I'm hearing."

"Oh, yes? From whom?"

"From those who know, Phil."

"What?" says Phil, refilling Little John's glass. "You've got a birdie in my group now?"

"Word travels. To interested parties. You know the process."

As Little John resumes sketching, his bulk sags over each side of the stool. Two of his lieutenants hover over him. Vito stands off to the side, and Phil, planting his elbows on the bar, inclines his face toward his guest.

"Word like that?" Phil says. "Ain't worth shit."

"That right?" says Little John, as if pretending to have just learned something, though still concentrating on the drawing.

Phil steps back but shows a bit of exasperation. "I told you, John. Trust me on this."

"I think you should appreciate my level of anxiety."

"I do, John."

"And I think you should share it."

"But I do share it."

"If it were my situation, I'd take care of it."

"And I am."

Cuitano finally looks up. "Not... the safe way."

"It's not your situation," Phil says coldly.

"Getting close to being that is what I'm telling you."

"You understand," Phil says, "the feds are not unaware of her existence. She disappears, and who are they coming for?"

"They don't seem overly excited about Aaron. Who has already disappeared."

"They're looking for him. So are we. But I'm sure you can see the difference."

"You're looking for him, you're saying?" Little John's bulbous nose wrinkles with distrust.

"Every day," Phil says.

The door opens suddenly. Sam Brno appears with an overalled workman.

"Sorry," Sam says. "Didn't know anyone was in here."

"Who the fuck are you?" Phil says.

"I work for Abigail. Plan says we put a smoke detector down here."

"What's your name?"

"Me? Sam."

"Sam." Phil goes to genial. "Later, okay?"

"Sure." Sam leaves with his workman, who closes the door.

Little John gives Phil a look of, What the hell! Phil says, "We gotta live too, John. Like everyone else. Maybe if you had told me you were coming...."

The fat man makes a harrumphing sound and admires his doodle, a surprisingly accomplished rendering of an MP5 submachine gun. He shows it to Phil. "The safe way," he says. "And I'd be doing you a favor. No trace, just like Aaron. But clean for you.

Lots of advantages here, Phil. Think about it."

Later that morning, a meeting assembles in Mac's office. The room has the same basic architecture as Alec's, but is otherwise worlds apart. It's a corner office with six windows, decorated, surprisingly, in a French provincial style to Mac's wife's specifications. Associates, like Alec, are given one-windowed cells, with standard fabrics and furniture. Also, the surfaces in Mac's room are clean—precisely because the materials littering the offices of Alec and other associates are summarized by them for Mac and other senior partners. Mac's office, moreover, is studded with the artifacts of great victories in court, and graced by photographs of grown children and their young progeny. Neither grandkids nor triumphs are probable for associates. They're expected to leave before either eventuality, if they haven't made partner in ten years.

Harvey Grand arrives first in all his finery. When Alec enters, Harvey extends his hand but doesn't rise. Harvey is known to say little at meetings, unless asked. Mac had once said of him, "He's a quiet man who sees evil everywhere, and it amuses him."

Harvey is not amused by Alec's report, however, nor by the fact that Macalister seems intrigued by the possibility presented.

"You want us to represent this woman?" Mac says.

"It's not such a crazy idea," says Alec.

Mac looks to Harvey who takes out his pad. "Current drug intake?" Harvey says. "About thirty, forty milligrams a day methadone. Does a gram of coke a day to prevent the methadone from blocking the pleasures of heroin. Then, of course, she does enough heroin and blow to keep her high. Comes to at least seven-hundred, maybe eight-hundred-fifty bucks a week. She'll be on the streets soon, if the mob doesn't take her out first. Hasn't paid rent in four months, and the landlord's already got a judgment filed against her."

Mac turns to Alec. "This fits our client profile?"

"She's not going to talk to us otherwise," Alec says.

Harvey flips a page in his notebook. "There's another side to this. Carrie's husband. Phil Anwar. He's got no record, which just attests to his power, because everyone working for him's got a rap sheet that unwinds like a roll of toilet paper. And Phil's grandfather's name isn't Anwar. It's Angiapello. I assume you've heard of this family, Mac."

"Mob family," says Macalister.

"With an interesting history. Recent history. After the granddad came Phil's uncle, a dandy called Don Giovanni, who ran the mob for twenty years, then retired. Which is unheard of. He's said to have fallen in love with the British lifestyle and moved to London. He handed the crown to Phil, but bloody warfare ensued. The result of that was a pax between Phil and a creep called Little John Cuitano, who controls most of New Jersey."

"You mean the mobs there."

"No, I mean the state."

"With Anwar in New York."

"The City, Long Island, bits of Connecticut, and whatever Little John doesn't own in New Jersey. Every U.S. Attorney in the tri-state has been trying to break up this organization for the last thirty years."

"And Anwar is connected to Martini?"

"Only through Carrie's connection to Martini's lawyer, Weinfeld," Harvey says. "So far as we know."

"You're saying—as we assumed from the start—the whole swindle was likely a mob job?"

Harvey shrugs.

Mac gets up and goes to the window. "So," he says, "we're trying to prove that Whitman Poole was taking from the Cosa Nostra. There's a shitload of witnesses—including Poole—ready to swear he wasn't. Jury believes that, our client gets hosed. On the other hand, we've got one witness who, with ten minutes of testimony, might be able to blow the whole fucking case out of the water, but she could OD any minute, or get shot." He swivels around. "Dunno, Harvey. Don't think this is a close one."

"You think what?" says Harvey. "That because you represent her she's gonna hand you Phil Anwar as the guy who bribed Poole? Let me tell you. Carrie married this guy when she was nineteen. He's been beating the crap outta her regularly since then and now has their kid, a four-year-old girl—a hostage Carrie never sees again in case she steps outta line. So you know what's more likely than her helping us? That she'll do anything this guy asks, including double-dealing you. On the witness stand. Just when you've got no way to bail out."

Silence for a moment as they consider that all-too-real scenario.

"I see the risk," Mac says evenly. "I see the upside. I'm going for the gain." He fixes again on Alec.

"I might have trouble finding her this time," Alec says.

"Wouldn't worry," says Harvey, his voice caustic. "You gave her money for drugs? She'll find you. If she's still alive."

TWENTY-SEVEN

Saturday morning. Alec, in the shower when the doorbell rings, wraps himself in a towel to answer it. Carrie's outside, looking up at him, fresh-faced from the cold air, a little high, and a bit bedraggled, wearing a gabardine coat over the same clothes he last saw her in.

"I could render myself into your state," she says with a grin, "or you could render yourself into mine."

He lets her in. "Shampoo's in the shower," he says.

Letting out a laugh, she takes over the bathroom. Alec dresses in the bedroom, listens to the sound of water running. Whatever, exactly, she had in mind with that invitation, he's resisting the temptation to find out.

Carrie's in the shower, a small tiled stall. She's thinking she hasn't fooled him much with her act of bravado. She's frightened and sick. She stands directly under the stream, allowing it to cascade down on her head and over her shoulders. Her face is hidden by a tent of water and hair, and her weeping, by the noise of the shower.

The leaves have turned late this fall, despite the mysterious appearance and disappearance of the one early snow. Shockingly colored things, they travel the air in the tangle of branches or decay in the wet grass. Alec leads Carrie to the same path he'd once walked with Darcy, up to the track around the reservoir. A nice, if inexplicable, distinction: when Carrie halts, leans her back against the wire fence and turns her face up to the sun, it stops his heart.

"My firm will represent you," he says, "if that's what you want."

"I don't care about that," she says. "I have two things to tell you. One's a gift from me to you."

He puts his hands high up on the fence, his face close to hers. She draws a breath to ground herself.

"You say your case depends on whether a stuffed-shirt asshole named Whitman Poole was taking bribes? Four times I delivered envelopes to him from Aaron Weinfeld."

"Did you really?" Alec utters under his breath.

"I thought you'd like that one."

"You know what was in the envelopes?"

"I typed what was in the envelopes. Checks. Each two-fifty large."

A rush of excitement mixes with fear for her. Alec comes away from the fence. "You're willing to say this on the witness stand?"

"Wouldn't be much of a gift if I weren't, would it? Only—"

"What?"

"Can a wife testify against her husband?"

"He's not a party to our case. But also, about something like this? Absolutely. You wouldn't be testifying about a confidential communication, much less the kind the rule is supposed to protect. You'd be testifying about your own acts—writing and delivering checks."

"Good." She stares at Alec intently. "The other thing I want to tell you is that, this afternoon, I'm checking myself into a hospital." After a moment of indecision, she adds, "I have a daughter, Alec."

His face shows nothing.

"I want her back," she says. "When I'm clean, I'll fight for her."

"Okay," he says.

"Okay? *Okay?* Do you have any idea what I'm saying? What's involved?"

"Yes," he says flatly. "I do. Believe me."

"Okay," she says, relenting. Then looks out over the reservoir. "I've got to get clean. For Sarah. For us. For me. We're not going to make it—you and I—if I'm not clean and sober."

"*We're* not going to make it?" he says.

"Oh, come on, Alec," she says, strutting past him. "Don't be slow!"

TWENTY-EIGHT

My name's George," says the little blond boy in short pants who has just been deposited in Sarah's room.

Sarah, in overalls, is sitting on her four-poster bed, dressing her favorite doll. "I *know* your name," she says impatiently, hunting for the doll's underwear in a stack of doll clothing. "I just heard it. Didn't you hear Nanny just saying it?"

"I'm almost five. How old are you?"

"Four-and-a-half."

"I'm older than you."

"So?" says Sarah.

"I live in the next house," George says.

"I know that too. I've seen you."

George, who is a bit shorter than Sarah, strides to the center of the room and looks around it. "You sure have a lot of toys in here."

Sarah, too, glances at her possessions, but without much pride or enthusiasm. The room is large, pink, and bright, and might have been furnished by F.A.O. Schwarz.

"All girl's stuff," George notes deprecatingly.

"Well, ye-ah," Sarah rejoins.

"You have a dog?"

"Vito does. I can play with him whenever I want to."

"Who's Vito?"

"He works for daddy."

George opens the lid of a bin of toys and starts rummaging.

"You have a doctor's bag?"

"No," Sarah says, as if it were stupid to have such a thing, but staring at the boy now with curiosity.

"I do."

"Why would *I* want that?"

"To play doctor, of course."

"Why would I want to play that?"

"It's fun. And, actually, you can do it without a bag."

"So how do you play?"

"I'll be the doctor, and you take all your clothes off."

"That's nasty."

"No, it's fun."

"Okay. I'll be the doctor, and you take all *your* clothes off."

George looks confused. "That's not the way you play."

Sarah slides down from her bed, holding the now fully dressed doll. "I don't like you. I'm going to tell Nanny to take you away."

"I shouldn't come here anyway, my mom says."

"Then why did you?"

"Because my babysitter's friends with your babysitter."

"She's not a babysitter. She's a nanny."

"What's the difference?"

"Boy," Sarah says. "You don't know anything, do you?"

"My house is bigger than yours."

"You're a big jerk," Sarah says.

"Well, your father's a gangster boss."

"What's that?"

"A very bad man."

"Who says?"

"My mom says. *And* my dad."

"Well, whatta they know? They're wrong," Sarah says, feet planted, arms akimbo.

"No they're not."

"Are too."

"Your father kills people," George says, his small eyes lit with excitement.

"He does not!" Sarah exclaims.

"He does too. And your mom doesn't even live here."

"Who says?" Sarah, clutching the doll, screams, tears welling in her eyes.

Phil bursts in. "What's going on here? Who is this kid?" Back to the doorway, he bellows, *"Nanny!"*

TWENTY-NINE

Sam, arriving at Abigail's office in Syosset, takes off his coat and hangs it next to hers on the coat rack. Abigail, at her desk, watches each movement.

"Thanks for coming in on a Saturday, Sam."

"I don't mind," he says, thinking she's sounding a bit strange.

He goes to the new steel desk she put in, catty-cornered to hers—all the while her eyes still on him. On his desk is a container of coffee from the diner next door. He opens it, takes a sip. Just the way he likes it, one sugar, very little milk. "Thanks," he says.

"We've got some catching up, paper-wise," she says.

"So you mentioned."

"I'm kind of interested… yesterday, you said—"

"I walked in on them," he says.

"Right, yeah, that," she says.

"You didn't want to talk about it on the phone."

She sighs, gets up, and leads him outside to the parking lot, which has a cluster of cars in front of the diner.

"You're thinking what?" he says. "They've wired the phones *and* the office?"

"I'm not sure is the point."

"You're the security expert."

"Yeah, but there are lots of ways to bug somebody."

"This is pretty crazy, Abigail."

"Who was there?" she asks, ignoring the admonition.

"Anwar and four other guys."

"Where in the house?"

"The bar in the basement."

"Yeah, that's where they'd meet," she says. "Describe the guys."

"Why're you so interested in this?"

"Who were the guys?"

"The one sitting was huge. Three hundred pounds, maybe three-fifty. Probably glandular. Ugly son-of-a-bitch."

"Little John."

"Little John Cuitano?" he says, sitting hard on the fender of his own car.

"Sounds like him, yeah. What were they talking about?"

"You know him, Little John?"

"We work for him."

"Oh, Christ," says Sam. "Him too?"

"Yeah."

"He's in New Jersey, I thought."

"And what?" she says. "We can't drive to New Jersey?"

"You're really plugged in."

"It's a lot of business, Sam. And I thought we'd been over this."

"It's freezing out here."

"I know. What were they talking about?"

"I didn't hear."

"Nothing?"

"Nothing," he says.

"Okay," she says. "You wanna go back in?"

"We're not finished," he says. "Cuitano and Anwar are both bosses."

"So?"

"Different families that don't always get along."

"And?"

"They fight, you're in the middle."

"I never take sides. No need to."

"Oh right," he says, as if indulging a child. "And they're always gonna see it that way?"

"We're nothing to these people, we're menials. We provide a service."

"So whatta you gonna do when one of those bastards asks for a service against the other? Like a little ole bug in the ceiling lamp? You give him what he wants, you're a player, and you're at risk. You refuse, they've got you down as unreliable, maybe even playing for the other side. So either way, you start measuring your life expectancy in what? Weeks, maybe. Days, probably."

She swallows hard. "It hasn't happened."

"Good. Get out before it does."

"I can't."

"You already know too much?"

"That's right."

There's an awkward moment in which Sam ingests what he's been told and Abigail considers whether to tell him more.

She says, "Because there *is* something else we do. Have done. I have. The company."

"I'm really not going to like this, am I?"

"No."

"Okay," he says dismally. "What is it?"

"Close to what you said. Tap phones."

"Oh, boy."

"The last one of those I did, for Phil… the guy was a lawyer."

"And?"

"He's missing."

"How long?"

"Too long."

"You mean, he's probably dead."

"Most likely."

"Great," he says. "That's the too much you know."

"Yeah."

"For which you also feel guilty."

"Very," she says.

"You didn't kill him."

"Not directly."

Sam rubs his face.

"Abigail, sell the business and move elsewhere."

"You're kidding, right?"

"No. I'm not."

"I gotta live, Sam."

"That's what I'm trying to make sure of."

She thinks about that for a while, then says, "Let's get a drink. I've got a bottle of Jack Daniel's at home."

"In the middle of the afternoon?"

"I know."

"And I don't drink," he says.

"Neither do I."

"Then what are we talking about?"

"I gotta draw you a picture?"

THIRTY

At a hospital in Queens, Alec and Carrie meet with a small round person with exquisitely formed purple lips, a Dr. Patel, who is actually there on a Saturday and will be her treating psychiatrist. In a tiny impersonal office, he explains the routine. Carrie will undergo detoxification for five days. Then, they will attempt to treat her. Then, they will see. He discreetly leaves them alone for a few moments after closing the door, whereupon Carrie grabs Alec and gives him a kiss. Their first. One unlike any other. So that he will never forget it.

Late Saturday afternoon. Alec, in running shorts, shambles down the embankment from the reservoir track. He is trying to imagine the sensation of detox. He has this picture of Carrie curled in agony on a bed. He has this picture of himself as he is at this moment, which makes him stop walking—tethered to a spot, like a goat, by the remembrance of a kiss that is all the more admonitory for the dark and sweet taste of it still on his lips. He replays in his mind their last scene in Patel's office, watching her go, her last look, wistful and self-mocking, flung over her shoulder. And that lovely kiss still curls in his brain, churning it to the consistency of jelly.

The scene is all too reminiscent. They didn't allow children to visit in hospitals, but Alec, age eight, somehow got in, found the room, saw his mother looking like someone else. Looking at him as if she didn't know him.

He stirs himself finally and makes his way toward the avenue. Joggers, strollers, bikers, skaters flow insouciantly the opposite way. It's like he's burst from a bubble of fantasy time, the kind cocooned by children at play. *What am I doing?* he thinks. *I don't recognize this person.*

THIRTY-ONE

Abigail and Sam lie naked in bed. It's her bed, and it's king-size. Sun spears through the blinds, slats both of them. He's lanky, with long slender legs and a little pot belly that stretches flat when he lies on his back. She has small ankles and thin legs, with a butt that pillows out surprisingly on her light frame, and dainty breasts.

"I used to have a beautiful body," she says.

He boosts up on an elbow. "Whatta you mean, used to?"

"Ha."

"What?" he asks.

"How long you been celibate?"

"That obvious?"

"I've seen hungry," she says.

"And I'm what, in your view? Ravenous?"

"Alters your judgment."

He falls back to the pillow.

"But a good start," she says. "For us. Considering."

"Considering my celibacy," he says.

"Considering the fact that it was our first time. First times are difficult."

"You know this?"

"Not from recent history, if that's what you're asking."

"No. I'm not."

Sam's eyes dart around. It's a spacious room filled with maple, florals, and chintz. Many purchases, many objects, all denoting a companionable couple.

"His name was Gus, your husband?"

"He was called Gus."

"Augustus?"

"Giuseppe."

"Ah," he says, now sitting up.

Silence.

"What?" she says.

"Just looking around. You really loved him."

"You're creeped out by his things being here still."

"No, only natural," he says.

"Even stuff in the bathroom? His razor? Shaving cream?"

"I understand."

"I can't touch a goddamn thing."

"We made love in this bed," he says.

"Big step for me."

"Which part?"

"Both. You. And the bed."

Silence.

"I put away the photos," she says. "Somehow I could do that."

"You put them downstairs."

"Well, I got them out of the bedroom."

"Should we talk about something else?" he says.

"Yes, definitely."

"Should we talk about the business?"

"No." She climbs out of bed, heads toward the bathroom. "Take a good look. We can talk about that."

"Your backside."

"My ass. Pretty big."

"Hell no, it's not."

She turns. "Big ass, small tits."

He rolls from the bed, stands before her. "Beautiful. Every bit of you. Truly beautiful."

"You just wanna get laid again."

"That too."

"Could happen," she says, going into the bathroom and

closing the door.

He drifts back to bed, lies on his back, looking around some more. The house is on a good-sized lot at the end of a street bordering what's called the Syosset Woods, some uncleared land, too swampy to build on and filling the windows with branches. Presently she emerges with a plastic pail full of men's toiletries.

"These I'll get rid of," she says, going to the foot of the bed. "Not the business. I come with the business. Because I leave, that's worse. Believe me, not even possible. Gus and I knew that going in. A deal with the devil, maybe, but we made it. So the question for you, Sam—you in or out?"

"Why not possible?"

"Just isn't, Sam. Think about it."

"What about me?"

"You could still leave. No problem. It's been done."

"There's something you're not telling me," he says.

"There's lots I'm not telling you."

"And will you?"

"When you need to know it, yes."

"You get to decide."

"How else could it be?"

"You could trust me now."

"It's not a matter of trust," she says.

He can't see why not, but says to himself, *Let it go, because ultimately it will make no difference to how you feel.*

"So in or out, Sam?"

"What do you think?"

"I like to hear it said."

He slides to the foot of the bed and hoists himself again to a sitting position. "Okay," he says, looking up at her. "I'm in for as long as you want me."

"Yes?" She tears up.

"Put the toiletries back. I may need them."

"Okay," she says with a wet smile.

"And we have to take measures."

"What do you mean?"

"If you get targeted—when it happens, we have to know it's happening."

She studies his face, gets nothing.

He says, "You know how to tap phones."

With widening eyes, she says, "What… are you thinking, Sam?"

"You're gonna have to teach me," he says.

"To wiretap, why?"

"I just said."

"You wanna tap Phil Anwar's phone?" she says, as if questioning Sam's sanity.

"You agreed you're at risk. And what you're not telling me probably increases it."

"And this is what?" she says. "A smaller risk?"

"If it's done right, sure. He travels, doesn't he? Away from home a lot."

"He'll know."

"He might find the tap, but he'd probably think it's the FBI. And if he rips it out, we'll know that. Because we'll be listening."

"Know, and do what?"

"Depends," he says.

"This is worse than crazy, Sam. It's suicidal."

"I don't agree, Abby. You tapped a guy's phone, and he died. Makes you a witness to a probable murder. Guy who did it might decide any minute, you're too big a risk. Which means he wants your name off the witness list—permanently."

She takes his head in both hands. "What you're thinking of doing… would be putting a bigger risk on yourself than on me."

"Trust me," he says. "I do know what I'm doing. The worst risk is to be in the dark."

THIRTY-TWO

She's in rehab," says Alec to Mac, who has perched himself on the credenza against the long wall of Alec's office.

"All right," Mac says. "We'll have her sign the affidavit when she gets out."

"Fine," Alec says in a tone suggesting the opposite.

"You have a problem with that?" Mac asks.

"How'll we use it, the affidavit?"

"The point of getting it, dummy, is so we never have to use it. You get witnesses committed on paper? It's amazing how reliable they become."

"I think we can trust her," says Alec.

"Oh, really? You're a trusting sort of person?"

"Forget it, fine. We'll get the affidavit."

Mac's glance isn't trusting, but he lets it go. "I'm afraid we have to fill in Shilling."

"Oh, well, shit!"

"For Christ's sake, Alec! The man's negotiating with the warehouse receipt holders."

"Well, you see, that's what I don't like," says Alec. "We go public with this, and we make her a mark. We put her at risk."

"Are you conflicted?" Mac asks with chilling sweetness.

"In the sense that I think the personal safety of a witness is more important than our personal gain? I wouldn't call that a conflict."

Mac, glaring for a moment, decides to cut Alec some slack. "Marius Shilling—kraut bastard though he may be—is co-representing our clients. Do you have any doubt that we have to at least inform him of this witness?"

"We should give him as little information as possible," says Alec begrudgingly, "and should control how he uses that."

Mac laughs. "Control? I'm all for it. And I'd like to think, kiddo, that I had more over you." He pushes up against the credenza. "Come on. Let's go."

"Why're we going to his office?" Alec asks, as he and Mac stride up Wall Street.

"Like to put this info out on the telephone?"

"Of course not, but he could come to ours."

Mac broadens his smile. "We're the supplicants. He's got big news—even bigger than ours, I gather—so we have to go get it. Go fetch."

"I assume you're kidding."

"Only in part. Besides," Mac adds, "I'd rather be in that prick's office, nosing around his papers, than have him in mine. And I thought his place might interest you."

"Been there."

"Yeah? What did you observe?"

"A law firm," Alec says.

"That's it?"

"This one's different?"

"From ours. Operates like a tribe of gorillas. Control the food source, you control the tribe. And the allocation of the money. If you want to."

"The food source being the clients," Alec says.

"What else?"

"And our firm?"

"The opposite extreme. We're a fucking Athenian democracy. And we split the money by lock-step progression."

"What does that mean?"

"Three tiers, from youngest to oldest. Complete equality of distributions within each tier. Only small differences among them. No partner with executive power."

"How's that even possible?"

"Because the standards for making partner are almost impossibly high. So the partners *are* equal. Any one of them could run an army, or a nation. And we're not scrounging for work. We've got too much of it. So we're not willing to give someone power because he can bring more of it in."

"You know," Alec says, "it might be a good idea to get some of that information out on interviews."

"About how hard it is to become a partner?" Mac says with a laugh.

"Everyone knows *that*. The rest of it."

"People pick it up. You just did."

"And Shilling's still out there hustling for clients?"

"In his case, mainly West German clients. They love the son-of-a-bitch. He comes on like a Prussian general, with his dueling scars and his shaven head, and they eat it up. But the prize, for him, would be the general representation of U.S. Safety."

They confront the shorn-headed one in his personal conference room, forty-two stories above Wall Street. Shilling is holding a meeting with his associates, lecturing them by tapping his dueling saber on a blackboard covered with notes. He pauses to hear Mac's report, then pooh-poohs the idea of an affidavit from Carrie. "At the trial, if we have one, we might want her as a witness, but, even then—" Shilling whips the sword through the air between them with a stagey laugh. "I have doubts as to the utility of an affidavit. More downside than up, I should think. Suggests too much pre-arrangement with the witness, too much intimacy."

At the word "intimacy," Alec inwardly cringes.

Mac says, with menacing affability, "You giving me trial advice, now, Marius?"

"Is that a problem?" says Shilling, his own attitude coy. "You're above taking advice?"

"I'm completely open-minded. To those who know what they're talking about." Mac smiles innocuously—at Shilling, then at his associates, who now form an open-mouthed crew.

"The client," purrs Shilling, regaining his seat, "evidently believes that I do."

Mac sits in the next chair, and juts his jaw close to Shilling's. "You want to steal the client, dude? Then make your move. But until it's yours—so far as the trial is concerned—stay out of my way. Okay?" Big broad grin.

Shilling's eyes flutter. "So far as my negotiations with the East Coast banks are concerned, there's been a development that rather changes things. I doubt, Mac, that anyone's gotten around to telling you yet." The man smiles, inviting others to relish the knife-cut that Mac is on the B-list for news. "The fact is, Whitman Poole has fled. Flight, as you probably know, is seen by the courts as an admission of guilt. Much more revealing and effective than an affidavit from the afflicted Miss Madigan."

For Alec, who has joined Mac at the table, surprise and relief rout feelings of discomfiture.

"The banks know this?" asks Mac, masking his own surprise.

Shilling smiles again, disingenuously. "Of course, *they've* been told."

"Makes your job easier, then," Mac says, rising from the table and signaling Alec to leave with him. "And the sooner you do it, the sooner I can go about doing mine—litigating with Si Rosenkranz and the rest of the Dark Side bar."

"Oh, that case might settle too," says Shilling as Mac heads off.

Mac turns, openly furious. "Have you been authorized to talk to Si? Behind my back?"

"I didn't say that, Mac."

"Shilling," says Macalister with a tone of disgust, "you mess with that—I'll take that fucking dueling sword of yours and ram it up your Teutonic rectum!"

Alec, trailing Mac out the door, sees Shilling's associates in nearly convulsive acts of grin-stifling.

THIRTY-THREE

On the tarmac of U.S. Safety's storage tank facility in Bayonne, Gen. Marcus Rand, topcoated but bareheaded, surveys the place as if it were a battleground strewn with bodies. About a hundred yards away, a younger, taller, sturdily built man in a navy pinstriped suit leaves a touring party to join him. They confer for a moment in the shadow of one of the tanks, while the wind whips their hair and garments. Rand gesticulates in anger at the news being imparted; the younger man, while delivering it, adjusts his Clark Kent glasses and combs his thick black hair with his fingers. Then they spot Frank Macalister and Alec Brno, both dressed for the weather, walking toward them from their car.

"I thought Ben Braddock was coming," Rand says.

"Couldn't make it," says Mac.

Rand's mouth forms an expression of distaste. "Frank Macalister, Alec Brno: Brett Creighton, chief operating officer." This by way of introduction.

The men greet each other, and Rand says to Macalister, "You know what's happening?"

Mac and Alec plainly don't.

"Tell 'em," says Rand.

"Our stock's in free-fall," Creighton says.

"How far?" Mac asks.

"In half a day," says Creighton, "we lost twenty-eight percent of our value—at which point the stock exchange suspended trading."

Rand asks Macalister sharply, "You know what's causing this?"

"I'm surprised it's taken this long," Mac says. "The institutions are dumping your stock."

"Well, no shit, Macalister. The question is why. They don't like our side of the case, or they don't like our lawyers?"

Mac gives a grim laugh.

"This amuses you?" Rand says.

"Only in one sense. Strips the mask off Rosenkranz's face."

Marcus Rand, often given to Delphic utterances himself, is intolerant of such pronouncements by others. "You care to tell us what that means?"

"Sure," says Mac. "What Si wants at trial—what he thinks more than anything will help him win? Getting seen by the jury as the champion of the little guy, the stockholder. But of course that's bullshit. The reality is, Si wins and the judgment comes out of the pockets of the little guys—because that's who your present stockholders are. And it goes primarily into the pockets of the fat cats—the funds, the insurance companies, the institutional investors—the people who have just sold out."

"The jury will know this?" Rand says.

"I do my job—and I will—the jury will know it."

Rand frowns; Mac looks as if nothing has happened. It's Alec's role to say nothing, unless called upon, just listen and learn. And Alec appreciates the opportunity. Two very powerful men, each having risen as high as he wants, keeping sharp by sparring. But there's another man present whose role is to smooth things.

"Do I correctly understand," Creighton says with a smile, "that you and my old friend Marius Shilling are not getting on as famously as we might have hoped?"

"So he's your friend."

"We were in the Army together. He's German by birth, but of course he fought on our side."

"Fought?"

"Well, we were in Washington. Intelligence, as I gather you were, Mac, though you, I hear, were in a more active theater."

Mac, ignoring this, says, "If you're a friend of the man, give him a message. I have no idea how he's doing in his negotiations with the East Coast banks, because, oddly enough, he doesn't consider it to be within his job description to keep me current. Up to now, that hasn't seriously interfered with what I'm doing, and frankly it's not likely to. So that's an issue for you to deal with, if you care to. Up to you. But what you get him to understand—what you damn well get him to understand—is that, so far as the trial is concerned, there's one case, meaning one ship, which means one captain. You want two captains running your ship, you've charted a course for disaster. And if that's what you want, I'm out. I'm not trying a case being sabotaged by the client. You got that?"

Rand and Creighton exchange glances. "Shilling is not the captain of the ship," says Rand finally.

"Very well," Mac says. "So let's take the tour you promised me and get the fucking ship into port."

THIRTY-FOUR

Carrie, in the ward, waits by a pay phone, her hand on the receiver, her eye on the clock. She strangles the first ring, as the clock strikes noon. "Looney bin," she answers.

"On the stroke," says Alec admiringly. "How are you?"

"On a pink cloud, honey. Clean. Clean and sober! Can you believe it? I did it! I actually did it!"

Carrie beams at Alec with a luminous smile. They sit facing each other in a hospital cafeteria painted, floors and ceiling, institutional green. In her white cotton pajamas and pink-striped robe, she looks as confectionary as a peppermint on a Christmas tree.

Dr. Patel, spotting Alec while crossing the hall, waddles over to their table to join them. He takes a seat, spreads his hands, purses his fabulous lips. "We can't keep her here, you know. We have schizophrenics here, psychotics. We can treat them. But there's nothing we can do for an addict."

"I thought there were programs—"

"Oh, yes," Patel says, interrupting. "Very effective. For some. Not, I'm afraid, for our Carrie. She's too clever for the programs. Outsmarts them. She plays the program."

Carrie makes a comic guilty face, as if it were funny.

Alec, not amused, says, "I'm afraid I'm not clear on what that really means."

The doctor looks at Carrie, who gives him an expression of indifference.

"What it means," Patel says, and thinks for a moment. "She

knows the right things to say, the right things to do, and she dutifully says and does them. Then she tries to bribe a night maintenance man to bring her cocaine."

"It was a joke," Carrie says.

"Did you do that?"

"I wasn't serious. I just said."

He looks to Patel whose expression is disbelieving.

"So what're you saying?" Alec asks, beginning to get angry. "There's no chance of her staying clean?"

Patel gives this a philosophical shrug. "What are the odds on a miracle?" he says. "For, you see, it is a miracle that we need."

"A what? This is a goddamn hospital. You've got a sick person, you treat her."

"What I'm telling you, my friend, is we can't. Precisely because this is a hospital. Not a rehab facility, which, in my opinion, is what she needs. A reset. A complete overhaul. It's not done in a week. Or here. You understand?"

"Look at her," Alec says. "She's clean, happy."

"Oh, my dear boy." Patel rises, smiles weakly and leaves.

Alec watches the little doctor part the crowd now entering the cafeteria. He can barely stand to look at Carrie, because he knows Patel is right.

His mind is filled with the memory of a conversation guiltily overheard when he was nine. His father in the kitchen of their small apartment seeing a doctor out, arguing with him, as Alec had just argued with Dr. Patel. There was no medical fix for addiction then, and there's none now. No one's devised a method for extracting the gene. It's just stupid to fall in love with an addict. You either cast them adrift or they'll pull you down with them. Of course, a kid has no choice.

At the end of the visiting hour, as Alec says goodbye to Carrie at the threshold of her room, she pulls him inside and shuts the door behind them. She then kisses him full on the mouth, pushing him back against the wall.

"Your roommates could come in any second," he says.

She shakes her head, no, emphatically.

"You've made a deal with them?"

She shakes her head, yes, just as emphatically, and pulls him down onto the bed.

"We can't do this, Carrie."

She says, "Shh! We have ten minutes. Just hold me."

Feeling little volition to do otherwise, he wraps his arms around her, and they topple together, both holding on tight.

THIRTY-FIVE

I t's basically simple," Abigail says, holding up a small silvery object having the circumference of a dime and the thickness of a
nickel. "It's like plugging an appliance into an outlet on the wall.
Except instead of an outlet, you plug it into the telephone wire
you're tapping."

Her Formica kitchen table is cleared of everything but the
equipment she needs for the tutorial, which is quite professional.
For a moment, entering into it, she suspends her judgment about
the lunacy of the scheme.

"Why not plug it into the phone?" Sam asks.

"People do. But then it's obvious, too easy to find. Best way?
Open the wall, put it on the wire."

"When no one's looking."

"They could be looking," she says. "As long as they think
you're doing something else."

Sam laughs. "Okay, how do you plug it into the wire?"

"Easy." With an electrician's knife, she slices the cover from
a long strand, exposing the red- and green-coated wires within.
"See the green has the positive charge, the red the negative, and
they go this way into this gizmo." She cuts the wires and shows
him how the ends connect to the bug. "Takes a couple of minutes, at most. Then tape the whole thing like this. Voila! Phone
tapped."

"Then what?"

"The device transmits by radio waves."

"How far?"

"Theoretically ten miles, but you'd want the recorder to be

closer, to be sure."

"Like here," Sam says. "So we'd want the recorder in your house."

She heaves a big sigh. "Yeah. Like here."

"I can collect the tapes and do the listening."

"Terrific," she says, returned to her senses with renewed dislike for the whole plan.

He gives it a moment. "It's not wonderful," he says. "I never said it was wonderful."

"Right," she says. "They have to be changed often, the reels do. They don't hold that much."

"They run constantly?"

"No, the recorder is voice-activated."

"Okay, I'll do that too," he says. "Change the reels."

"Guess you're going to be around here lots."

Sam gets up from the table, helps himself to water from the sink. "Is that a bad thing?"

"No," she says. "It isn't. It's the only thing good about this."

THIRTY-SIX

Alec is in Milwaukee, about to leave a seedy hotel room for a deposition at the federal courthouse. The case is another he got assigned to after reading about it in the newspapers: the one in which the firm's principal media client, Telemarch News, was sued for libel for accusing the police chief of a local township of stealing the department's Christmas fund for underprivileged children. Alec's there to depose the cop.

Carrie reaches Alec by phone as he's packing his lit bag. She's standing, amongst upturned furniture and debris, in a bare-walled apartment. "I wish the hell you'd been able to come for me."

"What's wrong?"

"There's nothing left. Most of my clothes are gone, so's the TV, all the dishes."

"What?" he says. "You've been burglarized?"

"You go into rehab, the word travels the street. The cokeheads break in, steal everything."

He snaps his bag shut. "You have someplace to stay tonight?"

"I suppose I could go to my mother's." Carrie had told him about her parents. Her father, a small-time criminal lawyer and alcoholic who regularly beat up her younger sister because "Jessie talked back." Her mother, a nasty piece of work, who once carted the girls to Ireland, sponging off relatives for a year, then returned them to New York and a life of mutual hatred.

"Great choice," he says.

"Actually," she says, "I'll be all right here. No one's coming back. There's no more to take but some furniture, and that's worthless."

After a pause that gets awkward, Alec says, "My apartment... on the ledge at the top of the door frame? There's a key. You can stay with me for a while. I'll be home tomorrow night."

Another pause, even longer, that Carrie breaks. "Alec, you sure?"

"Yeah," he says. "I'm sure."

"Big fucking step."

"Just come. We can talk about it."

"I dunno," she says.

"You have to think about whether you want to?"

"No, I don't have to think about whether I *want* to."

"So what is it?"

"You don't know half what there is to know about me."

"So you'll tell me when I get there."

"I'll come tomorrow," she says. "Maybe late."

"Why not today? If you're worried about the key, I can call the super."

"No, no. It's just... today, I've got to see if I can track down any of my stuff. And tomorrow... there's one more thing I've got to do."

THIRTY-SEVEN

S arah arcs her swing cautiously between the seawall behind her and the foot of a long hill. Phil, gently pushing, encourages his daughter to go higher. She stares out, with large, brown, questioning eyes, toward the main house of the estate, to its side lawn. She sees Vito playing with his dog, Friday. *He's lucky to have a dog*, she thinks. She's not allowed to have one. She's told when she's older, maybe. She bets her mommy would let her have a dog. Her eyes fix on a figure, just coming from the house, who Sarah thinks may *be* her mom. She can't be sure. She's been imagining her mother everywhere and is always disappointed.

Carrie, catching sight of her daughter, begins to run. Sarah flies off the swing with a shriek and runs toward her. "Mommy!" the child yells. The two hug each other, kiss, then hold on for dear life. Phil observes the scene with a seigneurial expresssion before crossing over to take charge of it.

"Rehab looks good on you, sweetheart," he says. "Took a lot of guts, what you did."

Carrie pulls back. "You know?"

"I keep tabs. What do you think? I'm not interested?"

"Third rehab in two years." Her tone is self-lacerating.

"Whatever it takes." He smiles. The man can be charming.

"Go play, honey," Carrie says softly to her daughter. "I'll be right there." But Sarah, who has captured Carrie's leg, is not inclined to let go of it.

"Go on, sweetie," says Phil, his voice sharp. "It's okay. Go play with the dog."

Sarah obeys—too quickly, thinks Carrie. She watches her

daughter, whose walk up the hill seems mechanical, then, unconsciously, slips into a little-girl role herself. "I can't be separated from her any longer, Phil. It's not human. We at least have to share her."

Phil, nodding as if in agreement, says, "Come. Let's go up to the house and talk about it. We'll get Nanny to come down."

Carrie looks back at the house she had once lived in with this man. Phil, reading fear in her look, laughs reassuringly. "Beautiful place. Still. Right?"

It's not how she remembers it.

"Come on," he says. "Don't be ridiculous. You want to work something out, or not?"

THIRTY-EIGHT

As Alec arrives from Milwaukee, mid-afternoon, a chubby receptionist leaps up from her chair. "Judge Braddock says you're to see him as soon as you get here." She rearranges a plaid skirt which got twisted from long sitting, and her pale eyes glisten with the importance of her message.

Alec casts an eye at his luggage.

"He said," the receptionist quotes, "'Don't even let him drop his bags off in his office.'" Her expression is apologetic.

In the secretarial compound next to Judge Braddock's corner suite, Madge Harlan, who has worked for the judge her entire adult life, holds up a cautionary finger. A plain-faced woman in her fifties, she scorns hair dye, makeup, or pretense of any sort. "You look like shit," she says to Alec, her eyes conducting a head-to-toe appraisal. "He's on the phone."

"I'll wait," says Alec, dropping his bags by a chair near her desk.

"It's personal, his conversation." A touch of disapproval. "May take a while."

"Want to give him a note I'm here?"

She gives Alec a look, as if to say, *You can't be serious.* Then she says, "You're working on the U.S. Safety case, right?"

"Right," he says, settling in the chair.

"You know…." She lowers her voice. "A lot of the service staff here have their savings tied up in U.S. Safety stock."

"What? How did that happen?"

"Some guy… a broker… came through here a few years ago. Friend of one of the partners. It was a new public offering.

Seemed safe."

"Why?" asks Alec, having a hard time believing this.

She grimaces in self-reproach. "The name. U.S. Safety. The guy." Same grimace. "I know. World-class stupid. Couple of people bought, and it kind of spread. Getting in on IPOs, in those days... it just looked good. Sort of thing you read about, people getting rich on new stock offerings, but not an opportunity for service staff, usually. And the firm said it was okay—almost a perk." She looks away. "I cashed in my savings bonds."

"Jesus!" Alec says.

"Yeah."

"The stock price has already halved," says Alec. "We lose this case... it'll go to zero."

"I know. So don't lose." She glances at the light extinguishing on the phone. "He's off. You may go in now."

Ben Braddock stands at his desk with the *New York Law Journal* spread out before him. As Alec walks in, he hears the telephone ringing behind him, then the intercom buzzing on Braddock's desk. Miss Harlan's voice on the squawk box says, "Judge Kelly, calling from Washington."

"I'll call him back," says Braddock. Then, not looking up, "You remember that Mexican divorce we got for Nelson?"

"Rockefeller?" Alec says.

"No. The Lord High Admiral of the fucking fleet. Of course, Rockefeller. You leave your brains in Milwaukee?"

"Probably."

"Some shit-for-brains judge, in a case defended by Louis Nizer, has just invalidated all Mexican divorces. Can you beat that?" He stares hard at Alec, as if this might be somehow Alec's fault. "I think I'll call the little prick."

"The judge?"

"No. What the hell would I want to talk to that asshole for? He's already published his opinion. Nizer! We gotta be damn sure that little prick appeals."

Braddock, getting a dial tone on his squawk box, dials the number himself.

"Mr. Nizer's office," croons a woman's voice in a tone meant to conjure up images of client heaven.

"Put him on," commands Ben Braddock.

"Judge Braddock?"

"Yes, ma'am. Put him on."

"You do know, Judge, that Mr. Nizer doesn't simply take calls. If there is something you'd like to discuss with him, he asks that you write it in a memorandum to him, and he'll call you when he can."

Braddock reflects for a moment. "Fine system," he says to the box, giving Alec a wink. "Wonder, ma'am, if I might dictate a brief message to you, and then you could show it to Mr. Nizer when he has a spare moment?"

"Well," she says, uncertainly. "I suppose that might be all right."

"Excellent! Ready?"

"Yes, sir."

"You have your pad in front of you?"

"I do."

"Dear Louis," says Ben. "Kiss my ass!"

He disconnects and holds his watch up to Alec. "What do you think? Two minutes, max?"

Frank Macalister walks in. "We got news," he says.

Braddock motions him to wait. The judge looks at Alec. Mac looks questioningly at both of them. The phone rings, and Braddock picks it up on the box. Shrieking out of it is a voice Mac recognizes, "Ben! I didn't know it was you!"

"It's okay, Louis. I've got important people in here now. Have to call you back." He hangs up with a laugh and turns to Mac.

"Was that Nizer?" asks Mac, joining in the laugh.

"Who else? What's the news?"

"That German bastard," Mac says.

"Shilling."

"Who else?" Mac says, mimicking Braddock's growl.

Braddock says to Alec, "Those two guys! Like John Wayne vs. Erich von Stroheim." He swings back to Macalister. "The war's over, Mac. We won. And Shilling was here. He was on our side."

"You love the guy?"

"I don't hate him 'cause I think he's a Nazi."

"Great."

"I hate him 'cause I think he's a prick. And what's he done now? Pull off a settlement with the East Coast banks?"

"Five-hundred-million," says Mac.

Braddock thinks for a moment. "I'm not sure I like that."

"Caps the damages in the stockholder suit. U.S. Safety can't be liable to Rosenkranz's clients for anything more than it pays out in settlement to the banks."

"Yeah, but!" Braddock says. "Big fucking *but!*"

"No jury's likely to award one point two billion dollars in damages," Mac observes. "Five hundred million? That they might do."

Braddock looks at Alec. "You understand this?"

"It's pretty clear," says Alec.

"And either award would bankrupt the company, as well as the directors. So!" Braddock takes in both men with his glance. "Your job, young fellows, has just gotten a bit more challenging."

THIRTY-NINE

Carrie arrives at Alec's door with her right cheek twice the size of her left, and her right eye purpled like a hunk of raw liver.

"My God!" he says. "Who the hell did this?"

"You ain't seen nothing." She stumbles into the apartment and drags herself into the bedroom. "I need to lie down," she says. "I stood all the way here on the subway."

She pulls off her dress and flops face down on the bed, in nothing but her panties. Her slender back and the backs of her legs are ridged like a bike track: crisscrossed welts of angry subcutaneous tissue. "I think we should go to the hospital," Alec says hoarsely.

"No point. He's a professional. It's the one thing he's good at. Beating people up. Maximum pain—and humiliation—without permanent injury."

"Your husband."

She plunges her head into the pillow.

"Why?" Alec asks, dropping to the edge of the bed.

"When I checked into the hospital, I gave them your name. As the person to call, in case. Bad mistake."

"This is jealousy?"

She twists her head around. "No-oo. A warning, more like."

"Not to see me?"

"Not to talk to you. About… the things I've already talked to you about."

"The checks? Aaron Weinfeld? Whitman Poole?"

"Yeah."

Alec rises from the bed. "All right, let's get the son-of-a-bitch."

"What're you gonna do? Whack him with a subpoena?"

"Put the goon in prison."

"You don't stop a guy like Phil with court papers. Or police. Or prisons. He's got a fucking army." She lays her head once more on the pillow. "And he's got my daughter. Sarah. I need her back." Carrie begins to cry.

Alec goes to hold her, gently, around the shoulders, his mind working it out. "The U.S. Attorney's office," he says, "has been after this guy—and this mob—for years. You've got the evidence that can put him away. Maybe permanently."

Carrie sits up. "You in for that, Alec?"

"What do you think?" he says, throwing his hands out. "I'm going to push you to nail him, then leave you alone? Let you disappear into witness protection, while I stay here pretending I had nothing to do with it?"

"It'd be smarter," she says.

"I'll call Ray Sancerre, the U.S. Attorney, in the morning."

"No," she says, thinking rapidly. "Not yet."

"If we're going to do it, why wait?"

"In about three weeks, Phil goes to Europe. He won't take Sarah."

Alec senses where this is going and gives a look of warning.

"He doesn't have legal custody," she says. "He never bothered. And I've as much right to her as he does."

"Just grab her?" says Alec. "Why not? If Phil's own army's not big enough, every mafioso in the country can help him hunt us down."

"We've got three weeks before he goes. Three weeks to live like normal people."

"Before becoming target practice for the mob."

"Before whatever," she says.

FORTY

Carrie's things, salvaged or new, migrate into Alec's apartment. Pastel cotton things, outer and under. Skirts and sweaters and capri pants. Arrid, Maybelline, Tampax, Halo, Gleem, Adorn, and Chanel. It's like a flowering in his cabinets and closets. Indeed, in Alec himself. For two weeks she's been clean, seems at peace with herself and with him. She travels to meetings in the "rooms" twice a day, and to gym or dance classes at the Y. On evenings when Alec's at home, he studies her as she reads, her legs folded under, her sharp knees jutting out, white to the bone, her head bent down, torso curled, strands of hair drifting over her forehead. All this close observation deepens his feelings but does little to explain them.

He watches her at rest, her books and clothes about. He watches her stretch out lean, incurving her spine like a yawning cat, reach, stride, stand in thought for an arrested moment. He watches her watching him.

Contentment in routine, he thinks. Waking each other up, making the bed, cooking meals, washing dishes. People can live entirely on this level, moving instinctively like lizards from need to need, sunning themselves, pleasuring, using routine like rocks. Yet everyone's taunted by biological facts. Peel open the cranium, he thinks, a computer works away powered by organic batteries, with nucleotides in the cells reproducing themselves presumptuously without our awareness or consent. There's more that drives the rest, he thinks; there simply aren't any useful names for it.

When they are quiet with each other, as when he watches her read, or when they lie still in bed not yet asleep, Alec feels it, the idea about her he's waiting for. But, like a bear, he's cautious before crossing the clearing, before entering the dark hole in his brain where it will fit.

One night, Carrie asks about Alec's parents.

"My mother's dead," he says. "My dad..."

She coaxes the thought out with a look.

"We don't have much of a relationship," he says.

They lie side-by-side in bed. At this angle her hip bone is her largest vertical protrusion.

"What was your mother like?"

"Absent," Alec says.

"She abandoned you?"

"That was his version."

"Your dad's? And you've no idea? How old were you?"

"Nine. Maybe just ten."

"What did she die of?"

"Pneumonia. Probably brought on by cirrhosis of the liver."

"You know this?"

"I saw the records."

"You went looking for her. Did you find her?"

"Only the records."

"Wow. Jesus. What's the problem with you and your dad?"

"Having nothing in common."

She gives Alec a look.

"I go out there," he says. "We have a beer. We have nothing to say to each other. We watch a ballgame. I leave. As soon as I can. Because my impression is, he wants me to leave."

"He doesn't say that?"

"No. The opposite. He acts hurt."

"Maybe it's not an act."

"Believe me."

"Is he angry at you?"

"Maybe."

"Something to do with your mom, maybe."

"Could be. We were close, I remember that. They weren't."

"What's he do?"

"Reads. Anything. The older the better. Histories, poetry, plays."

"I mean, for a living?"

"A union guy for years, an organizer. Almost always away. I lived with relatives after mom died, I barely saw him. Now he's with a small firm doing house security systems."

"And before your mom died," Carrie says, "he was away, she was drinking?"

"You got the picture."

"So you were taking care of your mom."

"In a manner of speaking."

"A nine-, ten-year-old kid. Waiting for someone to take care of him. You see some connection in all this to us?"

"The problem," he says, "with easy insights—"

"Is that they're often very insightful."

"Not in this case," he says.

"Like we go deeper," she says, lifting up and peering down on him.

"I would hope."

"Like this—" she laughs, grasping his bare thigh—"unbelievably physical, hot-brained reaction of two otherwise sensible people?"

"Like that."

"Hmm," she says, settling back. "I know about that."

"And this calm, which is lovely."

"Before all hell breaks loose."

"Hell," he says, "is what we're putting behind us."

FORTY-ONE

A law office late at night is neither raucous nor quiet. People there don't wish to be there. They tend not to gab or visit or laugh—they just finish what they must and leave. So the sound level is low. It consists mainly of a barely discernable hum, audible only to dogs and young lawyers.

Alec is working with his door closed. When his phone rings, he expects Carrie to be calling and picks up.

"Hello."

"This Alec Brno?"

"Yes."

"I'm the guy whose wife you're fucking."

Alec allows the phone to drift away a bit, as the terror of this call goes through him like a spear.

"Be stupid to hang up," Phil says.

Alec says nothing.

"What?" says Phil. "You don't like my calling you at the office? You rather I call you at home? Or maybe drop by? I could do that. That little basement you live in."

Is this really happening?

"Cat got your tongue, asshole?"

"You want to beat me up, Phil? Is that it? Or is it only women you like punching in the face?"

"What's going on here, Alec? You've convinced yourself you're in love with her?"

"Are you jealous?"

"Or maybe you're just fucking her to get evidence."

"You finished?"

"Listen to me! Hard! Right now, I've got no reason to hurt you. In fact, if Carrie really likes you, keeping you breathing gives her another reason to behave. But the thing is, Alec, any time I want, you're gone. That's not a challenge for me, you understand? And her—" he laughs—"all I need to do is deliver a package. She does herself."

Alec listens to the hum, too alarmed by the threat just made to say anything.

"In fact…" Phil says again, letting it drift, and hangs up.

Alec holds onto the dead receiver as if he's been stun-gunned into paralysis. Then he bolts from his seat, grabbing his coat, thinking it may already be too late.

In Alec's apartment, every light blazes, but Carrie's gone. He calls out her name, checks the bedroom, then the bathroom, where he sees what he expected to find. A hypodermic needle lolls in the sink. It looks alive, ready to move. Like a gigantic water bug from hell.

Half-past twelve, Alec stares at soundless images on a TV screen. He's in a chair in the living room with one hand on the telephone. When it rings, it's a wrong number.

Alec lies in bed, tossing, every few minutes glancing at the clock. It's two forty-three a.m. He gets up, pulls out the yellow pages, and starts calling the hospitals.

Alec goes through the motions of the day. He travels to work, does some, returns home, eats what's in the refrigerator, and waits for a call. By eleven, he's asleep in the living room chair. At two in the morning, he drags himself to bed.

Past a receptionist and a bullpen of young assistants, Alec barrels into the inner office of Harvey Grand.

"Alec? You look like shit."

"Why do people keep telling me that?"

"Because it's true?"

Harvey's office is low rent. Near Penn Station, an old loft. Battered wood desk, fire-sale hotel chairs, and sofa. Volumes of New York case books on the shelves, law school diploma on the wall, no other decorations. Harvey has no shame when it comes to billing clients. Doubtless his office is designed to state that their money isn't going into the furnishings.

"I want you to help me find somebody," Alec says.

"Is this business?"

"It was. Now it's personal."

Harvey wags his head with pity. "You mean her."

Alec's silence confirms it.

"You've gotten tangled up with a drug addict—a mobster's wife—*and* your principal witness in a case coming up... when?"

"Two, three months. She may not have to testify. Whitman Poole's fled."

"You think it matters? To how this looks? To how it will affect you?"

Alec stares at him numbly, and Harvey comes from behind his desk. "Mac will have your ass for this. Braddock too. Make partner? You'll be lucky to keep your job. What the fuck are you doing, Alec? Is this a rescue fantasy? You're supposed to be smart."

Alec sinks into Harvey's sofa. He knows all this. For him, at the moment, it's beside the point. "Will you help me find her, Harvey, or not?"

"She's gone missing. Addicts do that." He sits across from Alec and the sofa sags at his end. "How long?"

"Two days."

Harvey nods. Alec looks sick.

"Let me tell you what I'm hearing," Harvey says. "Here's this… kid, really. Estranged wife with a lot of information in her head. The capos don't like that. The only thing keeping her alive is Phil, believe it or not. He may actually care for this woman."

"As a punching bag."

"Whatever. I'll track her for you," Harvey says, "but she'll probably call you before I can find her. She's been bingeing two days? Long enough for her not to give a shit about getting yelled at by you."

"That's what I want, you think? To yell at her?"

"It's the normal reaction. And she'll take it. A lot easier than peddling her tushie on 10th Avenue."

Alec, face dark, gets up to leave.

Harvey says, "One more thing. Rent a new apartment. Under another name. You hear me?"

Alec, home in bed, turns off the light. Then lies there sleeplessly. Head splitting, muscles tight, body resistant to any tricks for relaxing. Two hours like this. Then the doorbell rings.

It's Carrie, strung out and twitchy. She breezes in. "Sorry," she says, speech slurred, but putting on an act again. In the middle of the room, she finds the back of a chair, steadies herself. "Bit of a relapse. Almost died. Need a shower, darling, rather desperately. Then we'll talk, and you'll tell me how angry you are."

He thinks of Harvey predicting an outburst from him. Not Alec's style. He bottles it, which is worse.

He fixes coffee, lightheaded now with mixed anger and relief. He listens to the shower noise and tries to imagine the sort of nightmare she's just lived through.

He has a tray on the bed when she emerges in his bathrobe.

"When did the drugs start?" His tone is sharp. This is not the question he most urgently wants answered, but it will do.

"Twelve," she says, going to a mirror with a hairbrush. "Maybe thirteen, no later. All I needed? A beer at a party. Then, booze, pot, coke, pills. Slippery slope, usual progression." She pulls the brush down hard in her hair. The shower has apparently revived her strength.

"The heroin. When did that start?"

Where have you been? Whom have you been with?

"The heroin was Phil. But I wasn't exactly kicking and screaming."

"What *were* you doing?"

"What was I doing?" Her laugh sounds like a cry. "I'm an addict. That first hit you think, *so this is what I've been missing.* You think, *I can control this, take it or leave it.* Until your life turns to shit."

Her lids press together as if reacting to a migraine. "Some people—a beer, several drinks, a joint—then they can leave it alone. But with addicts—one taste, there's no more 'leave it alone.' You're on automatic pilot."

He looks skeptical, which she sees in the mirror. She turns. "You're not getting this," she says.

"I understand it well enough."

"No. I don't think so," she says, her voice rough, unfamiliar. "The thing about addicts is—active addicts—there's no peace for them. No joy. There are only demons. When addicts look like they're resting, their demons are screaming." She starts picking at her arm, and Alec realizes she's gouging herself. On her forearms, deep red pits.

"What are you doing, Carrie?" he says, leaping up, no release for his anger.

She stares at him. Still picking. Pride beaks on her face like a plate. "I call my demon *Iago*. You probably think that's pathetic, self-dramatizing. But let me tell you, the name fits. Iago is pure evil. He wants me to live in the streets, so he gets me to bring the streets into the apartment. He wants me to abuse anyone who might love me, so I'll lose their support. He wants me to use! He's furious when I deprive him. And his tricks to deprive me of anything but the drug are diabolically clever."

"Carrie...." He seizes her wrists, stops her hands from picking at her skin, but she wrenches free, thrusts her face at him.

"See, Alec, what you don't understand—addicts will do anything to get high. I live to get high. Everything I see makes me want to use!"

As he reaches again, she grabs his wrist, holds it out. "Even the veins in your arm."

She rakes her teeth against the inside of his forearm. He lifts her by the neck and shoulders and slams her to the wall. His hands grip her throat. She pounds his chest, crying out with frustration, "It's hopeless!"

"No, it's not," he says, hands sliding down her, no longer caring about whom she's been with. Like wounded animals they cling.

FORTY-TWO

Jim Velsor, managing director of the Metropolitan Outreach Program, has a cubicle office in a building on 6th Avenue housing a conglomeration of private clinics. Inside the cubicle, Carrie sits rigidly on a straight-backed chair. She's already been interviewed. From the doorway, Velsor, wearing a black polo shirt, pants, and sneakers, beckons Alec to join them.

Velsor is a long, thin man with faded blue eyes and straight black hair. He has the look of an often-rehabilitated addict, which is to say, skin discolored like a patchwork of grafts.

"Metropolitan Outreach," Velsor says, admitting Alec and shutting the door, "has two locations. Detox is done here. After-wards, patients are brought to our facility in New Jersey. It's near Morristown. Rural. Lots of grass, trees, fresh air. And good food."

Alec, taking the one other chair, glances at Carrie. She has the look of a sparrow dropped down a chimney: a little stunned, frightened, making herself small. "Sounds good," she says.

Velsor plunks down on the front edge of his desk. "The cost is seven-hundred-fifty dollars a week."

"That's more than I make," Alec says.

"We can arrange a payment plan."

"We'll have to arrange something," says Alec.

"The detox is five days," Velsor says. "It's safe. Relatively safe… if you're honest with us."

Alec says, "She's already detoxed this year."

"Not unusual," Velsor says. "And not a problem. What is…" He stares at Carrie as if not quite believing what she's told him. "Daily methadone intake, twenty milligrams, right?"

She gives this a tight nod.

"Anything higher, Carrie, the detox is too dangerous. You could have a seizure. You do understand this?"

Carrie is silent.

Both men are staring at her.

"I get it, I get it!" she says.

The men exchange looks.

Alec asks, "What are the odds? On recovery?"

"Well...."

"I'd really like a no-bullshit answer to that."

Velsor again fixes on Carrie. "She knows. The numbers aren't good. I can't be sure yet whether she wants to stop. Whether it's taken enough away from her yet."

Carrie fires out of her chair. "Oh, really!" she says. "My daughter, my pride, my self-esteem!"

Velsor's heard it before—or something like it—from too many people, including himself. "There's always more to lose, Carrie. That's the goddamn truth." He gets to his feet. "I'll leave you two for a few minutes."

As Velsor exits, Alec closes the door. "What is your methadone intake?"

"Don't ask," Carrie says.

"As if it's meaningless? You heard what he said."

"It's okay," she says stepping close to him.

"Not okay! What are you doing, Carrie? Some form of penance?"

"I want this, Alec. He's wrong about..." She flutters her hand. "All that."

"Then get the methadone level down on your own. Gradually."

She looks as if she might cry. "I can't."

Alec, protesting, feels her hand covering his mouth and her slight frame gluing itself to him. Velsor returns, and she wraps her arms around Alec's waist even harder, digging in her chin and elbows and refusing to let go.

Alec, returning the hug, looks helplessly at the psychologist. Velsor says gently, "Carrie." He taps her on the shoulder, and she breaks the clench.

"Ri-ight," she says, as if nothing had happened.

"We ought to get started," he says. Then, to Alec, "You all right on the money end? One of our administrators is waiting to talk to you."

"I'll work out something," Alec says.

Velsor nods sympathetically.

The two men shake hands, and Carrie, giving Alec a movie-ish brave smile over one shoulder, follows Velsor down the hall.

Heading home in a cab, Alec thinks back on the scene he's driving away from. Once again, Carrie's in rehab. Being detoxified. Lying somewhere in a hospital, demons screaming in her head. And Alec can't help her, can't talk to her, can't do anything but wait, while imagining the pain she's in. Which he does throughout the night, the morning, and going to work. Where no one knows or cares anything about it.

Alec's secretary, Joni, a Gina Lollobrigida lookalike from Bayonne High School, makes him listen before he can even get to his coffee. "Judge Braddock called. I took it down verbatim, and I quote. 'When you see him, you get his ass in here, pronto. You hear? Not even a pee first.' " Bowlegged in black tights, she smirks fondly at Alec. "Pretty clear message. Doesn't seem to vary his theme much, does he?"

Frank Macalister is two steps ahead of Alec into Braddock's office, where the presiding partner is pacing. "Shilling called me last night at home," he says, swinging on Macalister. "Tried you first, but apparently doesn't have your M.O. You gotta start laying off the sauce, Mac."

Macalister waves his hand dismissively.

Braddock, frowning, goes on. "Seems this no-goodnik, Whit Poole, has returned. Hurts our case. You agree?"

"Of course."

"Way I see it, despite all the money, it's a simple issue for the jury. Warehousing tons of oil is essentially a no-risk business, if the guy managing it has any brains and is honest. And this guy Poole had come highly recommended. So if Poole was being bribed to defraud the directors, then they and the company were not at fault. They were victims too. But if Poole was stupid—honest, but stupid—then our clients, the people who hired him and left him screwing up, are gonna end up paying for this mess. You agree with that?"

"I do," says Mac. "The legal issues are more complicated, but that's what it boils down to for the jury."

"How much more complicated?" Braddock spits out in the general direction of Alec.

"Oh, Christ! A hornets' nest. U.S. Safety ran the warehousing business through a subsidiary corporation—so the first set of is- sues concerns the permeability of the corporate veil."

"And?"

"Permeable as hell," Alec says. "I think we can ignore the fact it even existed. The company did, which is the problem."

"So. Next set of issues. As to the directors."

"They can be liable to the corporation—for simple negli- gence. And the stockholders—courtesy of Si Rosenkranz—are asserting that claim derivatively, on behalf of the corporation. The directors' negligence would consist of either hiring an in- competent like Poole, or letting him do business with a felon, or just failing to discover Martini's scheme. Or the directors could be liable for gross negligence—in other words, recklessness—in which case the claim is more serious."

"You mean fraud."

"Right. To prove fraud, the stockholders have to show that the company's financial reports were not only wrong—and they plainly were off by more than a billion dollars—but that the errors were published with intent to defraud the stockholders. The directors' problem is, to publish erroneous financial information recklessly is the same thing as publishing with the intent to defraud, as a matter of law. So, if the directors were reckless, they are also guilty of fraud. And the stockholders' fraud claim is a direct one, not only against the directors, but also against the corporation, which is legally responsible for the acts and omissions of the directors."

"Which is the claim Rosenkranz is pushing," Mac says. "He's got little real interest in the directors. They don't have enough money. He's after the corporation and its insurance policy, which overlaps with and subsumes the smaller insurance covering directors' liability."

"I see," Braddock says. "I was wondering why no one was asserting that our representation of both the corporation and the directors was a conflict, at least on the stockholders' derivative claim."

"Well, as a technical matter," Alec says, "on the derivative claim, Shilling represents the corporation. Although it's a nominal representation, because the corporation is only a nominal party on that claim—and, most importantly, Si is probably going to drop the claim. He thinks it will only confuse the jury."

"So he'll try only the fraud charge, based on a theory of recklessness," Braddock says.

"Exactly," says Alec. "It's the one way Rosenkranz has to recover directly against the corporation and grab the insurance money."

"Does Shilling agree we're likely to win this case before the jury if Poole was bribed by Martini, and lose if he was just stupid?"

Mac shrugs. "We don't talk very much."

"Hey! Way to go, Mac. You and co-counsel in a five-hundred-million-dollar case. Don't talk? Don't fucking talk?"

Madge Harlan opens the door. "Marius Shilling. On one, Judge."

Braddock flips on the speaker. "Marius? You hear from that son-of-a-bitch Poole? What's he saying? Why'd he run?"

"That the shame was just too much for the poor man." Shilling's accent crackles in the box. "Being blamed for being negligent—'And maybe I was,' he says."

"How convenient for Rosenkranz," notes Alec.

"But," Shilling says, "you have the means to break down Poole's story. I mean the girl. Carrie Madigan. She gave Poole the checks from Martini's lawyer, Weinfeld. And she's working with you, right?"

Braddock and Mac both turn to Alec.

"We'll get back to you on that, Marius," Alec says.

Mac's eyes open wide.

Braddock hangs up the call, cutting off Shilling's response. The judge gazes at Alec.

"She's in rehab," Alec says, lowering himself slowly into a chair.

Braddock says, "You have something to do with this?"

"Yes."

Mac, still standing, arms folded over his head, says with a frightening sweetness, "Are you sleeping with her?" At Alec's expression, Macalister looks skyward. Then he starts walking. Halfway out the door he explodes. "Fucking hell, Alec! I told you!" The door slams so hard that the paintings rattle.

Braddock, ignoring that outburst, says to Alec, "You realize what you've done?"

"Yes."

"Could totally compromise our calling this woman."

"I know."

"Could ruin you."

"I realize that."

"You have some other way of breaking down Poole's story?"

"Yeah. I think so."

"Then you better get to it," Braddock says. "Now!"

FORTY-THREE

On a noisy corner in Hell's Kitchen, as all manner of humanity streams by, Alec and Harvey hurriedly confer. "If Raffon's in his office," Harvey says, "there's a chance he'll spot us from his window up there on the third floor, in which case, by the time we get up the front elevator, he'll have flown the coop."

"You know this."

"Trust me," says Harvey, stepping into the phone booth. "So what we do, we make damn *sure* he's looking for us." Harvey slots a dime into the phone, dials, and Alec can pick up his side of the conversation. "Carl, you sit tight, you hear? We're coming upstairs."

Smiling to himself, Harvey leads Alec onto the south side of 49th Street. They stroll casually into the front hall, then dart outside, hugging the facade of the building, so as not to be seen from the third-story window, and go to an alley door between this edifice and the next. They then rattle along steel steps into the alley and wait but two minutes. Bursting out of the back door, past fan exhausts, old duct work, and bundles of trash, chugs Carl Raffon, smack into Harvey Grand's arms.

"Where you going, little man?" Harvey laughs at the confounded, still struggling, putative escapee.

"Shit!" says Raffon, straightening himself up, glaring, pursing his lips.

"So whatta you say, Carl?" Harvey says. "We stay out here with the garbage, freezing our asses off?"

Begrudgingly, Carl leads them upstairs. He's a chinless man, with a widow's peak of black, greased hair. His dark blue, white-collared shirt is worn with a pinstriped suit, sharp but threadbare, and a dull red tie. There are people who are frog-faced, horse-faced, or who look like a fish. Carl Raffon resembles a weasel. Thrust back into his hole-in-the-wall office, he glares like a weasel in a trap.

Alec and Harvey lean forward on metal chairs, no doubt rented as a set with Carl's desk. Through the one window blinks one word on a neon sign, "Dancers." The room smells sour. It might be the building, or Carl.

Alec says, "We want you to help us, Carl. And we're willing to pay for your time. I understand your fee is one hundred dollars an hour. For this—"

Raffon breaks in. "You wearing a wire?"

Harvey rises with indignation. "A wire? Christ! What the hell good would a wire do us? Jesus, Carl! Think! I told you. For this, we need testimony, not wire transcripts. We can't put hearsay statements in evidence. We need you live. On the stand."

"I'm not doing it, Harvey. I'm really not that fucking stupid."

"What are you afraid of, Carl?"

"What the fuck do you think?"

"What do I think? I think you were paid off by the Angiapellos to look the other way. That you know they funded Martini. And that you're scared shitless. That's what I think. What do you think, Carl? That you can avoid having to tell that story in a courtroom? Not fucking likely."

"I think you're wearing a wire," Carl says in a monotone.

"Well, suck my dick!" shouts Harvey, ripping off his jacket. "You can just put your slimy hands all over me and find out. Go ahead. Cop a feel. You'd probably like it."

Raffon produces a nasty grin. "No, him," he says, pointing to Alec.

"Me?" Alec laughs.

"Get up, kid!" Raffon commands, enjoying it.

Alec, still laughing, rises to his feet, takes off his jacket and suffers the little weasel feeling around for a wire Alec's not wear-ing. "What I don't understand," he says, with Raffon's hands in his armpits, "is how you're avoiding telling the truth to the DA."

Carl hesitates for less than a second, but it's enough for Har-vey to pounce. "So that's what's happening. You've got a deal with a prosecutor. The DA? Or is it the U.S. Attorney? What are you getting, Carl? Immunity? Witness protection?"

Satisfied Alec's not wired, Raffon returns to his seat. "I'm not talking about this."

"Why the hell not?"

Carl shakes his head glumly.

"Hey!" says Harvey, settling back into his chair. "Be enlight-ened, man! Working with them doesn't stop you from testifying for us. And you want to deal with us. Because in witness protec-tion, you know what you get? A pot to piss in. Some menial job. Beneath your talents, Carl. You're gonna need some serious cash."

"Am I."

"I think *so*!"

"And that's where you come in?" Carl says sardonically, but with a glimmer of interest.

"If you're wise, we do," says Harvey.

"To the tune of, say, what?"

"Well, that depends, doesn't it. On who you can deliver."

Raffon emits a derisive grunt, with his thin lips pressed together.

Harvey says, "Use your head, man. Once you testify for the government, you're out there. Exposed. The wiseguys find you, they'll kill you. They can't kill you twice. You might as well make some money on this to fund yourself in hiding. And we can't do this without making a deal with the government ourselves—who, once they arrive at an agreement with us, will protect you in our trial too."

Carl's eyes widen a bit. "How much?"

"I told you, depends on who—"

"How 'bout Phil Anwar?" he says.

Harvey, coolly, says, "With what evidence?"

"He was there," Carl says, as if commenting on the weather. "We met. With Poole. But it was Phil who was running it. Poole just took orders."

Alec says in a low voice, "Who told you not to probe the tanks?"

"Phil, of course. The scam may have been Martini's idea, but Phil banked it and took it over."

Alec and Harvey exchange a brief glance.

"Okay," Harvey says, "that's valuable testimony, I won't kid you. And we won't disappoint you on the money. Also, we'll expect nothing from you—nor, of course, can we give you any-thing—until we've made our arrangements with… who was it you said you're working with?"

Raffon nervously sucks on his teeth. "I didn't."

Harvey gives him a big, friendly, questioning smile, as if to reaffirm the obvious.

"Ray Sancerre," Raffon finally says. "U.S. Attorney."

"Good," says Harvey. "With him, then."

The three stand, shake hands. Carl says, "I wanna see some money on this soon—or you get nothing!"

"We'll be in touch," Alec says. "No pun intended."

In a taxi on their way to the office, Harvey opens his shirt and removes the wire he's wearing. They listen to the recording on his portable tape player. It sounds as if Raffon is sitting with them in the back seat of the cab.

FORTY-FOUR

London. The Ritz. Listening to piano music gently crest the many tea-time conversations, Phil surveys the honeyed elegance of the room, the glistening service, the balletic deportment of the staff. The guests comprise an ill-assorted lot of tourists and bankers. The financial men are dressed, as is Phil, by Savile Row, but, unlike him, they are totally at home in—indeed, knowingly contribute to—the theatricality of the scene.

Phil's companion, a compact, elderly man with pocked skin and thick glasses, reaches for a cucumber sandwich. "I love this city," he says.

"For the afternoon teas?" Phil says.

"For all of it. What? You don't like London?"

"Not particularly."

"You don't know it."

"I rarely come here, you're right."

"I'm an outrageous anglophile." The older man brushes back some white hair with a gesture that doubtless became reflexive back when there was more of it. "Strange doings, eh? For a Sardinian?"

"I'm surprised you haven't joined one of the clubs."

"Whatta you saying, haven't joined? I have. Two of them. I like this better, though. The hurly-burly. The show. The humanity."

Phil thinks, *He didn't ask me to London for tea at The Ritz.*

"I love to watch the excess," his uncle says. "*Other people's* excess." He squints at his nephew. "You understand what I'm saying? Not ours. Not our excess. We *feed* on other people's excess."

"Of course."

"I hope you understand, Phil."

"Why wouldn't I?" Phil says, beginning to feel put upon and annoyed.

"That's the question, isn't it?"

"Is it?"

"There's reason to believe, Phil, you've been indulging in excess."

The maitre d' sidles over to their table. "All well, Signore Angiapello?"

"Excellent, Gilbert. As always."

"So nice," Gilbert mutters, nodding to Phil and shuffling off to another table.

His uncle says defensively, "I come here twice a week. It's the only reason he knows who I am."

"My first time," says Phil.

"Within our world—" wistful smile—"I'm still referred to as Don Giovanni."

"You certainly are."

"A name—historically—associated with excess."

"Never as applied to you, Uncle."

The old don nods and removes his glasses by their heavy black frames.

"I supported you, Phil."

"And I owe you."

"Not only as head of the family. I supported you in this oil deal. Put my own money in it."

"Which will be returned to you, Uncle, twenty times."

"At what cost, Phil?"

"We're good, Uncle, don't trouble yourself."

"Not what I'm hearing, Phil. I'm hearing about excess. Greed. You maybe went too far with this? Took too much? Got too public. And you're maybe too exposed? This young wife of yours? A junkie, I hear."

"You've been talking to Little John?"

"He calls, yes. He's very respectful."

"He's not an objective informer."

"I understand. He wants your turf, your businesses. So I have to weigh what he says carefully. But the facts, Phil. The facts are the facts. You took a lot. You got people excited, many bankers, the federal authorities. And in general, you've made yourself too visible. Like a celebrity. Out of vanity, which is a form of excess. What's more—and worse—this young woman, this junkie, you got her involved. She knows things no junkie should be trusted with."

"I'll take care of it."

"Yes? How will you do that? Because in a situation like this there aren't that many alternatives."

"Respectfully, Uncle, there are ways of silencing people, which don't involve sticking legs in a barrel of cement."

Don Giovanni gives his nephew a skeptical glance. "A woman like this can do anything. She's too big a risk, son."

"I'm not having her killed."

"Then get her under control. You're losing respect over this. In our world. Where it matters."

Phil is silent.

"And what about the civilians you used on the job?"

"Under constant surveillance, Uncle."

The maitre d' saunters back. "More tea, Mr. Anwar?"

"You know my name?"

"Naturally, sir. You're well-known here. If I might venture to say, a celebrity."

FORTY-FIVE

Vito answers the front door of the Long Island mansion, looks Sam over, says, "Whatta you want?"

"I should have called, maybe?" Sam says.

"I dunno. Whatta you want?"

"There's a fault in the system."

"A what?"

"Something's not right in the burglar alarm system we installed. Let me show you."

"You know this how?"

"We have a monitor. In the home office. A mouse chews the wire, something—could be anything—we pick it up, come to fix it. Is Mr. Anwar at home?"

"No, he ain't."

"Maybe I should come back then?"

"Shit, no. There's a problem, fix it."

Vito stands aside to let Sam in. Vito's dog, Friday, is alert behind him.

"The most likely place," Sam says, "is the basement."

"Okay," says Vito, "let's go."

Sam laughs. "You want to keep an eye on me."

"What the fuck you think?"

"Let me get my stuff from the car," Sam says.

When he returns, Vito leads the way to the basement, turns the lights on, says, "So where we looking?" Friday seems to be following all of this, turning his attention from one man to the other.

"Well, the wires, of course. I may have to open up some of the boards, but don't worry. We installed them, can put it all back, no one will notice."

"You do what you have to do."

"Right."

Sam gets to work. He feels along each exposed section of the wire. Slowly, meticulously, he unscrews the wall panels and feels inside. Vito gets bored, goes for a beer in the fridge under the bar. Friday, curled up on the vinyl tiled floor, watches intently. When Sam pulls out wires, Friday barks, and Vito looks up.

"Isn't that the telephone wire?" Vito calls out.

"Yeah, of course," says Sam. "We work off the telephone wires. How else you think the alarm goes to the central system?"

"Hey, buddy. I'm not a fucking mechanic."

"Okay, found it. Here's the problem. I've got to splice this wire. Want to give me a hand?"

"What the fuck I look like? I should hold your tool?"

"No. Never mind. I can do it. Just thought if you came over here I could explain exactly what I was doing."

"Why? So I can do it myself?"

"Forget it. Relax. I'll be out of here in five minutes."

Friday barks again for no reason Vito can fathom, but he believes animals in general to be unfathomable.

In Abigail's kitchen, she asks, "So which one did you use?"

"The FM transmitter," says Sam.

"Safer."

"No click."

"And Phil's still in Europe?" she says.

"He wasn't there."

"Vito hadn't a clue?"

"Don't think so."

"You're really out of your mind," Abigail says. "This is an insane risk."

"Big risk. For both of us. There's only one I can think of that's bigger."

"Not knowing what Phil's thinking."

"That's the one," he says.

FORTY-SIX

Friday morning, Alec drives to New Jersey in a pounding rainstorm. Regular visiting hours, he's been told, are on Sundays, but Kendall, Blake, Steele & Braddock has already laid claim to him seven days a week. He succeeded in negotiating this one weekday off for moving—into the new apartment he's found on East 87th Street—because even the partners know that movers, unlike lawyers, do not work on weekends, except at multiples of their normal rates. So his belongings move uptown as Alec drives west.

In Alec's head is the message from Carrie, scribbled and mailed. "Hi, darling. I'm fine. I got through everything thus far in pretty good shape, but don't come out here yet, okay? I'm going to need just a little more time—to get human. I love you lots, and I'll look forward to seeing you. God, I'll look forward to that!" But she hasn't called him. Or come to the phone when he called. In more than two weeks.

He turns his rented car into the parking lot of the facility. Metropolitan Outreach looks like a summer camp in the hills. Low, clapboarded main buildings and cottages dispersed on rolling, grassy grounds surrounded by woods. If it had rained here, it hadn't melted the snow that still streaks the land in ice-bound clumps of random design. It's nearly noon. As Alec walks from his car with a package of food, groups of young, fresh-faced patients stream out of several of the outlying buildings, heading toward the dining hall or the cottages.

In a corridor of the main building, Carrie makes her own way painfully on recalcitrant limbs. She's forced to stop from time to time, to take hold of one leg and pull it forward, then drag the other, as other inmates scurry past. They stare at her, she thinks, not only because of her unusual gait, but because her general appearance frightens even hard-core addicts. It frightens her. She's ninety-four pounds, gray-skinned, and gaunt. She doesn't want others looking at her. Especially Alec. Who miraculously appears through the front door holding a package. Which, when he sees her, he drops.

"I told you not to come," she cries as he runs to hold her.

In the pine-paneled dining room, at a table at which they're left alone, Carrie gazes at Alec with dark, sunken eyes.

"Detox took longer than anyone's, ever."

"I know. Velsor told me."

"I look totally hideous. Like some creature in a body-snatch movie."

Alec empties the package of gourmet tins and bottles and a loaf of French bread. "You look fine," he says.

"Are you blind?" she says.

"You're recovering. That's what you look like. Which, to me, is beautiful. Should I open the pâté?"

She covers her mouth as if she might vomit.

"Well, you'll get better now," he says.

"Yeah," she says, in a forced upbeat tone. "Gotta be something better than this."

What they hadn't been told is that the people in charge would give them thirty-five minutes, tops. The rules forbid Carrie even sitting in Alec's car, much less leaving the premises. So they sit on the sofa in Carrie's cottage, holding hands. Carrie says, "I'll make this up to you." Alec says, "I would have made the trip anyway."

Her Brunhild-sized counselor walks in on them and is introduced. She says to Alec, "This is a very sick young woman."

Back on the highway, this time going east, Alec thinks about that statement, about how sick Carrie is. *How many people have told me this? How certain they all are. Doesn't seem to change anything.*

And no one should know better than Alec how quixotic the dream is of changing her. But he can't help dreaming the dream. He can't help seeing her sober and settled—with him.

I don't have to understand it, Alec thinks. *The fact is we're joined at the brain.*

Alec laughs at himself. *It's better to get detached, outside oneself, see the humor in the human condition.* Tears come to his eyes. It's not funny at all. He's never felt so totally helpless.

"I'll think of something," he says aloud to himself.

FORTY-SEVEN

Phil, at dinner at Ponte's in the printing district, has a feeling of well-being. Just back from London, he's surrounded by loyal lieutenants at a restaurant to whose owners and staff he's more important than the mayor. He has enjoyed, as a result of his venture with Martini, nearly a doubling of his wealth. And, despite the admonitions of his uncle, almost all the loose ends—Poole, his crew, Martini himself—seem to be staying in place. *You can't kill everyone*, he thinks with some amusement. *Not immediately, anyway. Looks bad.*

As for Carrie… well, he has a plan for her too.

Little John wheels in with his entourage. He waves to Phil, settles his group across the dining room, then comes over. Phil nods to Vito, who vacates his seat.

"You good, Phil?"

"Splendid, John. You?"

"Just the one thing."

Little John, his big butt slopping over Vito's chair, spreads out the napkin, removes a pen from his breast pocket, starts doodling a submachine gun.

Phil grabs the pen and says to the look of astonishment on the fat man's face, "I've got one thing too, John. My uncle. He's an old man. At peace with himself in a city he loves. I don't want anyone—even you, John—disturbing that man's equanimity. *Capisce?*"

Little John seems to recover himself. "We at war, Phil?"

"I'm trying to avoid that."

"By shoving me around?"

"I needed your full attention."

"Be careful, Phil," says Little John, rising slowly. "My full attention may be more than you want."

"Are you threatening me?"

"Giving advice. Just be careful."

"Oh, I will," Phil says.

FORTY-EIGHT

Alec, crouching over a stack of documents on the floor of his office, has his mind on other things.

It's Sunday morning. He's there in khakis and a blue button-down shirt. Joni, in pedal pushers and a frilly blouse, is typing at her station outside his office. Alec is literally up to his ass in documents strewn over chairs, credenza, desktop, and floor, but the stack in front of him is the most important. It consists of monthly reports on the operations of the warehousing subsidiary and other memoranda submitted by Whitman Poole to the management of the parent company. Any hint in them of the Martini fraud would constitute the proverbial "smoking gun" and effectively end the lawsuit. Not, of course, favorably.

What's preoccupying Alec more, however, is how matters stand with Macalister. Alec played the Raffon tape for Braddock, who grunted approval, but Mac was elsewhere at the time. Alec's not even sure he himself is still employed by the firm, let alone still on the case. He raised the question with Braddock who told him to discuss it with Mac. Wonderful. Discuss it with a guy who won't see him or take his calls.

Mac, Alec learns, has been in Miami, so Alec couldn't just walk in on him either. But his secretary tells Alec that Mac is scheduled back last night.

Alec pulls the first document off the stack and gets distracted by the intercom. Joni's voice: "Mrs. Macalister on one."

He's not expecting calls, much less from *Mrs.* Macalister.

Grabbing, cradling the phone, *"Evelyn?"*

He pictures her: tall, athletic, still lissome. Out of place at firm dinner dances, in her strapless evening gowns and diamonds;

easier to visualize playing tomboy roles in B-Westerns, which was, in fact, what she'd been doing before meeting Mac during the war. By that time, she was entertaining the troops. Alec has learned more about their relationship from Evelyn, whom he sees only at firm parties, than from Mac, with whom he works almost every day. She's open; Mac's closed. But now he can't seem to get her to talk.

"Evelyn?" he repeats.

"Alec?" It's a whisper.

"Evelyn, what's wrong?"

"Mac wrecked up his car last night. Drove it into a fucking tree. In the driveway of his fucking golf club."

"Jesus!" says Alec. "Is he—"

"All right? No, I'd say he's definitely not all right. The surgeons have just finished putting him back together. He'll live, they tell me, and he'll walk—not very well, all pinned up. And I had a lovely night too, thank you."

"My God."

"It's pretty bad."

"I can't tell you how sorry I am. Should I come out there? Is there anything I can do for either of you?"

"No, Alec. Really. I didn't…. Look. I'm just so… we've got to get Mac to stop drinking. All of us. Everyone who loves the son-of-a-bitch. Or he's going to kill himself. I mean… shit! Fifty miles an hour in the fucking driveway!"

"What hospital?"

"Alec, don't!"

"Is it Greenwich?"

Silence.

"That's where you're calling from, isn't it?"

"There's nothing you can do for him."

"I'll be there in thirty to forty. For you."

They sit in the lobby of the vast hospital atrium on low, wood-framed, soft leather chairs. Evelyn, in profile, yawns like the sleep-deprived beauty she is, sun-blanched from Aspen. Her clothes have an expensive, rumpled quality: the sort of pants made only by designers; the kind of oversized, floppy, camel-colored turtleneck sold only in pricey specialty shops. Sun flaring through the windows irradiates the curve of her cheekbone, the tightness of her skin. She and Alec are conspicuously not talking about the man lying in a private bedroom upstairs in a state of drugged unconsciousness.

It's a hospital built by rich people for their own kind and all the lesser locals having the right insurance. Over Alec's shoulder is the Harry B. Helmsley Medical Building, funded by the real estate tycoon, and over Evelyn's, the Olive and Thomas J. Watson, Jr. Pavilion, a gift from the son of the founder of IBM, and the leader of its current worldwide ascendancy. Apart from guards, who are an acre away, and a surprisingly small number of passing visitors, they're alone.

Alec says, "If you came with the ambulance, I could give you a lift home."

"Someone's coming from the house, Alec, with a change of clothes. No point going home, I can't sleep."

"What about eating something?"

"Here?" She kicks off her loafers, laughs, curls her legs under her.

"Coffee?"

"All coffeed out, thank you."

"Where are your children?"

"Hither and thither."

"They know?"

Evelyn shrugs.

"But you've called them?" Alec says.

"Let's not talk about my children, shall we? They're away at school, they're fine. I don't want them running back right now."

"Nor me, running up here."

"No, I'm glad you came." She reaches over, grips his knee. "You know what it's like. Living with this sort of mess."

Her remark surprises him.

"I'm not thinking only about your childhood," she says, releasing him.

"Ah."

"Mac's told me about… this woman. He's furious with you, which I thought was a bit ironic. To say nothing of hypocritical."

"With her, it's something worse than alcohol."

"Worse? That's debatable. These people—whatever they take—*they* escape, that's the purpose of it. We don't get to escape." She slurs the last few words, then closes her eyes.

It's obvious what she meant by the first "escape"; not so clear about the second. But he can't ask her; she's fallen asleep.

After several minutes, her eyes open, and she smiles. "I do that. Catnap."

"All's fine."

"Is it?"

"With Mac, now, yes, I think so," Alec says. "He's survived the worst. This may be the shock he needs."

"Ha! Shocks! If only they'd work, we'd have them administered by machine."

"Something will work."

"What about on you?" she says.

"Me?"

"Yes, Alec, you. Working for an alcoholic, living with a heroin addict, raised by woman with a drinking problem."

"Wow."

"Sorry."

"You see a pattern?" he says, trying to keep it light.

"I see a problem."

"A problem we share?"

"Yes. Aren't you tired of it, Alec?"

"I didn't ask to be assigned to Mac."

"You could ask for a reassignment, or leave the firm."

Alec rubs the back of his neck without answering.

"But you won't do that," she says, "will you?"

"No," he admits.

"Because you like it."

"There are other considerations."

"In addition to the fact that you like it."

"Yes."

"What about the girl? You knew about her going in, right?"

He hesitates. "Mostly right."

"Plaintiff rests his case, your Honor."

Alec smiles. "Things are more complicated than that, Evelyn."

"Oh, yes?"

"Did you know about Mac's drinking, going in?

"Of course. I did it with him."

"But you got out. Of the drinking."

"I'm not an addict."

"Me neither," he says. "Somehow didn't get the gene. Don't even like the stuff. So we try to help them, right?"

She laughs. "Oh, right."

"There must be some drugs, experimental, whatever."

"Sure. There are. Experimental. Makes you hate the taste of alcohol. God knows what the side effects are. Must be something like that in the works for heroin. And that's great. If you can get 'em to take the pills—and, bear in mind, the more they love the booze or smack, the stronger their aversion to the antidote. But what're we doing? Just substituting one drug for another."

"What about treatment methods?"

"He's tried 'em all. Sauna detox, meditation, yoga, fasting—fasting was a ball—vitamin therapy."

"AA?"

"He's been. Not a take for Mac."

"Sheer willpower?"

"Great idea. Tried that too. You ever try living with that? Lasts about a week, if you're tough. Then you start begging him to begin drinking again."

"I can't believe it's hopeless."

"Not for you, Alec. That's what I'm trying to tell you. For me. It's hopeless for me. Maybe you can't escape your own demons, but you sure as hell don't have to wallow in hers... or, for that matter, his."

FORTY-NINE

Carrie, in sweat clothes, walking from classroom to cottage, is hailed by Jim Velsor, who approaches out of breath. "Hey, looking good, Carrie! And in better shape than me, obviously."

"Human again, if barely," she says.

"You've put the work in," he says. "Including the detox, it's been five weeks. But I came over to tell you. You have a visitor."

Her face brightens, and she pushes past Velsor, without waiting for him to tell her more.

Over the hill, from the direction of her cottage, strides Phil Anwar, his overcoat open and swinging, his face wreathed in a smile. Carrie stops, the life pumped out of her. Phil, towering, clamps his big hands on her shoulders. "I want you back," he announces, as if he thought she feared he might not.

"Or," she says, "any other woman you can flog with that stupid belt of yours."

"I mean it, sweetheart. New beginning. Your terms. Everything the way you've always wanted it." He touches her face, and she pulls away from the one hand still on her shoulder.

"It's not as if I'm unaware," he says lightly, "of… the violence in me." His expression conveys deep remorse. "I'm told recognizing the tendency is the first step to controlling it. I'm sorry for the past. I'm working on it, love. Getting help. But I need your help. And Sarah needs her family—together."

"Sarah needs her mother, Phil. She needs time with me."

"Not under the present circumstances. The present circumstances are—" his face scrunches up, as if he's searching for the word—"unstable."

"What does that mean?"

"Must we really?"

"I want to know what the hell you mean."

"Okay, sweetheart, sure. Right out on the table. I know perfectly well how you've been living, my darling. *With whom* you've been living. Let's just forget about that, is what I'm saying. It's in the past. There's blame, so far as Sarah is concerned, but it's not all yours. I acknowledge that. The thing is, the way you were going—that can't keep happening. I'm not going to allow it to keep happening."

"What the hell do you mean, allow?"

"You don't come back, love? This guy you like so much, this lawyer bastard? You're gonna find him in a Dumpster somewhere. Minus the back of his head." Phil's high-voltage smile laced with melancholy. "That's just the way it is."

FIFTY

Gen. Rand gives thought to Alec's report on the progress of the litigation. Alec waits for the man to speak. Mac's chair is conspicuously empty.

"There've been settlement discussions?" the general asks.

"There have been two, yes," Alec answers.

"What's Rosenkranz's current offer?"

"Four-hundred-fifty million."

"That's the limit on our D-and-O insurance."

"Not a coincidence," says Alec.

"Right. He wants it all. The greedy bastard wants every cent of the insurance money."

Alec sits back. "When we talk about settlement, sir, you and I...."

"Yes?"

"There's arguably a conflict."

"There's no conflict," snaps Rand.

"The appearance of one, which, legally, is the same thing."

"Explain."

"Settle at Rosenkranz's figure, you'll personally owe nothing. The insurance company picks up the tab. Litigate and lose, you'll be wiped out, as will all the other directors."

"And if we take Rosenkranz's figure, the insurance company will bless this?" Rand asks with some asperity.

"Pretty close. They're willing to go to four hundred. They figure they'll save fifty million plus counsel fees."

"My God! They think we're dead in the water? No chance at all?"

"They like certainty."

"And what do you say?" Rand gives Alec a hard stare.

"I think we'll win." He says it levelly.

Rand barks out a laugh. "Well, I should hope so. Look! I haven't moved from what I said at the outset. I'm not giving those bastards one fucking cent. And with Ben Braddock trying the case—I assume he will, after Mac's accident—we should be fine."

Twenty minutes late, Alec rushes from the parking lot to Carrie's cottage from which Brunhild is emerging. "She's gone," says the large woman without breaking stride.

"Whatta you mean, gone?" Alec calls after her.

Her departing back shrugs indifference.

Inside the cottage, there's no one in the parlor or downstairs lavatory, and no response to Alec's calling up the stairwell. He heads toward the main building.

Jim Velsor, pinning a notice up on the bulletin board, says, "Alec? You looking for Carrie?"

"Yeah, hi Jim. Have you seen her? We were supposed to meet at her cottage at one-thirty."

"She left this morning." Velsor gives Alec a glance, as if no longer sure of him. "Guy said he was her husband."

"What?"

"He paid her bill."

For several seconds Alec can't breathe.

Velsor says, "She left of her own volition. That's certainly what it looked like."

They stand there a moment unguarded. In Alec, the news distends his face with pain. "Right," he says and lurches off. Then throws a look back over his shoulder. Velsor wears a puzzled expression, as if to say, *She comes with one guy, leaves with another— what the hell's going on?*

Alec's rented car is parked on the edge of town. He's on a pay phone with Harvey, who's saying, "What makes you think it wasn't voluntary?"

"Look," Alec says, "I know her, okay? I need home addresses. He's got a place on Long Island, North Shore, and an apartment in Manhattan—I think Central Park West."

Harvey says grimly, "Then what's your move? Stalk both addresses?"

"I'll need phone numbers too," Alec says.

"Telephone stalking! Much better! Should increase your life expectancy—by about five minutes."

"Just get me the information, Harvey. Okay? Please?"

"Okay, kid," Harvey says, then pauses to say more, but Alec has already hung up.

"Ben."

"Marcus."

"Good of you to come to my office."

"Why's that?" asks Braddock.

"Well..."

Braddock laughs. "You think it elevates your status? I know you military fellows care about such things."

"And you don't," says Gen. Rand archly. "Beneath you to give it any mind at all."

"On the contrary," Braddock says. "I think my coming to your office raises your status tremendously."

"Which, no doubt, will be reflected in your bill."

Braddock smiles. "I leave billing to younger partners."

"Speaking of whom..."

"Ah," says Braddock. "You've heard about Mac's accident."

"Everyone's heard about Mac's… accident. I simply wanted to confirm that you, personally, would take charge of the lawsuit."

"I've always been in charge of the lawsuit."

"I think you know what I mean."

"I'll oversee the case," Braddock says.

"We want you to *try* the case, Ben."

Braddock waves his hand at this. "That's months in the future."

The door opens to admit the one man in the company having the rank to walk in on this meeting. "Judge Braddock," he says. "Brett Creighton. Good to see you again." They shake hands, and Creighton eases his frame into one of the unoccupied wing chairs.

"You two know each other, then?" says Rand.

"We frequent the same charity affairs," Braddock says. "Dragged by our respective spouses. Or do you go willingly?"

"Depends," says Creighton with a smile.

"I asked Brett to join us, Ben. As a director and future CEO of the company, he is one of your clients."

"Delighted," Braddock says.

Creighton pulls his chair in closer. "Marcus and I have talked at length about the importance of this case, not only to the well-being of our company, but to its viability. And I don't mean simply winning the case sometime in the future. I mean shoring up the market appraisal of our future, giving the shareholders who have stayed with the company—who have not sold out— the confidence that we are doing everything possible to win. And while I'm not a trial lawyer, Ben—I'm a simple accountant—I do realize the importance of appearance in a case like this."

"Appearance?" says Braddock, chewing on the word, as if unfamiliar with the concept.

"Marius… Marius Shilling… has suggested the possibility that you might be thinking of turning this trial over to a junior associate."

Braddock looks at Creighton without expression.

"Apart from the impact such a move would have on the judge—" Creighton interrupts himself. "We simply want to make sure that you can free the time from your crowded schedule to devote yourself to this case. That's not unreasonable, Ben. For litigation of this magnitude, we have the right to expect the top counsel in your firm, not an inexperienced associate. You see my point?"

"I do," says Braddock, getting up. "And I will lavish upon it all the attention it deserves."

"What about an assurance?" Rand snaps.

"Marcus. When I head out this door, I will endeavor to walk the eight or nine blocks to my office. I can give you no assurance that I will arrive there safely or at all. What I can assure you of is that my firm is populated by the best and smartest trial lawyers in this city—and, most probably, the country. Collectively, we will give you the best defense that money can buy. So you consider whether you want that. Okay?" he says, grinning once out the door.

Alec at home, waiting for the phone to ring, leaps when it finally does.

"Harvey?"

"Yessir."

"Whatta you got?"

"What you asked for. Whatta you expect?"

"So let me have it."

Harvey lets out a troubled grunt. "I gotta tell ya. I put a tail on her this afternoon. Saw her take her kid to the playground with a bodyguard. She did not look unhappy, Alec. I'm not sure you wanna be messing with this. And as far as the case goes, she's off limits now. We can't trust her. Thankfully, we've still got the other witness, Carl Raffon."

"What do you mean, she didn't look unhappy?"

"What I said. Playing with her kid, laughing."

"She's putting it on for the kid."

"You think that, fine. I was there. You weren't. Which is where you should stay. Away from her."

"You're thinking about the case."

"Of course I'm thinking about the case."

"This doesn't have much to do with the case," Alec says.

"Well, that's where your head should be, boy. Braddock was summoned today to U.S. Safety. I gather he refused to commit to try the case personally. And he didn't rule out the possibility he might turn it over to you."

"*What?*"

"You heard me."

"To me?" Alec says. "Not one of the other partners?"

"If we have a list of happiest clients..." Harvey begins.

"Doesn't include Gen. Rand."

"Got that right."

FIFTY-ONE

Alec arrives at his office at eight fifteen in the morning, which is early for lawyers who work late. Joni, in greeting, starts by reading a message that's already a half-hour old. "Judge Braddock—"

"I know," says Alec. "Don't even stop at the men's room."

She shrugs apologetically.

Braddock is pacing as Alec walks in. "You know what you lack?"

Alec sits on the sofa. "We've been through this. A reputation."

"So what's taking you so long?"

"Well, there was that price-fixing case—"

"Yesterday's news. Generally, you need three hits. Three big cases with headlines before anyone takes you seriously."

"Then I've got a ways to go."

"Fortunately, from your standpoint, there's an exception to the general rule. It's the mega-case. Immediate worldwide attention. Front page every day. Lots of photographs. Television news clips. Interviews. You getting all this? Is it sinking in?"

"As applied to me?"

"There someone else here?"

"Just you and me," Alec says.

"That's what I thought. And you know what's on my trial calendar now?"

"Your schedule's impossible?"

"So how the fucking hell am I supposed to try your goddamn diesel oil case? You think of that? You and that goddamn lush you work for? And every other partner here is in the same position. Too damn busy to deal with what we had before to take on

Macalister's slush pile now."

Alec knows it's an act, can see where it's going thanks to Harvey's warning and still doesn't believe it.

Braddock descends wearily to his desk chair. "I never intended to try that case. It's either Mac from his hospital bed—or you."

Alec takes a deep breath. "The U.S. Safety case," he says, as if repeating a proposition too incredible to be taken as true. "Me."

"There something about this you're failing to grasp?"

"The client sitting still for it, for one. How'd you pull that off?"

"I haven't," says Braddock. "That you're going to have to achieve for yourself."

He shoves at Alec across the desk a batch of court pleadings. "This case. Definition of mega. Don't fuck it up!"

FIFTY-TWO

Phil's apartment spans the entirety of the tenth floor in a new high-rise condominium on Central Park West. The fashionable prewar co-ops on the Upper East Side wouldn't seriously consider him. Knowing that, Phil didn't bother to apply. Under condominium rules, however, no board approval was necessary, and in any event would not have been a problem. On the contrary, the building he bought into was happy to have him. Their problems, at the time, were with unions. And, upon the closing of the deal on Phil's apartment, those problems suddenly disappeared.

Phil breakfasts late in a small sun room off the kitchen offering a view of the park. The doorman, a slow-witted young man named Benny Forcaccio, rings up from downstairs. Benny is a cousin of Joey Forcaccio's, who is the opposite of slow-witted and a rising star in Phil's firmament. Benny owes his job to Phil and attaches great significance to any request Phil makes, however small. The present office is simply to announce the arrival of Carrie's father, Conner Madigan, which Benny does with the solemnity appropriate to a convocation.

Phil has summoned Conner after not having laid eyes on him for almost a year. And he notices—it's unmistakable from the unsteadiness of the smile, the flabbiness of the face—that the interval has been rocky for Mr. Madigan.

"Have a seat, Conner," Phil says without further greeting.

"Good to see you, Phil," says Conner, doing as he's told.

"Coffee? Breakfast?"

"Oh, no, I'm just fine."

"Eat a big breakfast, do you? Early riser? Maybe, this hour, you'd like a bit of… sherry?"

"That'd be just grand, Phil, thank you."

Phil goes to a wall cabinet, inspects some bottles on the shelf. "Or something stronger, perhaps?"

"Wouldn't mind," sings out Conner.

"A bit of the Irish, is it?"

Conner stammers, "It's a little early, but… a bit of the Irish? Couldn't say no to that, couldn't."

Phil brings a double shot of the drink to the table.

"Thank you," Conner says, raising his glass. With eyes rolling to the ceiling, he sips primly.

"My pleasure, sir." Phil butters a wedge of toast, takes a bite of it. "Asked you to come, Conner, because of your daughter."

"Carrie? She a problem?"

Phil grins. "It's funny. Most parents would say, 'Is she all right?'"

"Well, I know she's all right. All cleaned up now. After five, six weeks in that rehab."

"So you're current?"

"Of course I'm current. I'm her dad."

"Thing is, Conner, I don't like her attitude. For instance, she's been cheating on me."

"No!"

" 'Fraid so."

"Oh, Jeez!" he says.

"Yeah. Pretty flagrant. Some kid, a young lawyer. She moved in with him."

"Jeez, I didn't know, Phil."

"She's back here now."

"So that's okay, then?"

"Hardly. She doesn't want to be here."

"I'm so sorry, Phil. I don't know what to say."

"Well, for one thing, sorry's not going to cut it."

"I'd do anything to help, Phil. You know that. Let me have a chat with her."

"A chat, you say. You think that might help? Somehow, Conner, I don't think you do. That's just sop for me, right?"

"Tell me what to do, Phil, I'll do it."

"You're not drinking, Conner?"

He reconsiders his glass. Head back, he takes a belt.

"The point is," Phil says, "there's nothing you can do. It's I who must do something. To you, I think."

Conner's eyes widen.

Phil laughs. "Heady. This feeling I can do anything I want… to you, to your daughter. You know, I still beat her on occasion. Tie her down, lash her with a belt."

"I gotta go, Phil."

"I don't think so, old man."

Conner, looking sick, turns his head in the direction of the bottle.

"Like another?" Phil asks, rising and plucking Conner's glass en route. "The beating doesn't help. Doesn't change her basic behavior." He fills the glass to the brim, then plunks it down in front of Conner, spilling some on the tablecloth. Then Phil lowers himself into his chair, observing the now terrorized lawyer. "So I've decided on something different." Phil smiles, throws his head back and shouts toward the open door, "Vito! Get the fuck in here!"

In seconds, the henchman appears. "Vito, you know Conner Madigan?"

"Sure," Vito says.

"Ask my wife to join us, will you. Tell her her dad's here."

"Sure, boss," Vito says and leaves.

Phil pours some coffee, gives Conner another smile. In a few moments, Carrie and Vito come into the room. She's still in her bathrobe. Her face is bruised. "What the hell're you doing here?" she says to her father.

Conner shrugs, too frightened at this point to say anything.

"Here's the thing, sweetheart," says Phil. "This house isn't sweet. It's a drag to come home here. I think it's you. So I asked myself, what haven't I tried? And somehow that makes me think: this old sot, how many blows to the head could he take and survive? I don't know if you give a shit, but we can find out, and in any event it's an interesting question."

FIFTY-THREE

Alec stands on the Avenue of the Americas, having just emerged from the subway. He's hatless, feels the wind whip his face and hair, but he's not quite ready to cross the street. There, occupying half a city block, rears a new glass tower of forty-two stories built as a monument to the power of Telemarch News— and to its founder and chief executive, Jocko Rush. When Alec enters that building, his life will unalterably change. Either of two possibilities, success or failure, will play out on a worldwide stage. There's nothing in between, and there'll be no escaping the limelight. He wonders how many novitiates in any profession are given such a conspicuous rite of passage. The sensation in his gut is a mixture of presentiment and dread.

Lawyers would kill for the chance Ben Braddock had just handed him. To Alec the blessing is mixed. Before leaving the office, he calls Harvey.

"There it is, boy," Harvey said. "Your test. Race for the roses. Good timing. Should take your mind off the other thing. And prevent you from acting suicidally."

"You'll keep the watch?"

"What do you think?" Harvey said dourly, having been asked this too many times.

"At the first sign of trouble—"

"Yes?"

"We'll go in."

"And do what?"

"I'll think of something."

"Oh good," said Harvey. "Had me worried."

For the general counsel of a company the size of Telemarch News, Bill Templeton has a relatively small, spare office. Danish modern desk and credenza. No files, no books, no clutter. Suits him, Alec thinks.

They've worked together before: the Milwaukee libel case, other defamation suits; and Alec has often sat in for Bill to read copy before putting an issue of one of the magazines to bed. Alec wonders how it became his lot to become involved with so many addicts. Templeton is what Macalister calls a "dry drunk"—an alcoholic whose brute power of will crushes the drink out of each day, but not the desire. His fingers still stretch with a tremor. His fleshy face always looks as if powdered after a raw shave. He smokes Lucky Strikes, two packs a day. He speaks in whispers delivered staccato. He makes huge decisions, daily and fast.

Telemarch runs six TV stations and publishes twelve magazines, half on a weekly basis. At any given time, more than one hundred libel actions pend against it, and it has never lost or settled any. Braddock, Macalister, and other Kendall, Blake partners have either won such cases or forced the claimants to capitulate. But these were cases made easy because, as each article had gone to press, Bill Templeton had made the right decisions about what could and could not be published.

The man rarely smiles, and greets Alec without doing so. "What do you know about Leland Franks?"

"What's been in the news," Alec says, taking a seat. "He purports to have the 'as told to' autobiography of Spike Ikuda—supposedly 'told to' Franks by Ikuda himself."

"And what do you know about Ikuda?"

Alec shrugs. "Again, news accounts. Megalomaniac. Recluse. Creator of—what do the Japanese call it?—a *zaibatsu*. Electronics companies, media giants like yours, hotel chains." Alec pauses, weighs his words. "Jocko Rush's main competitor."

Templeton doesn't blink. "Ikuda hasn't made a move yet, but Franks and Franks' publisher have just sued us for an injunction."

"To stop what?" Alec asks with some surprise.

"Our news magazine—"

"*World Week?*"

"Right, our hard news magazine. Saturday night—tomorrow—we're printing an article exposing the Franks manuscript as a fraud. It'll be on the newsstands Monday morning."

"I thought you were serializing the manuscript in *Flash?*"

Templeton finally breaks a smile. A small one. "We made that deal. Provisionally. To get, shall we say, closer to the situation. The catch was, we could walk away if the manuscript proved phony."

"And you now think it is."

"We know it is. We've just found what Franks copied it from. A bio written by a guy named Tanaka who actually knows the facts. He worked for Ikuda for thirty years—helped build the empire—and then the two had a spat. Apparently, Tanaka offered the manuscript to a couple of publishers, which is probably how Franks got it—it's how we did—but then Tanaka thought better about publishing and pulled it back. Franks added a lot—publically known stuff—but the Tanaka material is what gives it enough authenticity to let Franks palm it off as Ikuda's own work. Half the people in the world seem to believe that. We're doing a side-by-side. Print passages of the Tanaka manuscript alongside Franks' so-called autobiography. That should be the end for Mr. Franks."

"Why doesn't Ikuda disclaim it?"

"He issued a press release doing just that."

"And?"

"Until he says so in person, few will believe it."

"And he won't surface."

"Which is what Franks was gambling on, until we came along."

"Great story."

"We like it," says Templeton, rising. "So I assume you know

how to defeat a claim for an injunction?"

"Sure," Alec says.

"Good. There's an executive committee meeting going on now down the hall. Jocko's office. I'll bring you in. You'll tell 'em how you'd do that."

"This minute?"

"Little less, actually," Templeton says, consulting his watch. "Shall we go? It's the other side of the building. The one with the view."

Alec's walking down the hall listening to Templeton, all the while trying not to panic, putting thoughts together on the fly, focusing on the timing, the judge, the possibilities of appeal. Too quickly there's the door. Then they're in, with no signs of their being noticed. An elongated table, a gaggle of suits, everyone talking, smoke billowing from ashtrays and lungs.

The CEO's office is an eight-window corner expanse surrounded by a honeycomb of rooms for dining and caucusing, and an outer chamber for Rush's secretaries and staff. Bushido items line the spare, white walls. Samurai robes, samurai swords, and other Japanese artifacts are hung up like paintings.

As he and Templeton stand waiting, Alec brings back what he's been told about Rush, mainly by Macalister. Once a reporter, Mac had mentioned, with an extraordinary brain for numbers, a mania for acquisition, and the sort of energy that engulfs people like a tornado. Starting on the staff of a small newspaper in New Zealand, Rush had somehow raised the capital to buy it. Then leveraged the paper into enough cash to buy a radio station. Then TV. Then many more of each all over the world. Within two decades, his brand of media had put its spin on the culture of four continents. Still, when Alec meets the man, and he rises up only to Alec's chest, Rush needs to prove something physical with a handshake grip that crushes the ends of Alec's fingers. "So you're the young warrior whom Ben Braddock brags about."

Two chairs have been cleared at the end of the table. Bill Templeton and Alec each take one, Templeton lighting up one of his unfiltered cigarettes. Rush himself continues to stand, balancing a sheathed samurai sword he had plucked off the wall. "I wanted Ben to do this case himself. You know what he told me? That you'd do it better. That you're the smartest young lawyer in New York. And that he'd carry your bag. Is any of that true?"

"The bag part, probably."

Jocko laughs. "Bill, I trust, has filled you in?"

"He has, yes," says Alec.

"Piece of cake, right?"

Alec hesitates. "No, I wouldn't say that."

"What?" Rush utters with a show of surprise. "Franks is a swindler. A fucking con man. This is a news story. What about the First Amendment?"

"You can write what you want about Franks, but if you want to prove it with a side-by-side, there's a competing policy," Alec says. "Copyright."

"Copyright?" storms Rush, slamming the sword to the table. "On a fraudulent manuscript? You can't be serious!"

"The problem is timing," Alec says. "The court hearing is scheduled for an emergency session tomorrow morning, Saturday. You go to press tomorrow night. The trial judge will probably rule against us. We need time to make an emergency appeal on a Saturday afternoon. Which cuts out the time for an evidentiary hearing—even assuming the trial judge would allow one. So we have to win immediately in the appellate division on the papers. And all we have is our paper allegation that the manuscript is a fraud. Without live witnesses—and without the time for these judges actually to read both manuscripts side-by-side, this is not a slam dunk."

"How much of the thing do they have to read, for Christ's

sake? Look at four or five passages and you know that Franks is a plagiarist."

"He'll probably claim Tanaka plagiarized from him."

"That's absolute bullshit!"

"No doubt. But you can't cross-examine an affidavit. And if there's no evidentiary hearing, in effect, for the time being, it's taken as true."

"But you will win the case," Rush asks.

"I'll win what I think you need," says Alec.

"Meaning?"

"How much of the Franks' manuscript were you planning to print?"

Rush looks down the table at the magazine's managing editor. "About a thousand words. That right, Miguel?"

Miguel Rivera, the editor, nods. Rush looks at Alec.

"Okay," Alec says. "A thousand words. You got it."

"What about the copyright problem?"

"Just went away. With the doctrine of fair use. Assuming we can find some appellate judge who understands it."

"Why you so sure we're losers in the lower court?"

"The judge," says Alec. "I know him."

FIFTY-FOUR

There's been a development," Braddock says as Alec walks into his office.

"Oh?"

"Actually, it happened late yesterday, but we didn't get notice until today. Ikuda's intervened. He also wants an injunction—both to stop the Franks' book from being published and to stop our printing any part of it."

"Who's representing him?"

"Dave Lipschutz."

"Bronx clubhouse," Alec says. "That's probably how the judge got appointed."

"You know him, Lipschutz?"

"He was on the other side of something Mac did last year. What're his grounds?"

"Libel," Braddock says. "And exclusive right to his own bio."

"Pretty baseless."

"Not at the trial-court level."

"No, they could argue anything there."

"So, whatta you need?" Braddock asks, sitting back in his desk chair with a deliberate show of ease. "In an appellate judge?"

"We get to pick our own judge?" says Alec.

"This is the appellate division. Still in the dark ages. No emergency judge is designated. You got an emergency? Go find a judge yourself. On a Saturday."

"A single judge can stay an injunction," thinks Alec aloud. "Not reverse it, but stay it until the full court can review weeks later. Right?"

"Right."

"And a stay on a Saturday afternoon is all we need to go to press Saturday night."

"Now you're getting on top of the problem. So what kind of judge do you need?"

"First of all, he can't be a Democrat. Dave Lipschutz is totally plugged into Tammany Hall. Secondly, we need a smart judge. We've got the better case. Be nice if we had a judge who understood it."

"You also want someone who knows something about copyrights."

"Yeah, great," says Alec. "In state court? A smart Republican scholar of a federal doctrine? You're going to tell me there's somebody up there who meets those criteria?"

"Of course. Teddy Krane. Big copyright expert before going on the bench. Won a huge case in that field. Landmark decision."

"He's ideal!"

"Yes, he is," Braddock says.

"There's a problem. I can see it in that look you're giving me."

Braddock laughs. "Yeah, there's a problem. Case he won was against your client, Telemarch News. And he won it by defeating the very doctrine you're planning to assert—the fair-use exception to a copyright."

"The Zarenga film case," Alec says. "The estate of the guy who had been filming a documentary about Trotsky at the time of the assassination. Telemarch wanted to publish two or three frames of the film, arguing it would be a fair use. The Supreme Court ruled otherwise."

"That's the one. You remember the facts, but not the lawyers."

Alec says carefully, "You were on the other side?"

"Whatta you think?" Braddock says with a smile. "You win every case?"

"Our facts are a lot better than they were in Zarenga."

"A bit. So are you going to call Mr. Justice Krane, or am I going to have to do that for you, too?"

The trick about not being nervous, Alec thinks, as he dials Justice Krane's chambers, is not to think about all the things that should be making you nervous. It also helps that the thing you're in charge of is the front page story of every newspaper in the world.

Alec tells the judge's secretary why he's calling, and the Hon. Theodore Krane immediately takes the call. Listening to a complicated situation netted out tersely causes the jurist briefly to pause.

"I'll be at home tomorrow afternoon," Krane says. "If your papers are in order—which includes proof of appropriate notice to your opponents—I'll hear your application for a stay. In my living room. I'll put my secretary back on to give you the telephone number and address."

While Alec waits, he muses over an interesting fact. Not even Krane had any doubt but that an injunction would be issued by the trial court judge, Robert Locklear, the judge in Alec's first trial. Not the brightest star in a dim constellation, and Tammany to the core.

Alec, still at his desk and surrounded by case books, puts in a call to Harvey at home. "Sorry."

"Why?" says Harvey.

"Calling you this late."

"I'm watching the ballgame. It's not as if I have a life outside the office."

"Oh, Jesus," Alec says, "I really am sorry."

"Lighten up, kid. I'm just kidding."

"Are you married? Christ. I should know that."

"Not at the moment."

"You've been married."

Harvey lets escape a big dramatic sigh. "Oh, yes."

"Has the sound of more than once."

"This is why you called?" Harvey says. "To discuss my marital history? And where are you, anyway?"

"The office."

"Right. As I expected. I thought Braddock was doing the papers for you."

"He is. Has. They're great."

"So all you gotta do tomorrow is stand on your feet and talk, right?"

"Right."

"So what the hell are you still doing in the office? You ought to be home, getting some sleep."

"Why haven't you called me about Carrie?"

"Because there's nothing to tell you. There's someone with her every day. But there's nothing to report, because nothing's changed. She looks okay. The kid's okay. Mom and kid on the playground. Not exactly earth-shattering news."

"Suppose I were to approach her?"

"Before your court appearance, or during it?"

"Not funny. Right after."

"You gonna bring the TV cameras?"

"I hadn't planned on it."

"Well, the guy who watches her is not employed by me. Vito is his name. He works for Phil. I suspect he knows what you look like."

"So what's he gonna do? In the middle of the park?"

"To you? Then? Probably just shoo you off. Especially if you bring the cameras. What Phil might decide to do later? To you? To her? Couldn't tell you for sure. But Phil Anwar is a notorious sadist. He's got the muscle to get you on a table. He takes pleasure in inflicting pain, and he's not overly fussy about killing people. So it's not exactly high on the list of risks you ought to be thinking about taking."

Sam, at home, listens to recordings from the tap on Phil Anwar's phone. Some of the conversations are Vito's, some involve other staff, some are Phil's. None are illuminating.

With the tapes droning on, Sam watches a basketball game, audio off. It would seem Phil assumes his line is tapped. He makes veiled references to people, places, and things. At the end of the day, Sam has trouble listening to as much as a half hour without nodding off.

Since this is work he does only in his own apartment and now spends half his time at Abby's house, Sam's falling way behind, and it worries him. Not as much as moving in with her, however. That really scares him, although it's not as if she's asked him to do it. He's guessing it probably scares her too.

He checks the clock. Nearly eleven. Another beer would put him to sleep for the rest of the night. He resists it and turns up the sound on the tapes.

Doorbell. It's Abby. Cold as hell outside, and she's coatless. Hair windblown. "Busy?" she says.

"Get in here, you'll freeze!"

"I should have called."

Inside, she gives a disparaging glance to Sam's earphones and recorder. "If we're not getting anything out of this, let's stop it."

"We are getting something," he says.

"Oh?"

"Phil's having a lot of trouble with his young wife."

"Great," she says sarcastically.

"Phil might say something. Vito might."

"I'll tell you what's likely," she says. "He's seen you. He can easily find this place. Anyone checking on you, seeing this equipment—"

"I thought we might broaden the coverage. Tap Little John too."

She does a double take. "Are you totally out of your mind?"

"Abby, for Christ's sake. You just told me you're worried Phil might send a man here. Just 'cause he once saw me in his home. You read that story in this morning's *News?* Missing people connected to the mob, a bunch of them, including Aaron Weinfeld, right? How many people, other than you, know that Phil wanted Weinfeld's phone tapped? That makes you valuable to Little John and dangerous as hell to Phil. You wanna go missing too? You're now more vulnerable than Weinfeld was, and he's probably at the bottom of the ocean."

FIFTY-FIVE

I t's a cold March morning when Alec steps into a cab. Stoically, he rides it downtown, spies the commotion going on in front of the courthouse and gets out on the west end of Foley Square.

Crossing a small park of tall, spindly trees, he watches the press mob swarming over the courthouse steps, vans in front, camera equipment being assembled. He stops for a moment, takes a deep breath, and looks up. Black limbs pattern a pewter sky, like an abstract canvas. The sun is up there somewhere between the branches, behind the cloud covering. The crowd's here for Ikuda, but in a couple of hours, they'll be swarming the lawyers. He heads for the courthouse. The reporters let him pass with only mild curiosity. No one knows yet who he is, and he looks straight ahead. Wind swirls in the square like wet paint.

Lawyers are haranguing a bleary-eyed judge. He wants no reporters to witness this, so the argument is in chambers. Having not had the time to recover from his hangover, much less study the papers, he looks put upon and confused. And Justice Locklear's appearance has not otherwise improved. He is still a round man in a bulging vest, who's slouched in his chair and peers at you like a hound dog. For all the comprehension he reflects, the attorneys before him might be speaking in tongues.

Leland Franks has somehow conned Marty Levinson into representing him. Marty is a shaggy little man who has won more death-row cases than any other lawyer in history. And, predictably, he argues for the injunction on the ground that the planned

World Week exposé of the Franks manuscript would infringe his client's copyright on that work. The publishing company lawyer, Chisolm Knorr, wags his square jaw in harmony with Levinson's point, adding that, without an evidentiary hearing, the court could not accept as true Telemarch's allegation that the manuscript is a fraud, undeserving of copyright protection.

Locklear turns to Dave Lipschutz, the man probably responsible, through his Tammany connections, for having the judge assigned to the case. Lipschutz's client, Ikuda, owns no copyright on Franks' manuscript, which Ikuda has himself denounced as fraudulent, or on the work Franks plagiarized, which Ikuda claims is defamatory and an invasion of privacy. So Lipschutz argues that the prospective *World Week* article—though he's never seen it—must be based on both manuscripts, is likely enjoinable on both grounds and should therefore be stopped by a temporary restraining order until the court has the opportunity to study it. Locklear glances at Alec, as if the jurist agrees.

"Can't do it, your Honor."

"Oh, really!" says the judge, stirring himself into an upright position. "Why is that, Mr. Bruno?"

"The doctrine prohibiting prior restraint. One of the oldest First Amendment principles—and the most clearly established."

"I wanna stop this article, counsel—I just issue the order."

"Which, Your Honor—and I say this with all due respect to the court—would be overturned by the appellate division in approximately twenty minutes, the time of a cab ride uptown."

"You planning to take such a cab ride, Mr. Bruno?"

"At one o'clock, your Honor."

Locklear looks at him cagily. "I may not rule by one o'clock."

"Then that's appealable."

"My not ruling?"

"Of course," Alec says. "The *World Week* printing deadline is tonight. Which means everything has to be submitted this afternoon. Everyone knows that, especially the hundred or so press people waiting outside. Holding a prospective injunction over our heads all afternoon would itself impose a chilling effect. And when a trial court deliberately delays an injunction until the last minute before the enjoined act can be taken to prevent an appeal—that itself is an appealable event. At least by mandamus. Basic rules of appellate procedure."

"It might be just a temporary restraint."

"Makes no difference, your Honor. No prior restraint means no prior restraint without a clear and present danger to the nation. Even the threat and delay of such an order is appealable, as I just said."

Locklear says warily to Lipschutz, "You know about such a rule?"

Lipschutz, shaking his head, looks uncertain.

"Would your Honor like authority on the point?" says Alec. "I take it that the appealability of a deliberate attempt by a trial judge to avoid an appeal is of interest to your Honor."

"No, it isn't!" Locklear snaps. "Why should it be? I'll have my decision out well before one o'clock!"

FIFTY-SIX

Back in the office, waiting for Locklear's decision, Ben Brad-dock says to Alec, "You actually have cases on the appealability of trial judges delaying rulings to avoid appeals?"

Alec shrugs. "No. Looked last night. Couldn't find any."

Braddock, smiling, says, "More balls than brains."

"I dunno. If I couldn't find any, Locklear's not likely to."

"Which means, for this bluff to work, he's got to believe you're smarter than he is—and not bluffing."

"Right."

"And he was the judge when you bluffed J.J. Tierney out of his underwear in that price-fixing case."

"True. But before the bluff, I did get Tierney on a real document that he hadn't remembered."

"So which does Locklear remember?" Braddock muses.

"If either."

Madge Harlan walks in, white-faced and excited. "Call from the courthouse! The judge has issued an injunction!"

Braddock looks at his watch and laughs. "You step in shit, kiddo."

Alec leaves to call Lipschutz, and gets him on the first ring. "You heard, Dave?"

"Yeah, have. Sorry, Alec, but we both know it's only the first round."

"What I was thinking."

"So," says Lipschutz smoothly, "looking ahead, knowing one of us would want to appeal, I've lined up an emergency judge in the appellate division. To hear us this afternoon. He's available in his apartment at two-thirty."

"Who'd you get, Dave?"

"Lester Coogan."

"Wasn't he the former Tammany leader in the Bronx?"

"Hmm," says Lipschutz. "I think he might have been."

"Thing is, I'm going to be moving before Teddy Krane at one-thirty. You can join me in his apartment if you like—this call is notice."

"Krane? He's a Republican!"

"Only nominally."

"I've already lined up Coogan," Lipschutz sputters.

"I'm the appellant, Dave. It's my appeal. All I need is any judge of the appellate court to stay the decision below. So you go to Coogan's apartment, if you prefer. But if Krane issues the stay, doesn't matter what Coogan does until the full court can be assembled."

Alec steps out of the Checker cab, leaving Ben Braddock to deal with the driver. It's the protocol of the firm: "first chair" never pays. And Braddock is observing the rule to the letter. Alec, waiting, gazes up at the white brick high-rise. "Whatta you doing?" says Braddock. "Thinking about the ways you can fuck up this case?"

Alec play-acts a look of disdain.

Riding up in the elevator, Braddock sniffs. "You think too much."

"No doubt," says Alec.

Amazing, Braddock is nervous. He thinks we could lose this.

They get out on the twenty-second floor. No trouble finding the apartment; reporters spill out of it into the hall. The Hon. Theodore Krane, enthroned on the wing chair within the bay window of his living room, gazes out on the more than dozen lawyers occupying his sofas and floor. Krane is a professorial sort of man with thinning hair, a high-domed forehead, and a trim-waisted medium frame. His khakis and pink, open-collared, button-down shirt distinguish him from the lawyers in suits. He has the demeanor of a host who wants to move on with the party so he can clear all these people out of his home.

Marty Levinson argues the copyright point. Alec counters with the obvious proposition that copyrights are given only to original works, not to plagiarized manuscripts.

"And how," Krane asks, "within the approximately one hour you've given me to rule, am I to determine that this seven-hundred page manuscript submitted by Leland Franks is nothing more—or little more—than an act of plagiarism?"

"You obviously can't," says Alec, "but I have here two things that will allow your Honor to rule in a lot less time than an hour. The first is an eight-hundred-page manuscript by a man named Tanaka. He worked for Ikuda from the days their business operated out of a garage. When they split, Tanaka wrote this tome. His agent sent a translated version to two top publishing companies before it was withdrawn. Almost certainly, Franks got a copy from somebody in one of those publishing houses."

"Eight hundred pages, you say." The judge holds up the manuscript and gives Alec a look that says, *You surely don't expect me to read this.*

"I show your Honor the Tanaka manuscript," Alec says, "only to verify the second item—which is a side-by-side layout of about twenty excerpts from the Franks manuscript and the Tanaka passages that Franks stole from. As your Honor will quickly see, they're virtually identical. Same anecdotes. Almost the same words."

On the judge's coffee table sits an ashtray milled with a replica of the scales of justice. Marty Levinson lifts it above his head.

"Yes, Marty?" says Krane.

"There are a lot of people in your Honor's living room at the moment, but none of them, so far as I know, is named Tanaka."

Levinson carefully returns the ashtray to the table. "So right now, we have only Mr. Brno's statement that such a person exists, much less that he wrote this manuscript. In other words, Mr. Brno offers us classic hearsay. And the vice of hearsay is that the actual witness, whom we're being asked to believe—Mr. Tanaka—is not here to be cross-examined. And if he were—assuming he exists—he might well tell us, under vigorous cross, that it was he who copied his manuscript from the manuscript written by Mr. Franks—not vice-versa."

"Mr. Brno?" the judge says. "Would you like Mr. Levinson to pass you the scales of justice?"

"Don't need them, your Honor. I have the doctrine of fair use."

"I thought we'd be getting to that."

"It's the way the copyright laws reconcile the conflict between the act's restraint on the publication of copies and the First Amendment's prohibition of restraint on publication. So even if your Honor were to assume that the Franks manuscript were genuine, we'd still be entitled to publish our opinion to the contrary and support it with excerpts from both manuscripts. As a fair use."

"I happen to know something about this doctrine."

"I know you do, your Honor."

"I suspected you might. And there are limits to this doctrine of fair use. Very important limits."

"And we're well within them. In the Zarenga Films case, for example, Telemarch News published without license the entirety of the film that gave it any value—the several frames showing the assassination. Here, we're publishing a few excerpts from an eight-hundred-page book."

Justice Krane looks Alec in the eye. "How many words?"

Alec hesitates for only an instant. "Twelve hundred, your Honor."

"I'll give you a thousand."

Alec opens his mouth to protest, but the judge comes down hard. "Don't push it, counsel!"

"Right," says Alec with a smile.

"All right, everybody," the judge says. "You heard it. I'm staying the order of injunction below. Telemarch can publish one thousand words from the Franks manuscript. You'll have my opinion on Monday."

The lawyers are silent, but shouting reporters throng the hallway, and several try to interview Alec and Judge Braddock on the elevator going down. On the pavement outside, Braddock pushes Alec into the TV cameras and mics.

A blonde with big lips rattles out the first question. "You won a great victory for the First Amendment! How does that feel?"

"These are pretty standard doctrines," Alec says. "Prior restraint. Fair use. Most people are aware of them."

"Apparently not Judge Locklear."

"Oh, I think he was aware of them," says Alec. "Just had a problem applying them to our case."

FIFTY-SEVEN

Conner Madigan sits alone at the bar in Callahan's Tavern, his pub of choice on Staten Island. He likes the actual wood the bar is made of. After two or three Irish whiskeys, he can stare at it for hours and often does. He thinks he sees meaning in the grain, as one would in the spatter of Jackson Pollock. There's no one to talk to at home. His wife's gone back to Ireland, maybe permanently. On balance, he prefers her being there than here. His younger daughter, Jessie, has skipped to L.A., and good riddance to her, too. *She's a mouth on her, that one!* But Lord knows, he's run out of conversation with Mike, the bartender, whose last name may or may not be Callahan. Conner's never bothered to ask. And there's no one else in the entire establishment.

Until Vito walks in.

Conner's not surprised. He'd been wondering how long it would take.

Vito pulls up the next stool. "What the fuck you still doing here?"

"In this bar?"

"In this city, you shithead!"

Mike, a hirsute young man, comes over. "Whatta you have?"

"Ginger ale," says Vito.

Mike shrugs and goes for the bottle.

Vito says, "The man warned you. I was standing right there."

"This is my city."

"Oh, yeah?"

"Damn straight."

"Check your deed, counselor."

Mike deposits the drink before Vito. "Two bucks," he says.

Vito laughs and hands him the money. "I was wondering how you made a living in this place."

Vito sips his drink as Mike goes to the cash register. "So he wants to see you again."

"*He* being your boss?" Conner says haughtily.

"Not good to get smart with me," Vito says. "Better just to come along."

"I'm not really in the mood."

"Your going or not going… doesn't really depend on your mood."

"That so? You think you can drag me out of here? My friend over there would call the cops in ten seconds."

"Well, let's put it this way. You can come on your own, no fuss, or, while your friend stands there with his dick in his hand, I can carry you out like a bag of shit. Put a real hurt on you. Because, with the booze in you, the usual amount of force's not gonna be enough for you to feel it the way I need you to feel it. So I'd have to do some serious damage. But, counselor, that's my job. I'm real good at it. It's what I'm paid for, and I'm paid very well. So I go either way on this. Choice is yours."

"You're bluffing."

"Now you're giving me a preference." Vito removes from his pocket a set of brass knuckles and places it on the bar. "You know where I found this? Place on Canal Street. The thing's an antique. But it's terrific. Protects my hand and, of course, is very painful for the guy stepping into it."

Conner steps off his chair with an effort at dignity. "You enjoy this?" he says. "Working for a man like that? Strong-arming? Dirty work?"

"You call it what you like, counselor. I take pride in my work. How many people can really say that?"

Carrie Madigan sits on the edge of her bed in her room in Phil's apartment. It's a sizeable room with its own bathroom, big windows, views of the park, floral wallpaper, blue velvet draperies. The furniture is Colonial, made of maple; the bed, a four-poster. She's bought many things for Sarah's room, nothing for her own. Everything, including the toiletries, has been purchased by Phil's housekeepers from lists written out by Phil. In one corner is a Magnavox TV in a large maple cabinet. It's on without the sound. She's just put Sarah to bed and has nothing to do, but she's not watching the screen. She's in a prison, she feels caged. The prison is a version of hell, and she has no good idea how to get out of it.

Beneath a false bottom in a dresser drawer is a small bag of heroin. There's another in a talcum container in the back of a bathroom cabinet and a package of needles in the top shelf of her closet. Efforts had apparently been made to "hide" these items so she would find them. Her mind is numb—less with longing for the drugs than with hatred for the man who put them there. It's as if the latter works against the former. The hating is so strong it reinforces her will not to give in. The last detox and all those weeks of rehab, after all those failed attempts, put her in a good place. Hating Phil will keep her there, so far as the drugs are concerned, but she wonders whether it has left her the capacity to enjoy anything else in her life.

Phil lets her go to meetings, which seems inconsistent but probably isn't. Most likely, the way his mind works, he's proving to her that there's no antidote to her dependency. While she's in the room, with Vito outside waiting, her mind sometimes fantasizes escaping through a back door, just running away. But, of course, she can't do that. Not without Sarah. And running to Alec would get both of them killed.

There's a knock on the door, and then Vito intrudes. He apes his boss in all things, including rude behavior. Phil pays no respect to her privacy, neither does he. "Phil wants you. Get up."

She regards him with contempt, then rises. There's really no point in not.

The living room presents a tableau appropriate to a B-movie gothic. There's Vincent Price in the form of Phil. There's her unfortunate Da, alone on a small wooden chair in the middle of the carpet. He's not tied but probably too drunk to do anything but maintain a precarious balance to avoid pitching headlong onto the floor. He looks like a waxen image of himself, too terrified to speak. There's the coffee table in front of him loaded with implements. *What are those—knives?*

"I've gone to some trouble," Phil says, "so I'll need you to watch this."

"What are you doing," Carrie says. "You crazy?"

"Hardly. Vito, I think maybe we start with the needles. In the eyes. That may be enough for this time."

"You're outta your fucking mind!" Carrie screams.

Even Vito looks skeptical about this.

"It's training, Vito. Like you trained that dog of yours. If one thing doesn't work, you try another."

She flies at Phil, but, with the back of his hand, he whacks her in the face, which sends her sprawling.

All the time, this strange silence from Conner.

"Boss," says Vito.

"What?"

"Look at the guy."

They do.

"Jesus Christ," Phil says.

Carrie, sitting up on the carpet, screams, *"What?"*

"I think he's croaked," Vito says.

Phil inspects more closely. "I think you may be right."

"We scared the dumb bastard to death."

Carrie jumps up, looks at her father, screams again, *"Oh, no, no, no, no!"*

"No doubt we did him a service," Phil says. "Man with a heart like that."

Carrie's in a dream, where people stick needles in eyes, kill by fright, no one listens or cares.

"All right, Vito," Phil says. "Get Benny from downstairs to bring up a mail sack. Dump this carcass somewhere. Out to sea is always best." He turns to his wife. "See what you did? This was totally unnecessary. Who'm I gonna have to bring in now? That lawyer boyfriend of yours?"

FIFTY-EIGHT

Alec's phone rings at eleven-thirty that night, waking him up. It's Bill Templeton, Telemarch's general counsel.

"You better get down here."

"What's going on?" Alec asks, trying to shake himself into full consciousness.

"A runaway client."

"Jocko Rush?"

"No, the managing editor. Miguel Rivera."

"He wants more words?"

"You got it," Templeton says with exasperation.

"I'll be there in twenty minutes."

"Make it fifteen. Don't even dress. We are that close to mayhem, or contempt of court."

Almost midnight. The Telemarch lobby: vast, empty, crypt-like. The barrenness of the place presses on Alec's headache, as does the hum of a polishing machine operated by an unseen porter. In the chrome plating of the elevator door, Alec stares at a rippled image of his face: pale, haggard. A security guard on the thirtieth floor escorts him to the editorial wing.

Miguel Rivera, a second cousin of Diego Rivera, the Mexican painter, is a large man, thick through the shoulders and bald on the pate. Standing in his office, his attitude toward Alec is pugnacious. "We need eleven hundred words. That's it. Not a word less. I don't give a shit who you are, or what you say. We can't reach Jocko. I'm in charge. It's my decision, and I've made it."

"You like the idea of going to jail for contempt of a court order?" Alec asks. The question is rhetorical. Every reporter Alec's ever known couldn't wait to be martyred for the First Amendment. Rivera's eyes simply shine.

"Right," Alec says. "How are you counting the words?"

"What do you mean, how are we counting? One at a time. How else?"

"Are you counting articles and conjunctions?"

Rivera's eyes narrow, and he turns to one of his editors. The answer doesn't surprise him. "It appears we are."

"Do the recount," says Alec. "Then we'll talk."

In ten minutes a group of assistant editors come in. "We're still three words over," one of them says.

Rivera's stance remains belligerent.

"You're not serious," Alec says.

"It's a matter of principle."

"Let me tell you," Alec says, his headache turning to migraine. "We got the one judge in the appellate division who would have stayed the injunction. You go in contempt of that order for even three words, the rest of those judges will bring the house down. Not simply on you. On the whole goddamn company. The fine will be—I promise you—e-fucking-normous! I would not want to be the corporate officer who has to go before the board and try to explain how three words were worth all that money. And who made that decision against clear legal advice as to exactly what would happen. You understand what I'm saying?"

Rivera, not pleased, turns to the assistant editor. "You can cut three words?"

"Not a problem."

Rivera's curt nod completes the editing process. Templeton says to him, as the assistant editor leaves, "He's right, you know, Miguel. It's not a good risk. The point is made with half the quotes we use."

"Lawyers!" says Rivera.

"It's not lawyers who're the problem," Templeton flares back. "Particularly, good lawyers. It's judges like Locklear and the system that puts them on the bench. Turn your magazine on that one!"

"Wouldn't sell."

"Right. So once again, the public gets what it deserves. And so do you, my friend."

FIFTY-NINE

Templeton calls Monday morning while Alec is trying to clean up his office.

"Can you get up here this afternoon?" Bill says. "Around two?"

"What now? Rivera's on another rampage?"

"Rivera? No. He's so covered in kudos, he'd grin if you kicked him in the balls."

"So? What's happening?"

"Don't ask so many questions. Just get your ass up here."

At the stroke of two, Alec opens Templeton's door.

"Ah, Alec," says Bill, as if surprised to see him. He gets up. "Come on," he says, heading out of the office.

"Whoa! Where we going?"

"Jocko wants to see you."

"You going to tell me what it's about? Or do you get off on watching me sweat?"

"Just follow me, will ya? Christ, you're getting to be a pain in the ass."

The door opens on the same executive committee assemblage that had confronted Alec on Friday. Except this time, they're looking at Alec as he walks into the room, and there's a smile on everyone's face. Jocko, standing at the head of the table, says,

"C'mere!" indicating the one empty seat next to his. As Alec sits, Jocko lifts off the wall the largest samurai sword in his collection and places it in its scabbard in Alec's hands. "It's yours," says the chief executive.

Alec looks around the table at faces grinning now even harder and feels as if he's elevating from the chair.

Jocko, laughing, says, "Speechless, huh? I thought of asking you to kneel and dubbing you Sir Alec, but, what the hell! That's a bit over the top."

"And this isn't?" Alec says. "I'm overwhelmed, Jocko. Thank you."

"I like my warriors to win," Rush says in a tone whose jocularity is underscored with intent.

As if on cue, the meeting gives Alec a standing ovation. Even Bill Templeton, with uncharacteristic enthusiasm, joins in.

"So how does it feel?" asks Marius Shilling, leading the way around the crowded tables. "Seeing your photograph in the papers, your face on the telly? Exhilarating, right?"

"Life goes on," Alec says.

"Bullcrap," says Shilling. "You must be floating on air."

Alec laughs, taking a seat at a table against the wall in the Down Town Association dining room where Shilling has invited him to lunch. He glances at the high damask-swathed windows, the dark wood paneling, the leather upholstery. Little has changed here, he thinks, in a century. And the atmosphere is palpable: the hush of money, the weight of power. A waiter, an ancient retainer, takes their orders for lunch, meaning he snatches up a slip of paper on which Shilling has scribbled their selections.

"Don't underestimate the significance of publicity," Marius says. "It's a prize beyond price."

"You and Braddock," says Alec.

"Ben would know."

"You have any idea how simple that case was? Legally?"

"Matters not, my boy. No one understands litigation from press accounts anyway."

Alec laughs again. "Maybe so."

"At any rate," says Shilling, "I'm offly glad you could join me for lunch."

It takes Alec a second to crack "offly." "Blue Points and Dover sole?" he says. "A bit better than a sandwich at my desk."

"There is something particular I wished to discuss with you."

"About our case?"

"No," says Shilling. "In fact, not about our case."

He looks disappointed in Alec's lack of response.

"Are you all right?" Shilling asks.

"Sorry. I seem off? I'm kind of distracted at the moment."

"Anti-climax?" Shilling suggests.

"No, no. I'm sorry. A personal matter. You were saying there was something…."

"Particular. Yes. It's a bit delicate, but I think well within the bounds of propriety. The question I'd like to put to you is, have you ever considered making a lateral move?"

"A what?"

"There are advantages to doing so, you know."

"You're talking about my leaving Kendall, Blake?" says Alec.

"You wouldn't be the first," Shilling says.

"Well, of course not. But—"

"How long do you think it will take you to become a partner there—*if* they take you in? Another six to eight years? Look, Alec. I like planting seeds. Kernels of ideas that perhaps wouldn't otherwise enter one's head."

"Are you making me an offer?" Alec says, faintly amused.

"I love your directness. We haven't even had our first course. Yes. Let's be direct. I'm making you an offer. Come to my firm,

I'll make you a partner within two years. With the classic proviso, of course."

"That I don't screw up."

"Precisely."

"I'm flattered, Marius, but no."

Shilling looks stupefied. "You don't even want to think about it?"

"I don't even want to talk about it."

"My, my, so precipitous. You think Kendall, Blake so superior to my firm?"

Alec doesn't answer.

"You know," Shilling says, "the financial rewards of partnership are a good deal more flexible in my firm than they are at Kendall, where partners are paid on a lockstep basis, by class."

"I actually did know that," says Alec.

"And, in our shop, only one person decides on the distributions each partner receives."

"That person being yourself?"

"I have that privilege," says Shilling, with a bow of his head.

"So in your firm, it pays to stay in your favor."

Marius looks at him inquiringly. "All right. Let's table the subject. You will find, my friend, that I am not an irresolute suitor." He gives Alec his warmest smile. "And 'no' is not an answer I readily accept."

"I may stay for lunch then?" says Alec, glancing at the waiter bringing their oysters.

"Ha!" Shilling says. "I love it! I hope, my dear friend, there will be many lunches. Many!"

SIXTY

An early spring can startle you, conjured out of yesterday's cold ground. *But everyone adjusts,* thinks Carrie. *To the cruelty of April.* She admires her daughter seriously at play. *Or is it just me?*

Sarah plays. Carrie watches. In the park. How normal, mother and child.

No one plays with Sarah, however. No other mothers come over to have a good chat. Carrie can see why. She's marked, and not only physically. *I no doubt appear to be looking at nothing, at least nothing of this world. No one likes a woman with a blank stare in her eyes, let alone purple cheekbones.*

Vito, sunning on a bench near the sandbox, removes an enormous cigar from the pocket of his leisure suit jacket and lights up. Nannies give him furious looks. Young mothers start drawing their children away. With a sigh, Vito, not totally insensitive to naked contempt, stalks off, out of the playground, to a bench on the encircling path.

On the other side of the playground fence, about thirty yards away, Alec watches it all. Carrie and her child have removed their jackets in the sun, and Carrie wears dark glasses. She sits on the side of the sandbox, one hand aimlessly sifting, while Sarah plays a few feet away.

Seeing Vito leave, Alec heads toward them.

In his vision they float among the daffodils outside the far gate. He sees Carrie, not that surprised, fixated on him as he comes near. Easing down beside her, he feels exhilaration laced with dread.

She speaks in a fierce whisper. "This is not a good idea, Alec."

He sees the bruises beneath her dark lenses. "He's hurt you again."

Sarah looks up from her digging with momentary interest. A streak of sand glints on her small, pale cheek. Carrie gives a furtive glance to the playground entrance.

"He'll kill you Alec, you understand? It means nothing to Phil to have someone killed."

"We'll get a court order. Put him in jail if he comes within twenty feet of you."

"Court order! Please!"

Spying Vito lumbering back into the playground, she grabs their jackets. "Go away, Alec. You have no idea of the trouble you're making."

"I can protect you," he says, barely recognizing his own hoarse voice. "Come with me. We'll leave the city."

Carrie shakes her head vehemently, at the same time pulling Sarah from the sandbox, brushing her cheek.

"Carrie, please listen to me!"

A few steps away, she turns. "I can't do this," she says, balancing Sarah and jackets in her arms. She then pivots toward Vito, who is glaring at Alec, while grinding his cigar into the pavement.

"What the hell's the goddamn point, Carrie?" Alec calls as she hastens away.

Women at the swings stare openly at Alec, then down at the ground with embarrassment for him. Another young woman, blond and imperious, having just entered the playground with twin five-year-old boys, says to them sharply, "Go play!" They're off. Then, turning on Alec, she says, "What the fuck was that?"

It's like stepping into another life.

"Darcy! Jesus! What're you doing here?"

"What am *I* doing here?"

"Who're those kids?"

"Those kids are my sister's kids. I am their aunt. I therefore have a perfectly good reason for being in this playground. And it looks very much to me like you don't."

"I have to go."

"And leave me guessing for the rest of my life about what I've just seen? And, more to the point, heard?"

"I'll call you."

"The hell you will." She swings back toward the gate, stops, and beckons. "Alec!"

"Timing sucks."

"That's not my fault," she says.

Darcy thumps down on the bench vacated by Vito and stares Alec into settling on the other end.

"Now tell me about this melodrama I just witnessed."

"Freakish coincidence, your being here," he says, his mind not on this conversation.

"No doubt. But I was."

He wants to be off.

"Goes to show," she says. "Can't believe what you read in the papers. Here I was thinking you're leading this fabulous life, slaying dragons in every courtroom, becoming trial lawyer of the year, or whatever they call it, and what's the reality? You're screaming *Stella* in the park at some woman with a kid. Who is that woman?"

"You wouldn't know her."

"Obviously. So who is she, and how do *you* know her?"

"It's a long story."

"Did you know her before we broke up?"

"No."

"So couldn't be that long a story."

"Aren't you worried your nephews might run off?"

"They're fine. That's what the gate's for. And they don't listen to me, anyway."

"Darcy, I will call you, but this isn't the time, I really—"

"No you don't."

"I gotta go!'

"Alec! Who the hell is she?"

He takes in the sky, finding no solace. "You've heard of a guy named Phil Anwar?"

"No. Should I have?"

"He's what they call a capo. Mafia. The boss of the mob here in New York."

"Okay. I suppose someone's got to be that. And this girl has something to do with him?"

"She's married to him."

Darcy regards her former boyfriend as if he were a total stranger. "And you're in love with her?"

"It's complicated."

"You're lusting after some mobster's wife?"

"We were living together."

"Were you? Brilliant! And now he's got her back?"

"That's right. It would seem… by coercion."

"Jesus, Alec."

"It's not pretty."

"It's not sane. Not for you. But you won't listen to me either, will you? Like those kids. Look at 'em! I think they're ganging up on some four-year-old. I better break that up."

"See ya."

"You *won't* listen to me, will you?"

Alec's laugh is directed at himself.

"You're in a bad hole, Alec. You damn well ought to be climbing out of it."

He watches her go, having never before felt such a rift between the normal world, which she represents, and the dystopia which he's inhabiting.

Phil often works in the paneled study of his Central Park West apartment, in lieu of his office downtown. It depends very much on the paintings he's in the mood for. Here he keeps several Fauve works, notably a Vlaminck bridge scene with flaming water, and a Derain forest of twisted trees. That morning's news from his source in the U.S. Attorney's office makes the Fauvists more fitting company.

The word is that Sancerre has a witness on Phil and will soon be convening a grand jury. Phil's made a study of the subject of grand juries. Originally they were devised to protect ordinary citizens from the influence of the evil prosecutors of the Crown. Grand juries ensured that no man could be indicted and made to stand trial unless a group of his peers said it was fair. Now the reality is that any grand jury is easily sent in any direction the prosecutor cares to point it. These people generally aren't very knowledgeable or bright; they're almost never shown any conflicting evidence that isn't discredited or overwhelmed; and defense lawyers are never allowed in the room. So the system is used by the prosecution simply as a means of forcing testimony from unprotected witnesses in advance of trial on a transcript that defense counsel don't even get to see, unless the prosecution decides to use it. All this is done under the fiction that grand jury secrecy benefits the accused—a banner waved frequently by prosecutors and courts without acknowledging the irony involved, much less the hypocrisy of which they're all guilty.

Grudgingly, Phil admires the whole setup. Screw the accused with a system supposedly put in place for his protection. It's exactly what Phil would do were he on the other side.

Phil's source also states that he will keep his eye peeled for the identity of the witness and that, in the meantime, Phil should be exceptionally careful. Phil makes a mental note. When this guy's usefulness ends, get rid of him. Terminally, if necessary. It's a huge mistake to lecture Phil on the obvious. He hates condescension and can spot it a mile away.

The pressing question is, who's the government witness? Could be any of his own men, his own wife, Whitman Poole, or any of Poole's men, although they shouldn't know enough to matter. On balance, he suspects Carrie. And it's getting progressively depressing to have her around. Problem is, having just gotten rid of her father, the time is not propitious for Phil to dispose of his wife.

He thinks he has a better idea. But before letting her go, on his terms, why not have a little sport with her—send her off with something to think about.

SIXTY-ONE

In Ben Braddock's office, it is Alec who is pacing.

Braddock says, "So you are involved with this woman."

"I'm in love with her," Alec says.

Braddock sniffs. "Drug addict," he says, as if listing her credentials. "Mafiosa. Excellent choice. Not even counting the fact that she's already married. To a murderous thug."

"You know the DA—"

"Quite well. And I'd happily call him. And then what? What's he going to do? Give you and your girlfriend protection twenty-four hours a day? Forever? He'll say, 'Get a court order, and call me when he violates it.' By which time you won't need protection. You'll be dead."

"So anyone who wants to can raise an army, come after you— even warn you he's going to do it—and no one can do anything to stop the violence."

"That's about right, except who needs an army? All you need is a gun."

"Great world."

"Civilization's a thin veneer, my friend. And the system of justice designed to preserve it? Even thinner." Braddock shrugs at the unhelpfulness of his own observation. "Look, Alec. You love this woman? Leave her alone."

Alec's gesture declares this to be out of the question.

"Then take her and her child to some little town somewhere, and hide."

Alec likes this no better.

"Good," says Braddock. "It's not what I want you to do either.

What I want you to do is to try the goddamn diesel oil case."

"What does Rand want?"

Braddock takes out the *Times*, which is still running the dregs of the Ikuda story on its front page. "You remember that first lesson I gave you?"

"The one about ink."

"Ink. Exactly. So what do you suppose? That damn fool, that puffed-up general you represent, he sees your picture in the newspapers, and guess what? He believes what he reads. About you. I told you. Doesn't have to be true. He's now telling his friends he's got the hottest young trial lawyer in the city."

They both notice Madge Harlan standing at the open door. "There's a call in your office," she informs Alec. "From a Miss Madigan. She says it's urgent. You want it switched in here?"

"No, I'll take it there," says Alec, already on his way, as Ben Braddock watches with a pitying frown.

"Carrie?" Alec, holding the phone, swings his butt at the door to his office to close it.

"You still willing?"

"Yes. Sarah too. I'll get a car. We'll leave town."

"I'm not sure I can travel."

"What happened?"

"Just hurry," she says. "Take a cab. To the church nursery school at 85th and Park. I'll be outside."

As Alec pulls up in a taxi, Carrie sits on the church steps with Sarah. They have one suitcase between them. Sarah looks puzzled and a little distraught, as if she knows something's amiss, and her mom's not telling her what is going on.

Alec gazes at Carrie inquiringly as he loads her suitcase into the trunk. "Where're the heavies?"

"He's letting me go."

"With Sarah?"

"No."

"You just took her out of school."

"A bit early, yes."

Alec feels a bit dizzy.

Carrie says, "Let's go, Alec. Even my clothes hurt."

In the back of the cab, she hands Sarah to Alec and sits on the edge of the seat.

"Where we going, Mommy?" asks Sarah, not at all comfortable with this situation.

"To Alec's house, darling. Alec's a friend of mine."

"He was in the park."

"That's right, sweetheart."

Alec leans forward to face the child. "Should we get some ice cream, Sarah? What do you say?"

She gives this serious consideration. "What flavor?"

"Any you like."

"Pistachio," Sarah concludes.

"Excellent choice."

"Buy a gallon," says Carrie. And in a sardonic whisper in Alec's ear, "We can feed it to Phil when he comes."

SIXTY-TWO

At five-forty in the afternoon, Sam is asleep on the La-Z-Boy in his front room. Two things happen almost at once. An ambulance siren startles him awake. Then on the recording that put him to sleep in the first place, a voice recognizable as Vito's starts mentioning Alec's name.

To Sam, it's more likely than not he was dreaming. Groggily, he rewinds the tape. No mistake. Vito is talking to a man named Dominick. He's chortling about a lawyer named Alec and the things Phil will do to him. How he will mutilate and dismember him and revel in every scream. Sam, momentarily transfixed, doubles over and heaves his lunch at the floor.

Sam and Abigail have serious conversations, typically, in her kitchen or her bed. That afternoon, Sam arrives, hustles her out to his car, turns the heater on and relates what he's just heard.

She says, "How on earth does Phil Anwar know your son?"

"I think," Sam says, trying to get a grip, "as far as I could piece this together—and as crazy as it sounds—Alec is somehow mixed up with Phil's wife."

She stares at him for a moment with incomprehension. "Is that even possible?"

"It's that case Alec's working on. They seem to have gotten involved, somehow. The problem with these goddamn tapes is that they give you incomplete information."

"I can't believe this," she says. "It's fucking surreal."

"I have to tell Alec what I have—about the recordings. I have to warn him."

"If he's sleeping with Phil's wife, I think he knows he's in trouble."

"So whatta you saying? I shouldn't talk to him?"

"Dammit, Sam. I don't know what you should do. You just hit me with this. What I do know is that somebody's gonna get hurt, and I don't want it to be you."

SIXTY-THREE

Phil's downtown office is on the twenty-seventh floor of 40 Wall Street. His several rooms there are furnished in light woods and heavy draperies. On the walls hang paintings by very good American Impressionists: a street scene with flags by Childe Hassam, a beach scene by Edward Potthast, and a sunset by William Merritt Chase. Phil brings the bankers and lawyers in for his legitimate deals. It's the one-upmanship that amuses him. His paintings are better than theirs.

He keeps no permanent staff there, though, and answers his own phone.

At least one of them. The one whose number only several people in the world have. So he's surprised when it rings.

"Phil?"

"Yeah, John?"

"We need a meet. Tonight at the latest."

"I'm having dinner in town."

"I'll join you."

"Look forward."

There was no need to say when or where.

Alec's new apartment, rented while Carrie was in rehab, is on the sixth floor of a doorman building on 87th between Madison and 5th. Its living room has a dining alcove from which, through a small side window, one can glimpse Central Park. There's also a good-sized bedroom with a view of the street and a kitchen just large enough to turn around in. Alec hoped to stop by the apartment for about five minutes, throw some of his own clothes into a suitcase, grab a car at a rental agency, and get them all out of town. Carrie insists, however, that she's in no condition to travel.

Instead, she spoons Sarah ice cream at a leisurely pace, tucks her in for a late nap on Alec's sofa, and then sprawls face down, under the covers, in Alec's bed, all her clothes piled on a chair. Throughout these movements, he's allowed a brief glimpse of the crosshatched pattern Phil made of her back, and it sickens him.

It's also frightening as hell. The fact is they're defenseless in this apartment. Phil could arrive at any time, with henchmen, guns—strap them down; tape their mouths; torture them as long as he wanted. *Maybe he won't with his daughter in the next room,* Alec thinks, but that idea seems more wishful than real.

Alec sits on the edge of the bed, not letting Carrie sleep. He needs to know what's happened, he says, so that he can even begin to consider what they should do. In a strained voice, Carrie recounts Phil's visit to the rehab facility in New Jersey and how he got her to leave immediately by threatening Alec and promising vehemently to stop beating her.

"Why didn't you tell me?" Alec says.

She turns her head away on the pillow.

"Phil never gave you the chance. And never kept his promise," Alec concludes.

"Seems I'm not the kind of person to whom keeping one's word matters."

"But he let you go."

"After he killed my father."

"He did *what?*"

"I saw it happen."

"He murdered your father right in front of you?"

"Scared him to death. Literally. Threatened to put out his eyes with knitting needles."

"Good God, the man's totally demented."

"He would have done it," Carrie says. "Da knew that. It's what killed him."

"I'm so sorry. About your father, and that you had to see it."

"I don't know how I feel. Shock. Still in shock. And hate. I hate that man as sick as he is."

Alec is trying to think through some kind of plan. "Phil has this address?"

"Not from me."

"He'll want his daughter back."

"Oh, yeah."

"And now you're a witness to a murder."

"Except Phil never touched him. And Da was dead drunk. I'm no lawyer, but I can hear Phil saying, 'Isn't it probable the man was too drunk even to hear the threat, and simply died of natural causes?'"

"He beat you up again. What was that for?"

"You think he needs a reason? He likes to do it, and he does what he likes."

Alec gets up, goes to the window facing the street. "It's not smart being here, Carrie. I could be out now getting a car. Or even a van. You and Sarah could sleep in the back while I drive us to Ohio or Colorado or wherever." He turns, and she's fast asleep. He shakes her harder than he intended.

"Alec, stop! I can't move. Tomorrow. We'll go tomorrow."

Swearing silently, he watches her pass out.

Then goes into the kitchen, dials Harvey Grand.

"Yes?"

"I have them here, my apartment. Carrie and her daughter."

"Jesus Christ."

"Can you get me a car?" Alec asks.

"For tonight?"

"Tomorrow morning."

"Why not tonight?"

"She can't move."

"I'm coming over."

"Harvey, no. Just the car, please. We're okay for now. In a new apartment—as you advised. Phil has no idea where we are."

Alec hangs up and regrets it. *Why didn't I accept his offer of protection? Stupid pride?* His brain isn't working well, but he thinks, *If we don't leave here, it wouldn't have helped, bringing in Harvey. Either we all die or no one does.*

Sarah's wide eyes are watching him. "How come you got a sword?" she says, pointing to Jocko Rush's gift hanging above her on the sofa wall. "Do you fight bad guys?"

"Something like that." He flops down next to her. "How 'bout some apple juice?"

"Can I see it, the sword?"

"Sure," he says, bringing it down from the wall.

She carefully touches the sword handle, attracted by its spiral striations of turquoise and amber mesh. "Is it very sharp?"

"Probably the sharpest sword ever made."

"Could you take it out of that thing?"

"Out of the scabbard, no. Way too dangerous."

"Where's my mommy?"

"Sleeping in the bedroom. Want to go see?"

"Will I wake her up?"

"You might."

Sarah presses her lips together and then shakes her head.

"What about that apple juice?" Alec asks.

"Yes, please."

He brings it to her in a glass. She drinks slowly, measuring him with each sip.

"Hey," says Alec. "Want me to read you a story?"

"*Curious George*," she says without hesitation.

"Don't have that one, I'm afraid, but I do have one I saved from when I was your age. *Peter Rabbit.* Should we try that?"

"Okay."

Alec, finding the book on the shelves, sits next to her and

starts reading. The story holds her in thrall. She especially likes the part where the rabbit is threatened by Mr. McGregor. "Stop thief!" Alec reads with a flourish.

"Again!" says Sarah, her squeal pure delight.

"Stop thief!" Alec reads even more dramatically.

"Again!"

Alec grills a hot dog for Sarah and puts two TV dinners in the oven for Carrie and himself. He ends up eating both dinners alone. Carrie is not to be awakened.

He and Sarah watch television for a while. Alec's bought a new DuMont set, and it's wired to an antenna on the roof that gives pretty good reception. After an episode of *Mister Ed*, Sarah falls asleep again on the sofa. Alec rechecks the door chain, wedges a chair under the handle, and moves a bookcase against the chair. He has little faith in any of these precautions. Even less in the night doorman, whom Alec once caught sleeping, or in the lock on the back door to the building, which can be opened, Alec has discovered, with a penknife. He thinks again about calling Harvey. Then about waking Carrie, and no matter what her protests, dragging her and her daughter off to a car rental office, and speeding out of New York. Then, with anger at his own fear, his thoughts rebound. *Why is it a given Phil knows where we are? And even if he does, it's a crowded Manhattan building. He's not going to commit violence here. Surely not with his kid in the next room.*

Alec stands with his back against the bookcase. He hates being this frightened. He goes into the bedroom, watches Carrie breathing evenly in a deep sleep. *What the hell are we doing here?*

Downtown, Phil dines either at Ponte's in the printing district or Sloppy Louie's in the Fulton Fish Market. Both places have corner booths plated with his name, released to other parties only after eight thirty. Phil shows up by then or not at all, and on

Friday, which this is, only at Louie's.

Normally, Phil invites Vito plus two or three others to sit at his table. Tonight, he's alone but not for long. Little John enters, dispatches his own men, and takes the seat opposite Phil.

The head waiter immediately displays for their admiration a bottle of the house's best pinot grigio. The waiter pours, the men taste and approve. When the waiter leaves, Little John says, "I've been offered a deal. On the diesel matter. U.S. Attorney's Office."

"To give them who, John? Me?"

"Of course."

"This is Sid Kline?"

"That's right."

"And?"

"And! Whatta you mean and?"

Phil laughs. "You gave them nothing. But this thing worries you?"

"It's not so simple," Little John says. "They have other witnesses. Most times, they say that, it's bullshit, but here they know too many details. Someone's talking."

"Then why do they need you?"

"They're not offering me much. They don't expect me to take the deal."

"So whatta we talking about, John?"

"We're talking about somebody talking."

"I doubt that," says Phil.

The large man stares glumly at his wine.

Phil says, "This is Sancerre. It's what he does. He pokes you, gets you to poke me, sits back, sees what happens. If he had something, he wouldn't be playing."

"What about Poole?"

"What about him?"

"He's a direct link."

"And?" Phil says. "That warrants a bullet in the head?"

Little John shrugs.

"Okay," Phil says. "Let's take the case of this guy, Poole. Perfect example. They have absolutely nothing on him or any of the men working for him. We made sure. And we were careful. And while no one other than Poole knows much that Sancerre doesn't already know, no one in the group has any incentive to tell him fuck-all. You start killing people—especially Poole—and suddenly what? You change everything. You double the government resources and scare everybody shitless. I mean everybody. Martini, Raffon, spreads like leprosy."

"They're already scared."

"Right. Scared enough to keep their mouths shut. You let them know we might take them out anyway, we'll scare 'em right into witness protection. You know why?"

Little John frowns.

"You know why?" Phil repeats.

"Don't fuck with me, Phil."

"Because they'll have no place else to go."

"I get the fucking point. What about your wife?"

Phil regards Little John with a cold stillness.

"I hear she's not with you again. Not living in your house."

"She's controlled, John."

"She took your daughter, I hear. You allow that?"

"For a time."

Little John drinks, considers the bouquet, and takes another sip. "Do you know where she is? This very moment?"

"I know exactly where she is."

"Then—"

"My dear friend. Do you think for one minute I'd allow this situation to go uncontrolled?"

"Look," Little John says. "A man and wife, that's personal. I know that."

"I'm glad you do, John."

"But I'm your friend, Phil. I think about your best interests. You could have any woman you want."

Phil waits, says nothing.

"This one—and I say this as your friend, thinking only of your interests—she may be bad for you. The worst kind of woman for someone… such as yourself."

Little John smiles, which creases the fat in his face into rolls. "I have a cat I'm fond of. Not an affectionate animal, but great manners. Very proud, very clean. However, every now and then, he catches another little animal outside and drags it into the house. A mouse, a chipmunk, a bird. He doesn't kill it. Keeps it alive for as long as he can to torture it. Loves to toy with it, cause it pain. It's not an attractive trait. It decreases my love for him."

"I'd get another cat, if I were you," Phil says, while signaling the waiter to come over for their orders.

Little John sits stoically until the waiter leaves. Then he says, "I may do that."

"All right."

"Now we've talked it through."

"And I've heard you," Phil says.

"I'm not sure you've caught my meaning, however."

"Oh, I got it, Johnny. I got it, believe me."

"Don Giovanni agrees with me."

Phil raises an eyebrow. "You and my uncle?" he says.

"We're also related. He and my mother were cousins."

"Second cousins."

"Still blood."

Phil forces a laugh. "I know the man a lot better than you do. I'm fine, he's fine. I talked to him in London."

"Well, he's here now," says Little John.

It was, as intended, a slap in Phil's face.

Phil says coldly, "Here? Where?"

"New Jersey. I set up a house for him."

"You set up a house? He asked you to do this?"

"He did."

"What are you telling me, John?"

"I'm telling you, none of us have any patience left with this situation, Phil. Y'know what that means, no patience?" He gets to his feet, knocking over his chair. "We're not gonna let it keep happening."

Having turned off all the lights, Alec lies down fully clothed on top of the covers, next to the still-slumbering battered beauty in his bed. He listens intently to every creak in the building, every moan of the wind, every twang and strain of the elevator cables, every rattle of the doors. He analyzes each sound for inflections of danger. This night, he thinks, will turn into a nightmare. The point then dawns on him: It already has.

Three hours of listening. The other sixth-floor dwellers have returned home. The elevator stops moving, and the street sounds prevail. From sheer exhaustion, Alec falls into an agitated sleep, despite the near certainty it's not going to be restful.

SIXTY-FOUR

Roughly shaken awake, Alec sees colors. Red for terror. Bright blue in flashes for the screams in his throat. The black feels like drowning, of which Alec was dreaming. Drowning in gasoline, because that's the smell of Vito's meat hook of a hand mashed over Alec's face.

Then flipped, one arm locked behind him, face mashed in the mattress, Alec cannot see the goon holding grips on his wrist and neck. Phil, he can see. Phil turns the light on with one hand, rams Carrie down with the other. Phil with his scalpeled features, workout body, and black silk turtleneck. Phil says very softly, "Either of you wakes the child, you will not walk unassisted from this room." Releasing Carrie, he directs her. "Get your ass outta bed! Now! Do it!"

"Phil, Jesus! I'm not wearing anything!"

"Get the fuck outta bed!" he says, grabbing her and pulling her up by the armpits.

Which is how Alec discovers the kind of hold being placed on his arm. When he struggles, Vito almost breaks it off, pushing Alec's face harder into the mattress. But Alec can, with a wrench of his head, still see Carrie made to stand on the carpet, stark naked, within the full sight of two other men. Reacting, he feels another screeching pain through his shoulders. Carrie's face is dreamy, as if this isn't happening.

Phil says, "You two, I own you now. And you play by my rules. Rule No. 1: Sarah comes with me, and stays with me. No visitation, no weekends, no court battles. You're out of her life. Rule No. 2: nobody testifies. I don't care who subpoenas you; you testify, you die. You think about testifying, you die. Both of you. Got it?"

Not getting an answer, he grabs Carrie by the hair. At her look of pain and blind hatred, he yanks her scalp upward, until, screaming, she dances like a spastic puppet, with flailing arms. "I asked you a question!" he says.

"Okay!"

Released, she collapses to the floor.

"And you?" Phil says, turning on Alec.

"You sick fuck!"

Phil nods to Vito who calmly dislocates Alec's shoulder. With Alec's shriek of pain, Sarah starts crying in the other room. Phil goes to her, Vito in his wake. Alec, despite the agony, crawls after them, seeing how easily his furniture barricade had been pushed aside and the door chain severed.

"Hush, baby," Phil croons to his daughter. Propped on his chest, she peers over his shoulder.

Alec, from the floor, gives her a wink, thinking, *It's amazing what we do for the innocence of children.*

Sarah smiles. "Stop thief!" she exclaims with glee, leaving the apartment in the arms of her father.

Alec blacks out until more pain wakes him.

Carrie has grabbed Alec's arm. "Stay still. I know how to do this."

She pulls his arm straight down hard, popping his shoulder back. He screams and again passes out.

She says to Alec, as if he were awake, "Well, we know what we have to do now."

Alec picks up the car, a four-year-old blue Chevy, at a lot in Flushing. Harvey arranged for the purchase, so Alec knows the engine's reliable. He and Carrie also accede to Harvey's insistent advice:

to take separate routes, on different subways, Alec to Flushing, Carrie to Gun Hill Road in the Bronx. Where Alec, waiting for her as she comes out of the station—thinking all this subterfuge to have been superfluous—spreads a map out on the hood of the Chevy.

He and Carrie had talked through the night, after Alec had regained consciousness, remarkably free of pain.

"It's one of their favorite things," she explained. "No mess, no fuss. Just tremendous misery until the shoulder's popped back in, which is easy enough, if you know what you're doing."

Although he wouldn't have predicted this, it was now fairly clear, Alec thought, what Phil had in mind, leaving them the way he did. Carrie, on her own, might hate Phil sufficiently to try to send him to a prison cell from the witness stand. It was also the simplest way of regaining custody of her child. But it wasn't something she'd do, in all probability, at the cost of Alec's life. So Phil let Alec remain among the living. Killing his own wife, moreover, was never a good risk. Phil had the obvious motivation, to stop her from talking, and no alibi that would stand up. No doubt, he could arrange to be elsewhere at the time she went missing. But who would believe, in any event, that Phil took care of such matters with his own hands?

Given this standoff, Alec thought, he and Carrie could have stayed in New York, but for one thing. There was absolutely nothing to stop Phil from invading their apartment and beating up both of them whenever he pleased.

Again, they talked about witness protection. For Alec, Phil's brutality only strengthened the reasons for putting him in prison and going into such a program with Sarah. It appeared to have the opposite impact on Carrie. She said she simply wanted to flee. And Alec wanted what Carrie wanted. The injury done him would permanently weaken his shoulder. What Phil did to her, short-circuiting her rehab, could trigger the overdose that would end her life.

On the Bronx street, before getting into the driver's seat of the car, Alec folds up the map, looks skyward. The sun is blazing, though the air is cool. "We'll take it in easy stages. Stop outside Boston somewhere."

"No," she says, grabbing the handle to the passenger seat door. "Let's go straight to Maine."

"You can stand that? All that time in the car?"

"I'll deal."

"You know," he says over the roof of the car, "unless something changes, I think we're all right."

"All right?" She looks angry and incredulous.

"I mean, you don't have to surface. My trial, the criminal case. There's another witness. They should leave you alone." Misreading her look, he adds, "Except for the custody proceedings. Which I'll start as soon as I get back to the city. We will get Sarah back."

"Jesus," she says.

"What's the matter?"

"You still think you can fix everything with court papers?"

"You have a better idea?"

Carrie opens the door and gets in. "Yeah," she says. "Buy a gun."

So saying, she slams the door shut.

Phil's on the phone in his study when Vito appears in the doorway. Phil waves him forward, finishes up. "What do you have?" Phil asks.

"Harvey Grand, the gumshoe? Bought a car this morning from a dealer in Flushing."

"The dealer, he's one of ours?"

"No, but he owes us."

"The car wired?"

"Sorry, boss. We got to this guy too late."

"And they've skipped. In the car."

"Looks like. Should we try to get a tail?"

"Waste of energy," Phil says. "In a few days, they'll write a check, use a Diners Club card, register for a new phone, utilities, something. We'll find them. No rush. The farther away they are right now, the better."

Vito stands there thinking. "You knew they'd skip?"

"Of course."

"You wanted them to?"

Phil laughs. "Sometimes, Vito, you surprise me."

Sarah, bursting into the room, goes directly to her father, leaving the nanny in the doorway. "When's Mommy coming home?" she wants to be told.

"Oh, sweetheart! Mommy's gone on a long trip."

"Where?"

"Y'know, I'm not sure right now. But we were just talking about that, Vito and me. We'll have word soon."

"She go with Alec?"

"I believe she did."

"He's funny."

"Yes, he is."

"A real scream," Sarah declares, drawing upon her trove of TV idioms.

"Also true," agrees Phil with a grin.

As Vito heads off, Phil calls him back. "Tonight, we'll need about five men. The best."

Vito again stands motionless. "Carrying?"

"Whatta you think?" says Phil. I say I want the best, I want them useless?"

Abigail's at her desk mid-morning when Sam barges into the Syosset office. "I can't find Alec," he says. "Can't reach him anywhere."

She glances at the wall clock. "He might be on a subway."

"I've been trying him since seven this morning. Office and home."

"He could be out of town, Sam."

"Not according to the office. Where he's expected."

"Let's try the office again."

"I just did. Third time this morning."

Abigail gets up, goes to him, leads him outside into the sun. They stand together in the parking lot. She says, "There's nothing to be done now, Sam."

"I know."

"Ridiculous to go to the police. There's nothing to tell them, except we're afraid, and who we're afraid of."

"I know."

"And for Alec—we have no idea what we're stepping into, interfering with."

"I know, Abby. But it's not a wonderful feeling."

"Helplessness."

"Right. That."

"Let's go in," she says, wrapping her arms around her. "It's starting to get cold."

"Crazy weather."

"Thirties tonight, they're saying."

"Just a front," he says. "Two days, spring again."

"I heard that, right."

"So we're talking about the weather," he says.

"Yeah, Sam. Let's go inside. Bore whoever's listening."

SIXTY-FIVE

Between Providence and Boston, Alec says, "No one could possibly be following us."

"That's probably right," Carrie says, taking another peek out the rear window. "So you want to stop? Is that what you're saying?"

"I could use the sleep."

"Sure, let's stop then." Her voice is dreamy.

"You want to go on," he says.

"I want… I think you know what I want."

He takes his eyes off the road for a second to look at her. "No, I don't."

"Right."

He says gently, "What is it, Carrie?"

She huddles into herself. "I had a bad night too."

Phil and his men travel in two black vans. Vito drives one of them with Phil sitting in front. In the second, right behind them, five armed men are crammed in uncomfortably. Everyone wears black gear and leather gloves. A battle unit, thinks Vito. Men trained in actual combat. This is what Vito loves, what he was born to do. Like the good old days, which weren't that long ago. The days when they clawed back their territory street by street. He'd love to reminisce about that, relive the good times, but Phil's not talking. In one of his moods. It's not nerves. Phil gets cold when he thinks about killing people. And Vito suspects Phil is especially cold now, given who's likely to be on the kill list.

The night itself is cold, maybe just twenty, twenty-five degrees. Crazy weather. Snow in November, thaw in December, then frigid nights in early spring. Everything's fucked up, even the weather. It's keeping the cars off the road, though. The highway is virtually empty. Some sixteen-wheelers—you keep out of their way, let them go by with your headlights shining up their exhausts. Phil wants the heat off, so it's freezing in the van. But it's good to be keyed, psyched. *Coming back*, Vito thinks, *we'll be warm.*

Little John has his own favorite restaurants when dining in New Jersey. He varies the pattern for security purposes, and he expects his principal men to eat with him on these nights.

Their dinners are convivial. Though there's good reason to fear Little John, he's an expansive host who's easily humored by good food and wine and loud jokes at other people's expense. Unlike Phil, who limits himself to a dedicated table, Little John prefers commandeering an entire restaurant. Dining out with his crew, he has an extreme antipathy to civilians.

His new favorite is Buccatoni's, an upmarket *ristorante* atop a hill on a twenty-acre plot near Morristown, run by the young chef Nicky Buccatoni and financed by Little John. For their dinner tonight, the New Jersey boss wants something special to honor his guest, Don Giovanni. So Nicky creates a tasting menu of extraordinary delights. Little John is more than pleased: with the meal, with his investment, and, most of all, with the plangent honor of hosting the family's *éminence grise*.

In about a week, Little John will move in on Phil. It will be bloody, but quick, beginning with the assassination of the capo himself. And it will succeed, Little John believes, because of the planning and because all of the other families will step aside. They will do this, because Don Giovanni has given his blessing.

Little John calls Nicky and his staff out from the kitchen, congratulates them in front of the assemblage and asks his men to comment on the courses they preferred and why. Little John enjoys talking about food. It is, in fact, close to his favorite subject. He suggests they go around the table, with himself going last, and with Don Giovanni choosing the best description.

The men are uneasy. They're not used to having a celebrity in their midst, especially an old man who says little and therefore seems all the more judgmental. They're familiar with Little John's games and will play along. But this kind of verbal description? It's designed to make clowns of them, and they know it.

Joey Sacco leads off. He thinks of himself as a comedian. And he thinks of something clever to say about the gnocchi, so he doesn't dislike the game as much as the others and begins with a smile on his broad face.

Which freezes when Phil and his men stomp in, brandishing MP5 submachine guns.

It is clear what's happening but still a shock. No wasted moves, no banter, Phil's people start shooting at once. Little John, Phil's target, is riddled to death as he attempts to rise from his chair. Some of his group leap up, get gunned down. One almost makes it out of the room before jerking in the air from the impact of volleys from three different weapons. The kitchen staff is slaughtered with the rest. Not a shot is returned. It comes at them too fast. Don Giovanni, allowed to observe nearly to the end, looks Phil straight in the eye and says, "Nephew?" Phil's response is the rattle of his gun, which turns the old man's face into chopped meat.

At the conclusion of the blood bath, only Nicky is left standing. He looks ashen, says nothing, and stares at Phil.

"Collaterals are unfortunate," Phil says.

"Yes," says Nicky.

"We'll let the locals deal with this… carnage. They should be here…. Oh—" Phil glances at his watch. "Five, six minutes. Want a lift?"

"No, I have my car, thanks," Nicky says.

"So you all right?"

"Yeah. Sure."

"Where were you tonight, when all this was happening?"

"My condo. In town."

"That's for certain?"

"Yes!"

"You have someone who can vouch for that?"

"My friend."

"Male, female?"

"Does it matter?"

"No," Phil says with an oddly wistful inflection, and opens fire. The first blast goes into Nicky's gut. When he hits the floor, Phil's second barrage splatters the chef's brains on the carpet.

Phil turns. "Vito!"

"Yes, boss."

"I didn't like his response."

"Yeah. Me neither."

Phil recalls Little John's doodled napkin, appreciates the irony of the sketch. "I think we've been here long enough."

"Car's running, boss."

SIXTY-SIX

In the Massachusetts town of Newburyport, Alec and Carrie find a
room and crash, sleeping until midmorning. Carrie says at breakfast, "I need to find a meeting."

"I'll wait," Alec says.

One call, she finds it, and is back in a little over an hour. On
the road by lunchtime, they reach Down East Maine by nightfall.

Off the highway, on a scenic route, a sign points to a town
named Reefer's Harbor. "Surely," says Alec, taking that road, "the
name of a person, not a crop!"

"One never knows!" sings Carrie, her voice sounding hopeful.

The Inn at Reefer's Harbor has lots of rooms—in fact, all
twelve—available. Springtime in Maine? For vacationers, an
oxymoron.

They expect quaint; they get it. Also quiet, salt air, thick mattress, deep sleep. They breakfast at a place called the Acadia Tea
Room, a few steps from the inn. Everything commercial is on one
side of a narrow street down the middle of the Reefer's Harbor
peninsula. On the other side is the harbor, filled with fishing boats
and some pleasure craft, gulls swooping everywhere, as populous
as Central Park pigeons. The air has warmed somewhat during
the night. On the dock, a white-haired guy in a Forties suit buys
swordfish right off the boats. "For the canneries," their waitress
tells them. She's a pretty nineteen-year-old; the wood-paneled tea
room and its wooden booths, at least a century older.

"This may be it," Alec says over coffee. "No one in New York's
ever heard of this place. And it's close to Augusta and Portland.
With a change of name and a manufactured identity, I could fly

up on weekends."

Carrie gives him a look. She knows the kind of hours he works.

"Some weekends," he amends. When her face turns sour, he says, "What? You don't like it?"

"What's not to like? No friends, no lover, no kid."

"No drugs."

"Ha! Love the irony! Reefer's Harbor, no drugs."

"They're here, Carrie," he says, turning serious. "You want 'em, you can find 'em."

"I know."

"And?"

"Not for today," she says.

"Great." He smiles. "Let's find a house."

"So Phil can find us." As if that were the goal.

"He's not that good."

"Y'know," she says, "I think you're wrong. And when he comes, this time, I'm going to be ready for him."

"We're on that again."

"We are."

"With guns," he says, "it's the good guy who gets shot. The amateur."

"So let's turn pro."

"We both get guns," he says dully.

"Don't kid yourself, Alec. Phil's coming. At some point, he's coming. And when he does, the only thing's gonna stop him is a bullet in the head."

SIXTY-SEVEN

Alec, driving, shifts his glance from the road to the real estate agent, Ariel Huffman, a trim, fiftyish woman with gray eyes and a beak. She looks as at ease with herself as she is with her attire: the sort of colorful, loose-fitting items that can be purchased from an L.L. Bean catalog, and may well have been.

"I know the normal practice," Alec says. "Show clients the white elephants first. Maybe, for us, you'd go right to the house you think we're going to end up taking?"

She appraises him quickly. "In that case," she says, "turn off here."

The wheels screech, which doesn't daunt Ariel. They've turned onto a small country road, the homes mostly hidden by hedges. "There's a place at the Point," she says. "The very end of this peninsula. A tad out of your price range, but, well… you'll see."

They do. A few more turns and several hundred yards away. Rising over a jumble of weed trees and shrubbery, on a hill covered with sea grass that sweeps down to the bay, is a narrow, three-story cottage. It's built like a rectangular lighthouse, high for the view, ringed in fieldstone up to the first-floor windows, otherwise shrouded in weathered gray shingles and roofed in slate. Walking through the front hallway, being stunned by the view of the marsh and the bay from a wall of French windows at the end of the living room, Alec says, "We'll take it."

Carrie says, "Don't you want to see if there are any bedrooms upstairs?"

Alec says, "With this view, that's irrelevant."

Upstairs, in fact, bedrooms abound: three on the second floor, with a small deck outside the master bedroom, and a warren of servants' rooms on the third. The marsh to the south teems with birds, even swans. A football-field-size lawn, rolling west, borders on a meandering seawall, beyond which curls a small half-moon beach on the bay. Northwest there's a twenty-acre estate, belonging, they are told, to a family named Allingham.

"And who owns this place?" Alec asks.

"Boston family," says Ariel, beak tilted slightly, eyes still appraising. "Name of Scanlon."

"Would they consider a rental with an option to buy?"

"I should think so. They're building a larger place, I understand, in Marblehead." With a shrewd look at Alec, "And may be a bit overextended."

Alec turns to Carrie, though still directing his questions to Ariel. "So what are they asking for rent?"

"It's quite reasonable at five hundred a month, off-season."

"And how much more reasonable does your authority allow you to be?"

"I've just reached the end of my authority."

"And Mr. Scanlon?"

"He," says Ariel, "might be fifty dollars a month more reasonable."

"Fully furnished, of course?"

"Of course."

"Done, then," Alec says. "When can we move in?"

"Of course, have to check you guys out."

"Sure," Alec says and grabs a note pad from a desk in the bedroom. He hastily scribbles two names and numbers and hands it to Ariel.

One look, and she exclaims, "You know Jocko Rush?"

"He's my client. The other name is the senior partner in my law firm."

"Would tomorrow be soon enough?" she asks with a grin. "Have to confirm with Mr. Scanlon, get a standard lease form drawn up."

"Tomorrow would do splendidly. And, if you could, sale and option prices too?"

That night at the inn, Alec concedes, "I must have been out of my mind."

"We can't afford it?" Carrie asks.

He likes the "we," but it doesn't lessen the panic. "The problem is paying two rents every month. It'll wipe us out."

"Maybe we should just buy it," Carrie says, not really serious.

"Y'know," he says. "That's not such a crazy idea. Get a mortgage. The monthly payments on that might be less than the rent."

"It's a great house."

"It's a great house," he agrees.

"We can scrimp on everything else," she suggests. "No new clothes. No meals in restaurants."

"You're right," he says. "It's worth it."

Which panics her. "In hock to our eyeballs."

"Look at the bright side."

"The drive from the city being only eight hours?"

"We'll fly up," he says. "Keep the car here."

"What car? Who can afford a car now, let alone airline tickets?"

"If it gets too tight, we can sell in a few years."

"You'd never sell," she says. "You'd rob banks before selling."

"So whatta you think? We back out?"

"You kidding? I'd drive the damn getaway car."

Then they realize what they're doing. Making plans, like a couple.

"Let's just rent," Alec says. "Dealing with a bank right now may not be the smartest idea."

The next morning Alec signs a lease in Ariel's office, then they drive into Augusta for new pillows and linens. Food shopping they do at the market in Reefer's Harbor, which displays a wall of S.S. Pierce canned goods, including one special item, lobster Newburg, on which they feast for dinner. Their new kitchen comes fully equipped. Stove and refrigerator that function, despite being antiques. Table, chairs, flatwear, and dishes, each piece of disparate and ancient origin. The sink's porcelain is mainly intact, and the water runs clean. Ariel had seen to the electricity and telephone, putting both in Carrie's name, which they give as Reilly. Not a problem. People here are generally trusted at their word.

Cleaning up after dinner, making the big double bed, allows them to feel they belong there. With the lights out, they climb under the covers, hold on to each other, see the stars through the windows.

"What's that sound?" Carrie asks.

"I think it's the ocean."

"You can hear the ocean from here?"

"Yeah, I think so. The surf. Sound travels well here, especially at night."

"Good," she says. And they both think the same thing.

Monday morning, Carrie drives Alec to the airport in Portland. Nothing more is said about guns, though they both know that Alec has left her with enough money to buy one.

They are a bit of a spectacle at the gate, but when the plane arrives, Alec gets on it.

SIXTY-EIGHT

Among the many messages Alec finds on his desk are four from his father. Alec calls Sam at the Syosset office.

"Where the hell you been?" his dad wants to know.

"Away. Something I can't talk about."

"Well, I've got something I need to talk to you about. But not on the phone. I'll drive into the city."

"I'm up to my eyeballs, Dad."

"I'll be outside your building when you get home."

"It won't be early."

"Ten?"

"Probably later."

"I'll be there."

At about eleven-thirty p.m., Alec pulls up in a cab. Sam, as promised, is waiting. He's gotten friendly with the doorman and is sitting on a chair in the lobby.

Alec says, "Come on upstairs, and I'll give you a beer."

"Let's take a walk around the block," Sam says. "Your apartment is probably bugged."

When they turn the corner at 5th Avenue, Sam signals to a bench on the park side, and they cross the street to take it.

"You know," Sam says, after they both sit, "I'm now in the home security business."

"So you've said."

"One of our customers is Phil Anwar."

"What?" says Alec.

"It gets worse. I've got a tap on his phone."

"*What?*"

"So I know about you and his wife."

Alec jumps up. "What the hell're you talking about? You've tapped Anwar's phone? You outta your mind? That's suicidal!"

"And sleeping with his wife isn't? He doesn't know about the tap. He sure as hell knows you've run off with his wife."

Alec slumps back to the bench. "You don't understand anything about this, Dad."

"I understand he's going to try to kill you. Do you understand that?"

"Yes."

"And?"

"He won't do anything before the trial. Keeping the threat on me stops his wife from testifying."

"The trial in your case?"

"Yes."

"So that diesel thing, that was Anwar?"

"Right."

"And she was your witness. You got another one?"

"I think so. If I can pry him away from the U.S. Attorney. Which is the subject of our meeting tomorrow. Although he knows nothing about it."

"And how will you protect yourself after the trial?"

"Anwar will go to prison."

"Will he? And that makes you safe?"

Alec shrugs.

"You're not that naïve, Alec. He's the boss whether he's in prison or at home."

"Not if it's a capital crime."

"You're talking about those killings in Morristown."

"Among others," says Alec.

"You got evidence it was Phil?"

"Morristown, no."

"Anything?"

"Maybe."

"Maybe?"

"It's pretty obvious Morristown was Phil."

"There's been no charge," Sam says. "And I doubt there will be. Those were mob executions. Who cares? Also, murder—these kinds of murders—that'll be in the state system. Very slow. Frying Anwar—if ever—it'll take years."

"He killed Carrie's father. Made her watch it."

Sam says slowly, "Did he really!"

"But he might slip out of that one too, at least as a murder-one case."

"Why?"

"Look," Alec says, tired and losing his patience, "how are you even involved in this? I'm doing what I'm doing out of necessity. You? Putting a tap on the man's phone? What the hell is that all about?"

"My own necessity."

"Really? Of what nature?"

Sam sits back. "I suspect very much like yours."

They watch the traffic for a few minutes.

Sam says, "We're going to have to kill the son-of-a-bitch."

Alec's laugh has a bitter taste. "You're worse than Carrie," he says.

SIXTY-NINE

In a long, bent gallery of an office on Foley Square, Ray Sancerre, the United States Attorney, gives phone like a Hollywood agent. The chief of the Criminal Division, Sid Kline, broods at the window. Alec, being shown in by Sancerre's secretary, crosses over to Kline.

"He's on with a *Times* reporter," Sid says under his breath. "The guy works sixteen hours a day, fourteen of them on the phone with the press."

Hardly surprising. Alec had met Ray two years before on a Bar Association committee to which Macalister had had Alec appointed. One night, after a late meeting and a couple of drinks, Ray confessed to Alec his secret ambition. He expected to become president of the United States. As Alec now waits with Kline, Sancerre's once-bizarre fantasy seems not quite so preposterous. After becoming a partner of Marius Shilling's, Ray leveraged a Washington job into the chief prosecutorial position in New York and, within six months, was a media darling. Few prior holders of the office had been this colorful—or accessible.

Close to concluding his conversation, Sancerre smiles and waves at Alec. Then, after a final burst of conviviality, he hangs up, gets up, and greets Alec with a capacious smile. Despite his relentless attempts to enlist others in his ebullience, gloom hangs on this man like a cheap suit.

"Alec, good to see you!"

"You too, Ray."

"Diesel oil, right? That's what gives me the pleasure of your company?"

"Diesel it is."

"Big case! You're about to try it, I gather, with my former partner, Marius, consulting."

"That's right. In a couple of weeks."

"Want some coffee, a Coke?" Ray re-establishes himself behind the desk and buzzes his secretary. "Hold all calls—" wink at Alec—"you can."

"No, I'm fine, Ray, thanks. Actually, what brings me here is that we have a common witness."

"Oh? Who's that?"

"Carl Raffon."

Still smiling, Sancerre says, "Can't allow that, Alec."

"Really? Why's that?"

"Bad timing. Sorry."

Alec catches Ray's wandering eye. "You're not quite ready to indict Phil Anwar?"

Sancerre says, with no further pretense of affability, "You know I can't discuss that."

"Trouble is, Ray..." Alec pauses. "I can't change the timing. And Raffon, for me, is a material witness. So I think the judge will allow the subpoena."

"I don't think Raffon will be around to be served."

"Oh? How's that?"

Ray leans back. "Man does seem to travel. And, Alec. Without my dispensation, Carl does some serious time. No freedom. No license. His life turns to total shit. Think your offer measures up?"

"Suppose—just speaking hypothetically—Raffon did testify first in my case?"

Ray laughs—for the first time, genuinely. It's all the response Alec will get.

Alec says, "What are you worried about? Might look to the press as if we were out ahead of you guys?"

"Come on, Alec."

"I'm wrong? This whole thing's not about PR?"

Black looks. "Careful!"

"If Rosenkranz wins, my clients are bankrupt, fifty thousand people lose their jobs, and thousands of individual stockholders, many of them elderly people, lose their shirts. Rosenkranz doesn't give a shit about that—he personally stands to walk away with millions of bucks—but you ought to care."

Sancerre gazes at Alec for another moment without saying anything. "Is there a question pending?" he finally asks.

Alec, frowning, takes a portable tape player out of his briefcase and places it on the edge of Ray's desk.

"I really hope," says Ray, his words dropping like ice cubes, "that you haven't been taping this meeting."

Alec leans forward and pushes a button on the machine. Silence, except for the playback of Carl Raffon being questioned by Alec and Harvey. When Carl finishes incriminating Phil, Alec stops the tape. "You guys want to hear it again?"

Resumed silence, as if a weighted object had just fallen to the floor.

Ray's question is toneless. "What's the deal?"

"No prior release of this," Alec says. "No prior publicity whatever. I give you fair warning before Raffon has to testify. You get to issue your release that morning, the day before, whenever you want. Take full credit."

"And if that's not acceptable?"

"Then we've got a problem."

"I can't believe this," Sancerre says, looming out of his chair. "You're threatening me?"

"Certainly not," Alec says. "I'm simply giving you notice. I have a subpoena from Rosenkranz, which I'm required by the rules of court to comply with. It calls for everything I plan to use at trial. Up until this moment, I had no plan to use this tape, because I assumed Raffon would testify live to what he said on the tape. So I had no thought of delivering the tape to Rosenkranz.

But now you've given me reason to believe that I have to petition the court immediately, on the strength of this tape, for special discovery to track Raffon down, which means, unless you and I arrive at a deal, I have no choice but to turn it over to Rosenkranz."

Ray sits on the top of his desk. "And what possible incentive would Si have for releasing it to the press?"

"Who knows? But if he's got it, twenty-six other strike-suiters have it. Each has, what? Ten people working on the case? So now you've got more than a couple of hundred people who have listened to the thing and know what Raffon has to say. And at that stage, why wouldn't U.S. Safety itself want to publicize the tape? It shows that the company was swindled by the mob. So you see, Ray, it's not even a question of whether the tape surfaces at trial several weeks from today. You control whether this tape goes public tomorrow."

As soon as he returns to his office, Alec phones Carrie in Maine.

"We've got Raffon," he says. "I simply agreed to let Sancerre put out the press release and take credit for breaking the case. You, my dear, get to stay in Reefer's Harbor."

"I bought a gun," she says.

He says nothing.

"Alec?"

"I heard."

"I said I would. So I went into Portland and did it. A rifle with a box of ammo. Like buying fruit off a pushcart. That easy."

More silence.

"Alec?"

"You know how I feel about guns."

"I'm the one who's up here alone."

"I've told you, the people who get hurt by guns are the people who don't know how to use them. The people who need the protection."

"I've got nothing but time, Alec. I'll learn."

"This is not a great idea."

"I don't agree! Look! Phil's going to show up here. I don't know when, but he's coming. That's not guesswork. I know him. It's certainty. He's got to show us he can find us. Show us—" she mimics Phil's voice—"we belong to him. It's that primitive with him. And I can't live like that. Not anymore. He comes for me, I'm going to shoot the bastard. Okay?"

"What do you want? My blessing?"

"No. I want you. When are *you* coming up here?"

Braddock appears in Alec's doorway like a second sighting of Lazarus. "You'll be in the office this weekend, kid?"

Alec puts the receiver to his chest. "No, I'm out of town this weekend."

"Oh, really! Trial coming up in a couple of weeks, you're going out of town. That's nice."

Alec starts to explain, but Braddock cuts him off. "You're being given a chance. You fuck this up, how many more you think you get?"

"Zero."

"You got that right! Mac wants to see you. God knows why."

Macalister's room in Greenwich Hospital is the size of a luxury suite, with a fourth-floor view of foliage and white clapboard. The patient props himself upwards with a rattle of pulleys and wires. He's shaved, has some color in his cheeks, but his hair is thinner, his face gaunt. "Damn sorry sight. I know. But that's the way it is." Half his body is encased in plaster.

Alec says, "When is that thing coming off?"

"Scary, huh? Couple of days, actually."

"When you getting back to work?"

"Me? Maybe never. Which is too bad for you. You need all the help you can get."

"No doubt," says Alec, taking the Windsor chair at the side of the bed.

"Shilling called," Mac says. "Full of good wishes. Tells me he's offered you a partnership deal, which you turned down."

"That's right."

"Was that smart?"

"I don't know, Mac, was it?"

Mac laughs. "You've been called up from the minors, kid. Win the case, you're Rookie of the Year. Blow it, you'll be dispensing jockstraps in the locker room. No one's going to want you. Especially if your losing looks like it has something to do with that girl."

"So I should win, you're saying," says Alec, deadpan. "Funny, just got the same message from Braddock."

"I'm saying you should reconsider your priorities, Alec."

"I have my priorities straight."

"Really!" Mac says with a withering smile.

"Yeah, I think so."

Macalister again shifts position. "Ben tells me you're not even working this weekend."

"Mac, Jesus! She's just out of rehab. She's up there alone. She goes to meetings in Portland, but Portland's a city. There are dealers all over—"

"Tell me about it! Heroin. Alcohol. It's the same fucking thing. And it's not going to get any easier—I mean, for you— just 'cause she's been clean for a while. Maybe even worse with the strain. But here's the bright side. If you leave her now—and I emphasize *now*—most people would excuse it as a single youthful indiscretion."

"That your advice?"

"Ha! Look at me! You think I'm qualified to give personal

advice? I get out of here in ten days. Then I get to live like a cloistered monk. Outpatient treatment for the indefinite future. That's my penance. You screw up this case, I'm sure they'll figure out something for you."

"You got advice on that? How not to screw up?"

"Yeah, I do, as it happens. That I understand." He sinks back on the pillows. "You know what your biggest problem is? In the case?"

"Of course. We've talked about it. It looks like I'm representing the bad guys."

"Exactly. You represent a corporation. You represent fat-cat directors. They lost money, who gives a shit?"

"Whereas Si Rosenkranz appears as the lawyer for the stockholders."

"Good guys. Moms and pops."

"That's not the real story," says Alec.

"You have the numbers yet?"

"Pretty much."

"And was I right? What I told Rand that day in Bayonne?"

"After the news broke on the Martini story? Almost all the institutional stockholders bailed out, sold off their stock. Left the company in the hands of the individual investors."

"Yes," Mac says. "Yes. I knew it." He reflects for a moment. "So Si's clients are mainly the banks, the insurance companies, and the hedge funds. They're not getting much, but all the little guys in his group get totally screwed, especially if they hold on to all or part of their shares. Because if Rosenkranz wins, this company goes into bankruptcy. And after Si extracts his thirty percent of the judgment, after all the other bankruptcy claimants and lawyers stick in their beaks, the mom-and-pop shareholders—for their stock holdings—get *bupkis*. Zilch. Nada! Not even a viable business, 'cause that's now down the drain. That's reality. That's what you've got to get across."

"Right. And I can hear Si now. 'Whether plaintiff class

members are companies or individuals is not relevant, your Honor.' "

"You'll get it in," Mac says. "Si'll slip. He'll open it up. Just stay focused."

"You think my attention might drift?"

"I think it already has, kiddo. That's what I'm telling you."

SEVENTY

To get from LaGuardia to Portland, one has basically two choices. Take a puddle-jumper with three stops in between, or fly a shuttle to Boston, and switch to a puddle-jumper with one stop in between. Alec books the no-change-of-planes commuter flight. With no sleep in two nights but the catnaps on Braddock's sofa, he figures the three stops won't wake him; he'll sleep all the way.

Carrie wraps herself around him at the gate. Nice greeting. He could sleep in her arms. She drives home, and Alec dozes in the car.

Next morning, sun in the windows, great shower, Carrie makes pancakes, Alec thinks, *fool's gold*. Only a fool would disregard what's waiting for them on the other side of this paradise.

He outlines a pre-trial brief to the trilling of birds. On the deck off the bedroom, in the sun, he still needs a heavy sweater. This is Maine. But the wildlife is stirring in the marsh.

For lunch, they stroll into town. Off-season, the Acadia has plenty of booths. They order the house specialty, lobster rolls. On the shoreline of Maine, it would be stupid to eat anything else.

On the town dock, the same white-haired guy in the vintage suit is sitting on a bench waiting for the boats to come in. Alec and Carrie greet the man as they stroll out on the dock, and he gives them a nod. With his red face, white cowlick and big ears, he appears to be a fisherman dressed up for church.

"They're late today?" Alec asks.

"It's Saturday," says the man, as if that explained it.

"They stay out later on Saturday," Alec says, as if the man's explanation makes sense.

Which seems to amuse him. "You're the couple who rented the Scanlon place." At their look of surprise, he says, "This is not a very large town."

They introduce themselves, and the older man gets up to shake their hands. "Roscoe Harley's the name. And what the men do on Saturday here is harvest their lobster boxes. They'll be in any minute."

"You buy fish for a cannery, I understand," Alec says.

"Swordfish. The cannery's mine."

"You do your own buying."

"I'm not exactly Del Monte."

Carrie says, "Canned swordfish? Kind of unusual, isn't it?"

"Unique," says Roscoe. "I've got a monopoly. The market, however, is not what you'd call huge."

"A specialty item," she says.

"Swordfish in a can," he says, "tends to get mushy. I've got a process that keeps it fresh and firm. Try it. You can buy plenty in the market here."

"Interesting," Alec says.

"Oh yes?" says Roscoe, as if: *Interesting enough to me, all right, but why would you give a damn?*

"For one thing," Alec says, "what do you do with the bones?"

Harley gives him a sharp, suspicious look, then casts an eye up and down the dock, as if not wanting to be overheard. "Why do you ask that?"

"Dunno. Just occurred to me. Might have a use for some."

"Swordfish bones?"

"Yeah."

"Well, it's only the ones I buy from the sports fishermen that come in with bones intact."

"And those?"

"Clean 'em, crush 'em—" Another furtive look. "Dump 'em. Want to take some off my hands?"

"I've seen swordfish skeletons in museums. They're quite

large."

"Some of 'em, yeah. The sword can grow to three feet in length, sometimes more."

Walking back home later, Carrie says, "What was all that about, your sudden interest in fish bones?"

"Just an idea."

"Yes? And?"

"Still working on it. I'll let you know when something not totally ridiculous occurs to me."

Homes are large here, mostly clad in fieldstone and weathered shingles, sitting on two or three acres of rugged tracts, masked by trees and high hedges. Streets are narrow, blanched by winter, and empty.

They walk in silence until Carrie says, "I'm in prison again."

Alec says nothing, letting her finish her thought.

"But this time without my daughter, who I can't get."

"You will," Alec says, but Carrie's not following.

"I've figured it out," she says. "What I want to do is go back to New York, grab Sarah out of school again, and wait for Phil in your apartment every night, with my gun trained on the door. But I can't. Totally unfair to you. I can't let you sleepwalk through this big trial. And if I holed up in another apartment, Phil would probably go to yours first anyway. So I'm stuck up here. Whether the trial gives Phil reason to stay away or come after me—I can argue that both ways. So I wait for him here every night, and I'm the one sleepwalking through days. Kind of an existentialist nightmare, wouldn't you say?"

"We'll get past it."

"Right."

"We will," he insists.

"I'm not disagreeing."

"So let's enjoy what we have."

"You bet," she says.

He's been thinking Phil is happier with Carrie far away from the courthouse, at least until the trial is over, and will leave her alone unless she returns. Whether his butchering of Little John, however, suggests Phil's crazy enough to go after both of them now—that Alec can argue both ways too, and does. So they share the nightmare. Doesn't leave much joy for the days.

Sid Kline, in Phil's study, moves worshipfully from painting to painting. Vito bird-dogs his steps as if waiting for Kline to try to walk off with one.

"This is an amazing collection," Kline says.

"Yeah," says Vito.

"Are there paintings like this all over the house?"

"Look, I don't really want to talk to you, okay?"

"Sure."

Phil walks in. "Sorry to keep you waiting," he says to Kline. Then, "I've got it, Vito."

Phil takes the desk chair, Sid sits in front, Vito leaves with a bulldog mouth, closing the door.

Sid says, "Y'know this could have waited until tomorrow. Coming here on a Sunday night—"

"Better this way. You live on the Island. I'm not planning on being in the city next week. You got something to tell me. Why wait?"

"Indeed. And cutting through all the crap—I know you're not interested in the crap."

"Never the crap. Just the point, Sid."

"We've built the case, is the point. On diesel. We've got you cold, Phil. You're going to have to bargain a plea. In fact, we're closing in on Morristown too."

"Morristown?"

"Mass execution."

"Oh, yeah. Read about it. Isn't that a state matter?"

"Not if part of an interstate conspiracy, which this was."

"You're saying, mob guys?"

Sid smiles. "Yeah. Mob guys. Same mob guys who were in the diesel scam with you and Martini."

"Wow," Phil says with a grin.

"Yeah, it's a lot."

"Well, it's your claim. What we both know is, without evidence—some tangible manifestation of the fact you aren't just blowing this out your ass—right now it sounds exactly like the crap we were supposed to cut through when we started this conversation."

"Obviously, we have the facts."

"Not obvious to me, Sid. And as I just said. Facts—alleged or real—are one thing. Evidence is quite another."

Sid laughs. "True. But in this case, we have the evidence, or I wouldn't be here, Phil."

"Okay, in what form does this purported evidence come? I know you don't have documents, unless you guys wrote them yourselves. You still do that, by the way?"

"No, Phil. Never did. Not in my time."

"Then who's your witness?"

"You know I can't tell you that."

"What? He's going to testify with a hood on?"

"If we go to trial, you'll of course know then."

"Exactly. So why not tell me now? Unless this whole thing is a bluff. You bluffing, Sid?"

"No, Phil, I'm not. I'll tell you this. We have your Swiss bank accounts, with the sudden surges after the diesel thing started. And we have… let me just say, someone in your organization."

"Do you really!"

"Absolutely."

"Man or woman?"

"Woman?" says Kline, caught off balance for a moment.

"Yeah," Phil says. "Witnesses come in two varieties. And

unless you tell me it's not a woman, I'm going to have to assume you've been talking to my estranged wife, who's not exactly trustworthy right now. Nor qualified to testify against me."

Sid looks uncomfortable. "It's not a woman," he says.

Phil glances upward for a moment as if with a sudden thought. "There's something funny about this, right? If you were serious about a deal—"

"We're quite serious."

"Then what are you offering?"

"Big on the money. Very big, to make a splash."

"My money?"

"It's not really yours, Phil. Or, again, I wouldn't be here."

"And that's it? Pay a fine, and proceed past go?"

"We'd blink on Morristown, but there'd be some prison time."

"Like, say, what?"

"It's negotiable."

Phil barks out a laugh. "As I was saying, if you were really serious, you'd have a witness deeply sequestered and you'd be able to give me his name. Because without a name, I can't take you seriously, Sid. You know that."

"I'll tell you what. Unique deal. This off the record?"

"Always."

"You sign a plea bargain which lays out the facts. Then I give you a copy of the witness's sworn confession. If there's any material difference in the story, the plea gets rescinded, and it's never usable in evidence. By its terms."

"This, in your opinion, is a good deal?"

"Best."

"Sid! What are you thinking? I've suddenly gotten stupid?"

Kline looks offended. "Whatta you mean? There's no downside to this deal. And it won't be on the table for long. Train's leaving the station."

"Oh, bullshit. *Train's leaving the station!*" Phil mimics. He sits back, gives the matter some further thought. "You know what this sounds like to me? Sounds like you're jumping the gun. You're not ready. But something's pushing you to act before you are. What is it, Sid?"

"Wrong track, Phil. The offer's a bit unusual, but—I won't kid you—you're a big fish."

"Wait a minute. I see it. The Senate vacancy. Your guy wants to announce. He wants to be senator on my back." He gives Kline a face of mock expectancy. "That's it, right?"

Kline gets up. "Sorry I wasted your time."

"Hell no, you didn't. It's been great. Nothing on tonight nearly this entertaining. Not even Ed Sullivan. I checked. So anytime, Sid. Great fresh material, love it."

Kline's house is a ten-minute drive. He's divorced, lives alone in a five-room ranch, and has one phone which is in the bedroom. He dials an unlisted number.

"Hello?"

"Ray?"

"Who the fuck else?"

"It didn't work," Sid says.

"No surprise."

"We may lose the witness now. We should've put him in the program."

"He wouldn't go, you forget that?"

"We could have pushed him harder on that."

"And lose him," Ray says. "He would have flown."

"So what did we accomplish with this?"

"Sid. How often I have to tell you? We shake the tree."

"And I'm saying, our witness may fall out of the tree. Break his fucking neck."

"So," says Sancerre, as if he finds the subject unendurably boring, "if that happens..."

"What?"

"Right after your meeting with Phil… pretty good inference."

"Jesus, Ray."

"What?" says Sancerre, now losing his patience.

"The guy may be a creep…."

"He's a fucking flake. You think I'm going to risk my career on a lowlife like this coming through? Examined in the civil case first? I didn't like the whole setup. Did you like the setup?"

"I don't really like setting *him* up."

"You didn't hand over his name, did you?"

"Of course not."

"Then stop worrying. How's Phil going to identify him? There are too many possibilities. Besides, he's not likely to move on the guy right away. For the reason I said. It's too soon after his conversation with you. He'd be the obvious suspect."

"That right?" Sid says. "What about Morristown? A fucking blood bath. Who the hell's a more obvious suspect than Phil? You see him nervous about that? And why the hell should he be? We know goddamn well it was Phil. But can we prove it? We don't have shit."

"You getting upset, Sid? Over that… flake?"

"It's not about the flake."

"Oh?" Kindly tone, wanting to understand. "What's it about?"

"It's about the process, Ray. Our process."

"We live in the world, Sid. Our process is of that world. And it's a tough world. No one should ever think otherwise. Least of all the flake."

"Who, after all, isn't reliable enough from our standpoint."

"That's right."

"So we throw him out of the boat."

"Now who's mixing metaphors?" Ray says. "We're not throwing anybody."

"We're not exactly protecting the man."

"That's his fault."

"And he should know it?"

"He does know it. I guarantee it."

Silence.

"All right," Ray says. "I'll have someone call him. Re-offer protection."

"Who… will you have make the call?"

"Why? Now you don't trust people in our office?"

Sid, ignoring this, asks, "We have anyone else even close? Another witness?"

"I'm working on it, Sid. Still working on it."

SEVENTY-ONE

Vito and Joey Forcaccio snare Carl Raffon fleeing. He's downstairs from his one-room apartment on a side street in the Lower East Side. Having just packed up the trunk of his Oldsmobile convertible, Carl rushes to get the key into the ignition and instead fumbles it onto the floor. Vito and Joey don't bother forcing the door. They slice open the canvas top of the convertible and pull Carl up and out of it, with Carl squirming in their grasp like a weasel. People stare and keep going, despite Carl's screams. Getting involved isn't safe in New York and it's considered to be very time-consuming.

Across town, Phil is waiting in an old refrigerator room in the meat-packing district. The butchery once there has shut down. But meat hooks are still affixed to the walls and dangle from ceiling trolleys.

Phil doesn't have to wait long. Vito and Joey arrive with their prey before schedule. Carl's been cuffed by the boys and held upright. He'd be screaming still, except they've taped his mouth. But his eyes bulge. A mistake Carl makes. It gives Phil an idea.

He says, "You know what happens to pigeons, Carl. Bad things happen to pigeons. So guess what, pigeon? They're about to happen to you."

A loud hum of protest erupts from the now thrusting, frenzied figure being held by the two men.

Phil proceeds. "I think we should make a statement here. I want what happens to you to be graphic. People should be moved by your plight. I want them not only to understand it intellectually, but to feel it. You know what I mean?" Phil waits. "Probably not. So try to stay with me. You see those meat hooks. I'm gonna yank one into the back of your head and thread it through one of your eyes. If I miss, I get another chance. In golf, we call that a mulligan. In Latin, we call it an *in terrorem* effect."

Carl lunges with all the force in his body against the clamp of the henchmen, which leaves him sagging on his knees on the cement floor.

"Take the tape off, Vito. Carl wants to tell us how he's feeling about all this."

Vito's method of tape removal isn't gentle, so Carl has further reason to scream.

"You've understood what I just told you?" Phil says.

"Phil, Jesus! I haven't told anybody a damn thing."

"Wrong tack, Carl."

"All the good work I've done for you, Phil. You wouldn't do this."

"Do what?"

"What you just said."

"You think I'm joking?"

"You're not that… vicious."

"A challenge!" says Phil. "Whatta you think, boys? Am I joking, bluffing?"

Neither say anything, but Vito shakes his head, no.

"Put the tape back on," Phil says.

SEVENTY-TWO

For Alec, the plane ride Monday morning is a bit of an out-of-body experience. He's flying to New York, but part of him never leaves Maine. In his mind, he's still clinging to Carrie. Like she clung to him at the gate.

At LaGuardia, he doesn't get far. No further than the newspaper rack of the Union News kiosk. There's Carl Raffon, big as life, on the front pages of the *Daily Mirror* and the *Daily News*. Except Carl's no longer living. According to the story, he was found hanging from a meat hook in a freezer on Jane Street. The hook was rammed into the back of his head, out through his left eye.

Alec buys both papers. "Typical of a gangland execution," the *News* article reads. And, obviously, a warning to other prospective witnesses. Alec knows of only one.

So does Shilling, whose call comes in as Alec opens the door to his office. "We'll need the girl now, Carrie Madigan."

Alec's tone isn't pleasant. "You think the Angiapellos have run out of meat hooks?"

"I have that covered, no fear. As it happens, I was at a dinner party this week with my former partner, Ray Sancerre."

Alec now totally loses it. *"You told Sancerre about Carrie?"*

"Alec, what's the matter?"

"You fucking crazy? You trying to get the girl killed?"

"On the contrary. Ray will put her in the witness protection program, which I'm told is damn good."

"Yeah? Whatta you suppose Carl Raffon thinks about that?"

Alec hangs up, furious, blood pumping. He gives it a minute, then dials Carrie in Maine. Tells her about Raffon, Shilling, Sancerre.

"So you've got no witness," she says.

He says nothing.

"Me then!" she says. "I'll come back, nail him, get Sarah back, go for witness protection."

"You're safer not testifying. Just sit tight. As yet, no one knows how to find you."

"Not testify."

"That's what I'm saying."

"I don't testify, you lose your case."

"Ri-ght. Just what I want—to risk your life so I can win my case. Phil killed Raffon two days ago. If he were worried about you and knew where you were, he'd have been there by now."

"What about all those people—you said, thousands—who will lose their jobs, their savings?"

"So I won't lose," he says. "I'll figure something out."

"Alec?"

"Yes."

"As soon as this is over, no matter what the outcome, I'm getting my daughter back."

"Yes."

"Even if I have to grab her and wait for Phil with my gun."

"It won't come to that."

"But if it has to?"

"Trust me, please. I will figure this out."

At U.S. Safety, in a large office with a view of New York Harbor, Alec and two younger associates are preparing Brett Creighton to testify at trial, when Alec's secretary transfers a call from Ray Sancerre. Alec takes it in Creighton's adjoining conference room.

"Alec," says Sancerre. "Think we need another face-to-face."

"Tied up, Ray, sorry. I'm with witnesses every minute until we start the trial."

"Carrie Madigan. You know where she is?"

Alec, off guard, doesn't answer.

Ray says, "I know you know who she is, Alec. Your firm's gumshoe made a deal on her behalf with the ADA handling her drug case. So, you know where she is?"

Alec now doesn't hesitate. "No."

"We can make the same deal we made on Raffon. You get to call her first in your case."

"Fine," says Alec. "You find her, I'll call her."

"Why is it I'm feeling you're blowing smoke up my skirt?"

"Overly cynical?"

"I can subpoena you."

"And waste both our time."

"Lie to me under oath, I can put you away."

"Nice threat," Alec says. "Nice story. Telemarch would love it."

Pause.

"All right, Alec. I'll find her," says Ray. One could hear his mind working—the impulse to deliver his pet lecture on obstruction of justice warring against the Telemarch threat. He hangs up.

Alec calls Carrie. "Stock up on groceries," he says.

"I know. I was halfway out the door when you called."

"Sancerre is unleashing the bloodhounds. As U.S. Attorney, he gets the cooperation of every local sheriff in the country. In about two hours it won't be safe to be seen anywhere there are cops."

"I know this, darling."

"Okay, I won't hold you."

"You may hold me as much as you like," she says.

"This," he says, "is getting extremely sappy."

"Wish to contribute?"

"Go!" he says.

"I'm out of here."

"No, wait. One more thing. I want to ask you to do something you'll consider weird."

"I don't know, darling. I've got quite a range."

"Remember that guy we met on the dock... what was his name? Roscoe Harley."

"The swordfish man."

"Right," he says. "Make him an offer. Say we'll be willing to take delivery of about two hundred skeletons, not crushed."

She says nothing for a moment. Then, "You're kidding, right?"

"No. Not kidding."

"You've thought of something not ridiculous to do with them?"

"I have," he says. "But I'm going to have to show it to you."

"This is a test," she says.

"Of faith."

"Where'd you like 'em?"

"Backyard?"

Alec is meeting with the younger associates when he's summoned to Braddock's office. "With the team?" Alec asks Madge, who's delivered the summons.

"He said you. I'd come alone."

Alec heads for the senior partner's office.

"You working this weekend?" are the first words out of Ben's mouth delivered over the morning's *New York Law Journal*. Tilted back, newspaper up, legs sprawled over a corner of the desk, the former judge is a half-hidden figure.

"Not here," says Alec.

The newspaper comes down. "Really. Not here. Where your team is. Where the documents are. Where you could have the witnesses, if you wanted them."

"I don't need them. Or the documents. Or the team."

Ben's legs hit the floor. "You know what you're doing?"

"Yes."

"You're setting up a situation where, if you win, you're okay. Marginally, because you winged it, but okay, because winning excuses much. You lose, which is the far more likely scenario…."

"And I'm gone."

Braddock wags his head mournfully. "Gone? You're unemployable. You're toxic fucking waste. After you win ten, twenty big cases, maybe you can afford to boot one. At your stage, for you to break in… you need this win. The firm needs it—for trusting you—and for redeeming an unforgivable mistake. Almost half the service staff of this office, the secretaries, the messengers—you know what they've done?"

"Yes, but I didn't know you did."

"Don't kid yourself, son. Ain't nothing goes on here I don't know about. You lose this case, those poor bastards will be wiped out."

Alec says, "I can't be here this weekend."

"You mind telling me why?"

"Sorry. I can't tell you why."

Braddock gives him another sorrowful wag of the head, and the re-raised newspaper is a signal to get out of his office.

At the airport gate, Alec says to Carrie, "That disguise is ridiculous." She's wearing a blond wig.

She kisses him on the mouth and whispers in his ear, "I walked by six cops who are looking for a dark-haired woman. They hadn't a clue."

Making for the front entrance of the terminal, Alec says, "I thought we'd agreed I'd take a cab."

"Actually," says Carrie, "I don't know what you're doing here. Don't you have a case to try next week?"

The car is parked a few feet away. "I have to deal with the fish bones. You got them?"

"You're not going to believe it."

"You didn't get them?"

"Oh, I got them all right," Carrie says. "You've never seen any-one as happy as Roscoe to deliver anything. What you won't be-lieve is what they look like in our backyard."

Close viewing is put off until morning, although the stench of dead fish pervades the night, as does the howling of every cat in the neighborhood. Twin mounds of skeletons. Hundreds of them. Many with heads, many in bits. Like an offering in the sunrise to a sea god.

They find a wheelbarrow in the basement. It takes them hours to cart the bones down to the small beach in front of the seawall. It takes the rest of the day to sort out the whole ones, clean them and lay them out on the lawn to dry. The local hardware store has fulfilled Alec's order. He makes the pickup early that evening. Gets some looks hauling the cans out of the store. But this is Maine. No one questions his need for ten gallons of phosphores-cent paint. People like their walls to glow in the dark, that's their business.

Sunday is cloudless. Alec and Carrie roast as they work in the full glare of the sun. The basement had offered up not only the wheelbarrow but an old tub they also haul down to the seawall, and then fill, for starters, with four gallons of the paint. Dipping all the bones in the tub and drying them in the sun take them to midafternoon. Then the big job: dispersing the painted bones over the marsh.

That night, Alec and Carrie go up to a third-floor window to admire the effect. It's dazzling, literally. In a random pattern, throughout the marsh, the swordfish bones luminesce in the moonlight with a light greenish sheen, as if the marsh itself were an organism being X-rayed. Or a parchment of celestial runes.

"Takes one's breath away," says Carrie.

"Yes."

"Quite an artistic conceit."

"Anything moves in that marsh," Alec says, "it breaks the plane of fluorescence. And we'll see it. Better than depending on lights, whose wires can be cut."

"But why swordfish bones?"

"Because of the artistic conceit," he says.

She looks up at him dubiously.

SEVENTY-THREE

Back in New York, on the day before trial, a fissure in Alec's composure tears open, and panic flows in. The verdict against him is ruinous—to the stockholders, the Kendall, Blake service staff, and Alec personally. The newspapers mock him. The firm fires him. No other will have him. Carrie leaves him. Phil tracks him down....

What stops the free fall is anger. At himself for his weakness. At Phil for sadistic brutality. At Si and his smarmy troupe, painting themselves as the champions of their own victims, and getting away with that fiction—getting rich on it—in case after case.

Alec calls Carrie, looking for calm.

"What's it like up there?" he asks.

"Lonely. What do you think?"

"I meant outside."

"You trying to trick me? I do go outside. Around the house. No one sees me, don't worry."

"I'm sure it's fine," says Alec, wondering whether it really is.

"You worried about your bones? *Dem bones, dem bones,*" she sings.

"Still in place?"

"Still there. Still beautiful. And they protect me. I can see if a chipmunk moves out there. A field mouse!"

"A large rat."

"Blow his head off!" she says, jest ending with a grim little tone-twist.

They're silent for a moment.

"Almost over," Alec says.

"I know."

"We'll come through this, have Sarah back, be all right, you'll see."

Another silence.

"Carrie?"

"I know. Just do it!"

Rosenkranz's final settlement offer is delivered that afternoon. A meeting to consider it is scheduled for Gen. Rand's office. On arriving, Alec is surprised to learn that it's a meeting between only the two of them. Rand has already gotten Creighton's opinion, and Shilling's.

"And what do they think?" Alec asks.

"I'm not telling you."

Alec laughs. "Which way do you think it would push me?"

"I figure you for a contrarian."

"In fairness, sir, almost no one tries these cases. No one wants to. Either side. The risks are too high before a jury, and there's too much at stake. Also, Rosenkranz and his crew are finally down to where the insurance companies want to settle."

"And is that what you want?"

"Personally?"

"Yes."

"Of course not."

"Right," says Rand. "And you know what paying out four-hundred-million would do to our rates?"

"Up fifty per cent?"

"Try double that. Maybe triple. Which we can't afford. We're in twelve different businesses operating at the margin. We need low insurance rates to succeed. U.S. Safety is mainly a banking and small-manufacturing operation. We do not make large profits. We do need insurance, and it's not an insubstantial part of our costs. Double our rates, I sincerely doubt we'd survive long term. Triple 'em? We wouldn't last four years."

Rand stands up, goes to the window. "Come here," he commands, and Alec joins him. "Those people down there," Rand says. "Scurrying around. Most of them work for people like me. I make bad calls, they pay. I don't like that. Especially if the decision I'm making is to bail out my own ass by settling with insurance money. You getting my drift?"

"I am."

"Do you know the average length of time our employees have worked for the company?"

"No."

"It's the longest of any company on the Big Board. Over sixteen years. That's our average. That includes brand new employees. Which means most of our work force has been with the company for more than twenty-five years, many for thirty-five years. You think I'm going to put those people out of work with an improvident settlement?"

"No."

"Right. So you tell me. Now. On the eve of trial. Are our chances of winning this case realistic?"

"They are."

"I don't want bullshit," Rand says. "I want an honest appraisal."

"I've just given you one."

"Do you believe you'll win?"

"I do."

"Then, goddamnit..."

"Do it."

"Right! Do it!"

SEVENTY-FOUR

A bigail is planning a romantic picnic. *To take our minds off things,* she thinks, *to live!* One of the estates she services has a strip of sand on Long Island Sound. The owners, still in Palm Beach, called Abby for additions to their security system before their return to New York. The job is done on a balmy spring day which ripens into a sultry evening. When they wrap the work, she surprises Sam with a basket of food and a blanket for them to sit on.

The mood, however, isn't as cheerful as she had hoped.

"Okay, Sam, what?"

"Food's terrific."

"Cold lobster, yeah, I should think."

"Alec's trial starts tomorrow."

"I'm sure he'll do great," she says, snapping a claw off.

"Yeah, he's a smart kid."

"So?"

"So. Whatta you think? It's like watching a time bomb set to go off in his lap who knows when."

"You're talking about Phil. But he's made no move."

"He will."

"You've heard something more?"

"No," Sam says, spreading his hands on the blanket. "Phil hardly ever uses that phone now. It's who he is. His history."

"All right… so where's this going?"

"Where? Where can it go? Alec needs protection."

"Which you're thinking you'll provide?" she says in mounting decibels of incredulity.

He doesn't like the tone and doesn't respond.

"You're saying that Phil has to be removed as a threat."

He looks past the small beach over the flat water of the sound. From here, Connecticut is a purple blur. "Permanently," he says.

"Oh, Christ," she moans.

"There's some other way?"

"Well, that way's kinda outside your range, don't you think?" Sam shrugs.

"Even if you didn't get yourself killed, and somehow got him, they'd charge you with murdering the guy. Think of the irony!"

"It'd be self-defense. I'd make sure of that."

"You told me when we first met—"

"I know," he says, catching her eye. "But remember… I made a distinction. Between protecting myself and someone else."

"So whatta you going to do, Sam?" says Abigail, now angry. "Live in some closet in his house until you can jump him with a gun?"

"Maybe."

"What am I talking to, a crazy man?"

"How would you handle it, a guy who wants to kill your son?"

"I'd go to the cops. That's what you do."

"Cops, great. Phil and his family have been killing people for forty, fifty, maybe sixty years. It's the family business. You think his father went to prison? His grandfather? Or Phil himself? And you think my showing up at a police station's going to send him there? More likely be a death warrant for the both of us."

Abigail finally puts the claw down, having done nothing with it but wave.

"All right, look," he says. "I'm sorry. You went to trouble over this meal."

"You're making me sick," she says.

"I'm sorry."

"I'm already a widow."

"You think of me that way?"

She looks at him with horror.

"I don't mean as dead," he says. "As a husband?"

"You've got all the privileges."

"And none of the obligations, you're saying."

"I understand you're worried about your son…."

"I'm better trained than you think."

"Trained? You're one guy!"

"I was in the Army."

"What? You never told me."

"Nothing much to tell. It didn't go anywhere. But I learned how to use weapons."

"When? Thirty years ago?"

"Not quite."

"Sam! Think about what you're doing here. Think about… me."

"I am," he says. "Believe me. I think mainly about you."

"Oh, yeah?" She looks right at him. "Then stop thinking about what you've been talking about."

"I think we should get married."

It takes her a second to react. "Helps if you're living."

"Don't worry."

"Right. As if what? There's nothing to worry about?"

SEVENTY-FIVE

In the courthouse elevator, Alec ascends slowly with a pride of lawyers. They don't know him, wouldn't care if they did, are submerged in their own cases, weighed down by their own concerns. Each man, breathing heavily, lugs a file folder full of documents under one arm with a briefcase dangling from the other. For nearly unendurable seconds, all are trapped in a graffiti-marked, battle-scarred, claustrophobia-inducing box. When the door opens, they scatter—to the dilapidated courtrooms to which the most prosperous city in the world relegates the administration of justice.

Alec enters Justice Kaye's courtroom. It holds a mob scene of lawyers, paralegals, reporters, courthouse gadflies, and court personnel. Shilling is there, and, since he goes almost nowhere unaccompanied, is surrounded by his entourage. He has no function here other than to kibbitz, yet has more lawyers with him than Alec's entire team, which consists of two first-year associates. Making his way to the counsel table, Alec greets them tensely.

They merely nod in the midst of unpacking. First-years have one function at trial. Manual retrieval. Something comes up for which lead counsel needs a document, or a line of testimony in a deposition, the associates' job is to find it. Instantly. And they do, more often than not. Because they think their careers depend on it. And because they think their lives depend on their careers.

Braddock is also there, watching. Not from the counsel table—that would undermine Alec—but from the second row. Alec, spreading his papers on the table, glances back at him. Braddock's expression would be appropriate at a funeral.

Rosenkranz makes his entrance, trailed by his motley band.

He greets those in his path—mainly reporters—like a politico working the tables. His entrance gives rise to a buzz in the room, a heightened expectancy that moves the crowd to fill up the rows of seats. Alec thinks for the hundredth time, *How do these guys get away with it?* As a result of the machinations of strike-suiters like Si, thousands of stockholders are suing themselves for the privilege of paying the lawyers.

"*Oyez, oyez,* the Honorable Justice Jacob Kaye, presiding! All stand!"

Everyone does, with soles scraping vinyl, bags shifting, the judge swooping in, the ritualistic chorus from the lawyers, "Good morning, your Honor."

"Good morning, gentlemen. Be seated, please."

The bailiff is already herding twelve prospective jurors into the box and twelve alternates into the first row of benches. Judge Kaye begins delivering his set speech of which Alec, at the table furthest from the jury box, can hear very little.

The room is high-ceilinged, with big windows and horrendous acoustics. Microphones, though prevalent at concerts and riots, have yet to be introduced in courtrooms. Lip-reading is helpful if the speaker is looking your way. Kaye, naturally, is facing the jury.

Alec studies the group and the information sheet identifying them by address and occupation. Seven women, five men. All remarkably attentive to the judge. Five of the women are middle-aged, one elderly, one, a model, young and quite pretty. The men range from white-collar to blue, to a guy actually wearing a sweatshirt. There are two Asian women, six Caucasians, and four blacks, the latter groups equally divided by sex.

Rosenkranz is invited to examine. State system. Lawyers, not judges, conduct voir dire. And abuse it. Unless judges crack down. Kaye, however, will let Si do what he wishes, barring the outlandish. So, under the guise of voir dire—which is designed to check out the objectivity of jurors—Si begins making his first opening argument—which, of course, is designed to prejudice them in his favor.

Si is smooth, easy to like, with his crinkly grin, going for simplicity. He says, in order to know whether any prospective juror might be prejudiced by any aspect of the case, he has to tell them the "facts." Which are, according to Si: more than a billion dollars of oil allowed to disappear—and with it the investment of his clients—because of the recklessness of this huge corporation and its elitist board in getting involved in this high-risk, low-profit business, in not taking the most rudimentary precautions, and in hiring, as manager, a notoriously incompetent crony of one of its directors. Might these "facts," Si asks, bias any juror against his clients?

Not a word, of course, by Si identifying his real clients as the financial institutions that dumped their U.S. Safety stock upon learning of the swindle. Nor is Alec, who now stands to conduct his own voir dire, free to shed light on that subject. Si has not opened it up. He has simply left the implication that he's representing the "little guy."

So Alec says, "Okay. Now you've heard one side of the case. Let me ask you the most important question I can ask. Is there anyone here who feels he or she can't keep an open mind until hearing the other side?"

No one would admit to such close-mindedness, and no one does.

Alec next tells them a bit about the warehousing business, acknowledges that running it profitably would require some competence, but then asks everyone to open his or her mind to another point. "This case, as you will see by the end of the trial, has nothing whatever to do with the facility manager's competence. It has everything to do with the man's honesty. To explain," says Alec, "let me put these three questions. Suppose you own a storage tank facility in another state, and you call up the manager and say, 'Charlie, that third tank from the left—I'd like to know whether there's oil in there, or whether it's empty.' To get an answer you can rely on, how smart does Charlie have to be? All he's got to do is look inside the tank. This is not rocket science. What you need from Charlie is for him to call it like it is. Second, if you need Charlie to be honest, who would you pick? Someone you or your partner knew well and believed to be honest, or some individual neither of you had ever met? And third, would you, as a juror, be prejudiced against someone who answered these questions the same way I'm guessing you just did?"

Alec then seeks and gains the court's permission to poll the prospective jurors individually on whether any would be prejudiced against his clients because one was a large corporation and another a famous war hero. As each juror rises and swears to the absence of bias on either count, Alec, out of the corner of his eye, sees Si give a grudgingly admiring nod.

During a brief recess, Alec, still seated at the counsel table, finds Judge Braddock looming over his head. Alec knows the question in the senior counsel's mind.

"No challenges," Alec says.

"Reasoning?" asks Braddock.

"I like the mix, and no one's extreme."

"There are poor people on there."

"Doesn't bother me," says Alec.

"That's it?"

"No. You challenge, you run the risk of resentment. Some juror left on will identify with the guy you bounced off. And figure out you did the bouncing. Especially if it's a poor person."

Braddock, turning, goes back to his seat. Had he disagreed, Alec figures he'd still be there.

Si, for whatever reason, has apparently arrived at the same conclusion, not to strike anyone. He and Alec inform the clerk.

"*Oyez, oyez!*" The judge swoops back in. Five-minute recess to the second. Kaye's showing off for the press.

"I understand there are no challenges," says the judge. "I will therefore swear in the jury."

He does, and every member of the jury seriously incants the oath.

"Mr. Rosenkranz, you may begin your opening statement."

As if he hadn't already delivered one.

Si goes slowly to the lectern, conspicuously without notes. He repeats unabashedly—then hammers—his major themes.

Alec shows nothing. He's learned this from Mac. No grimacing, no scoffing, no expression of any sort. And no note-taking. You just sit there. You wait patiently. You hear of your clients' "greed," their "indifference," their "cronyism," their "reckless departure from the standard of care that stockholders have a right to expect of directors," and you say nothing, show nothing, react in no way at all. Until it's your turn. And then—

Alec walks to the lectern. Not as slowly as Si did, but also without notes. He thinks how much more effective it would be to stride to the rail of the jury box and speak right in their faces. But only movie judges allow this. In real courts, you address the jury from a distance. It's up to you to form the words to bridge that space.

There are certain things a defendant's lawyer must say, and Alec says them. Like telling the jury whom he represents. Like noting that the plaintiffs have the right to open and close—first word and last—which is meant to be, and is, a terrific advantage. "Why them, not us? Because they have the burden of proof! This is their lawsuit. They've claimed it, now they have to prove it. We don't have to say anything at all.

"But we will," Alec stresses. "We want you to hear the whole story, not just part of it. And, as we talked about before, for you to be objective and fair, it is important for you to keep an open mind until we've had our turn. Until all the evidence is in."

He stops to make sure all eye contact is still in force. It is. This jury is alive. Ready for his most important point.

"It's up to you to judge the credibility of witnesses. You are the sole judges of whether a witness is lying or telling the truth.

And in judging credibility, you are entitled to use your common sense and experience."

He pauses again. "Credibility is a critical issue in this trial. Plaintiffs are resting their case on a key witness, the manager of the oil tank storage facilities. Two years ago, when we hired him, we had no reason to doubt his honesty. But a lot has happened in two years. Now we certainly do have reasons to doubt his honesty and his testimony, and we will show those reasons to you. And if you're not persuaded he's telling the truth—if you, too, doubt his testimony—then you should find for the defendants. For without this man's story, plaintiffs' case falls apart. And as I've said, and as his Honor will tell you later—plaintiffs have the burden of proof."

All jurors are attending to what Alec is saying, but the guy in the sweatshirt is frowning. Already, he's not buying it. He likes Si. On the other hand, the pretty model is giving Alec a look that says, "I'm on your side." This happens. Alec knows. Jurors go with the lawyers they like. Decisions based solely on the evidence are myths. So, however, is consistency. Minds change.

"Now let me get to the facts," Alec says, looking straight at the model, not at the guy in the sweatshirt. Alec knows he's not going to win him over; she is. Inside. Where she can say things— at length—that Alec could not get away with.

"We are dealing here with a gigantic swindle, pulled off by a man named Sal Martini and the thieves who conspired with him. A lot of people lost money, including my clients. If my clients had actually been reckless in allowing it to happen, then they would deserve the blame, and perhaps the ruination of their lives and their company. But if this swindle happened because a person they had reason to trust conspired with crooks to defraud them, then my clients are the victims of the fraud, not the perpetrators—and no more blameworthy than any other victim."

Alec nods to Harvey, who rises from his seat in the back row and opens the doors to the courtroom. In march two messengers from Kendall, Blake, carrying a twenty-foot steel rod which, with everyone's eyes on them, they bring to the courtroom well and place in Alec's hands.

"Careful with that, counsel," cautions the judge.

"I have it, your Honor. It's very light." Alec turns back to the jury. "Diesel oil, as I'm sure you know, is stored in huge storage tanks. Each tank has a door at the top. Why? So you can open it up and find out what's inside. You do that—" Alec hoists the rod over his head—"by sticking one of these long poles down there to make sure there aren't any false bottoms. And by checking when you pull the pole out, to see what's on it." He rests the pole on the floor.

"Not very complicated, is it? You stick the pole in, you pull it out, you look at it, you touch it, you know—you absolutely know—whether you've got oil in there, or water, or air. Or maybe, even, a false bottom.

"Plaintiffs say that our not learning that Sal Martini filled these tanks with saltwater—or created false bottoms—was grossly negligent. I say, ladies and gentlemen—and I think you will find—that we weren't negligent—we were robbed! For empty tanks to be reported to us as full ones, Martini needed the full criminal collusion of people we were entitled to trust. In other words, we were the victims, too. We were conspired against. And if you understand, from the evidence, as I think you will, that that is what happened—or if plaintiffs fail to prove it didn't— then, based on the instructions as to the law his Honor will give you at the end of the trial, you must find for the defendants."

Alec spots Braddock who gives a barely perceptible nod. It means—and Alec so understands it—you've said enough, sit the hell down!

"Thank you, ladies and gentlemen," says Alec. "I know you'll do your jobs."

As Alec returns to his seat, Justice Kaye turns abruptly to Si.

"Mr. Rosenkranz, call your first witness."

"Thank you, your Honor," Si says, rising. "Plaintiffs call Brett Creighton, the Chief Operating Officer of U.S. Safety."

SEVENTY-SIX

In a private dining room of an eating club three blocks from the courthouse, the defense team lays siege to a buffet lunch. A small television in the corner drones local news, which only Harvey Grand is watching. Marius Shilling does most of the talking, to which no one gives much attention. Alec ignores him completely while trying to think through his examination of Creighton. Then Shilling asks Alec a direct question. "How will you get that analysis in, the one we did of the stockholder list? The one showing how all the funds sold out?"

Everyone turns to Alec who takes a moment to refocus. "Not through Brett," he says bluntly. "At least not now, not on cross. Probably, in our case-in-chief."

Shilling looks unhappy. "Why not offer it now? Brett's our best witness. And why call him back?"

"Kaye won't take it now."

"Why not?" asserts Shilling.

"Because Si hasn't opened the subject, Marius," Alec says with asperity.

"You think," says Shilling, in a patronizing tone, "that we're not allowed to identify the members of the plaintiff class?"

"That's right. We're not. Class reps, yes; other members, no. So unless something happens to change things, the judge won't take it now. It's beyond the scope of the direct." Alec turns to Creighton. "On the other hand, Brett, there is something you can do now that might help us when we offer it later."

"Oh, shit!" exclaims Harvey, riveted on the TV.

Alec, swiveling, gets poleaxed by the image on the screen: a photograph of Carrie's child, Sarah. Not hearing the words, he leaps to the set and juices the sound. A newscaster is saying, "We repeat. If you have any information regarding the whereabouts of this child, please call this number immediately."

Reciting the number to himself, Alec storms off without noticing the surprised looks in his wake. The telephone booths in the club lobby are empty. He directs a club operator to dial the number at once.

FBI agents' voices, especially on the phone, are often indistinguishable from machines. This particular agent has been programmed to achieve a single objective: not to impart information about the child, but to obtain it about the identity and location of the caller. Alec hangs up on the man in mid-question, and has a call placed to Maine. The phone rings eight times without anyone picking up. The club operator asks whether Alec would like her to continue ringing. Alec thanks her and says no.

Too damn late, he thinks. Carrie's in flight, or they already have her.

Watching Rosenkranz questioning Creighton, Alec tries not to think about Carrie and Sarah. Tries to focus on what's going on.

Si, Brett. Brett, Si. Cerebral tennis by players who return everything with style. Although, as between two self-assured men, Brett has an advantage. His charm is inbred. After all, it was Brett's forebears who barred Si's from the best jobs, neighborhoods, and clubs. And Brett's condescension begins to get under Si's skin, until the blister becomes visible to the jury.

"If I've done my arithmetic right," says Si, with a trace of acidity, "in this warehousing business of yours, the risk of loss to you was five hundred times the anticipated gain. Is that correct?"

Brett smiles. "With basic honesty in the operation—"

"Is the arithmetic right, Mr. Creighton?"

"You have the numbers right, Mr. Rosenkranz, but, as is often the case, the numbers tell only part of the story."

"Well, let's get the rest of the story. When you took U.S. Safety into a business with this high an exposure to loss, did you once consider the best interests of your individual stockholders? Did you warn them of the risk?"

Justice Kaye glances at Alec, who's looking innocent. Si may have just opened up the subject of the stockholders' identity as well as given Brett the platform for a speech.

"Mr. Brno?" the judge asks.

"No objection, your Honor."

Si, staring at Alec, senses the trap he's walked into.

Creighton, sensing from the judge and his own counsel that it's appropriate to proceed, says, "As I just started to testify, we thought the risk—"

Si interrupts. "How did you happen to hire Mr. Whitman Poole as manager of this warehousing business?"

"Objection, your Honor," Alec says, rising. "The witness should be allowed to complete his answer to the prior question."

Si scoffs. "It wasn't responsive, your Honor. If Mr. Brno wants the witness to make speeches, he may try that on cross-examination. Provided it's within the scope of my direct."

"I agree," says the judge. "Objection overruled. You may answer the pending question, Mr. Creighton. Do you have it in mind?"

"Yes, your Honor," Brett says. "Mr. Poole was highly recommended by one of our board members, Dr. Lionel Harding, who is the president of Princeton University."

"Mr. Poole was, in fact, Dr. Harding's college roommate, right?"

"That is true."

"And had Dr. Harding told you," Si asks, "that Poole had been fired by both Alcoa and the Jones and Laughlin Steel Corporation?"

"Dr. Harding believed—and we certainly did—that Mr.

Poole's separation from those companies had been voluntary."

"Did you check? Did you or anyone in your company call either of those companies to find out?"

Hesitant for an instant, Brett says, "No."

Si gapes at the admission, lets it hang in the air. He does not ask why—the cardinal sin of examining a hostile witness. And he does not otherwise give Brett a chance to explain his answer.

"Did there come a time, Mr. Creighton, when your board became alarmed at the exposure building up as a result of this huge quantity of diesel being stored in your tanks and all the warehouse receipts you had issued to cover it?"

"I wouldn't say alarmed, no."

"You called in Mr. Poole to explain the situation, did you not?"

"As part of his monthly report, naturally."

"And you learned that the oil had been supplied by a company owned by one Sal Martini, is that correct?"

"No. Mr. Poole told us that there were many companies storing oil at our facilities."

"All of which, you learned, were owned by Sal Martini?"

"Almost all. We learned that from the banks, as it happens. Who knew they were loaning money on Martini's oil from the beginning."

"The same Salvatore Martini who was twice convicted for frauds very similar to this one?"

Alec is on his feet, but Creighton keeps talking. "As I've been trying to tell you, Mr. Rosenkranz, if Poole was honest—and we had every reason then to believe he was—it doesn't matter who supplied the oil. That's why the banks were willing to deal. Except for fire, which is covered by insurance, there's almost no risk that a bailed commodity, such as diesel, will be lost."

"No risk? How lovely." Si laughs, then grandly announces, "I have no further questions of this witness."

"Counsel?" the judge says to Alec, as Si sits down.

"I do have some questions, your Honor, thank you," Alec says, staying on his feet. "Mr. Creighton, did Dr. Harding review Mr. Poole's résumé with the board?"

"Yes, he did."

"And did Dr. Harding tell you that Poole's separation from his two prior employers had been voluntary?"

"He either stated that explicitly or made it very plain in context that that had been the case."

"And did you rely on that?"

"We did."

"Now, Mr. Creighton, I want you to take a few moments before answering the next question. I want you to think about it and be sure. The question is, did you or your company have any reason whatever to doubt Mr. Poole's honesty when you hired him?"

"None whatever," Creighton says without pause. "Dr. Harding, who himself is a man of complete rectitude and one of the most distinguished educators in the country, had known Mr. Poole since their days together as undergraduates, and vouched strongly for his character and integrity."

Alec, glancing at the jury, allows that answer to sink in. It was a question he had had to ask, although the answer was predictably self-serving. And the jurors' reactions range from cool to noncommittal. Early days, thinks Alec, continuing.

"Mr. Rosenkranz asked you some questions about risk and risk ratios. If the person running the warehouse business is honest, what is the risk of losses on warehouse receipts?"

"Essentially zero, as I've already said."

"Why is that?"

"We're warehousing oil. Its market price may go down, but our warehouse receipts are based on the quantity of oil, not its value on the market, so we have no risk of market loss. Also, we're not talking here about the safekeeping of, say, diamonds— small, valuable objects that are relatively easy to hide and walk away with. We're talking about the storage of vast quantities of material. No significant tonnage can be removed from under the nose of an honest manager without his knowing it. Certainly not without his detecting it immediately thereafter. Systematic checks of the tanks—the most basic form of security—would disclose any loss at once."

"How are such checks done?"

"As you've shown everyone. You stick those rods down into the tanks."

"And did you rely on Mr. Poole for having such checks done?"

"Of course."

"And did he tell you they were performed?"

"Regularly. And that there was no shortage, no problem."

"Until the Martini fraud was detected, did you or your company have any reason to doubt Mr. Poole's reports?"

"We did not."

"Did the banks eventually ask your permission to check out the storage tanks at Bayonne, New Jersey?"

"They did."

"What did you tell them?"

"That our manager had the tanks checked every week, but that we had no problem with their checking on their own. It was in this same exchange that we got the details of Martini's involvement."

"Why were the banks suddenly so nervous that they asked to check the tanks on their own?"

"The market price of diesel had started to fall. I just mentioned, my company, U.S. Safety, had no market risk. Our obligation was to return the tonnage that had been stored there. But the banks had loaned money on the security of that tonnage. When the market price fell, their security was devalued."

Alec, pulling two copies of a document from his stack, says, "your Honor, may I hand to the court and the witness copies of our first exhibit, which has been pre-marked as defendants' exhibit one for identification."

Si rises. "I object to this, your Honor."

"Approach!" the judge says.

As both counsel arrive at the bench, they're surprised by the appearance of Marius Shilling, elbowing his way between the two. Justice Kaye says, "Now, what's this all about?"

Si says, "Looks like merely a couple of lists—prior stockholders, present stockholders—but it's a straight sympathy play, your Honor. Has nothing to do with the merits. They want to show that the financial institutions sold out and that the company is now owned by individuals—and that's totally irrelevant. It's also completely beyond the scope of my direct examination."

"Counsel?"

"Mr. Rosenkranz just opened it up, your Honor. He asked the witness whether he'd ever considered the best interests of his individual stockholders—"

"I remember," Kaye says, wagging his head negatively.

Shilling asserts, "And we should be allowed, in any event, to identify the parties, your Honor."

"This is a class action," says the judge. "You can identify the named plaintiffs, but not necessarily other class members. Certainly not when the obvious purpose is to sway emotions. I'm going to exclude this."

Alec whispers directly into Shilling's large ear, "Show nothing! Act like it doesn't matter!" Then, turning, going straight back to the lectern, "Thank you, Mr. Creighton. No further questions."

Nor has Si, although he thinks about it for a second. And as Alec sits, the bailiff hands him a note, which he scans as the judge leaves the courtroom. In his secretary's scrawl: "U.S. Attorney wants you to call him ASAP."

SEVENTY-SEVEN

Alec, on a pay phone in the courthouse corridor, spreading dimes out on the shelf, gets put through to Sancerre.

"You're in serious trouble, Alec," is the not-too-friendly greeting. "A witness you know to be material to a criminal investigation, and who was hiding from us, is living in a house in Maine on which—guess who holds the lease?"

"Where is she?"

"Heading to the city. But, Alec, you know I could prosecute you for this. Obstruction of justice."

"What about your lying to her on TV about the danger to her daughter?"

"Standard procedure. But you lied to us! That's illegal! We're the government!"

"All right, Ray. Stop screwing around. What do you want?"

"She says she's not going to help us without talking to her lawyer first."

"And you're saying you'll prosecute me unless I sell out my client by pushing her to cooperate with you. You want to put that in writing, Ray?"

"Calm down, fella."

"I'm in the middle of a trial, Ray. I've got to get back."

"Want to see her?" Ray asks.

Alec seems distracted. The jury looks bored. Si, staring only at the jury, punctuates his next question with a roar.

"And did there come a time," asks Si, "when you had to fire

the man named Whitman Poole?"

A little blimp named Simpkin, the assistant marketing director for Alcoa, eyes Si slyly and then the jury. "I did," he pronounces.

"For what?" Si asks.

"For turning our best sales region into our worst. In six months," he adds petulantly. "And for turning in some rather dubious entertainment expense reports."

"Dubious in what way?"

"It appears that the person being entertained by Mr. Poole on company money was none other than Mr. Poole."

Si, nodding with satisfaction, announces he has no further questions, and Alec hesitates, as Judge Kaye looks down from the bench. Both Simpkin and the next witness, Quince, had been placed on the list at the last minute, way after the deadline for informing opposing parties of prospective witnesses. The purpose of the deadline is to give each side the chance to depose the witnesses before trial. Alec's motion to bar the testimony of Simpkin and Quince was denied, as he expected. But when he asked for the right to depose them, the judge denied that motion on the ironic ground that there wasn't enough time before trial. Alec, rising, and about to fly blind, glances back at Ben Braddock, who smiles. *Like the good old days*, Alec can almost hear Braddock thinking, *when there was no pretrial discovery at all. When trial lawyers had to earn their livings by using their wits.*

"Good afternoon, Mr. Simpkin. My name is Alec Brno, and I represent U.S. Safety and its directors in this action. First, may I ask, did you interview and hire Mr. Poole for his initial job with Alcoa?"

"I hired him. A number of us interviewed him."

"Right. And did you promote him two years later to branch manager, and then regional manager?"

"Yes."

"So it would be fair to say that, for a period of at least two years, you trusted Mr. Poole and were happy with his performance."

"Ye-es," Simpkin answers, finding no way to deny it.

Alec can't resist sneaking a glance at Braddock, whose impassivity is all the assurance he needs. "No further questions, your Honor."

Si looks uncertain, then shakes his head.

"Thank you, Mr. Simpkin," says the judge. "You may step down."

Thaddeus Quince, sales manager for Jones and Laughlin, is called and walks to the stand. A precise, fussy man, he inspects the chair in the witness box before sitting upon it.

Si runs Quince through the same drill he employed with Simpkin. And the answers are the same, because Poole did to J&L exactly what he had done to Alcoa: perform adequately enough at first to get some promotions, then mail it in, along with some phony expense reports.

Alec's turn.

He asks whether Quince, before interviewing Poole, had read his résumé.

"I had his CV, yes."

"CV meaning *curriculum vitae?*"

"Of course."

"Meaning résumé?"

"Yes," says Quince, impatiently.

"And did Mr. Poole's résumé list his prior employment at Alcoa?"

Now Quince becomes a bit wary. "Yes, it did."

"Did you call Mr. Simpkin or anyone at Alcoa regarding Mr. Poole?" Alec holds his breath.

"No, I did not," Quince says.

Alec can imagine Braddock thinking, *Thou shalt never, ever, ask a "why" question of any adverse witness on cross-examination!*

"Why not?" asks Alec.

"Because," Quince says, looking down his long nose, "such

calls, in my experience, are worthless. You never get straight information. Prior employers are too worried about getting sued—and too anxious to be rid of anyone they dislike—to queer his chances of employment with anyone else."

"No further questions," Alec says, as if the answer just uttered had been self-evident.

Si's face is a storm cloud of disgust. Justice Kaye dismisses the witness. With court breaking for the day, amid the commotion of lawyers packing lit bags and reporters snagging interviews, Ben Braddock pulls Alec off to one side. "You violated the one rule of cross-examination that is absolutely inviolate. The wrong answer to that question could have lost the case. You have an explanation?"

"It worked?"

"Not good enough."

"The CV thing, and the way he looked at the chair before he sat down. Fastidious. Grandiose. Guys like that—they never admit they fucked up."

Braddock's face betrays a faint smile before he bursts out with a laugh and walks away.

A high brick building of styleless mass houses the Manhattan office of the Federal Bureau of Investigation on an otherwise residential stretch of 3rd Avenue. No signs indicate the function of the building. No formal entrance welcomes the public onto its floors. Yet the people working there are responsive to public needs, especially those asserted by a U.S. Attorney with the realistic ambitions of Ray Sancerre.

At a security desk inside, Alec stands facing two humorless young men in dark suits, white shirts, and dark ties. Together they wait, in silence, for the word to come down from upstairs that the person corresponding to the name Alec has given them is indeed expected at seven p.m.

The word is finally delivered. An escort is formed by two other dark suits to bring Alec to the thirteenth floor, no nonsense being indulged here about skipping unlucky numerals. Led into a small room of minimal furnishings, with the door closed behind him, Alec is surprised to find Carrie alone. She goes right into his arms and breathes in his ear, "I love you, and this room is wired."

"Are you okay?" he asks.

"Yeah. I heard the newscast and ran to the phone. I'm sorry."

"You had no choice," he says. "A message like that to a mother! It's the ultimate dirty trick."

He leads her to the embrasure of the window, which he guesses is as far away as they can get from the likely placement of the bug. The room is a vacant office, in basic government drab— metal desk and chairs, dung-colored carpet—designed to suck the soul out of anyone required to work there. Its single window is on the back courtyard of the building.

"They want me to testify to a grand jury," she whispers. "And they want me to testify in your case too. Why?"

"I'm not sure."

"Should I?"

"The grand jury… they're not going to give you an alternative. Not a good one, anyway."

"Then I might as well also testify in your case. Phil can't shoot me twice."

Alec, not liking it, says nothing.

"I can nail his ass," she says. "I can send him up. It's what we've talked about."

"Now you're trusting the system?"

"Y'know… we've got nothing to lose here."

Alec canvases all the possibilities he can think of, which is hard, not having slept in three nights.

Carrie says, "I'm going to do this. I want to do this."

A sharp knock on the door, and Sancerre enters, with Sid

Kline in his wake. "So that's a deal?" Ray says. "Full witness protection. For both of you, if you like." He twirls a chair around and plunks down on it, resting his arms on the back. "Complete immunity for Carrie."

Carrie's look to Alec says, *yes*.

SEVENTY-EIGHT

Morning. Court has resumed. Si is examining Whitman Poole, who treats the experience with the superciliousness of a critic. Alec listens as he studies the man: the slicked-back golden-streaked hair, the asymmetrical eyes, the fleshy bulb of his nose, the pointed chin, his demeanor smug and sun-roasted against a gleaming white button-down shirt.

"When you retained Mr. Raffon," Si intones, "to, as you say, ensure the integrity of your procedures, did you check his references?"

"Y'know," says Poole, "I didn't. Obviously, I should have. I really kick myself about that, and I have no real excuse. Just flat-out negligent."

"Part of Raffon's retainer was to keep a running check on the quantity of oil in the tanks?"

"That's right."

"Did you or your staff keep tabs on what he was doing?"

" 'Fraid not."

"Really!" Si says, as if surprised. "Why's that?"

"Y'know, I've asked myself that a million times. Once more, there's just no excuse."

"Overworked, possibly?"

Poole laughs. "Wish I could claim that! But y'know," he says, turning to the jury, "it did teach me a great lesson. In my new job, I'll never be that careless."

"No further questions, your Honor," says Si with the air of a man who has now proven his case.

Alec feels the eyes of a packed courtroom as he rises. Then, one pair of eyes, especially. Turning, he sees Frank Macalister, balancing on crutches, slip into an aisle seat. Mac gives him a grin that rattles Alec for an instant, before he shifts his attention again to the witness. Poole smiles as if his conscience is clear.

"When you came in as manager of the warehousing facility, Mr. Poole, there was a routine, was there not, for checking on the oil in the storage tanks?"

"Of course." Same ingenuous smile.

"And that routine involved more than just opening the flap door at the top of the tanks and looking in, did it not?"

"Yes," says Poole.

Alec hefts the twenty-foot rod from the floor, drawing a gasp from the benches. "You used this pole, right, or one just like it?"

"The men did."

"Foolproof, right? For catching false bottoms?"

"I should think, yes."

"If there are false bottoms in tanks, stick this pole down, and you'll find out, right?"

Sarcastically: "Right."

"Yet, Mr. Poole," Alec says, lowering the rod back down to the base of the rail, "there were in fact false bottoms in some of the tanks in all your facilities."

Si's on his feet. "Is that a question?"

Alec addresses the judge. "Of course, and the obvious answer makes the point, your Honor, that alleged gross negligence—or recklessness, which is the same thing—has nothing to do with this case. Someone had to order the men to stop checking these tanks with these poles."

"Save it for your closing argument, counsel."

"All right, your Honor." Alec turns back to the witness.

"So, Mr. Poole, were there false bottoms in some of the tanks at Bayonne and all the other facilities you were employed to manage?"

"Yes," Poole says, as if it meant nothing.

"And most of the tanks in those facilities were filled with salt-water where there was supposed to have been diesel oil, correct?"

"Yes."

"And are you a defendant in this action, Mr. Poole?"

"No, I'm not."

"U.S. Safety and its directors are being sued for what is alleged to have been your gross negligence. Do you have any idea why *you're* not being sued for your alleged gross negligence?"

Poole pretends to consider the question. "Because I don't have any money?"

"Really?" says Alec. "None at all?"

"Not a farthing."

"Do you know what the statute of limitations is on an action for negligence?"

Poole glances uneasily at Si. "Three years?"

"In other words, you know you can still be sued by the stockholders for negligence?"

Poole slowly nods his head. "Yes."

"Yet you are quick to admit negligence. Has someone—perhaps someone in this room—ever explained to you how useful it would be to his case if you made that admission, and promised you that you would not be sued if you did?"

Alec looks at Si, and so does Poole. Then so does the jury. Si sits there as if contemplating the stripes on the flag. Poole, now confused as to how to handle the question, finally mumbles something under his breath.

"Sorry," Alec says. "Didn't quite hear that."

"I don't remember," says Poole, still sotto voce.

"You met with Mr. Rosenkranz, before this trial?"

"Yes."

"And did he say something along those lines?"

"I don't remember."

"He might have said something along those lines? Promising you that you wouldn't be sued, if you admitted being negligent?"

"Might have." Poole looks sick.

"What is your present job, Mr. Poole?"

"I run an amusement park in Florida."

"Who owns it, Mr. Poole?"

"It's a limited partnership."

"And who is the principal partner?"

"I'm not sure I know."

"Would it surprise you to learn that his name is Angiapello?"

"No. But few things surprise me."

"I'll bet," says Alec. "No further questions, your Honor."

"Mr. Rosenkranz?" says the judge.

"No redirect, your Honor. And the plaintiffs rest their case."

"You may step down, Mr. Poole." Justice Kaye looks at Alec. "Counsel?"

"May we take a brief recess, your Honor?"

In the counsel room, amid boxes of documents and small office machines, Braddock, leaning on the table, says to Alec, "Despite the brilliance of your cross-examination of that liar, you've got no fucking choice. You've got to call her. Now!"

"It wasn't brilliant. It was standard, okay? But it's all we need. You saw the jury. They hate that guy. They know he's lying. It's obvious he's lying."

The door opens. It's Macalister, swinging in on his crutches. "Whatta you think, this door's made of steel? Everyone can hear you guys down the fucking hallway."

Braddock pays him no attention. "She's here, right? Ready to go on?"

Alec says, "The FBI people have brought her over."

Macalister, looking from one to the other, says, "What? There's some question about calling the girl?"

"We don't need her," Alec says. "There's no point risking her life."

"I thought she was the principal government witness in the

criminal case against Phil Anwar," Mac says. "That's not going to risk her life?"

Braddock shrugs. "It's academic. You don't put her on? Shilling will. Creighton blesses this. And they've persuaded Rand. They cooked it up last night and called me. Shilling, I suspect, has been talking to his former partner, Sancerre."

Alec looks at Braddock with anger. "And you accept this?"

"Frankly, Alec, I agree with it. It does not appear that we're putting the young woman at any more risk than she's already in. And if that's true, you don't bet an entire company on a single throw of the dice—*i.e.*, your cross-examination of Poole—brilliant or otherwise."

Alec looks at Macalister. "Ditto," Mac says. "And Alec. You do not want her examined by Shilling. He'd fuck it up. We'd end up with a mess. She might even react to that pompous ass by changing her story, which would lead to a perjury indictment. If she's going to testify anyway, which is certain—"

"I get the point," Alec says.

"Defendants call Carrie Anne Madigan." Alec, making the announcement, turns to the back of the courtroom, but Rosenkranz intercedes.

"May we approach?" says Si.

Convening at the bench, at the judge's beckoning gesture, Si says, in lowered voice, "I heard about this witness for the first time last night. From Mr. Shilling."

Marius, to Alec's annoyance, joins the conference. "Yes, your Honor. I called him."

"But I've had no chance," Si says, "to depose this witness, to investigate her—I haven't the slightest idea who she is, except for the limited information given to me by opposing counsel last night."

Shilling says, "There are several witnesses Mr. Rosenkranz has already called whom we weren't given the right to depose before trial. It should be a two-way street, your Honor. And Miss Madigan has just become available to us. Produced by the FBI, your Honor. She's the key government witness in a criminal case about to be filed against racketeering in this state. And we could not have called her without a witness protection deal from the government that we got only last night."

Justice Kaye looks down on all counsel. He frowns; he doesn't like it; he feels boxed. "I'm going to allow this," he finally says. "Si, you feel you need more time after she finishes on direct, I'll consider giving you a recess for a couple of days."

Rosenkranz looks sour. "And give the jury those days to let her direct testimony really sink in!"

"In the light of the history here, Si…. I am not—I repeat not—going to permit a mistrial over this. Or give the defendants a basis for appeal."

Carrie's already walking in as the conference breaks. Her trip to the witness box, with her eyes locked on Alec's, causes a sufficient stir in the room to force the judge to gavel it quiet. She wears a long black skirt, a silk blouse, and a tweed jacket, none of which Alec has seen before.

She sits demurely for the administration of the oath.

Alec says, "Could you state your full name for the record, please?"

"Carrie Anne Madigan."

Alec brings out her Irish birth, her educational background, her employment with Aaron Weinfeld, her marriage to, and estrangement from, Phil Anwar. Some jurors know who Phil is. The model knows. Two of the men. Alec can see them register it. He says, beginning to color, "There's something else I think the jury should know. Could you tell them, please, of your relationship with me?"

Her smile is radiant. "We love each other. We plan to be

married."

Alec cannot control the blush. It spreads, deepens, turns purple. Finally, he just gives in to it, thinking it probably won't do him any harm. Most of the jurors are grinning.

"You know what I'm about to ask you?"

"Yes," she says. "We've been over it. Whether my testimony is influenced by our relationship. And the answer is, no. I told you everything before we had one. What happened, happened."

"Have you ever met a man named Whitman Poole?"

"Oh, yes. Four times."

"Can you identify him?"

She points right at Poole, whose face displays a succession of tics. "The guy in the first row, in the white button-down shirt."

"Please describe the circumstances in which you first met him."

"I delivered an envelope to him from Aaron Weinfeld. About two years ago."

"Did you have any conversation with Mr. Poole at that time?"

"Sort of. When I handed him the envelope, he asked whether I knew what was inside of it."

"And what did you tell him? In fact, why don't you simply describe the rest of the conversation?"

"Okay. I said that of course I knew what was inside. I typed the damn thing. Then he said, 'You're Phil Anwar's wife, aren't you?' I said I was, and he said, 'You'll be the eyes on this, then.' I think he had some idea that Aaron might be trying to cheat him, and that I'd be available to tell Phil. Anyhow, he seemed extremely pleased that the amount was right, and said, 'This baby's going right into a Swiss bank account.'"

"What was the amount of the check?"

"Two-hundred-fifty-thousand dollars," she says.

There is a small, albeit collective, utterance in the courtroom.

"And later, you made further deliveries of checks to Mr. Poole?"

"Three more."

"The four totaling?"

"One million dollars," says Carrie.

"Before Aaron Weinfeld made out these checks to Mr. Poole, did he receive any funds to cover them?"

"Oh, yes."

"From whom?"

"From companies owned by Phil Anwar."

"Who is a member of the Angiapello family?"

"Yes. He's the current boss."

Alec pauses. Carrie's words, utterly believable, have taken the air from the room. *The case is won now*, he thinks. The dead silence confirms it. It's as if everyone is embarrassed to confront the man still squirming there; the one caught lying through his teeth.

"Did Mr. Weinfeld ever tell you why these checks were being given to Mr. Poole?"

Everything happens at once, in a sort of delayed, anticlimactic reaction.

Si Rosenkranz jumps to his feet. "Your Honor, I object!" Poole shoots up, bolting out of the courtroom. Harvey Grand lunges after him. Almost everyone in the courtroom is standing, jabbering at each other, and gesturing. Carrie, having rushed from the witness chair, grabs Alec's hand. The judge adds to the pandemonium by barking into it, and pounding his gavel for quiet. Alec and Carrie follow Harvey out the door.

In the outer hall, Poole, half-pinioned by Harvey, tries to fight his way free. Three FBI men pounce, pinning Poole to the floor, then cuffing him.

Out of nowhere, seemingly, Ray Sancerre appears, trailed down the corridor by a dozen reporters, cameras blazing, TV crew in their wake.

"This," says Ray to the TV lights and camera, "is the opening wedge in a major crime-busting onslaught that we've been planning for months. And we've just arrested Phil Anwar in his home."

SEVENTY-NINE

When order is restored, Alec and Si are invited to a robing room conference. Rosenkranz requests a week's continuance.

"You really think that's necessary, Si?" Justice Kaye asks.

The old lawyer takes some time before answering, no doubt considering his next case before this jurist. "No," he says finally. "You're right. No point."

The lawyers regroup in the courtroom. Mac and Braddock approach Alec. "It's over," he says.

"Good," says Braddock abruptly, as if having lost patience with the whole affair. Mac smiles, sits, shakes his head a bit at Alec, as if to say, *you lucky bastard.*

There's no cross-examination of Carrie; both sides close; summations are pro forma; and the jury watch takes less than an hour. It appears that the model has been elected forewoman, and she's grinning, while the man in the sweatshirt looks glum.

"Have you reached a verdict?" the judge inquires.

The model stands, enjoying her role. "We have, your Honor. We find—unanimously—for the defendants on all counts. We also find—though we weren't exactly asked—that Mr. Poole is a crook who should be punished."

There's an after-party at the client's office at which Rand and Creighton make brief appearances, Braddock and Mac none, but Shilling and his entourage celebrate as if they were solely responsible for the victory. Alec, not even knowing how to reach Carrie, tries Harvey with no success.

Finally he goes home to an empty apartment and, without turning on lights, plunks down on his sofa, letting the day play out in his mind. Rand and Creighton had said all the right things. Braddock and Macalister had said little, but they were plainly relieved. For Alec, the elation is gone—routed by anticlimax, laced with loneliness, soured by worry and fear. Drowsiness wins out at four in the morning, and that victory is entirely welcome.

EIGHTY

The phone wakes Alec. It's Harvey Grand.

"Congratulations!"

"Well, thanks," Alec says, still half-asleep. "Congratulations to you, too. Although, once Poole ran, only an idiot could have lost that case."

"Alec."

"What?"

"Turn on the news. They've given Phil a deal. He gets three weeks of liberty before going up."

Alec's suddenly wide awake, and the doorbell's ringing.

"Hold on, Harvey, will you?"

Alec goes to the door. Carrie, looking bedraggled in the same clothes she wore at trial, tears in. "Have you heard?"

"Just. I'm on with Harvey."

He goes back to the phone in the bedroom. Harvey is saying, "You got a car?"

"No."

"I'll be over there in twenty minutes," says Harvey. "You'd better take mine."

Alec hangs up, and the phone immediately rings again. Sancerre.

"Got some bad news, Alec," says Ray.

"I just heard."

"So you understand then."

"Understand what?"

"Or maybe you consider it good news. No criminal trial, no witness protection."

"You've got to be kidding," Alec says.

"Sorry."

"And you're giving that animal three weeks to come after us?"

"He wouldn't be that stupid. It's to put his shit together. And he wanted five. Three was a good deal. Plus seven years and twenty mil, which is a first for an individual. If we'd tried the bastard, what with delays and appeals, he couldda been out on bail for more than a year."

"But you'll put him under surveillance," Alec says.

"Waste of time. All we care about is keeping him in the country. The airports are covered. For him and fifty others. Not a chance he'll get out."

"I don't believe this, Ray."

"Look, don't worry. We're giving you and Carrie FBI protection."

"For how long?" Alec asks. "And how many men?"

There's a long pause before Sancerre answers.

Carrie's glued to the TV when Alec returns to the living room. Without averting her eyes from the screen, she says, "Phil gets three weeks to put his affairs in order? Can you believe this? His affairs! They're putting him in prison because of his goddamn affairs! But first they're giving the bastard three weeks to make sure he can run them from his cell? I mean, for crying out loud!" She finally turns to Alec. "Where the hell are we? Bedlam?"

"It's worse than you know. Ray just told me. You don't qualify for the witness protection program after all because the government doesn't need you to testify now. In other words, you gave the testimony in my case that scared Phil's lawyers into making the deal that Ray wanted from the outset. So we've been used. Phil pays twenty million bucks—biggest fine in the history of that office—plus goes up for seven years. Ray gets the credit. You get the equivalent of nothing. One FBI guy for three weeks."

Carrie looks dazed. "They just told me to go home."

"This is my fault," Alec says. "I didn't see it coming."

Grimly, Alec pulls a suitcase out of the hall closet.

"Where we going?" she asks.

"Into our own witness protection program."

"Meaning what?" she says.

"What it sounds like," says Alec, tossing the suitcase onto the bed and opening a dresser drawer. "Middle America someplace."

Carrie, not liking it, says at the doorway, "What about Sarah?"

"When Phil goes to prison—"

"I'm not doing this," she snaps, already agitated. "I'm going to Maine."

Alec puts down a shirt. "Phil knows where that house is. By now he knows."

"Right," she says. "That's the point."

"You're gonna what? Sit there and wait for him with your rifle? That's absolutely crazy."

"Crazy!" she says, jutting her small jaw right under his nose. "Six years with Phil, I got plenty of crazy. Now it's my turn. I'm giving it back."

"You're gonna get yourself killed."

"I'm already dead! You think being tortured by that asshole and humiliated at his whim is living? You think running is living? Being deprived of my child? Your wonderful system doesn't protect me, Alec. There's nothing to protect me. Face it! Understand it! It's that fucking primitive!"

He resumes packing. "I certainly don't want you out there alone."

"Then come with me."

He throws some more clothes in the suitcase, then stops to think.

He's staring at the suitcase, she's staring at him.

"You don't touch a gun, okay?"

"Whatta you mean?" she says.

"You stay out of harm's way."

"And what'll you do?"

"You'll see. Trust me."

Sam and Abigail get the news of Phil's plea bargain on the car radio, heading toward a job. They're on Sunrise Highway. Sam, who is driving, pulls off the road into the parking lot of a hamburger joint.

"Let me see if I can reach Alec," Sam says. "There's a phone in there."

He's back in five minutes.

"No answer," he says. "Home or office."

"You left word?"

"At the office, yes."

"So whatta we do?"

"I've got to find him," Sam says.

They cancel their appointment, go back to Abby's house where Sam is now spending most of his time. He calls Alec's office again, gets the receptionist. "I should have asked," he says. "When do you expect him?"

"Hold on, please."

She takes forever, in Sam's estimation.

"Sorry to keep you waiting, sir. Mr. Brno is on vacation, at the moment, with no indication as to when he'll return."

"This is his father. Do you have a number where he can be reached?"

"Sorry, sir, we don't."

"An address?"

"No, sir. I mean, we couldn't give it out if we did, but… we don't actually know where he is."

EIGHTY-ONE

Reefer's Harbor, as the season approaches, attracts the overflow from more popular Maine resort towns. Day-trippers like the harbor street, which is authentically scenic; the beaches, which are rarely crowded; and the T-shirts sporting the town name. While the cottagers resent and look down on all interlopers, the tourists, simply happy to be there, smile benignly at everyone they meet.

For Alec and Carrie there is no joy to be found in the place or its people, whether residents or those who drive by to gawk. And the latter cause fear. Any car on their street, anyone even strolling past, sends Alec to a window and Carrie poised at the phone.

Twice they drive into Portland. In the basement of the local gun shop, the proprietor operates a shooting range and gives lessons. It turns out that Alec, once he learns how to prevent Carrie's rifle from dislocating his weakened shoulder, has reasonably good aim.

They also buy a rope ladder from a naval outfitter and hardware store outside of town. The guy who runs that place tells them he's sold bushels of rope ladders to the big summer hotels that still dot the coastline of Maine. Most of them were built eighty years ago without fire escapes.

Larry Stahl is the agent given the job of protecting them from sunset to sunrise—others take various shifts during the day. Larry is a scrawny man with nappy blond hair and moist red lips who roams the property once an hour, but otherwise sits silently at the edge of the marsh on an aluminum-framed chair without visible form of entertainment.

"What would you say to a thermos of coffee, Larry?" Carrie asks every night. To which Larry responds, "That would be real nice, ma'am." Which is the extent of the intimacy they attain with the man responsible for their lives.

Sleep is erratic, fitful when it comes, disturbed by nightmares that color each day darkly and deepen its horrors. There is a surreal feeling to living like this, with the certitude of retaliation from Phil pitted against the likelihood of ineptitude from Larry.

And every day they have the same argument. Alec insists that Carrie's agreement to stay out of harm's way means that she'd agreed to go elsewhere, such as the outlying motel at which he'd reserved and already paid for a room. She rejects this interpretation and refuses to move. " 'Out of harm's way' means only that, if there's a line of fire, I'm not in it. And I won't be. Besides. You're the lawyer. You want precision? Don't use vague terms."

"Phil won't come here only to kill," Alec says. "You saw what he did to Raffon."

"You're telling me about Phil? You think there's some crazed rotten thing about him I don't know?"

They're in their bedroom. It's close to midnight. There's nothing more useful to be said on the subject. But they say it again and again, until they're too tired to say anything. Then they imagine the worst in fitful dreams.

Sam's made no progress tracking Alec. Neither lawyers nor secretaries at Alec's firm have any idea of his whereabouts. Madge Harlan thinks Ben Braddock might, but he's in Scotland, making himself inaccessible. None of the travel agents the firm uses lists Alec or Carrie on client lists. And several of the doormen in Alec's building have refused to let Sam upstairs.

He says to Abigail, "The horror here is, Anwar probably knows where they are."

She says nothing; they've both realized this possibility for days.

"Maybe I can catch the doorman who saw us together, slip

him a twenty, something. Maybe even sneak in the back way, get upstairs, and jimmy the bolt on the front door."

"Okay," she says dully.

"In the meantime, there's something you can do."

"Okay."

"Listen in on Phil's line."

"Oh, God."

"I'm current on the recordings, except for this morning. So catch up, and then go live. I'll call you as soon as I get to the city."

Phil Anwar loves judging talent, spotting the keen ones early. And he's been watching young Joey Forcaccio. In Morristown, Joey was cool, probably shot twice as many as anyone else, and without any show of emotion. He performed well, by report, in the Aaron Weinfeld matter, and, under Phil's personal observation in the dispatching of Carl Raffon. Also, Joey is smart. On his own initiative, though with blessing from Phil, he's already set up a profitable prostitution service and a gambling house. But there are two problems with Joey. He's too short, a shade under five-foot-five. It's tough to command respect when everyone else is looking down on you. Moreover, Joey enjoys hurting women—a subject on which Phil feels qualified to render advice.

So Phil decides, before taking care of other business and going up to Fed Med, he'll give Joe a talking-to on the matter, sugarcoated with a drink in his basement bar.

Phil is playing bartender and talking while mixing the drinks. Vito, as always, stands by.

"So this is the thing," Phil says. "The object is obedience. What you need to do is instill fear. Make them not only understand in the head, but feel—feel viscerally, in the gut—that crossing you will have consequences they're not going to be able to take. You know what I'm saying?"

"Sure, Phil," says Joey. He bounces his stocky frame on his toes like a boxer awaiting the bell and sweeps a hand through his curly black hair. "But to do that—"

"Requires smarts," Anwar says. "That's what I'm trying to tell you. I'm not saying you don't lift a hand—but be smart about it. In the first place, take all your own pleasure out of it. With some of these women, beating the shit out of 'em feels good, maybe too good. Especially when they deserve it. But if you get to like it too much, that's not cool. You go past what's needed for obedience. Then you bring in the medics, the cops, trouble, you hear me?"

"Yes, boss."

"In the second place, since basically what you want is to scare the shit out of 'em, you've got to leave room for them to imagine how it could get even worse. You see? If you go the limit right off—" Phil stops. He's gazing at the far wall. "What's that?" he says.

"What?" Vito says. "Where?"

Phil circles around the bar to go to the wall in question. "This," he says, pointing to a square section of board near the ceiling that's come a bit loose.

"Boy, you got good eyes," Vito says. "What's his name, the guy who works for Syosset Security, was here... when? When you were in Europe, I think. Obviously the screws came loose on that board."

"Was here to do what, Vito?"

"I dunno. Fix something. I think... what? I think he said one of the wires got frayed or something."

Phil pulls the board off the wall, exposing the FM transmitter. "What the fuck's this?"

"A splice?"

"Vito, I love you, you know that."

"I do something bad, boss?"

"Sometimes—and it gives me no joy to say this—you're a fucking idiot!"

EIGHTY-TWO

S am? Thank God you called."
"I'm upstairs. Alec's apartment. If the address is here, I'll find
it."

"I've already got it," Abigail says. "Twenty minutes ago. Vito
gave it on the phone to some guy named Dominick."

"Just like that," Sam says.

"Yeah. Fell into our laps."

"Where are they?"

"A place in Maine called Reefer's Harbor. Sounds like a drug
port."

"Street address?"

"Two Deer Cove Road."

"I can remember that."

"Yeah, but Sam?"

"What?"

"Come home first," she says.

"Why?"

Silence.

"Abby, I'm not taking you with me."

"Come home. Let's talk about it."

"I don't have the time. I want to get up there."

"You got a gun?"

"I'll get something up there."

"I've got a handgun. A good one. Also a rifle. And lots of
ammo. Faster than shopping up there, even assuming they're
selling."

"How come you have guns?"

"Gus bought them."

Sam thinks for a moment. It's fitting together. "All right. I run in, you hand me a gun and ammo, I take off, no arguing."

Silence.

"Abby?"

"You bargaining with me, Sam?"

"No, that's exactly what I'm not doing."

"Just come home, will you! Please!"

She doesn't tell him that the line, Phil's line, went dead. Could mean anything. Why frighten Sam right now? She would drive off, but Sam has the truck. She could run to a neighbor's, but that might implicate an innocent person. Besides, Phil would likely go to Sam's place, not hers, if he suspects a tap. So getting Sam to her house is a good thing, she reasons. Besides, she doesn't want him in Maine alone.

Phil, Joey, and Vito pop Abby's kitchen door as she's taking dishes out of the dishwasher. She drops a porcelain platter, which smashes on the tile floor. She reaches for the countertop to brace herself only to launch a full bowl of soup, which somehow ricochets off the toaster onto her capri pants. Launching herself into the small den where she keeps the guns, she realizes belatedly, is a bad mistake. On a side table sit the recorder and earphones.

Phil looks at the equipment and laughs. He says, "Get in the bathroom, Abby."

"What?" she cries, her voice rising in panic.

"Upstairs," Phil says. "Master bathroom."

Abby shakes her head with disbelief. Joey whacks her across the shoulders so hard she crashes into the table.

"Up the fucking stairs," Joey says.

She starts screaming. Joey grabs her and tapes her mouth. Vito and Joey then each grab an arm, hoist her out of the den, and drag her up the staircase and into the one large bathroom in the house. She's made to stand with her back to the tub. Phil sits on the toilet-seat cover. Joey sits on the edge of the sink. Vito bars the door.

"So this is what's happening," Phil says. "And Abby, look at me! I need your attention. We're setting it up so it'll look like a suicide. You run water for a bath. Then you take all your clothes off and get in. Then—" Phil notices a small trash basket under the sink and bends down to retrieve it. "Whatta you know," he says, fishing out a straight razor. "What is this, Gus'? Perfect touch. Grieving widow uses late husband's razor to cut her wrists. Like found art. You know that concept?"

Abby bolts for the door, but Joe is too quick for her. He lassoes her in with one strong arm, and with his other hand grasps her right breast. She slumps down on the bath rug.

"Okay, Abby," says Phil. "Here it is. The boys can hold you down and strip you, or you can strip yourself. The advantage of doing it yourself is that you won't have this brute of a man feeling you up. Oh, and Abby. You know why this is happening. So let's get the show started."

Abby rips the tape off her mouth and screams, "Fuck you!"

She scrambles up again, and Joey slams her down.

"Guys?" Phil says, inviting them to begin. "We don't have all day. I want the clothes off, but not torn. Then put in the hamper. When you get her in the tub, use her own hands to make the razor cuts. Gets the angle right. I'm going downstairs."

"You don't want to see this?" Joey says, pulling Abby's top over her head and unhooking her bra.

"I've seen it," says Phil. "It's not that exciting."

Sam parks the car in the driveway and heads toward the back of the house. Smack in his eyes: the smashed-in kitchen door, the shattered platter, the spilt soup. Like a large cat in panic, he bounds through the rooms, looking for Abby, shouting her name.

He finds her upstairs. In the bathtub, sitting, trying to wrench herself up, her breasts bare, her pants tangled around her knees, a nasty bruise on her upper right arm. She can scarcely move—her hands are tied behind her back with her bra—or make anything but muffled sounds—her mouth is taped.

He yanks off the tape, frees her hands, lifts her from the tub. "This was Phil," he says, "and my fault."

He carries her into the bedroom, lays her on the bed, and draws some covers over her. She's breathing in gasps.

"You're in shock," Sam says, wrapping the blanket around her. "I'll get an ambulance here. No! Bring you to the ER myself."

"No hospital," she says, curling herself up next to him. "And it's not your fault. It's mine. For doing business with a creep like that. For ever letting him into my home."

It takes Sam a couple of seconds. "He's been here before?"

"Once," she says, then sighs. "No, twice."

"Why," he says.

She shakes her head.

"You slept with him?" he says.

"No! I'm not that stupid."

He sits up. "Okay," he says roughly. "Why don't you just tell me?"

And now she can't say anything, or even look at him.

"When?" he says. "Circumstances?"

"It's not what you think."

"Then tell me."

"Gus died, I was sick with grief. I was standing at the sink in an open nightgown. Probably crying. And there was Phil's face, right in the window. He'd come over to give condolences, explain what had happened on the boat. I thought he was being kind, but the prick then started telling me how great I looked 'in the raw,' as he put it, and made a pass at me. I screamed at him. He left. Next day he came to the funeral. Acted as if nothing had happened. I made a decision. I'd act that way too. And so I have. I'm sorry."

"Don't apologize to me."

"Who to? You're the only one I care about."

He gets up, tries to think clearly about it.

"So what does this do?" she says. "I disgust you?"

"What do you think?"

"I don't know, Sam!"

He holds the covers around her again. "Abby, for Christ's sake, you don't disgust me. I love you like my life."

She twists around to hold him. "Me too, me too," she says. Then shivers. "He's such a twisted bastard. This thing today was to scare me. He had me believing he was going to cut me to pieces in the bathtub, had two of his goons pull my clothes off, then at the last minute gives me a warning. As if he, the fucking executioner, had just changed his mind."

"Abby, calm down, stop talking for a minute."

"I want to kill him!"

"It's amazing he didn't kill you."

"I think he believes he doesn't have to."

Sam looks puzzled, and Abby takes some time before continuing.

She says slowly, "I never said anything about Aaron. I never said anything about Gus. I'm afraid of Phil, and he knows it. And there's something about that he likes. A lot."

"You've known he killed Gus?"

"No," she says. "Not known. Not for certain."

"And you still worked for him."

"That's why I had no choice but to work for him. He prefers watching me squirm to killing me, because he thinks he can trust me. And he can, up to a point. I'm not going to the cops. I just want to kill him. That's the part he hasn't worked out yet."

Sam's having a hard time with all of this.

Now," she says, "I think it's you he wants. He may have found out who you are and that it was you who put the tap on. He also knows where you live; he went there first and has probably gone back."

Sam relaxes his hold. "Okay, you need a doctor, if not a hospital."

"No, I don't. You're better than a doctor. And we have to leave right now. For Maine."

Sam looks at her, as if to say he's taking her nowhere but the hospital.

She says, "You leave me behind, I'm just going up on my own. I wanna kill that prick. And I've got three guns here. I'll give you one, and take two."

"You'll be the one who gets shot."

"Maybe. But I'll get a shot at him. I do know how to shoot."

"You'd be in my way, Abby."

"I'm going up there, Sam—with you or on my own. I'm dead serious."

Sam lets out a sigh of resignation. "An unfortunate choice of words."

"I mean it."

"It's Friday. The roads'll be jammed."

"Then we better get started," Abby says.

EIGHTY-THREE

On Whalley Avenue in New Haven, one of many clapboard colonials is inhabited by three young women from Bulgaria who are overseen by a generously built Chinese-American female, who works for a local hoodlum named Dominick. The young women are not physically restrained, but they have no money or papers and have seen what happens to escapees who get caught. Dominick, six-five and relentlessly toned, often works out in the basement of this very house. He does what he wishes with the girls, including whacking them around. But the beatings are relatively soft. The young women are, after all, his property. Nothing like the beatings he puts on those who try to leave him.

When Phil arrives with Vito and Joe, Dominick's burly hand collars the prettiest of the girls, pushing her forward at the door, like an offering.

"I wouldda met you guys up there, I told Vito."

"It's okay," says Phil. "You were on our way."

"Yeah, but Phil—"

"It's better, Dominick. This way we're all together. And you don't have to try to remember where you're going."

Dominick blinks. "I see. It's because I had to ask Vito for the address. I didn't want to write it down, and then I wasn't absolutely sure."

"Get your coat on, Dominick. There's a chill."

"Where's Ed?"

"He'll meet us up there."

Dominick gives Phil a long, questioning look.

Phil says with annoyance, "You getting a coat, or aren't you?"

"Sure Phil, but… maybe you'd like…." He gestures at the girl he still holds at the neck, a slight, dark-haired, frightened eighteen-year-old who understands what she's being proffered for.

Phil studies her expression, which is not unintelligent, and her body, which is clothed for the occasion in only a slip.

Dominick says, "She can take punishment. I've got a layout in the basement—"

The girl squirms, which picks up Phil's interest.

"Maybe on the way back," he says, turning toward the door.

About five miles south of Reefer's Harbor, there's a new motel with clean rooms. Sam and Abby check in a little past three a.m. Sam thinks, if Phil or Dominick, or both of them, are coming up with guns, they'll be driving, not flying, and will be arriving at about the same time. So it isn't likely to be happening that night. Or it's already over. Sam and Abby drive by the house to make absolutely sure, get out, case the property for about twenty minutes, finding Larry, the FBI man, asleep in his chair.

They move off toward the seawall and work out a simple plan. On the way to Maine, Sam had argued with Abby unsuccessfully about her being at the house at all. "I know the address, Sam. If I have to, I'll take a cab. Or you will." So, of necessity, the plan includes Abby. In fact, it's hers.

At sundown, she proposes, they'll park the car about a quarter of a mile away, walk to the house, hide in the marsh close enough to hear and see any trouble, and when Phil puts in an appearance with his thugs, creep out, take aim and start shooting. The point Sam gets Abby to give in on is that she'll fire the rifle from a prone position. Small comfort, of course. There'll be three, maybe more, experienced killers against two amateurs who haven't held guns in years, much less fired them. It's reckless for Sam to be there. He hates that she's tagging along.

The further complication is the swordfish bones. It takes a

few minutes even to make out what they are. "The place is littered with them," Abby says in a sibilant whisper. "What the hell is this all about?"

Sam gives it thought, then says, "Haven't a clue."

"You think the house came this way?"

"These seem freshly painted."

"He's your son."

"Doesn't mean I can figure him. Never could."

"But he's planning something."

"Looks that way."

"Does it change anything for us?"

"Can't see why it should."

"Should we tell him we're here?"

"No," Sam says. On that he's definite. Sam and Alec never saw eye to eye on anything.

They drive back to the motel in silence and sleep until Saturday afternoon.

Harvey flies up Saturday morning. "You two look like you could use some sleep," he tells them at the airport gate.

Alec grimaces.

"Just saying," says Harvey.

"Lovely to see you too, Harv," Carrie says.

On the phone, beforehand, they had offered either to drive both cars to the Portland airport so Harvey could head back in his Caddy right away, or to entertain him for a weekend of *Waiting for Godot*, as Alec put it.

"I'll spend the night," Harvey said. "See what that feels like."

"Not a wise choice," said Alec, "but a welcome one."

On the drive home, car windows open, air piney, salty, as crisp as autumn, Carrie leans back in the breeze, laughing, chatting with Harvey. Alec thinks, how normal it feels, in the midst of incipient panic.

Harvey, getting out of the car in the driveway, gives a low whistle. "This house high enough for you two guys?"

"We have an architect looking at adding a floor," Alec says.

"God bless you!"

They have lunch in the kitchen—sandwiches—then spend the day on the local beach.

Harvey declares the ocean too cold for humans. Alec walks alone on the shore, giving Carrie and Harvey a chance to talk for a while.

At dinner—lobsters, sweet corn, apple pie—Harvey tells stories. "The good old days," when Harvey was young and worked for the now-deceased, legendary partners of what was then Kendall, Blake, van Vleck & Steele. When there was no pretrial discovery to speak of, when lawyers engaged in trial by ambush, and when investigators such as Harvey therefore meant something. The stories are old; the denouement is surprising. "Our young friend here," says Harvey to Carrie, "is a throwback. He would have prospered in that era. Present-day rules simply level the playing field for the dull ones. More likely to do justice is the argument—and maybe that's right—but it's a lot slower and not nearly as much fun. Not as sporting."

"Larry," Carrie calls out through the kitchen window. "How'd you like a thermos of coffee?"

"No thanks, ma'am. I'm just fine tonight."

Alec says to Harvey, "They send one guy. It's ridiculous."

Harvey glances at Carrie. "The Feds say it's unlikely Phil's coming."

Carrie makes a scoffing noise.

"I agree with them," Harvey says. "Phil's not that stupid. It's too conspicuous."

Harvey, given his choice of bedrooms—among sixteen—picks one on the third floor, facing the street, but also next to the back stairwell of the house.

In the master bedroom, Alec and Carrie are alone and stare at the bed.

"You think Harvey's right?" she asks.

Alec shakes his head, no.

Carrie says, "I can see Phil using that argument—'I'm not that stupid'—in claiming he never came here. But actually leaving us alone? After threatening us? After my testimony sends him up? I don't think so!"

Alec, sitting on the window sill, makes a wry expression.

"What're you saying?" Carrie asks.

"You heard me say something?"

"What're you thinking?"

"You know what I'm thinking. You ought to be staying at that motel. As I'd arranged it. Where you'd be safe."

"We've been over this, Alec. Fifty times."

"It's not too late. There are two cars downstairs. Take one of them."

"Listen to me! I'm not doing that. This is not something you get to decide. Phil's coming, and I'm gonna be waiting for him."

"It's unnecessary."

"Not so. It's better with two. I won't touch the gun. I'll be out of any firing line. That's what I agreed to."

Alec, unhappily resigned, looks out the window at the glowing array of swordfish bones that carpet the marsh.

Carrie, leaning against the wall, slumps down to the rug. "I want to stop running," she says.

EIGHTY-FOUR

It's the middle of the night. In the large bed, neither Alec nor Carrie can sleep. They can hear their own breathing, the surf pounding a half-mile away, the breeze in the marsh reeds. After several hours, it sounds almost like peace. Then the bedroom door opens. Not oiled, it creaks. And they bolt upright.

Total darkness. Total terror.

A child stands at the threshold, wide-eyed and scared. "Mommy?"

It's Sarah, and Carrie runs to her, kneels, hugs her, looks over the child's shoulder. "Honey, how'd you get here?"

"Daddy brought me."

Alec, fear pounding in his temples, steps into the hallway, turns on the light. The hall's empty.

Then the lightning-crack sound of a single gunshot outside.

Carrie huddles over Sarah, shielding her. "Let's play a game, sweetheart. You remember in the book, when Curious George played hide-and-seek with the man in the yellow hat who was like his daddy?"

Sarah gives a tight nod.

"So that's what we're going to do, hide from Daddy. Go baby, hide! It's very important. Find a good spot and, whatever you do, wait for Mommy to come get you."

Sarah is far from convinced she wishes to play this right now.

"Go! Please, baby!"

Fright lines on her mother's face send Sarah scurrying. Alec throws open the screen door to the deck outside the bedroom, goes onto the deck, tosses the loose end of the rope ladder over the railing and scampers down. Carrie follows right behind him, flashlight in hand. They move quickly, quietly—without having to think about their actions because they've practiced them.

On the side lawn there's a body. Larry Stahl, lifeless, a bullet hole in his head.

Carrie stops, gasps, lets out a cry.

Alec pulls at her, adrenaline pumping out everything but fear.

Sam thinks: Egrets and other fishing birds can be invisible in a marsh in daylight. Despite a full moon, he and Abby, crouching low in brown and gray clothes, should not be detectable to the group thirty yards away.

If Sam and she can keep silent.

So they barely breathe.

They listen to the surf, the crickets. And they hear everything the would-be assassins say.

There are five men. Sam recognizes Phil's voice and Vito's. Sam and Abby are a bit deeper into the marsh, and Phil's group is between them and the house. Phil is explaining what each of his band is to do. Vito and a man named Ed are to go to the house, and stay there, entering from the first-level deck, then covering front and back. Phil, Joe, and Dominick will spread out on the perimeter of the marsh, in case Alec and Carrie attempt to escape that way.

"My guess," Phil says, "they want to come through here. They've got something planned for these bones. And when they do, if they have the child with them—and they probably will—they'll give up. We get them separated, then we separate the guy."

Vito's look questions whether he's to take this literally.

"Yeah," Phil says. "Like the wings off a fly."

"On our way, boss," Vito says, and he and Ed jog off.

In a few seconds, Sam hears them climbing onto the deck.

Phil signals to Joey and Dominick, and the three start moving apart.

Sam gives Abby a strained now-or-never look.

Another dread-filled moment, and he says, "Now!"

Gunfire at the house.

Sam and Abby step out and start tearing through the marsh, reeds slapping their faces. Sam yells at Abby, "Lie flat!" She doesn't. It's Joey they come upon first, waving his gun, trying to aim. They blast away at each other, point blank. Joey falls, his shot hitting Abby, who screams. Dominick, a huge target, appears from the reeds. Sam's shot gets Dominick in one eye. Then Phil is there lurching, firing at Sam, blasting him under the right shoulder, too fast for Sam's shot to land.

"What the fuck!" Phil says, standing over their still bodies, recognizing who's been shot. "Can't anyone take a joke anymore?"

Alec and Carrie enter the marsh near the seawall. They hear gunfire at the house and in the marsh not fifty yards away. Their plan draws them closer to exactly that danger spot. Alec almost trips on another dead body. Not Phil. Not anyone Alec recognizes, but Carrie does. "One of Phil's," she says. Then two bodies, one a woman who seems to be breathing, and—

"Oh my God!" Alec says.

"What?"

They hear someone else, yards away, cracking swordfish bones underfoot. Then they hear another gunshot. From inside the house.

They thrash through the marsh reeds, getting scratched, muddy, covered in sweat, blood—both in dark T-shirts and shorts—and, despite their sweat, both freezing. They know where they're going, get there, and wait. It's a small island of glowing bones where Alec, as quietly as he can, removes their rifle from its waterproof carrier. Silence. They can hear themselves breathing and try to stifle that sound. They hear more bones cracking. There is definitely someone else still threatening them in this marsh.

Their eyes have adjusted to the moonlight. Shapes are visible. Standing with Carrie in a ten-foot clearing, shivering, Alec screams silently at himself to get a grip. Tries to think. What the hell was his dad doing here, and who is that woman? He thought he saw his father still breathing. Could the gunshots inside the house have been fired by Harvey? Could he have gotten a weapon through airport security? Larry Stahl had a two-way radio. Did he have time to use it to call for help?

Someone's barreling through reeds. Getting closer. Some FBI guy? Harvey? In another small clearing twenty yards away, a large man bursts into view parting the reeds in front of him. Carrie catches him in the beam of her flashlight. Phil.

In a loose, flowing shirt and slacks, he casts a menacing shadow. "As you can see," Phil says, "I have a very effective weapon pointing at whoever is holding that flashlight."

Phil flips his own on. Half blinds them in its powerful beam, and glints off the barrel of Alec's aimed rifle.

"Never aim for the head," Phil says. "It's a fool's play. Too easy to miss."

"Thing is," Alec says, "I've got two hands on this rifle and a damn fine sight. You, one hand on a handgun. Carrie turns off the light, I dodge your light and shoot."

"Carrie, honey. Go on back to the house with Sarah. I finish here, I'll take both of you home."

She holds the beam steadily on Phil's face.

Alec says, "What I'm looking at, Phil, is your finger. I see it so much as twitch? My gun, locked on your forehead, goes off. You like the odds—take 'em."

"You got something to say I might want to listen to?"

"Yeah. We put the guns down. How 'bout that? And then either I kill you with my bare hands, or you kill me."

"While Carrie runs to the police," says Phil.

"Exactly. I'm gambling that, if I can't finish you myself, I can hold you off long enough for her to get there."

"You really that stupid?"

"We put the guns down nice and slowly," Alec says. "We release our grips and raise our hands."

Phil, looking around with bemusement, says, "What's the plan? You thinking of stabbing me with one of these—what are these? Swordfish bones?"

"Whatever works."

"Jesus Christ! You are that fucking stupid!"

"What I said was, we put the guns down. After that, we can use anything we find."

"All right, asshole. You want it, you got it."

Alec, still in the firing stance he'd been taught, starts lowering his weapon. Phil follows. Inch by inch. Eyes of each on the other. Until the guns lie on the ground. Equally slowly, the two men raise their hands.

"One more thing," Phil calls out.

"We kick the guns away?"

"I'll go first," says Phil, "and I'll trust you."

"Okay."

"I can trust you? You will do this?"

"You do it, I'll do it."

Phil, eyes staying on Alec, kicks his gun to one side. Eight or nine feet. A soccer swipe. And out of sight.

Alec, returning Phil's stare, does the same. Then dives for an object on his left.

Letting out a soul-searing laugh at Alec's apparent hoisting of a swordfish bone, Phil dodges Carrie's beam, throws his own flashlight to one side, and comes smashing like a rhino through the reeds. At Alec. With blood lust. Taking the long knife out of his pants leg as he comes. Not breaking stride. Eyes gleaming with the image of the kill.

Thump! Jocko Rush's samurai sword sinks to the hilt into Phil's belly, a residue of fluorescent paint ringing the hole in his shirt. The force of contact ripples through Alec's arms. Phil looks astonished as Alec pulls out the sword, and, with a grunt, Phil drops to the ground. He utters no further sound, his face a mask of speechless amazement until the life leaves his body and his eyes freeze.

Alec plunges the sword into the soft earth. Carrie sinks to her knees, stares blankly at the space above Phil, digs her nails into the dirt beside him. Slowly, Alec pulls her up, holds her. She can't look at him, can't look anywhere but the distances of her mind. With gentle insistence, he leads her from the marsh toward the house. The blare of sirens, the sight of flickering lights from approaching police cars rouse her from the trance.

Cops are everywhere.

"In the marsh," Alec says to one of them. "I think there are people alive."

"This your dog?" the cop says about the mongrel that's trailing him.

"Never seen him," Alec says, but as he heads toward the house, the dog, Vito's dog, Friday, peels off to follow him.

Lights now blaze from the first-floor windows. Medics are dealing with a body on the deck. Two men in white are attempting to resuscitate a figure that could be Harvey sprawled in the front hall of the house. Alec dashes there, struggling to get a glimpse of the man's face. Then he hears Harvey's voice calling out from the living room. "Hey, kid! Looking for me?"

Harvey is reclining on the sofa propped by a mound of cushions. He's smiling despite a shoulder wound that the medics have already bound up. Next to him is a shotgun. The body in the foyer is Vito.

Alec says, "How the hell did you get that shotgun through airport security?"

"Didn't," says Harvey. "You brought it up for me, dummy. In the Cadillac."

Two plainclothes cops come into the living room. The older

one, graying and bespectacled, is carrying Alec's samurai sword wrapped in plastic. "This yours?" he asks.

"Yes."

"Given to him," Harvey says, "by the CEO of Telemarch News."

"You're damned lucky," says the cop. "It's three feet longer than the knife in the other guy's hand. Went right through his bullet-proof vest."

"Did you find a gun on him?" Alec asks.

"A forty-five. Strapped to his back. I guess he thought he could get you with the knife."

Alec looks around for Carrie. She's not there.

The cop says, "I can see self-defense all over this, although we're going to want you to sort it all out at the station. But tell me now, why'd you paint the sword?"

Harvey says, "You see those painted swordfish bones out there?"

"Hard to miss."

"In the dark, some feet away, could you tell the difference?"

The cop looks down again at the sword. "Oh, I see," he says.

Alec, with a grim smile, points upstairs. "Won't be a minute."

On the second floor, Carrie makes her way down the hall. "Come out, sweetheart! Come out, come out, wherever you are!"

No response.

In the room decorated for Sarah, Carrie sees her—or at least her foot—sticking out from under the canopy bed.

Gently, Carrie lifts the child into her arms, and slides her under the covers.

"I won, Mommy," says Sarah, more asleep than awake.

"Yes, we did, darling."

Alec, confirming that Carrie and Sarah are all right, heads quickly back to the marsh. A young cop greets him on the lawn. "We found the two live ones," he says.

"You're sure? Two?"

"Yeah. Man and woman."

Two stretchers are being carried out of the reeds. Alec walks along with his father's. Sam is conscious. Looking up at Alec, he smiles.

"Why?" Alec asks.

"I'm sure you can figure it out," says Sam.

EIGHTY-FIVE

The local hospital, serving five small communities, is a four-story red-brick building, sitting on a promontory, about five miles up the coast. Sam has a corner private room with a view over marshes and salt ponds.

He says to Alec, who arrives near noon, "You cleaned and painted hundreds of swordfish bones just to disguise one samurai sword?"

"It worked."

"A lot of things might have worked."

"No doubt. And you put a tap on a mob boss's phone."

"That's right."

Alec gives him a long look, as if to say, *And that wasn't crazy?*

"Also worked." Sam says.

"Bad odds," Alec says.

"I didn't have much choice, son."

Alec gestures to the next room. "Abigail Vaccaro. She's your girlfriend?"

"That's right."

"Your doctor says she'll pull through."

"She got it in the hip," Sam says. "Will probably need a replacement."

"You try to stop her from coming?" Alec asks.

"Whatta you think?"

"Yeah, no, I know how that is."

"She had her own grievance," Sam says.

"I see," says Alec, not wanting to pursue it.

Alec strolls to the window, takes in the view. "Great room," he says.

"Aren't many people here."

"No. People seem healthy here. Not many gunfights." Alec turns, ambles to the end of Sam's bed. "Look, Dad."

"You want to thank me for saving your life."

"Yeah."

"You would have done it for me."

"True."

"Only problem we have is talking about it."

Alec smiles.

"Pretty funny," Sam says. "Two guys who make their living by talking."

"We're both salesmen, you're saying."

"Union shops, burglar alarms, somebody else's arguments, what's the difference?"

"Better than fighting about it," Alec says.

Sam laughs. "I don't know. Sometimes you just pardon the ravens."

"I'm rejoining the doves."

"That what you call it? What you do in a courtroom?"

"My boss calls it sublimated violence."

"No wonder you're good at it," Sam says.

From the railing of their second-story deck, Alec looks out over the point where the bay flows into the ocean. Behind him, Carrie and Sarah, bundled up in a deck chair and bathed in sun, have both drifted off to a light sleep. Friday naps at Carrie's feet. His attachment to mother and child has quickly become mutual.

At the seawall, the bay, blue-black like Parker's ink, is chopped to whitecaps by the wind, and stands of birch trees bend like dancers. Under a pale bright sky, the neighbors' grandchildren, five or six of them, scamper over the lawns, scattering swordfish bones, careless of snares and boundaries.

The children's cries ring out like squeals of mice and squirrels and trilling birds. Alec looks back at Carrie, who stirs, and smiles at him. Alec, smiling back, returns his gaze to the children playing in his yard. Seeing them on the afterprint of Carrie's smile, Alec experiences a series of extraordinary near-hallucinatory images: their own children, and then children of those children, playing on these lawns.

He leans down on the rail. Whatever the future, he thinks, it will, necessarily, be a product of this moment—and this place.

The wind picks up again, whipping through the tall reeds and grasses of the marsh. Carrie's now fully awake. "We should go in."

"Right."

"Are we going to be okay?"

"Absolutely," he says.

"Anything could happen now."

"Whatever, we'll be fine. Don't worry."

"Don't worry?"

"I'll think of something," he says.

Carrie laughs, for the first time in days.

Alec takes Sarah in his arms and looks back once more over the railing. He sees sunlight dancing on the reeds, as if the marsh itself were alive.